Beneath Your Beautiful

emery rose

Beneath Your Beautiful
Copyright © Emery Rose, 2018

All rights reserved. No part of this publication may be reproduced, distributed, or transmitted in any form or by any means, including photocopying, recording, or other electronic or mechanical methods, without prior written consent of the publisher, except in the case of brief quotation embodied in critical reviews and certain other non-commercial uses permitted by copyright law.

This is a work of a fiction. Any references to historical events, real people, or real places are used fictitiously. Other names, characters, places, and events are products of the author's imagination, and any resemblance to actual events or places or persons, living or dead, is entirely coincidental.

Editing: Chelsea Kuhel and Madison Seidler, www.madisonseidler.com
Proofreading: Monica Black, www.wordnerdediting.com
Cover Design: Sarah Hansen, www.okaycreations.com
Interior: Stacey Blake, www.champagnebookdesign.com

Dedication

To my daughters, Maddie and Lillie, you are beautiful inside and out.

Chapter One

Eden

I BRUSHED SNOW OFF MY DOWN JACKET AND LAUGHED AT THE inflatable Santa hanging from the porch rafters as I opened the front door. Trevor, one of Luke's housemates, was sitting on the sofa, feet propped on the coffee table, a slice of pizza in one hand and the remote in the other. "Hey, Trev." I took off my beanie and let my blonde hair tumble down. "Studying hard for finals?" I joked.

He tossed the pizza in the box and vaulted over the back of the sofa.

"Impressive. Do you do that for all the girls?" I teased.

He ran a hand through his mussed-up hair, his eyes darting around the room, looking at everything except me. "What are you doing here? It's Thursday."

I laughed. "I'm not allowed to stop by on Thursdays? Is that a house rule?"

"You usually have class all day."

True. I was playing hooky this afternoon. Luke's text sealed the deal. *Ditch your next class. I need you. Now.* He'd never asked me to ditch class for sex. I was so thrilled he was finally letting out his inner rebel, I practically sprinted here. "Is he in his room?"

"Uh, no…he's out."

I furrowed my brow. "He said he'd be here."

"Let's go for a beer. I'm buying."

"I'm still recovering from last night's birthday celebration."

"Hair of the dog."

Hangover sex would be a better cure, but I kept that to myself. "I'll wait in his room." I breezed past him. "Catch you later."

Trevor's hand wrapped around my arm, and he tugged me back.

"You don't want to go up there."

I looked up the stairs, dread gnawing at my stomach. "Why not?" I whispered.

"Just...don't do it."

I shook off his arm and quietly climbed the stairs. As I crept down the hallway, voices came from Luke's bedroom. His door was open a crack, and I stood outside it, straining my ears to hear.

"When are you going to tell her?" After three years of listening to Lexie's voice in the dark while we talked late into the night, I knew it well.

"Soon," Luke said. "I just need more time. I couldn't tell her on her birthday. And with finals coming up..."

"This is making me crazy," Lexie said. "I feel so guilty. Every time I look at her, I feel like she knows."

I didn't know. I had no idea.

This couldn't be happening.

"Don't cry, Lex. I'll talk to her. It's just...hard."

Oh God. When? How? I wracked my brain, trying to figure out how any of this was possible.

"Do you still love her?" she asked, sniffling.

I squeezed my eyes shut, holding my breath as I waited for the answer. "I still care about her."

He still *cared* about me? That was the best he could muster? In our senior year of high school, he'd begged me to come to

Penn State with him. Like the fool I was, I had followed him to college, telling myself art was just a hobby. I could do it without the fancy degree. Not that my dad would have paid for art school. Still, I could have at least tried to get in, and I would have figured out a way to pay for it myself. But no, I had tossed the art school brochures into the trash.

All because Luke was my first love.

"Luke…I…there's something I need to tell you."

"What's that?" His voice was muffled. Was his face buried in her hair? Was he holding her? Kissing her? My hands balled into fists, my nails digging into my palms. I struggled to get air into my lungs. My heart hurt so much, I could barely breathe.

"Promise you won't get mad," she pleaded. "It was an accident. I don't even know how it happened. But…I'm pregnant."

I leaned against the wall for support. Pregnant? She didn't know how it happened? Bile rose up in my throat. I swallowed the bitterness and squared my shoulders.

Rage flooded my veins.

I pushed the door open, slamming it against the wall. Planting my hands on my hips, I took in the whole scene. Luke was spooning her, and she was facing the door, a smug smile on her face. She was triumphant, and not the least bit surprised to see me. Lexie must have sent that text from Luke's phone. She was the winner, and she was thrilled at her victory.

Luke's face was frozen in shock, his brown eyes wide, his mouth hanging open as if I'd caught him mid-sentence. The short layers of his golden-brown hair were ruffled like Lexie had been running her fingers through it. I diverted my gaze. I couldn't bear to look at the boy I'd loved for five years. *Five years.*

"Did I interrupt?" I asked, surprised by how calm I sounded.

Luke rolled onto his back and covered his face with his hands. Coward. If their clothes strewn across the floor was any indication, he was naked under those covers. And now it became painfully clear why our sex life had dwindled over the past few months. He was getting it from someone else—my best friend.

"Eden...it's not what you think." He sounded so lame, I laughed harshly. "I can explain."

"Save it for someone who cares."

I loved you. How could you do this to me? And Lexie, that backstabber, had been my roommate since freshman year. I took her home with me for the holidays because she said her parents didn't care about her. I let her borrow my clothes. My friends became her friends, and now, my boyfriend was her boyfriend.

My heart was shattering into so many pieces, I didn't know how I'd put them back together. But I refused to give Lexie the satisfaction of seeing me break down. Time for action, not tears. I flung open Luke's closet and reached inside for a baseball bat. I chose the Combat Maxum, a bat for power hitters, and came out swinging. Lexie cowered, hugging herself for protection.

I laughed. "Don't worry, Lexie. You're not worth an arrest for assault and battery."

I walked out of the room, my head held high. When I got into the hallway, I sprinted down the stairs and barreled out the front door. I flew down the front porch steps and rounded the corner, my feet slipping and sliding on the freshly fallen snow as I skidded to a halt in front of Luke's silver BMW, a high school graduation present from his parents. Everything in Luke Prescott's life had been handed to him on a silver platter. An only child of doting parents who put him on a pedestal, he was spoiled rotten. They should have given their son values instead of material possessions. Who got a BMW for graduating high school?

I swung the bat, and it connected with the hood. *Crunch.*

Another mighty swing, and I took out a headlight. My body was coiled tight with rage. I needed to unleash it. Anger beat the alternative—curling up into a ball and crying enough tears to fill an ocean.

"Eden. Stop!" Luke yelled. I ignored him and swung at the other headlight. *Bam! Bam! Bam!* I kept swinging, metal crunching under my bat. Hell hath no fury like Eden Madley scorned. Not that I was a violent person. But I pictured Lexie's triumphant smile, and it fueled my anger.

I raised the bat, ready to inflict more damage.

Luke wrapped his arms around me from behind and dragged me a safe distance away from the car. "What have you done?" Luke wailed, sounding like a big fat baby.

"The same thing you did to my heart."

I struggled free of his hold and dropped the bat to the ground. Crisis averted, he moved closer to inspect the damage, brushing off the snow with his hands. It wasn't nearly enough. But defeat and heartache had drained the fight right out of me. "I'm sorry," he said, his back to me. He didn't even have the guts to look me in the eye. "I'm really sorry, Eden."

"Fuck you, Luke. Take your sorry and shove it up your ass." I strode away, shoulders squared and head held high, trying to hang on to any shred of dignity I had left. Tears lodged in my throat, but I swallowed them. On the way over here, I'd thought the snow looked pretty. Like being inside a snow globe. Now the snow stung my face, impeding my progress. I burrowed into my jacket and stuffed my hands in my pockets.

"Hey, Eden," Trevor called, jogging to catch up to me. He knew what was going on under their roof. I was the last to find out. Wasn't that always the way? "For what it's worth, I think you deserve a hell of a lot better. If you ever wanna grab a beer, call me."

I nodded and kept walking, choking back the tears. I unclasped the bracelet Luke gave me for my twenty-second birthday yesterday, tossed it on the ground, and crushed it under the sole of my boot. It had come in a blue Tiffany's box—a sterling silver charm bracelet with a heart medallion.

Chapter Two

Killian

I pulled out of Joss and slid off the condom, retreating into her bathroom. After I flushed the toilet, I washed my hands and used her fancy hand soap and my fingers to clean the makeup smears off her sink. The bathroom was cavernous, but apparently not big enough to corral all her crap—makeup, hairspray, perfume, lotions, and potions cluttered all the shelves and every available surface. Towels were tossed carelessly into a heap on the limestone tiled floors like she was waiting for the maid to replace them with fresh ones. I folded the towels and hung them on the rail. I wouldn't even know where to begin cleaning up the rest of the shit in here.

I returned to Joss's room, sidestepping a mountain of discarded clothes. She was lying on her bed naked, a lit cigarette clamped between her lips. Outside her wall of windows, Lower Manhattan was lit up like the Fourth of July. Joss lived in a luxury condo in Brooklyn Heights. I'd never seen her apartment in the light of day—never seen her in the light of day.

Joss never asked for pillow talk or cuddling. She had zero interest in a relationship, and that was the only reason it had lasted this long. She stayed out of my business, never asked questions, and didn't try to analyze me. But tonight, the sex just left me feeling empty. Or numb. I couldn't even find a word for this dull, aching nothingness. I didn't know why I came over tonight. It was a mistake, and I knew it as soon as I walked in the door.

She watched me through slitted eyes as I got dressed, the smoke from her cigarette billowing up and into the stale air. Joss once told me she had a huge trust fund. She didn't work, and I had no idea what she did all day. Maybe she slept, or shopped, or got manicures. I'd never cared enough to ask.

"Did you meet someone special?" she asked. She took another drag of her cigarette and blew smoke out the side of her mouth.

"You should know me better than that." She didn't know me at all, but I made the rules clear from the beginning. No personal questions.

She shrugged one shoulder. "Things change."

"Did they change for you?" I sat on the edge of her bed to tie the laces of my combat boots. I'd had them since high school and they were as worn and battered as I was. Much too young to feel this damn old. That line came from a country song I'd heard at Fat Earl's once. I hated that bar. My old man used to frequent it before the hipsters invaded, back when Earl was still alive and turned a blind eye. But even now, with a new owner and a different crowd, the place probably hadn't changed much. Country music probably still blared from the jukebox, and it probably still smelled like stale beer and fried food. My stomach still knotted with dread whenever I drove past it.

"I don't need you to love me," Joss said. *Love*? I bristled at the word. She never brought any of this up before, and I didn't know what prompted her to do it now. This had never been our deal, and now I knew for sure it was time to bail. "But I'm not stupid. You kept your eyes closed."

"Orgasmic bliss." A lie. It had gotten the job done, but it wasn't blissful. It felt like we were going through the motions, like two well-oiled machines. All mechanics, no emotions.

That's what you wanted, asshole.

"Bullshit," she said. "You were pretending I was someone else."

Wrong. I was pretending *I* was someone else. I stood and turned to face her. "Time for you to move on."

"Maybe I already have." She let a curtain of brown hair fall into her face to mask her hurt expression. Jesus. Did she think she was in love with some guy who called her at two in the morning for sex? She didn't even know my last name or what I did for a living.

"I never made any promises," I said.

Joss laughed, but it sounded harsh in her quiet room. "I knew the deal. But I still hoped…it would be different."

I rubbed the back of my neck and exhaled. What in the hell could I say? I couldn't pretend to love her. I didn't know what love felt like, but I knew this wasn't it. I never thought about her after I left. Never asked about her family, never asked what she did in her free time, never asked anything about her life. We met at a club six months ago. I was drunk and beyond fucked-up. She was looking for a good time with no strings attached. She brought me home, and we fucked. We'd been doing it ever since, but I'd never once felt the urge to get to know her better.

"I can live without the three a.m. booty calls." She jutted out her chin. "Besides, I deserve better. My shrink told me that, so it must be true."

She had a shrink. And she did deserve better. Someone who stayed the night and gave a shit. "I won't call again."

My hand was on the doorknob, ready to leave when her words stopped me. "You thought I didn't know you were Killian 'The Kill' Vincent, the champion of the Octagon?"

I stilled, my body tensing. I'd walked away from fighting right before I met her. The media had been all over it, so I shouldn't have been surprised she knew who I was, but she'd never mentioned it. And that was a good thing. I hated to be reminded of what I used to be.

"Someone at the club pointed you out the night we met," Joss said. "Do you really think I would have gone for you if you'd been a nobody?"

I was a nobody. What did she think would happen? I'd take her with me to my fights, let her bask in the limelight like those other nameless girls who attached themselves to me because of who they thought I was. None of them knew me. None of them wanted to know me. They just wanted to be seen with me—and fuck me. "I don't fight anymore."

"I know. And I'm disappointed. I wanted to be with a champion, but I ended up with a has-been loser who runs a stupid bar." She faked a yawn. "Boring."

All along, Joss had been fucking someone else. Okay, it was me. But sometimes, I felt like it was more of an alter ego. I'd been a showman who got the crowd loving me and rooting for me, chanting my name. An actor, playing a role, all swagger and bravado, but I'd backed it up with a grueling training schedule, and I'd delivered the goods. My brother Connor once asked me if I was fighting my opponent or my own demons. I didn't bother answering him. If I had, I would have said: *both*.

She turned her back to me, and I let myself out. I was relieved it was over, but I felt shitty about it. My old man would tell me it was the price I paid for having a conscience. He was born without one, but mine was big enough to take on the guilt of the whole God damn world.

"The ref called a clean hit," my dad said.

"I don't give a shit what the ref called it. I killed a man."

"Don't be dramatic. He's still alive."

"He's in a fucking coma."

"Stop being a pussy."

That was one of his pet names for me. Pussy. Idiot. Shithead. I believed some people in this world set out to destroy you just because they thought they could. My father was one of those people. But I learned a long time ago, if you didn't let anyone get close enough, they couldn't hurt you. Not in any way that mattered. It wasn't fists that did the most damage. It was love that could bring a man to his knees. A woman brought down Seamus Vincent, and he turned to the bottle to ease his pain. He was a nasty drunk with a selective memory. Sometimes, I almost believed he had no idea what he did when he was drunk. Maybe he didn't. What went on behind closed doors stayed behind closed doors. Who was I going to tell, anyway? The cops?

★ ★ ★

I took a few deep breaths and pressed the call button. She answered her home phone on the second ring. In the background, I heard a baby crying. Johnny Ramirez's baby—a boy he'd never gotten the chance to meet. "Anna."

"Who is this?" she asked, sounding wary. She knew who it was. I met Anna first, at a nightclub on top of the MGM Grand in Vegas four years ago. She quickly figured out I was a one-night kind of guy, but Johnny was a forever kind of guy. Six months later, they got married, and I was his best man. I toasted to their health, happiness, and a long life together.

"It's Killian. You haven't cashed the check I sent."

"Your money won't bring Johnny back."

"I know that." *Cash the fucking check. Buy something for yourself. For your son. Goddammit. Let me do something for you.* "Anna. Please."

I was begging for forgiveness, but she couldn't give it to me. I was the man who ruined her life, and nothing I said or did could ever change that.

"Don't call me again." She cut the call, and I punched a hole in the living room wall of the crappy house I rented in Greenpoint. I wanted to burn the house to the ground—set fire to the whole fucking world. But it wouldn't bring Johnny back. Nothing would.

I heard the front door open, and the rumble of a Harley engine in the hallway. Fucking Connor. Why couldn't he park it on the street? Instead of going through the hallway into the backyard like he usually did, he cut the engine. A few seconds later, I heard his voice.

"You got what I need?"

I stalked into the hallway, catching him by surprise. He grinned and gave me a mock salute. He was feeling good. *Too good.*

"Good deal. And throw in some extra pancakes for the crispy duck," Connor said to the person on the phone, no doubt for my benefit. "Catch you in thirty minutes."

Connor flipped his phone closed. A burner phone with numbers for "Chinese restaurants" and "pizzerias" that didn't sell crispy duck or pizza.

"Thought you'd be at work," he said, cracking his neck.

"Don't make that pickup. You don't need that shit. I'll get you into the best rehab money can buy."

He climbed off his bike and rested his helmet on the seat. "Go to work. It's just Chinese takeout."

I grabbed him by his black leather jacket and slammed him against the wall. He looked like the younger version of me—dark hair, olive skin, blue eyes. Same height, similar build. But his body was filled with so many toxic chemicals, it was only a matter of time before they killed him. Over the past year, he must have dropped twenty pounds. His motorcycle jacket, once fitted to his body, hung looser on his frame, and his face looked gaunt. "This shit needs to stop."

"Punch me if it makes you feel better." He jutted out his chin. "Go on. I can take it."

I released my hold and took a step back. I would never physically hurt Connor. Beating him up wouldn't solve anything. "What happened to you?"

"Same thing that happened to you. Life." He looked at my right hand. "Did you punch another hole in the wall? Did that make everything better?"

He brushed past me and took the stairs two at a time.

The bathroom door shut behind him, and I flexed my hand, not even feeling the sting from the cuts on my knuckles.

I was losing my brother, the only person in this whole fucked-up world I loved. But I didn't know how to save him. And I didn't know how to fix what was broken inside him.

Chapter Three

Eden

Six Months Later

ANOTHER BAR, ANOTHER REJECTION. I'D BEEN TO COCKTAIL bars, dive bars, nightclubs, and now this rooftop bar. They all wanted someone with experience. How did you get experience unless someone gave you a shot? I considered my options as I washed my hands in the restroom. I'd only been in Brooklyn for three weeks, but I was burning through my savings. Dreams didn't come cheap. Neither did crappy apartments in Williamsburg.

I studied my reflection in the mirror. Did I reek of desperation? I'd never had a problem getting a job before. I looked down at my outfit—a floaty floral mini dress and suede ankle boots. Maybe it wasn't sending the right message?

What is wrong with me? I used to have confidence.

"Hey," a girl said, coming into the restroom.

"Hey."

She stopped in front of me and gave me a big smile. She was pretty, with long auburn hair and a sprinkle of freckles on her nose. "I'm Hailey."

"Eden."

"I was sitting with some friends, and I may have been shamelessly eavesdropping. You're looking for a bartending job, right?"

I nodded, even though I was thinking I should expand my job search into other areas.

"It's all about who you know. Most of these jobs are taken before you even get in the door. But I happen to know one of the bartenders at Trinity Bar got fired last night so you need to get your butt over there pronto."

"Why did the bartender get fired?"

She shrugged. "Can't really say. I was too busy crushing on the other bartender, Zeke. He's total eye candy. Anyway… the guy you need to speak to is Killian Vincent. He's…" Hailey furrowed her brow and tapped her finger against her chin. When she couldn't come up with the words to describe him, she shrugged in defeat. "I'm not sure what he is. He's total eye candy too, if you like them dark and brooding. Personally, I'm more attracted to sunshine and light. To each their own. Give me your phone. I'll type in the info."

I handed her my phone, and she pulled up the bar on Google maps. "There you go." Hailey handed back my phone and smiled. "Good luck."

"Thanks. I really appreciate it."

"No problem. Hope I see you behind the bar next time I stop by," she said, disappearing into a stall.

Twenty minutes later, I was standing behind the cover of a white van across the street from Trinity Bar watching a guy talking on his cell. He backed up to the edge of the sidewalk and looked up at the hulking steel towers of the Williamsburg Bridge rising in the background, or the flat roof of the building, I wasn't sure. Whatever he was looking at didn't make him happy. He was pacing in a small area, like an animal trapped in a cage. A sleek, powerful animal.

A black fitted T-shirt accentuated his broad shoulders and biceps, the hem skimming the waistband of his dark jeans. A tattoo sleeve covered his left arm. Dark, unruly hair cut in long layers reached the nape of his neck. His profile was strong. Chiseled jaw. Straight nose. Prominent cheekbones. Even without seeing his face clearly, I knew it was beautiful. I couldn't seem to take my eyes off him.

This was Killian Vincent. I was sure of it.

When he cut the call, he pocketed his phone and raked both hands through his hair, holding the back of his head like his frustration was too great to contain. It wasn't the ideal time to approach him for a job, but I was going for it anyway. No guts, no glory. The worst he could do was say no. I squared my shoulders, held my head high, and strode across the street. My number one mission was to get a job.

One minute, my body was moving. The next, I was sprawled across the road, all the air knocked out of my lungs.

"Are you okay?"

I lifted my head, dazed. Stars floated in front of my eyes. When my head cleared, I was met with eyes so blue, they didn't look real. Like tropical water in exotic places I'd only seen in photos. Fringed by long, thick lashes almost too pretty for his ruggedly handsome face. His eyes locked on mine, and for a few seconds, everything went completely still.

"Are you okay?" he asked again. His gaze swept over my face, dark brows furrowed, and the world came rushing back. Ten feet away, a car was idling, waiting for me to get out of the way.

"I'm fine," I said, brushing gravel off my palms. Stupid pothole. How had I missed that? I scrambled to my feet. A searing pain shot up from my left ankle, and my leg buckled out from under me—the same ankle I sprained in a dirt bike accident when I was thirteen. The guy's arms wrapped around me, and I was pressed against his hard chest. He smelled *good*. Something warm and faintly spicy. Masculine. Intoxicating.

He moved to my side and slid an arm around my waist. "Lean on me."

I gritted my teeth and limped along next to him. I set down my left foot, and my leg wobbled. His arm around me tightened, and he muttered something under his breath. Before I could stop him, he slid an arm under my knees and lifted me off the ground, carrying me in his arms, his stride long and sure.

"What are you doing?" I asked, finally coming to my senses. I struggled to break free of his hold, but he didn't let go.

"Stop fighting me. You'll hurt yourself." His voice was deep and kind of gravelly. Sexy.

"You'll hurt yourself carrying me," I said lamely.

"You weigh nothing," he scoffed.

I didn't weigh nothing, but in his arms, I felt featherlight. I could feel the muscles in his arms flexing and the warmth of his skin through the thin fabric of my dress. His nearness made my head swim, but at the same time, he made me feel safe, like nothing bad could happen to me while I was with him. Which was weird. He was a total stranger.

He carried me into the bar, and in a few long strides, we reached a leather sofa. He lowered me onto it, his face hovering inches above mine. My breath hitched as I stared at his full, sensuous lips and the dark stubble on his chiseled jaw that gave the impression a clean shave didn't last more than a few hours. A kaleidoscope of butterflies had invaded my stomach, and feelings that lay dormant swirled inside me. He held onto me a few seconds too long before he released me and stepped away, running his hand through the messy waves of his hair.

"I need to take off your boot." Without waiting for my permission, he carefully removed my shoe and sock. I bit down hard on my lip to keep from whimpering. He was holding my bare foot in both his warm, calloused hands—strong, capable hands, with thick veins, and white scars on the knuckles. How did he get the scars? Maybe he had a bad temper and flew into rages. That should have scared me, but it didn't.

His touch was firm, but surprisingly gentle. He slowly rotated my foot, his dark brows knitted as he assessed the damage. Good thing I'd painted my toenails glossy coral yesterday. Which was a stupid thing to be thinking about. His fingers brushed over the tender spot just below my ankle, and I sucked in my breath, my hands curling into fists.

"You okay?" He lifted his eyes to mine, and my heart stuttered. A person could drown in those eyes. It was like being underwater and looking up at the sunlight.

"I'm fine."

He set my foot down carefully, like it was made of glass. "Just twisted. Not broken," he said, like he was an expert on the subject. "I'll get you some ice and clean up your knee."

I looked down at my knee. Blood oozed from it. *Ugh.* This was not going according to plan. I came for a job. Instead, I was playing the role of pathetic invalid.

"I'm fine. Really," I said quickly, swinging my legs over the side of the sofa.

He scowled at me. "Stay where you are."

"Don't go to any more trouble. I'm sure you have a million things to do, so don't worry about it."

He crossed his arms over his wide chest and glowered. Impressive. This guy took scowling and glowering to a new level of badass. "I have a shitload of things to do. But you fell right in front of me. You expect me to send you on your way and not help you?"

"A lot of people would have looked the other way."

"Yeah…well, not me." He averted his head and exhaled

sharply. "I'll be right back. Don't move," he commanded. I watched him stride to the back of the bar, noting his perfect V-shaped torso that tapered down to slim hips and a narrow waist. Greek gods had nothing on this man.

What is going on with me? Had I hit my head when I fell? I came to Brooklyn to find myself and make my own dreams come true. Lusting after this guy wouldn't help me do that. My heart was closed for business, and if my body betrayed me… well, that was too bad.

Job, job, job. Stay focused.

Chapter Four

Eden

Taking a few shaky breaths, I looked around the building. Exposed brick walls and high ceilings. A zinc bar with glass shelves of liquor and antique mirror splash backs spanned the wall across from me.

Sunshine streamed in from a set of open doors in the back, giving the distressed hardwood floors a honey glow. A warm June breeze carried the scent of mint and lavender and something sweet…was I imagining that? It was a bar, not an herb garden. I craned my neck to see outside. Whitewashed brick walls enclosed a paved courtyard, and dark green foliage twined around wood beams. A brightly painted food truck said Jimmy's Tacos.

The guy who I assumed was Killian returned, loaded down with supplies—ice pack, first aid kit, water, and a black hoodie slung over his shoulder. He set everything on the table and handed me a bottle of water and two Tylenol.

"Thank you." I washed the pills down with a few sips, closed the lid, and set the bottle on the floor next to my leather backpack. He must have brought it in. I certainly hadn't.

Rolling up the hoodie like a bolster, he propped up my ankle and placed the ice pack on it with a bar towel underneath. As he cleaned my knee, I stared at the scar on his neck, white against his bronzed olive skin. Thick and raised. Jagged like barbwire. Like someone went for the jugular.

He placed the damp cloth on the table and rummaged around in the first aid kit, coming out with antiseptic wipes. "This might sting," he said, ripping open the packet with his teeth. God, that was sexy. I pictured him doing the same thing with a condom wrapper. "Need a whiskey?"

I laughed a little. I could use a whiskey, but not because of my knee. Scrapes, bruises, and sprains were a regular occurrence in my childhood, thanks to my brother Sawyer who was great at coming up with acts of daring. Stupid me, I followed him into the fire every time.

"I'll be okay."

It stung a little, but once again, he was gentle. He tossed the wipes in the garbage can behind the bar and took a seat on the coffee table across from me. I sat up straighter and angled my body toward him.

"What's your name?" he asked.

"Eden. Eden Madley."

"Killian," he said, not bothering to mention his last name.

"I know. That's why I'm here." His eyes narrowed in accusation, as if I'd tricked him and he was trying to figure out what I wanted from him. "For a job," I said quickly, which didn't appear to set him at ease. "I heard you might be looking for a bartender. And I'm looking to be a bartender."

He rubbed his jaw and squinted at something in the distance. It looked like he was waging a battle with himself. "I don't put women behind the bar."

"You think it's a man's job?"

He shrugged. "Maybe."

"That sounds sexist, you know."

He scowled. "Bartenders stay late. Anywhere from two to four in the morning. Those are dangerous times."

"I live really close. Only a fifteen-minute walk from here, so it's no big—"

"*Walk?*" He looked horror-struck, as if I'd suggested jumping off the Brooklyn Bridge. "You're not walking anywhere at that time of night."

"Fine. I'd take a taxi. You can't discriminate against me just because I'm female."

He opened his mouth to speak, but I rushed in before he got the chance to shoot me down.

"If someone...*you*...just gave me a chance, I know I'd be good at bartending."

He shook his head. "You don't have any experience?" he asked, sounding exasperated.

"No. But I took a course. And I've worked a lot of jobs in the service industry. I was a server for a while, and I know how to use a register. I'm good with people. I'm reliable. Punctual. A hard worker. And I'm not usually such a klutz. I have no idea how that happened."

"It's the road." He whipped out his phone and typed something into it. "I'll take care of it." I got the feeling this guy could take care of anything. I imagined him calling and giving the city hell about the pothole on the road.

"Let me work for one night. If it doesn't work out, you can just ask me to leave. You have nothing to lose." I flashed him a big smile. He didn't look impressed, but I wasn't above begging. I really wanted to work here. Out of all the bars I'd visited, my gut feeling told me this was the right one for me. "Everyone needs to start somewhere, right? I'm just asking for a chance. Please."

"How old are you?"

"Twenty-two. How old are you?"

"I'm not looking for a job."

He was more man than boy, and he didn't look old, but he

didn't look young either. If I had to guess, he was probably my brother Garrett's age. "Twenty-six?"

"Twenty-seven in August," he said, unwilling to acknowledge I'd been right. He was still twenty-six and wouldn't be twenty-seven for another two months. "Are you in college?"

"I just graduated from Penn State in May."

"What do you do in your free time?" he asked.

Was this an interview or was he just making small talk? He didn't strike me as a small talk kind of guy. "Since I moved to Brooklyn, I've been checking out the neighborhoods. Taking photos. And visiting art galleries. I run every day. And I draw and paint." I wasn't sure why I said that. I *used* to draw and paint, but it had been six months since I'd picked up a pencil or paintbrush.

"Which artists do you like?" He tilted his head, as if the answer really mattered to him.

I didn't know what kind of answers he was looking for, or how this had anything to do with bartending. "I like Picasso. Especially his Blue Period. Frida Kahlo. Willem de Kooning. Rodin's sculptures. And the street art and graffiti in Brooklyn."

I stared at the black and grey inked tattoos on his left arm. I'd add them to my list of art I liked. Intricate designs, interwoven with thick swirls and chains. A shield of armor on his upper arm. An anatomical heart and dagger. A Celtic cross. A banner trailing down his forearm, with words written in script. Not English. Latin? I wanted to know what it said and meant to him.

"Why should I take a chance on you?" he asked, reminding me of the reason I came here in the first place.

I dragged my gaze back to his face. God, he was gorgeous. His face was a study in symmetry. My fingers itched to hold a charcoal pencil so I could sketch him.

"I'm looking for a fresh start." Something like recognition

flickered in his eyes, but it was so fleeting, I might have imagined it. "That's why I moved to Brooklyn."

"By yourself?" he asked.

I nodded.

"That's brave."

I wasn't sure about the brave part. So far, it was lonely. And a lot harder than I'd expected. "I really need this job. Brooklyn is expensive. And I can't go home. I just…can't."

He studied my face, and I wondered what he saw there.

"These are the rules. Number one: don't lie to me. Number two: don't steal from me. You ring up every drink you serve. You don't give free drinks to your friends. Number three: no drugs. If you break any of my rules, you're out. Got a problem with anything I said?"

"Are you offering me a job?" I asked, gripping my lower lip between my teeth to keep from smiling. His gaze dropped to my mouth and lingered there before he shook his head and looked away.

"I'm offering you a chance. Not everyone is cut out for bartending. So?"

"I don't lie, steal, or do drugs." The two times I'd smoked pot with Trevor didn't seem worth mentioning.

I held Killian's gaze until he nodded, satisfied I was telling the truth. My face broke into a smile, but he held up his hand to stop me from getting too excited. "You'll have guys hassling you. When they get drunk, they say and do stupid shit. I'm not saying it's right," he shrugged one shoulder, "but you're not unattractive, so you'll need to deal with that."

"I'm not *unattractive*? Are you always this charming?"

"If you're looking for Prince Charming, it ain't me, sunshine."

Sunshine? At least he didn't make any empty promises or

pretend to be something he wasn't. "I don't believe in fairytales. Or happily ever after. Prince Charming was an evil villain in disguise, and Cinderella was the doormat he wiped his feet on." His brows went up a notch. "So, don't worry. I'm not looking for Prince Charming. I'm not looking for a guy to sweep me off my feet either. I'm just looking for a job. And I can handle guys hassling me. My dad and two older brothers taught me how to fend for myself."

He raised a skeptical eyebrow. "Did they?"

"Yes, they did. My dad and brother are state police officers and my other brother is a Marine. I grew up in a testosterone-fueled house with enough badassery to rub off on little old me."

His lips curved into a smile, showing off his straight white teeth…and—oh God, dimples. *He had dimples.* But the smile faded all too quickly, as if he'd caught himself doing something he shouldn't, and the mask slipped firmly into place again.

"Any questions?"

I had a million questions, but I refrained from asking anything too personal. Now that I'd secured a job, I didn't want to blow it with my unfiltered mouth. "Why did you name it Trinity Bar?"

"I didn't. My partner did. His mother is from Trinidad."

"You have a partner? Does he need to interview me?"

"He's away. If you're still here at the end of the week, you'll meet him."

Thanks for the vote of confidence. "I'll still be here."

He gave me a *we'll see* look and said he needed to get me an application. When he disappeared around the corner, I removed the ice pack. Standing, I put weight on my left foot, testing it out. It still hurt, but not white-hot pain. If I taped it up nice and tight, I'd be good to go. I sat back down and pulled the first aid kit into my lap.

When Killian returned, I'd finished taping my ankle. I pulled on my sock and nudged my foot into my boot. It felt like it was two sizes too small now. On the inside, I was screaming in pain, but I schooled my expression.

"You need to rest your ankle," he said.

"I need to walk on it." I took a few tentative steps. This had always been Sawyer's method for dealing with an injury, so I should have known it would hurt like hell. I'd seen him tape up cracked ribs and busted knees, hiding them from the coach, and he always got back on that football field, pretending he was fighting fit. "I'm good to go."

He gave me a skeptical look and handed me the application. "Fill it out at home and bring it back."

I stuffed the application in my backpack. "Do you want me to start tonight?"

He looked at me like I'd lost my mind. I thought, maybe, I had. I hadn't felt like myself since I set eyes on him. "No. Come back tomorrow at five. Bartenders spend a lot of hours on their feet. If your ankle's not better—"

"My ankle will be fine."

He handed me a black T-shirt with white lettering that said Trinity Bar. I checked the label on the collar—men's medium—and held it up in front of me. It would fit me like a mini-dress.

"Just wear it for now," he said. "I'll call you a taxi." He motioned for me to sit back down, and I collapsed on the sofa, acknowledging defeat. Fighting him on this would just be stupid pride on my part. The fifteen-minute walk to my apartment would take me twice as long, and it wouldn't help my ankle.

"Where do you live?" he asked, his phone pressed to his ear.

I gave him my address and the cross streets, and he relayed the information before hanging up. "Five minutes."

Someone knocked on the door, and Killian opened it wide.

"What up, man?" the guy in the doorway asked, bumping fists with Killian. He pulled a pen from behind his ear and handed it to Killian, along with a clipboard.

"I'll let you know when the taxi's here," Killian said.

I nodded and gave him and the delivery guy a smile. "Thanks."

I watched through the open front door as Killian climbed into the back of the delivery truck. A guy with a dark ponytail and a beard called out a greeting to Killian on his way into the bar.

"Hey. I'm Jimmy."

"I'm Eden. Is that your taco truck?"

"Sure is. If you come back later, I'll make you the best taco you've ever eaten."

"Eden. Taxi."

Killian guided me out the door with his arm around my waist. He was tall, six-foot-three or four, and his physicality was overwhelming. At five-seven, I wasn't short, but he dwarfed me. I was trying to tell myself he was just being helpful, a good samaritan, and his nearness didn't mess with my head. He held the taxi door open, and I slid into the backseat, grateful to put some distance between us. Maybe now I could start breathing again. Before he closed the door, Killian handed me his cell phone. "Type in your number."

I entered my number and handed his phone back to him. My phone rang once and stopped. "Call me if you can't make it."

"I'll be here. And thanks for giving me a chance. I really appreciate it."

He nodded once, closed the door, and took a step back. When the taxi pulled away, I leaned my head against the seat and tried to process what had just happened. The only part that was clear was I had a job. Or, at least, a chance to prove myself.

The driver stopped in front of my building, a three-story brick rowhouse, and I fished some money out of my bag. I held it out to him as he held money out to me. "What's that?"

"Your change. Or the guy's change."

"He paid? For my taxi?" I asked, taking the money from his hand.

"You got a problem with that? Are you one of those raging feminists or something?"

"No. I mean, yes, I'm a feminist. But there's nothing raging about it." I rolled my eyes and pressed my lips together to stop myself from going off on a tangent. I'd had this argument too many times at my family dinner table. "I'm just surprised. That's all."

He snorted. "A girl who looks like you…I'd think you'd get plenty of free rides."

I gave him a two-dollar tip, more than he deserved for that kind of sexist talk, and slammed the door shut with more force than necessary.

Sweat beaded my forehead as I hopped up the stairs on my right foot, using the wood banister as a crutch. By the time I reached the third floor, I felt like I'd just scaled Everest. I let myself into my new apartment, double-locked the door, and pulled the chain. This place was secured like Fort Knox. When Garrett and my dad moved me in, they did a full security sweep and found it lacking. My dad installed an additional lock with a deadbolt and made me promise to be vigilant about locking up. If he had his way, there would be bars on the windows too. My dad texted me every day to make sure I was okay. He'd insisted on a code word if I was ever in trouble. How he'd rescue me from three hundred miles away was anyone's guess, but if it helped him sleep at night, I wouldn't begrudge him.

Tossing my bag to the floor, I collapsed on my white Ikea sofa—the only piece of furniture in my living room—and removed my boots and socks. My ankle was swollen, and the bruising had come up just below the ankle.

I stretched out on the sofa and closed my eyes, covering them with my arm to block out the late-afternoon sunlight and all the jumbled thoughts in my brain. But I saw his face and his body, his scars, and tattoos, so clearly in my mind, like it was burned into my memory. I could still feel his arms around me when he carried me, the flex of his muscles, the warmth of his body, his heady scent.

My ringing phone woke me. I blinked in the darkness and answered without checking the screen.

"Eden," Luke said, his voice briefly taking me back to another time and place before he and Lexie shattered my illusion of happiness. But reality crept back in, like always. "We need to talk."

"Go talk to your baby mama."

"We never talked about this, and I want to explain—"

I punched the disconnect key and hurled my new phone across the room. It hit the wall and fell to the hardwood floor with a clatter. *Smart move, Eden.* I hobbled across the room and picked up the device. Even in the dark, I could see the crack in the screen. Great. I broke my new phone. Six months later, and I was still throwing tantrums? I was better than that. This needed to end. Right here. Right now. My phone started ringing again, and I let it go to voicemail. He wouldn't leave a message. He never did.

Who gave him my number?

Ten minutes later, Cassidy's name appeared on the screen. Of course. "Why did you give Luke my new number?" I asked, skipping the greeting.

She sighed. "He kept stopping by my house and begging me." Cassidy had always been a sucker for Luke. Everyone was. "Did you talk to him?"

"No. I hung up, then threw my phone against the wall and cracked the screen."

"Did that give you any satisfaction?"

"A little," I admitted. "But now I have a cracked screen."

She laughed. "How's Brooklyn?"

"Great," I said brightly. Fake it 'til ya make it. But hey, I had an apartment. And a job. I was getting my life together. No more going off the deep end. No more crying in my beer. I wasn't wasting any more time or energy on that. I'd moved on. New life. New me. And a world of possibility, all my own making. "I scored a bartending job today."

"That's great," she said, but her cheer was forced, and that kind of hurt.

Cassidy and I had been friends since junior high. She had stayed in our hometown for college, but she used to visit me at Penn State all the time. Now she was working for an accounting firm and living at home to save money while working on her CPA. She had her whole life mapped out: get a job at a top accounting firm in Pittsburgh and marry a wealthy, handsome man. Someone a lot like Luke.

Despite the baby on the way, it didn't derail Luke's life or his future. In the fall, he'd be starting law school at Duquesne. He and Lexie were living with his doting parents, and I was sure the only thing required of her was to lounge by the pool and look after herself. And her unborn child. We couldn't forget that.

Chapter Five

Killian

"I HIRED A NEW BARTENDER," I INFORMED LOUIS AS I ONE-handedly stocked a shelf of vodka.

"Back up. I've been gone two days. And you fired a bartender and hired a new one?"

"Uh huh." I put my cell phone on speaker and set it on the shelf to work more efficiently. We had a system, and it worked. Nothing worse than a messy supply room when it was time to take inventory or you needed a bottle in a hurry.

"Do I get a vote in this?" Louis asked.

"You hired Chad, the thief. So, no. Your bullshit detector is warped."

Louis muttered something I didn't catch. It sounded a lot like, *"Killian, you're an asshole."*

"It needed to be done," I reminded him.

"Chad's my cousin."

"You don't like that side of the family."

Louis chuckled. "True."

Chad was pocketing the cash instead of ringing up the drinks, and I'd suspected he'd been doing it for a while. It wasn't adding up. The drawer sales didn't match the inventory on the nights he worked. Last night, I'd caught him red-handed, and he'd lied to me. Zeke saw it too, so I had a witness. Two out of three rules broken in one night. The rules were my idea. Louis is a good bartender, a good people person, and my best friend, but sometimes he's too nice and people take advantage of that. Now he leaves the dirty work to me. I don't seek out confrontation, but I don't shy away from it either.

Louis had always dreamed of opening a bar. Why, I had no idea. Running a bar was the last thing I'd wanted to do. But eighteen months ago, when he was ready to open this bar, he asked me to invest in it. I had the money, and I wanted to help him out, so I did. Business was good—Trinity Bar was one of the hottest bars in Williamsburg—but it took years to turn a profit, and I knew that going into it. I'd signed on as a silent partner. But I couldn't afford to be silent anymore. I had a lot of money tied up in this venture, and I had no other source of income now.

"Who did you hire?" Louis asked. In the background, I heard the high-pitched voices of kids screaming. Louis was down in Virginia Beach with his mom, two of his sisters, and their five kids. It was the first real vacation he'd taken since he opened the bar, and I had a feeling it would be his last.

"Uncle Louis," a little girl yelled. "Jordan pulled my hair."

"She kicked me," a boy said.

"You're a big fat baby," she said.

I chuckled as Louis let out a weary sigh. "Hey, Uncle Louis. See you Saturday."

"Saturday can't get here fast enough," Louis muttered. "Who's the bartender?"

"If she's still here by Saturday, you'll meet her."

"*She*? Did I hear you right? What happened to your 'no women behind the bar' policy?"

Another one of my rules, and I'd broken it myself. "Gotta run," I said, cutting the call.

Shit. I forgot to tell him about the quotes for the new roof. I texted him the bad news. He responded with a string of curses and a threat to return early.

Won't change anything. Stay and enjoy your family, I texted back.

"Zeke is in the house!"

I opened the liquor supply room door. "Liquor room," I said, unpacking a box of whiskey.

Zeke stopped in the doorway. "What's up? Do you need help?"

"No." Louis and I were the only ones with keys to the liquor room, and the only ones allowed to venture in here. If the bartenders needed a bottle during service, they had to ask one of us. It was a pain, but we'd had too many problems with theft to relax that policy. "I hired a new bartender. Her name's Eden. She starts tomorrow."

"Is she hot?" Zeke asked.

Is she hot? I couldn't think straight when she was near me. I wanted to keep her talking so I could listen to her sexy, husky voice and watch her lush, pink lips move. Long waves of golden-blonde hair tumbled down her back, and I imagined fisting it in my hand. Vivid green eyes like a cat…I never noticed eye color, but I noticed everything about Eden. Her slim, toned body, legs that went on for miles, perfect round breasts, and the sway of her hips as she crossed the street. The set of her shoulders, and the way she held her head high like she needed to prove she was confident. It worked, until she fell in that fucking pothole.

What possessed me to pick her up and carry her? It was my undoing. If sunshine had a scent, it would smell like Eden.

If it had just been a physical attraction, I'd understand that. But I wanted to know everything about her—who hurt her in the past and made her feel like fairytales couldn't come true. She looked like a girl who should believe in fairytales—the kind of girl who could live in one. After she'd left, I'd Googled

Picasso, focusing on his blue period. Then moved on to Rodin and scrolled through photos of his sculptures before I shut the screen, cursing myself.

What the fuck was wrong with me? I never let women mess with my head.

"She's off limits. I don't care who you screw outside of work. But keep it professional with the new bartender. She's permanently friend-zoned. Got it?"

Zeke grinned. His smiles came easy and often. He was one of my hires, and I'd seen enough to know good from bad within minutes of talking to a person. Zeke was one of the good ones, but he was working his way through every hot girl in the Tri-State area. I had no room to judge, but I didn't want him to hone in on Eden.

"She's hot," Zeke said, and I glared at him. He held up his hands and backed into the hallway. "But she's off limits. Got it."

I gave him a curt nod.

"Does the same rule apply to you?" he asked with a smirk. I wanted to punch him. But I wouldn't. I didn't let my fists do the talking anymore. I'd put that life behind me. New and improved Killian. I used my words now, although they were in short supply. Not a lot came out of my mouth.

Instead of punching him, I closed the door in his face and heard him laughing on the other side. "I still love you, man. You're da bomb."

God knew what I had done to earn his praise. Nothing I said or did ever offended Zeke. He was like Teflon. Everything bounced right off him. *Ping. Ping. Ping.* I'd love to walk a mile in his shoes and see what that felt like. Zeke was a rich boy from Connecticut. His parents loved him, and they just wanted him to be happy. He'd told me that in our interview when I'd asked him why he wanted to be a bartender instead of using his fancy college degree. "Why would bartending make you happy?"

"I'm a people person. Clearly," he'd said, giving me one of his shit-eating grins. "The thought of getting stuck in an office for the rest of my life makes me feel like I'm suffocating. And the way I look at it, your twenties are the time to explore yourself and figure out who you are and what you want out of life. When I leave work, I don't want the aggravation of thinking about it, you know? I just want to kick back and enjoy myself."

Well, good for him. If Eden was looking for Prince Charming, which she claimed she wasn't, Zeke was her man—a pretty-boy who used his charms and corny pick-up lines on all the women he served at the bar. He was a player, and he loved the game. Exactly the reason she was off limits to him. She was off limits to me for an entirely different reason.

The door swung open, and Ava poked her head in. "You're an asshole," she said, confirming something I already knew. She leaned against the doorframe, holding a bag of Cool Ranch Doritos bigger than she was. Ava was a foot shorter than me, tiny and delicate-looking. But appearances were deceptive. She was stronger than she looked. "Did you just slam the door in Zeke's face?"

I broke down the empty boxes, not bothering to answer.

"Good thing I love you so much," Ava said.

It was a good thing. Ava was a loyal friend and put up with my shitty moods and all my baggage. When she was fourteen and I was eighteen, I'd rescued her from getting bullied, and she'd been my most loyal supporter since. Even when I fucked up or hurt her feelings by shutting her out, she stood by me. Unfortunately, she sometimes took it too far. Ava was a social media whizz and took it upon herself to be the virtual Killian Vincent. She skyrocketed me to fame and built a huge following. On my insistence, she shut down those accounts, but you couldn't erase virtual history. In a moment of weakness, I Googled myself about nine months ago, and drowned my self-loathing in a bottle of Jameson.

"Have you heard from Connor?" Ava asked, ripping open the bag of Doritos. She asked the same question every day.

I rolled out my shoulders. "No." My job was to protect Connor and take care of him, but somehow, I failed him. Again. And now I didn't know where in the hell he was.

"He'll be back soon." Another thing she repeated daily, but her voice lacked conviction. Once upon a time, Ava was Connor's girl. He'd claimed she was his whole world, but the Vincent men had a knack for ruining everything good.

Two months and not a word from Connor. Three days after he got out of rehab, clean and sober, he disappeared. Five days later, he left me a voicemail from an unknown number. *"I'm going to find a way to make things better. Thanks for everything you've done for me. I'll make it up to you. Promise. Catch you later."*

Ava held out the bag of Doritos to me, but I waved it away. I hadn't touched junk food in years, but she always offered. For some reason, it annoyed her that I always refused.

"You're not training anymore," she huffed, stuffing a handful of Doritos in her mouth. She crushed them between her teeth like they deserved punishment for my refusal.

My diet wasn't as strict as it used to be, and my current workout sessions were a joke compared to the grueling hours I'd put in before, but I still didn't see the need to fill my body with junk.

"I saw Seamus earlier," she said, and winced like it physically pained her to mention his name. "He asked if I'd heard from Connor."

Seamus Vincent. My father's name didn't strike fear in me. Not anymore. But if he got to Connor before I did, that would be bad. Connor wasn't built like me, and I didn't mean size and bulk. He wasn't made to get his hands dirty. Connor was smart and sensitive. An artist. Sometimes I still thought of him as a sweet little kid with an innocence I tried to protect at any cost. But growing up in our house was a bad dream you couldn't escape no matter how hard you tried. Even though Connor rarely had a hand laid on him, it was no less soul-destroying. I wore his designs on my arm and my back. He used to keep his sketchbooks hidden under the mattress. Otherwise, they would have been ridiculed and torn to shreds. The name-calling didn't roll off Connor's back like he'd pretended it did. He'd internalized it, took it to heart, and believed every word.

His opiate addiction began when he was seventeen, but I'd been too busy chasing my dreams to notice the signs. When I was twenty, I made my UFC debut and dedicated all my time and energy to becoming the best, but it came with a price. I'd gotten Connor out of my father's house, but I was rarely home, so he'd been left to his own devices. By the time I'd found out he was in trouble, he'd moved on to heroin, and the shitty part was Ava had needed to clue me in. How the fuck had I missed something so obvious? To say I failed him was the understatement of the century.

Ava tucked her pale purple hair behind her ear. "Tell me about this girl you hired."

"Did you book that band?" I couldn't remember their name. Ava dealt with all of that.

"All taken care of. It's on our website, Twitter, Facebook… all the stuff you never look at."

"The building reg—"

"The file's on your desk. What's the deal with Eden?" she prompted, tapping away on her phone while she spoke.

"No deal. She needed a job. We needed a bartender."

Ava smirked and kept typing. *Tap. Tap. Tap.* Most likely, she was promoting the bar, making it sound like the place everyone needed to be even if they didn't know it yet. "Did Eden play the damsel in distress card? You're a sucker for that."

I wasn't a sucker for it, unless it was genuine. Eden didn't do it intentionally, but it had happened. I chuckled at the memory, and Ava's brows hitched up like the sound was foreign to her. "Are you planning to be her white knight?"

I was nobody's white knight, but when Eden crashed into my life, all my protective instincts had kicked into overdrive. Her eyes were clear and bright. Her face was unguarded, giving away all her emotions. If she had lied to me, I would have been able to read it on her face in an instant. But she wanted a fresh start, and I'd do my best to see that she got it. The best thing I could do for her was keep her safe from guys like me, and all the other wolves who would be hounding her.

Christ. What was I thinking? Did I need another person to worry about? Hell no.

Chapter Six

Eden

A GUY WITH SHAGGY BLOND HAIR AND EARBUDS TUCKED IN his ears joined me outside the door of Trinity Bar where my knocking had gone unanswered. He was good-looking in a pretty boy way, and I guessed this could be Hailey's sunshine and light. He looped the headphones around his neck and folded his hands as if in prayer. "There must be a God. Heaven just sent me an angel."

I laughed at his corny line, and he rewarded me with a grin.

"You need to use the secret knock." He whipped out his phone and sent a text.

"Are you Zeke?" I asked.

"My reputation precedes me. But I know we've never met because I'd remember." He waggled his eyebrows.

"I'm Eden. The new bartender."

"Whoa." He held his hand over his heart and staggered. "Didn't see that coming." He held up a hand and bowed his head. "Just give me a minute to recuperate."

I couldn't help but laugh again. "You okay now?"

"Yeah. The shock has worn off."

"Why is it such a big deal?"

"I'm just messing with you. The T-shirt gave you away." I looked down at the T-shirt I tied in a knot at my belly button. I paired it with cut-off jean shorts and plain black motorcycle boots. Trailer trash meets vintage shop. "Killian told me about you, so I guess we should stick to a professional working relationship."

"Sounds like a good plan."

Zeke snapped his fingers. "Damn. Now you'll always be the one who got away."

"I have a feeling you'll get over it."

He sighed. "Yeah. I fall in lust at least three times a night. It's an occupational hazard."

I shook my head, laughing as the door swung open, and a guy with a deep, dark tan and short dreads let us in. "This is Brody. Resident world traveler and slacker. Eden's the new bartender."

Brody bobbed his head. "Cool."

"That's all he ever says," Zeke stage-whispered as we followed Brody inside. "He's mono-syllabic."

"Heard that, dude. We're outside tonight. Watch your back."

Zeke laughed and wished me luck while pointing me in the direction of Killian's office. "Zeke is in the house!" he yelled on his way outside.

I followed the sound of voices and stopped outside the open door of a windowless office with a filing cabinet and shelves lined with binders. Killian was leaning against the desk, arms crossed, a scowl on his face. He was wearing an untucked black button-down shirt, the cuffs rolled up to his elbows, with black jeans and beat-up black combat boots. He looked like a rock star, and despite the perma-scowl, he looked as good as I remembered. Maybe even better. The girl sitting in the swivel chair across from him looked to be around my age, with long lavender hair and delicate features. She had creamy skin, and her black eyeliner was thick and winged. Bluebirds trapped inside barbed wire wrapped around her right bicep. She looked like a porcelain doll with a rocker edge.

They were so engrossed in their argument, they hadn't noticed me.

"Take down the photos of me," Killian growled.

"You're so weird about social media. The customers love seeing your pretty face. It's good for business."

He glared at her.

I knocked on the doorframe, announcing my presence, and they both swiveled in my direction.

Killian's eyes locked on mine, and all the air was trapped in my lungs. He held my gaze for a few seconds before rubbing his hands over his face, like he was trying to erase the memory. I knew the feeling. I'd done the same thing last night when he'd kept invading my thoughts.

"You must be Eden," the girl said. I turned my focus to her and nodded, incapable of speech. My heart was hammering against my chest so loudly, they could probably hear it. This was ridiculous. She gave me a smile that made me feel like she was in on a secret I wasn't aware of. "I'm Ava. The brains behind this operation."

Killian snorted, and Ava smirked at him.

"Nice to meet you," I told Ava.

"You too."

I dug around in my backpack until I found the folded application. Ava was watching me with curiosity, her head tilted, her index finger pressed against her lips. I smoothed out the creases, and Ava took the application from me. Fishing out the twenty-dollar bill from my pocket, I held it out to Killian.

"What's that?" he asked, arms crossed, making no move to take the money.

"Your money. You didn't need to pay for my taxi."

He jerked his chin at Ava. "Give it to Ava for her taxi tonight."

I offered her the money.

"I get paid a salary. I don't need taxi money."

Killian snatched the bill out of my hand and forced it on Ava. With a roll of her eyes, she pocketed the cash, grumbling, "You're an ogre." Though, her smile told me she didn't mean it.

"Come with me," Killian said, indicating for me to precede him. "How's your ankle?" His gaze traveled from the big scab on my knee to my ankle as we walked down the hallway. I made a concentrated effort not to limp.

"It's fine." My ankle still hurt a little bit, but I'd rested it all day and wrapped it. He gave me a skeptical look I chose to ignore.

I followed him behind the bar and stowed my bag in a cupboard Killian locked up. He introduced me to Chris, a tall, lanky guy wearing a backwards baseball cap, who was checking the lines for the kegs.

Killian showed me the setup and talked me through the wine list, all the different tequilas, seven craft beers on tap, and a selection of bottled beers. The hour flew by as I performed the opening duties on the checklist alongside Chris—chopped fruit for garnishes, filled the ice bins, stocked the clean glasses, set up bus tubs. When six o'clock rolled around, I was organized and ready. Or so I kept telling myself.

"Is Killian okay to work for?" I asked Chris, keeping my voice low while Killian went to unlock the front door.

"If you follow his rules, it's cool. He won't hold your hand, though. It's baptism by fire."

"Oh God. I don't want to go down in flames."

Chris laughed. "He won't let you get in the weeds. He's too much of a control freak."

Okay, still not setting me at ease. Talk about mixed messages. Was he a control freak or someone who tossed you into the fire to see how you dealt with getting burned?

Here goes nothing, I thought as a group entered the bar.

No need to panic. I've totally got this. All I needed to focus on was mixing drinks, serving them, and ringing them up. *How hard could it be?*

Turned out, it was harder than it looked.

Killian wasn't impressed with my mojitos. Apparently, I didn't bash the mint enough. He showed me how to do it the right way—his way. Not long after the mojito tutorial, I grabbed two bottles of liquor from the top shelf, spun around, and rammed into Killian's chest. He steadied me with his hands on my upper arms, but quickly dropped his arms to his side like my skin burned him.

"Sorry. Did I hurt you?" Stupid question. Killian was made of the same steel Sawyer was, forged by hours of exercise and conditioning. You didn't get a body like his without putting a lot of time and work into it. He was all lean muscle without an ounce of fat.

"When someone says *behind you*, pay attention."

"Sorry. I didn't hear you."

"Just take it easy," he said, his tone softer. "Nobody's life is at stake."

So, I stopped trying to rush around like a headless chicken, and it worked a lot better. Indie rock music was blasting from the sound system, and I'd gotten into a rhythm. I had a system working, giving a nod to the new customers to let them know I saw them, and serving the ones who'd been waiting the longest.

A man in the corner called me over. He was older than the rest of the crowd, early fifties maybe. A big man, all bulging muscle, with closely cropped dark hair and a hard face, like it had been chiseled from granite.

I set a paper coaster in front of him. "What can I get you?"

"Jack and Coke," he said, his gaze focused on Killian.

I mixed his drink, side-eying Killian, who was serving margaritas to a group of women at the other end of the bar. A lot of hair-tossing and giggling was being directed his way, but it was in vain. He was either oblivious or not interested. When I set the Jack and Coke in front of the man, he looked me up and down, his steel-blue eyes containing no warmth. "You been working here long?"

"It's my first night."

"You one of Killian's groupies?"

"Groupie? What—?"

The man shook his head and snorted in disgust. "He never learns, does he?"

"What does that mean?" I asked, even though I sensed I should just keep my mouth shut and collect his money. When would *I* ever learn?

"Beautiful women are nothing but trouble. He should know that by now. But he's never been the smartest boy."

Okay, I was dealing with a misogynist who just insulted me *and* Killian. What did he mean by groupie? I planted my hands on my hips. He raised his eyebrows, waiting for me to say something I'd regret. I bit back the words I was tempted to say and adopted a professional tone. "That will be eight—"

A hand on my upper arm guided me away. I looked up at Killian, whose gaze was fixed on the man. "Take a break. Jimmy will give you food."

"I need to—"

"Come back in fifteen minutes."

"But—"

"Go," Killian cut me off, his tone sharp and face stern.

Did he think I couldn't handle it? Killian turned his back to me and took my place in front of the man, blocking my view with his body.

"Got yourself a fancy bar with all these pretty people," the man said. "You don't belong here, boy. You ain't cut out for this life. And get a haircut. You look like a fucking pussy."

"What do you want?" Killian asked, his voice devoid of all emotion.

"When are you gonna smarten up and get back to fighting? It's the only thing you're good at."

Killian kept his voice low, so I couldn't catch any more of the conversation. Not that it was intended for my ears anyway.

Chapter Seven

Eden

A s I exited the employee restroom, I ran into Ava coming out of the office. "You're taking a break?"
I nodded.
"Me too. I'm addicted to Jimmy's tacos. It's a serious problem."

I looked at her rail-thin body and laughed. Ava was tiny, built like a ballet dancer, and a few inches shorter than me. "It doesn't look like a problem to me."

The courtyard was heaving with people crowding the picnic tables. Zeke and Brody were whipping up frozen drinks, and a group I'd served earlier was dancing under hundreds of fairy lights strung from the foliage-covered rafters.

We lined up behind a few people waiting for tacos, and I studied the menu on the side of Jimmy's truck. "What do you recommend?" I asked Ava. "Since you're such an addict."

"The chorizo. Or the shrimp and mole. Or the carnitas..." She stopped and laughed. "They're all good."

"I'll go with your first choice."

Jimmy took our orders, and a few minutes later, handed us our tacos in cardboard containers. My soft taco was loaded with guacamole, sour cream, cheese, lettuce, and salsa verde. "Come back and tell me it's the best taco you've ever eaten." Jimmy pointed at me. "Or no more tacos for you." He laughed to let me know it was a joke.

Ava and I found a quiet spot along the back wall and sat on the ground, our legs kicked out in front of us. While I'd been working, I'd forgotten about my ankle, but now that I was sitting, it was throbbing.

I folded my taco, trying to contain all the ingredients, as that man's words ran through my head. Why had he put Killian down? I wanted to swoop in and defend him, not that he'd allow that or even want it. I didn't even know Killian. Why did I feel so defensive on his behalf? And what kind of fighting was the man talking about?

"How's your first night going?" Ava asked.

"It's good. I'm having fun." Except for a few glitches and that man. Could he be Killian's dad?

I took a big bite of my taco, not realizing how hungry I was. It was delicious, and nothing like the Old El Paso tacos we used to make from a kit when we were growing up.

"How long has this bar been open?" I asked.

"A year and a half. But Killian didn't get actively involved until a year ago. He put the money in from the start, but he didn't spend as much time here in the beginning. Now, he practically lives here."

"Has he always been in the bar business?"

"He did other things too," she said vaguely.

I waited for her to expand, but she didn't. I guessed that was all the information I was going to get.

"So, what's your job here?" I asked, taking another bite of my taco.

"I do the social media and promotions. Book the entertainment, the accounting, general office work…whatever they need."

"Sounds like you really are the brains behind the operation."

She laughed. "That was a joke. It's a shitload of work

running a bar, and between you and I, Louis, the other owner, is a good front man. He's even-keeled, and an all-around good guy. But Killian is better at taking charge and running things." I heard the pride in her voice, but I couldn't tell whether she had a crush on Killian, was his girlfriend, or it was something else.

"Have you known Killian a long time?"

"Since ninth grade. Killian was a senior. I mean, I knew who he was before that. We grew up in the same neighborhood in Bay Ridge and went to the same school. But I didn't get to know him until he rescued me from getting bullied. Nobody messed with me after that. If they tried, they'd have to get through him first. Good luck with that."

I couldn't imagine anyone messing with Killian. Except, maybe, the man I served earlier. "I think I served his dad earlier. I mean...I just got the feeling..."

"Big man? Looks like a bull?"

"That sounds about right."

Her face darkened. "I hate that man. I don't know why Killian even talks to him."

I would have loved to have known more, but she was done talking about it. We finished eating our tacos, and I wiped my hands and mouth with the paper napkins. "I need to get back," I said, gathering up our cardboard containers.

"Yeah. I'm out of here."

As I dumped our trash in the garbage can by the truck, I told Jimmy it was the best taco I'd ever eaten. He gave me a thumbs up. "I'd never lead you astray."

When I returned to the bar, Killian's dad was gone, and he didn't mention it. The rest of the night went smoothly, and we had a steady but manageable crowd.

Now I was sitting alone on a barstool waiting for Killian, who had offered me a ride home. He hadn't just offered, he'd insisted on it. *"I'm driving you home. Wait for me."*

"I can catch a taxi."

"I'm driving you home. Take a seat."

"You can't just issue orders and expect me to follow them."

I wasn't sure why I'd fought him on it. Maybe it was the way he'd said it—in a brusque tone that implied it was his obligation, rather than his pleasure, to drive me home.

"Door's locked. I have the keys. Sit and wait for me."

He hadn't been kidding—he was no Prince Charming. But I didn't trust Prince Charming anymore, so I sat and I waited. It was quiet now, except for the hum of the refrigerators, but my ears were still ringing from the music earlier, and my body was buzzing with energy. I checked my phone as a text came through from Killian and smiled when I saw it was my schedule.

"Let's go," Killian said, striding past me.

I shouldered my bag and followed him outside. "You don't need to drive me home every night I work," I said as he pulled down the metal gate over the building. It wasn't like I didn't want him to drive me home. I just didn't want him to feel obligated.

"Are you going to fight me on everything?" he asked, sounding exasperated.

"No. Only if you're being unreasonable or acting like a bully," I said as we walked up South Fourth Street.

"I'm not a bully." A beat later, he asked, "You think I'm a bully?"

After working with him all night, I got the feeling asking someone's opinion was rare. "I don't know. You tell me. Are you a bully?"

"You're my employee. It's my job to protect you and make sure you get home safely."

Wow. My dad would be thrilled I was working for a badass

who considered it his duty to protect me. "Williamsburg seems pretty safe to me."

"Are you from Brooklyn?" Killian asked.

"No."

"Did you grow up in a city?"

"No."

He raised his brows like he'd scored a victory.

"Have you ever been to a frat party?" I asked.

Killian beeped the locks of a black Jeep Wrangler and opened the passenger door for me.

"No."

"Have you ever been chased by a bear?" I asked.

"What the fuck?"

I smothered a laugh and climbed into the Jeep, stowing my backpack at my feet. We fastened our seatbelts, and Killian turned the key in the ignition. Music pumped through the speakers, a band and song I didn't recognize. Grunge with cryptic lyrics. The song reminded me of Killian, although I couldn't say why. "What is this?" I pointed to his sound system.

"Bush. 'Greedy Fly.'"

We rolled down our windows, letting in the warm night air and the odor of asphalt and garbage—the smell of summer in Brooklyn. Killian was a fast driver. One hand on the steering wheel and the other on the gearshift, his face illuminated by the glow of the dash.

"You've been chased by a bear?" he asked, hanging a left on Berry Street.

"Yeah. It was my brother Sawyer's favorite family holiday. He's an adrenaline junkie and loved the rush. Luckily, he and I were good tree climbers."

"Jesus Christ. Who are you?"

"Depends on who you ask. My brothers used to call me a

trouble magnet. Only because I was Sawyer's partner in crime. Bad move. It usually left me scrambling for my life."

His chest rumbled with laughter. The sound filled the Jeep and echoed in the night air. It was the first time I'd heard him laugh, and it was the best sound ever.

"I never thanked you for the other day," I said. "For taking care of my ankle and knee."

He glanced at me briefly, then fixed his gaze on the road again. "It wasn't a big deal."

"It was a nice thing to do."

He shrugged one shoulder, dismissing it, like it was hard to accept a compliment. Storefronts, bars, and cafes passed by in a blur, and at this hour, the streets were ours. A couple stumbled out of Fat Earl's, a bar on the corner, and started making out against the brick wall.

"You can drop me off at the next corner. My street is a one-way—"

But he was already turning up North Fifth Street so he could take Driggs and drive down my block. When he turned down North Sixth, I directed him farther up the block. He stopped in front of my building and peered out the window at it. "Which floor are you on?"

"The penthouse. Third floor."

"You left your windows open."

"It gets hot and stuffy inside."

"Close and lock your windows when you leave. It's dangerous."

"Do you think Spiderman is going to spin a web and scale the wall?"

He scowled at me. "Close your windows."

"Okay."

"Okay? No argument?"

"Disappointed?" I asked as I unfastened my seatbelt and grabbed my bag, which had way more cash in it than I'd expected to haul in on a Tuesday night.

"Suspicious."

I laughed. "You showed me the error of my ways. Thanks for the ride."

"I'll drive you home when you work. Save you the taxi money."

"Where do you live?" I didn't want to get out of the car. I wanted to keep talking to him. Keep driving through the streets, listening to his music, and watching the city blur past our windows in a neon haze. "Is it on your way?"

"Greenpoint. And yes."

"Was that your dad who came in earlier?"

"Uh huh," he said, staring straight ahead at the windshield.

"I like your hair. You have great hair," I blurted out, and immediately regretted it. Why had I said that? Where was my filter?

He clenched his jaw so tight, I heard his molars grinding. "Next time I send you away, don't hang around eavesdropping. That conversation was none of your damn business."

"I know. I'm sorry. I didn't know—"

"Now you do," he said, his tone harsh and his jaw set. I knew all he wanted was for me to get out of his car and leave him alone, so that was what I did.

As I was unlocking the front door of my building, I heard his engine idling. I wasn't entirely surprised he waited until I was inside, but it was nice he cared about my safety, I guess. When I got inside, I watched through the frosted glass window as Killian pulled away, and I kept watching until his taillights disappeared.

Upstairs, I dragged out all my art supplies, set up my easel and stool in a corner by the living room window, and attached a fresh canvas to a piece of plywood with a bull clip. I squeezed the tubes of paints onto my palette, mixed the colors, and painted. Bold brushstrokes. Great washes of color. Curves and broken lines. Building up the surface and destroying it again. Moving the paint around on the entire surface. I kept painting, losing all track of time, until the sky outside my window was streaked with orange and pink, then changed to a pale yellow.

Out of the chaos, something resembling art began to emerge. When I stood back and looked at my work, the painting reminded me of Killian. It was wild and turbulent, dark, and tension-filled, with slivers of light showing through the cracks. A beautiful, chaotic mess.

Chapter Eight

Eden

"**W**HAT'S THIS?" KILLIAN ASKED, LOOKING AT THE Tupperware container I set on the desk next to his computer. He was sitting on the leather swivel chair, typing something. I noticed he used the hunt and peck method, typing with his index fingers.

"Chocolate chip cookies. They're for you. I mean, you could share, but I baked them for you."

He leaned back in his chair and pulled the container into his lap. "You baked them? For me?" The way he said it, you'd think I'd just given him the Taj Mahal. He pried open the lid and looked inside, a perplexed look on his face.

"Do you like chocolate chip cookies?"

"Yeah. I like them. But why?" he asked, his brows knitted, like he couldn't make sense of why someone would do something nice for him.

I shrugged. I wasn't entirely sure why I baked him cookies. I was in the grocery store, saw the bag of Nestle chocolate chips, and thought about the things Killian's dad said to him. Since I'd been the one to bring it up in the car, I wanted to make it better. When we were kids, if we had a bad day at school, my mom always baked with us. While we baked cookies or cupcakes or brownies, we talked about our problems, and by the time we'd finished licking the bowl and spoons, we'd always felt better. Chocolate chip cookies wouldn't take the sting out of his dad's words, but I offered them anyway.

"Just to say thank you," I said. "For giving me a job."

Ava walked into the office and did a double-take. She looked at the cookies, then at Killian, over to me, and back to Killian. "You're eating cookies?" She raised her brows as Killian took a bite.

He didn't answer, because it was obvious he was. "Wow. This is epic. Can I get a photo?"

Killian narrowed his eyes, but didn't respond. I didn't understand what the big deal was, and nobody bothered explaining it to me. But Killian seemed happy with his cookies, so that was good enough for me. It only dawned on me later—I'd never baked chocolate chip cookies for Luke.

★ ★ ★

My fifth shift at the bar, and I was starting to feel more competent. I was working with Killian and Louis, who was no stranger to the gym. He had a shaved head, his dark skin so smooth and glossy, I was tempted to ask if he waxed it.

Luckily, Louis was a good guy, and he was okay with Killian hiring me.

Although they co-owned the bar, the entire staff took their problems to Killian first. I didn't know whether it was because Killian was the dominant alpha male, a natural leader, or just a bigger control freak than Louis, who was more laidback and easygoing.

On the first night I'd worked with Louis, he answered the question without me having to ask. "Killian needs to take control of a situation. He doesn't know any other way."

"It doesn't bother you?"

"I let Killian do what he needs to do. But when he takes it

too far, I wade in and make nice with the people he pisses off."

I laughed. "But you guys are good friends?"

"Yeah. He's a pain in the ass, but he's good people, and I couldn't have done this without him."

In the past week, I learned a few things about Killian. On our drives home, we talked. I did most of the talking, but he didn't seem to mind. And every now and then, he came out with an insightful observation.

"Is art like therapy for you?" he'd asked one night, genuinely interested in my answer. Killian didn't make conversation just to hear himself talk, and he didn't waste his words on idle chit-chat.

"Yeah, it is. I guess it's easier to express your feelings through painting sometimes. You can take all the crap inside you and put it on the canvas. And believe me, I put a lot of crap on the canvas."

"I bet it's not crap," he'd said, though I'd had no idea what would make him think I was any good.

I also knew Killian worked out at the gym every day and ran in McCarren Park like I did, although our paths had never crossed. He appeared calm on the surface, but I could tell he worked hard to control his temper. I got the feeling he was hiding a lot inside, and he locked down his emotions, like Sawyer—like all the guys in my family. I should have been used to it by now, but I still felt compelled to dig deeper—one of my tragic flaws.

Since I'd moved to Brooklyn, I'd been doing a lot of soul-searching, not only trying to figure out where Luke and I went wrong, but what I wanted out of my life. Growing up in a small town, people labeled you and put you in a box. In high school, I played the role assigned to me. Head cheerleader dating the captain of the football team. Homecoming Queen. Younger sister of the wide receiver, the school's bad boy who left a trail of broken hearts in his wake. High school was a popularity contest I'd pretended not to play.

I'd always loved art with a passion, but I'd kept it private and never hung out with the artsy kids. I hung out with the jocks and cheerleaders and tried to reconcile those two very different people. College hadn't been a lot different. Similar people, similar setting, but on a larger scale.

Now, I was living and working at a bar in Williamsburg, a young, artsy, vibrant neighborhood, and nobody had any preconceptions about who I was. I could be myself, in all my flawed glory, and it was liberating. Taking charge of my own life. Figuring out what truly made me happy and surrounding myself with people I liked hanging out with.

I set a draft beer in front of a guy with a blond buzzcut and colorful tattoo sleeves and took his money. When I returned with his change, he and Killian were talking.

"You ever need a tattoo, come and see me at Forever Ink. Name's Jared." Jared reached across the bar and shook my hand. "You can see my masterpiece right there on Killian's arm."

"That's good advertising," I said. "His arm is a work of art."

Killian gave me a sidelong glance. "You think so?"

"It's beautiful."

Jared winked at me. "I like a girl who appreciates good ink."

"Eden's an artist," Killian told Jared.

I raised my brows. *An artist?*

Killian raised his brows. *Yeah. Because I said so.*

He said it as if I had paintings displayed in galleries. Meanwhile, the only thing Killian knew about my art was what I had told him.

"When's Connor coming back?" Jared asked Killian. "The shop's busy. I could use him."

Killian cleared his throat. "Soon."

"Who's Connor?" I asked. Killian tensed, and even though no part of his body was touching mine, I could still feel it. That's the way it was for me, though. I could feel him even when he was clear across the room. I'd never experienced that with anyone before, and I didn't understand why I was so attuned to his moods.

"Killian's younger brother," Jared said. "He's an artist too. A free spirit. Can't always pin him down."

Killian rubbed the back of his neck. The conversation was making him uncomfortable. Time for a subject change.

"I'm thinking about getting a tattoo," I said.

"Do it. Ink is encouraged," Jared said.

"You want a tattoo?" Killian asked, sounding intrigued by the idea.

I'd considered it before, but never that seriously. "Yes, I want a tattoo." Jared handed me his card, and I pocketed it.

A little while later, Killian asked where I'd get the tattoo. I placed my hand on my right hip, just below the waistband of my shorts. His eyes darkened, and I needed to turn away from him before I self-combusted.

Working this closely with Killian was proving to be difficult. His arm brushed against mine, sending a jolt of electricity through my body. His chest pressed against my back when he needed to move past me. We did this dance all night long, every night I worked with him.

It was after midnight, and Killian had changed the music to psychedelic trip-hop, giving the bar a chilled-out vibe. A guy walked in the bar and called me over. He had a preppy rich boy look—classically good-looking with brown hair cut in short layers. His gray, tailored suit looked like it had cost more than my rent. I cleared the empty glasses in front of him and wiped down the bar. He ordered a Tecate and a tequila shot. "Start a tab," he said, handing me his credit card. "Wanna do a shot with me?"

"No, thanks. I'm good."

I started a tab and set the beer and tequila in front of him. He downed the shot, set the glass on the counter, and ordered another one. I brought over the bottle and poured.

By the time I served four gin and tonics to a group farther down the bar, he was ready for another round.

"Bad day?" I asked, setting the beer in front of him. He'd taken off his suit jacket and slung it over the back of his stool.

"Shitty day. I lost a lot of money. I'm a trader at a hedge fund." I nodded like that made perfect sense, even though I didn't know much about the financial world, and it had never especially interested me.

"Other than the days when you lose money, do you like your job?" I asked, because job satisfaction was a topic that interested me.

"I'm good at what I do. And I like the money. Anyone who says they don't care about money is lying." He cuffed the sleeves of his white shirt, revealing a Rolex on his left wrist. "The one with the most toys wins."

"And I guess you want to be the biggest winner."

"I have a lot of toys." He flashed me a smile, confident in his ability to charm. I was sure a lot of girls would fall for it. But making money for the sake of it didn't impress me. Neither did bragging about his toys.

I left him guzzling his beer and moved on to other customers, but he kept calling me back.

"What's your name?"

"Eden."

"If you offered me an apple, I'd succumb to temptation."

"That was Eve."

"But the apple came from your garden, Eden."

"Don't hold that against me."

"I won't. My name's Adam, by the way."

"For real?"

He laughed. "For real. Adam and Eden," he said.

"It was Eve."

"Eve. Eden." He reached for my hand and pressed a kiss on it. It was a soft kiss, just a brush of his lips, but it felt strange, and not altogether welcome, so I yanked my hand away. Undeterred, Adam lifted his beer in the air, toasting me. "The beautiful Eve. I'll drink to that."

He kept powering through his shots and beers like he was on a mission to see how fast he could get shit-faced. Despite all his toys and money, he was in a bar, drinking alone.

"Eden," Adam shouted, a little while later. "I need you."

"Is that guy bothering you?" Killian asked as I rang up a drink order. I slid the tab under the credit card and looked over my shoulder at Adam. His eyes were glossy and unfocused. He had downed a lot of alcohol in a short amount of time, but now I was thinking he'd started long before he came in here.

"He's harmless. I'll cut him off though."

"I'll take care of it."

I grabbed his arm to stop him. He looked down at my hand, and I dropped it to my side. "I can handle this."

He frowned.

"Would you have stepped in if I were Zeke?"

"Zeke doesn't have guys hassling him," he scoffed.

"Hey, Killian," Louis said and we both looked over at him. "If you make yourself crazy over every guy who looks at her, you'll be too busy to serve the customers."

Killian ran his hand through his hair. "Fuck. This is exactly why we shouldn't put women behind the bar."

I rolled my eyes. Louis winked at me. Killian scowled. I

returned to Adam.

"I need more tequila," Adam said, slurring his words.

"You've had enough," I said firmly.

He closed his eyes and shook his head. "I need more." He opened his eyes and grabbed my hand again, but this time his grip was strong, and he tried to pull me closer. "I need you. Come home with me. You know how to make things better, don't you, Eve?"

I pulled my hand free. "No. I don't."

Killian growled. Yes, he growled. "Keep your fucking hands off her."

Adam leaned back in his seat and crossed his arms. "My hands aren't on her," he said, his tone surly. "You need to chill out."

Killian glared at Adam and followed me to the register, getting right in my space as I closed out Adam's tab. "That was unnecessary," I said, looking him in the eye. We were so close I could see the thin rim of black around the outside of his iris. Why did he have to smell so good? It was like he'd marinated in pheromones. I was tempted to take a few steps back to fight this chemical reaction, but I held my ground. "I told you I can handle him. Pounding your chest and acting like a caveman is not cool. Not to me, anyway." I wasn't overly impressed with Adam, but Killian didn't need to turn it into a major issue either.

He narrowed his very blue eyes at me. "It's my job to protect you from assholes. It's your job to serve drinks. Not to play shrink."

I rolled my eyes and stepped around the mountain of muscle that was Killian. Setting Adam's card and receipt in front of him, I handed him a pen. "Is he your boyfriend?" Adam asked.

"No." I could feel Killian's eyes boring a hole into the back of my head.

Adam jammed his credit card in his wallet and threw down a wad of cash for a tip. "Give me your number. I'll take you to dinner."

I shook my head no and reached for his tab and receipt. My pen still in his hand, he grabbed my arm and wrote his number on it. "Call me."

I had no intention of ever calling him, and I didn't want his number on my arm. But Adam smiled like we'd brokered a deal before he turned and stumbled to the door. "Goodnight, Eve," he called over his shoulder.

On our way home, Killian brought up Adam again. "That guy was all over you. I didn't like it."

Was he jealous? It was hard to tell with him. "I was trying to be nice to him."

"Too nice." He looked at my arm where Adam's number was still written in ink. "That's the kind of guy you like?"

"No, it's not the kind of guy I like." Adam had the same preppy golden boy look as Luke, and there had been a time when I was attracted to that type. But Luke and I had met young, and his douchebag behavior, his quest for power and money, and his sense of entitlement, hadn't been fully developed yet. Adam had already shown me that side of himself, and I knew it wasn't something I wanted.

"You didn't wash off his number," Killian said.

"I didn't get around to it." I'd been busy with my closing duties and had mostly forgotten about it. As soon as I got home, I'd scrub it off.

I expected Killian to drop the subject, but he pressed on. "Do you want him to take you to dinner?"

"Why does it even matter to you?" I asked, annoyed with this conversation and his persistence.

Instead of answering, he pressed his lips together. If left to him, the rest of the ride would be in silence.

"Hey, Killian."

He grunted. Caveman-style.

"Does it hurt to get a tattoo?"

Killian shrugged. "It just feels like a needle scratching your skin. Annoying more than anything. But it doesn't hurt. Not for me, anyway."

"Tough guy, huh?"

"Thick skin. Not as delicate as yours."

"I'm pretty tough."

"You're also stubborn. You'd probably say it doesn't hurt even if it does."

"Probably. I grew up with boys. They wouldn't have let me hang out with them if I'd been a big cry baby. Whatever they could do, I could do better."

"And were you…better?"

I laughed, thinking about some of the stupid stunts I'd pulled. Nine times out of ten they back-fired. Like that dirt bike accident. Sawyer and I built jumps in the woods behind our house. When I took the jump, I bragged, "I'm flying so high I can see straight into the next county." Unfortunately, I didn't nail the landing. "No. But not for lack of trying."

"Why doesn't that surprise me?"

When he pulled up in front of my building, I said, "You're only a caveman sometimes. When we do talk, you're a good conversationalist. And you're not charmless. I've seen you be quite charming, so I know you're capable of it and—"

"You don't need to lie to protect my feelings."

"I'm not lying. Underneath your tough exterior, I know—"

"I'm not a gooey marshmallow underneath. Don't fool yourself into thinking I am."

He could try to hide it all he wanted, but I knew he was a

good person. He'd defended Ava against bullies. He'd given me a job even though I had zero bartending experience. And Jimmy had told me Killian had recruited his taco truck for the courtyard. Before that, Jimmy said he had barely been making ends meet, but now business was good, and he had a steady gig.

I also knew the tattoos on Killian's arm meant something to him, and he wouldn't have inked his skin if they didn't. Someone broke his heart. Stabbed it with a dagger. Even though his face was usually shuttered, I'd seen fleeting moments when it wasn't. And in the short amount of time I'd known him, I'd started to care about him, and I had an overwhelming urge to protect all the feelings he tried so hard to hide. I didn't understand why. I just did.

"Where's your brother?" I asked quietly.

"I don't know." He rolled out his shoulders. "He's a runner. Takes off when things get hard."

I bet Killian would never run from trouble. I bet he'd stay and fight his corner, even if all the odds were stacked against him. "Everyone has their coping mechanisms."

"Guess so."

"If you ever want to throw some paint on a canvas, I can hook you up. It's good therapy, apparently."

He chuckled under his breath. "Thanks."

"Anytime."

Chapter Nine

Killian

Louis let out a low whistle. "That is one sweet ass."

I grunted. *Keep your eyes off her ass.* Since he was looking straight ahead, he wasn't referring to any of the women in the yoga session on the lawn.

I'd never seen her running in McCarren Park before, but now she was right in front of us, hooked up to earbuds, her blonde hair pulled back in a ponytail. Wearing those tiny sports shorts designed by men, I was sure of it. They left something to the imagination, but they showed off her best assets. A perfect ass and long, golden-tanned legs. She was a real runner, not a half-hearted jogger. Her stride was long and powerful, and she made it looked effortless, like that ankle had never been twisted or bruised.

She was a fighter, with the face of an angel and an annoying habit of calling me out on everything I said or did. Why couldn't she grasp the concept that I was trying to protect her from the sharks of this world? And anything else that could hurt her. Despite the voice in my head telling me I was wrong, a part of me still clung to the belief that I had the power to protect someone.

"I'm gonna go for her," Louis said. "Treat her to some sweet, sweet Louis time. You know what they say…once you go black, you never—"

I shoved him, temporarily shutting him up. He stumbled

but regained his balance and grabbed my bicep in a tight grip, effectively halting me. We didn't need to catch our breath. We'd been trailing Eden, and while she was a good runner, we usually ran like bionic men. This had been a walk in the park. "What the hell are you waiting for? I see the way you look at her," Louis said. "How long have I known you? In all that time, I have never seen you act like this around *any* member of the female population."

I started running again, jogging, really, staying a good distance behind Eden but close enough to keep her in my line of vision. She hadn't seen us. She was too in-the-zone. Louis caught up to me and I wished I had my music with me, so I could plug into it instead of listening to him talking shit.

Louis was a smooth talker and never resorted to violence to solve his problems. His mama had raised him right. She didn't desert her four kids when her husband walked out on her. She'd worked two jobs to put food on the table, and her kitchen floor was so clean you could eat off it. Somehow, she'd still found the time and energy to laugh and cook and fill the house with love and happiness. I couldn't hang out there as often as I would have liked, though. She'd thought I was a bad influence—turning up drunk with black eyes and split lips didn't sit well with her. I couldn't blame her for thinking the worst of me. I'd never done or said anything to sway her opinion.

"What's the deal with you?" Louis persisted. "You've never had a problem going after women before."

What *was* my deal? I didn't know why Eden had this hold on me, or what she did or said that made me want her like I'd never wanted anyone before. I listened to every word that came out of her mouth. If Eden read the back of a cereal box to me, I'd still find it interesting. She pushed me for answers, and I gave them to her. I'd never done that before. That was why I'd been keeping my distance. I didn't want to ruin anything. I didn't want to ruin her. She radiated light and joy and everything good in this world.

If she dug too deep, she'd find out how toxic I was, how much shit I was hiding. I was surprised she hadn't Googled me already. Maybe she didn't think she had any reason to. If she had looked me up, I'd know about it—she wouldn't keep it to herself. That wasn't her style.

"I don't go after women," I said.

"My mistake. They fall into your lap. But with this chick, you have no game, my man. You act like a sulky teenager. You think that's gonna score you any points?"

"I'm not looking to score anything," I said through gritted teeth.

"You need to stop punishing yourself. You deserve something good in your life."

Louis had never killed a man, much less hurt one, so he couldn't possibly fathom the crushing weight of guilt that sat on my shoulders. For three nights, I was on my knees, praying. God did not hear my prayers. Not my begging, bartering, or pleading. I'd spent a lifetime raging against an unfair universe, trying to right wrongs that weren't of my own making. Until the night my fists officially became lethal weapons and I was royally fucked. I did that all on my own, and I couldn't put the blame on anyone else.

"I know what the problem is," Louis said.

I didn't ask him to expand on that. He didn't need an invitation. He'd tell me anyway.

"You like her. You want her for more than just sex. Which is a first for you, so you're at a loss. Louis has you covered. What you need to do is man up and ask her on a date."

I grunted. I didn't date. Never had. He knew that. But he'd

nailed the problem. I didn't want Eden just for sex or a casual hookup, but I didn't know how to handle anything more.

"Dinner. You need to take her to dinner. Somewhere nice. Bottle of wine. Take some Louis Moro pointers. Nothing gets a woman more hot and bothered and in the mood for some good lovin' than—"

Eden spun around to face us with a big smile on her face. "You guys having trouble keeping up? Need me to slow it down?" she asked, giving us a big wink. "Or do you need some pointers on how to wine and dine a woman?"

Louis erased the distance between them. "Hey, Eden. Didn't realize that was you. Just giving my boy here some dating tips."

Asshole. I planted my hands on my hips, an open position that said I wasn't on the defensive, but I stayed right where I was and made no move to get closer.

"Yeah? Does your boy have anyone special in mind?" she asked, giving Louis a flirty smile. Jesus. It drove me insane when she used that smile at the bar. I didn't think it was calculated—it was just in the arsenal of her many smiles and gestures. Guys watched her every move as her hips moved to the beat of the music, mixing drinks like a pro now, laughing and talking with customers while I watched in stony silence. Prince Charmless, at your service. The way I acted around her, it was shocking she would even give a damn about me, but she acted like she did give a damn. I didn't know what to do with that.

In my life, there had been two kinds of women—the ones who wanted to fuck me and the ones who needed my protection. Eden didn't act like she wanted either.

"Nah," Louis said, with that deep, rumbling laugh of his. "Just general tips."

Her face fell a little, like she was disappointed, but she

plastered the smile back on. It was bright. It was brilliant. It was sunshine on a rainy day. A sheen of sweat covered her face and body, and my gaze drifted down to the tank top outlining her breasts. A perfect handful. I wanted to lick the sweat off every inch of her body. Feel her legs wrapped around me while I was buried deep inside her. I held my fist to my mouth and coughed to cover up the groan.

"I doubt Killian needs tips." She looked at me from under her lashes. "He seems to have it all figured out."

Louis chuckled. I grunted. Like a fucking caveman.

"Okay, well…see you guys later." She waved goodbye and breezed past us, running in the opposite direction.

Louis looked over his shoulder. She was gone. I didn't need to turn around and look for confirmation. The air wasn't as charged with electricity. "You see what I'm talking about, Romeo? You've got no game. But you can thank me later. I put the seed in her mind—"

"Saw Carmen the other day," I said, to shut him up. It was child's play. He was so far gone, it was pathetic. "She was looking good. Sweet ass. Perfect tits. Gonna get me some sweet, sweet Carmen." I ran my tongue over my lips and got a punch in the gut for the effort. "Once she gets a taste of the Kill, she'll be begging for another feel."

"Keep your hands off my girl," Louis warned.

"She said she's a free agent," I lied. "Louis isn't showing her a sweet, sweet time."

"Bullshit. She's mine." He cracked his neck. "We're taking a break. It's temporary."

"A break, huh? Oooh, that doesn't sound good. You need some advice, *Romeo?*"

He glared at me. "Are we running or standing around chatting like schoolgirls?"

I chuckled. "How about a race? You could work out all your sexual frustration."

"You get a hard-on every time you look at Eden."

Fuck, it was true. Louis smirked at me.

"See you at the waterfront," he said, referring to Transmitter Park in Greenpoint, where all our races ended. "I'll be waiting to collect my twenty bucks."

"In your dreams."

I was built for endurance, and for going the distance, but Louis had always been the better sprinter. His mother taught him to run from trouble. My father taught me to stay and fight until the bitter end.

I won the twenty bucks.

Chapter Ten

Eden

I ducked into Brickwood Coffee on Bedford Avenue just as the heavens opened, releasing a summer shower I hadn't anticipated. When I left my apartment, it had been hot and sunny. I ran my fingers through my sweaty hair, scanning the room for Ava. The shop was small, with rustic wood walls, and a ceiling made of vintage crates, the air rich with the aroma of freshly brewed coffee. Bearded hipsters hunched over laptops sat at a tall wooden table down the middle and a few customers were sitting at the round tables by the windows, but Ava wasn't here yet.

I stepped up to the counter and gave my order to a short, wiry guy with dark hair and red-framed glasses. "Could I get a large iced coffee, please? And leave room for milk." I indicated with my fingers how much room he should leave. He handed me a plastic cup and a marker. I drew a line and handed the cup back to him.

"Do you want the French roast, the Kenyan, the Costa Rican—"

"Which one is the smoothest?" I'd never been to this coffee shop before, and I didn't get so many choices at my local shop. "You know…without—"

"The bitter aftertaste?"

I smiled. "Exactly."

He held up his hand. "Leave it to me. I've got you covered."

"I trust you. You seem to know a lot about coffee."

"I'm a trained barista. Coffee is my life," he joked. "Anything else? Bagel? Muffin? Cinnamon roll?"

"No, thank you. Just the coffee."

"And a large black coffee," a voice behind me said. I'd know that gravelly voice anywhere. What was Killian doing here?

"Your usual?" the barista asked, his gaze sweeping over Killian who I hadn't looked at yet. The barista seemed to be appreciating the view though, and it didn't take a rocket scientist to figure out he was gay. "Or did you want to try—"

"The usual," Killian said, cutting him off.

The barista nodded. "Good choice." He was still staring at Killian, making no move to get the coffee. I needed to see what was so swoon-worthy, not that Killian wasn't always swoon-worthy.

I turned to look at Killian who was running his hand through his wet hair. My gaze traveled down from his broad shoulders to the wet T-shirt clinging to his body, displaying his toned, hard body, every muscle clearly defined. Good Lord, were those eight-pack abs? I'd obviously checked out his body before. How could I miss it? It was like a work of art, chiseled by a sculptor, but in a wet T-shirt it was even more spectacular. I was imagining him stripped bare of the T-shirt. Stripped bare of *all* his clothes. I lifted my eyes from his chest to his face.

Busted.

He was smirking at me.

"Did you just smirk at me?"

Still smirking, he stepped forward and handed the barista a twenty-dollar bill. In all the confusion of ogling Killian's torso, I forgot about paying.

"Hey, wait. I'll pay." I dug around in my bag and pulled out some cash, offering it to the barista who was already handing Killian his change. I tried to give Killian the money, but he scowled at me like I'd offended him.

"Thanks." I stuffed my money in my handbag and slid it onto my shoulder. "I'm meeting Ava. I didn't know you were coming."

"Same here." His gaze glided over my body, scanning me from head to toe, his eyes so heated I was surprised I didn't burst into flames. When he was done, he leaned in close and whispered in my ear, "Now we're even."

"Enjoy your coffee," the barista said. He handed us our coffee and gave me a sly wink.

Heat flushed my cheeks as I walked my iced coffee over to the service counter and busied myself with adding milk and two sugars. God, it was hot and steamy in here. It took me ten times longer than it should have to perform this simple task. My motor skills had been severely compromised, and Killian was standing too close to me, in all his wet T-shirt glory. Coffee made, we carried our drinks to a rickety table too small for Killian, let alone me and Ava. It was like the kids' table at Thanksgiving. I took a seat facing the room and slid my phone out of my bag. Nothing from Ava. I typed out a quick text and hit send. Help, I need back-up. ASAP.

Where are you? Killian is here.

Two seconds later, she replied.

I'll meet you at the gallery in an hour.

I frowned at my phone. Double-crosser. An hour? I'd be done with coffee and finished at the gallery by then. I sighed and slid my phone into my bag. Killian leaned back in his chair which he'd pushed back to accommodate his long legs and… well, the rest of him…and took a sip of his coffee, his eyes on me.

"Ava isn't coming."

Killian rubbed his hand over his face and laughed.

I arched my brows. "Was that funny? Did I miss the joke?"

"The joke's on us."

"Yeah, I guess it is." I was still thinking about yesterday when he and Louis were running in the park. I only caught the tail end of their conversation when I turned off my music. Was Louis talking about me or someone else? Louis tried to cover it up, so I figured it wasn't me. Besides, Killian didn't need tips. Women gravitated toward him and didn't seem to notice or care that he didn't turn on the charm. All he needed to do was show up and all the work was done for him. Was I so shallow? Falling for him because of his looks? No, there was a lot more to Killian—I just wasn't sure what it was. "You're probably busy so if you want to go..."

"Are you trying to get rid of me?"

"I was just giving you an out," I guided my straw to my mouth and took a sip of my coffee.

"What if I don't want an out?" he challenged.

I shrugged like it didn't matter to me one way or the other. And it shouldn't matter. But it did. I was happy he wanted to hang out with me. "Then I guess you can stay."

He chuckled and lowered his gaze to my right hip as if he had X-ray vision and could see through the fabric of my black tank dress. Didn't hurt, my ass. It was a lot worse than a needle scratching the skin. I couldn't imagine sitting through all the hours of tattooing like Killian must have done to get a full sleeve. I left the shop an hour ago with full instructions from Jared, puffy red skin, and a bandage covering my tattoo. I promptly went home and changed out of the shorts chaffing my skin into a dress.

"Did you go through with it?" Killian asked.

I nodded, unable to keep the smile off my face when

I thought about the set of wings on my hip. Killian's smile matched my own. I loved his smile. I loved the dimples and the little lines that crinkled around his eyes. Adorable.

"You're different outside of work," I said, observing his relaxed posture.

"Different how?"

"More relaxed."

"You caught me on a good day. It won't happen again," he joked.

I laughed. "Do you like running a bar?"

"It wouldn't be my first choice, but I'd rather run a bar with Louis than work for someone else."

"I can't imagine you working for anyone."

"Well, there you go," he said.

"What would be your first choice?"

"Stunt man," he joked, fixing his gaze on the hand holding my coffee. I didn't do a thorough job of cleaning off the paint. "What were you painting?"

"Just…an abstract painting. I paint a lot after work. I can't sleep when I get home."

"Neither can I."

"So, what do you do?" I asked, taking a sip of my coffee.

"Last night I watched a movie. Listened to music. Cleaned the kitchen. And fixed a broken cabinet."

"You were busy."

"Sometimes I do all those things at the same time. Just to keep it interesting."

I thought about what he said and laughed. "Wow, you have skills."

"Oh yeah, I have skills." He made that sound dirty. I was imagining what kind of skills he had that were in no way related to watching TV, listening to music, cleaning, or DIY. His mouth, hands, and body…they were all very much involved.

"I was talking about…you know, multi-tasking."

His lips twitched with amusement. "So was I."

My face heated, and the heat traveled south. I guzzled my iced drink to cool off. Stop thinking about Killian naked, running his warm, calloused hands over your body and…yeah, cool it. That would be a disaster. I worked with him and, more importantly, I was working on myself. Last night, in a moment of weakness, I stalked Facebook. I stopped posting months ago, but I hadn't shut down my account, so I still had access to all my old 'friends.' Luke hadn't posted anything in months, but Lexie more than made up for it.

After tripping down memory lane and poring over pictures of me and Luke at the prom, at Homecoming, at Penn State football games and tailgate parties, and a million photos where we looked like the happiest couple on the planet, I tortured myself with the present-day photos. Lexie at different stages of her pregnancy. Luke, the proud father-to-be, with his hand on her pregnant stomach. "He never misses a doctor's appointment. World's Best Daddy," she wrote. Lexie and Luke with his parents. By the pool. Family dinners. The baby shower—Cassidy and Lexie with their arms around each other. Traitor.

But I considered it a small victory that I didn't end up in a puddle of tears. When I shut my laptop, I concluded that I didn't envy their life. My greatest fear was getting trapped in my hometown for the rest of my life. Unfortunately, that didn't make the betrayal easier to accept.

Killian was watching my face. "So many loud thoughts. I can barely hear myself think."

I sighed, and it was also loud.

"That bad?" he asked, sounding like he genuinely cared.

"Yeah. I did a stupid thing last night."

"What did you do?"

"I stalked my ex-boyfriend." I wasn't sure why I was spilling my guts to Killian all over the coffee shop, but he didn't seem fazed by it.

"Literally?"

"Virtually."

He took a sip of his coffee. "Was he your Prince Charming?"

"Once upon a time. But someone else got the happily ever after."

"He's an idiot."

I laughed a little, but I didn't want to talk about Luke with Killian. I wanted to talk about Killian. "What does your tattoo say?"

He looked at his arm, as if he needed confirmation. "Non Desistas Non Exeiris. Never give up, never surrender."

I thought about it for a few seconds. It sounded familiar and then I remembered why. "You inked your skin with a line from *Galaxy Quest?*"

He shook his head. "Yeah."

"That's awesome. My brothers would love that. They were so into that movie. We watched it so many times, we knew all the lines."

"Connor used to love it." He looked at me like he was seeing me for the first time. "But nobody ever guesses it's a movie reference."

It was a stupid movie, but if you took the humor away from the quote it had a deeper meaning. I got the feeling Killian wouldn't ink his arm with those words unless they meant something to him. Maybe it was his life motto. Never give up, never surrender.

"What's your tattoo?" he asked.

"Wings. For my mom. I'm not sure if I believe in Heaven,

but I like to think that if there is a heaven, she's an angel, watching over me." I scrunched up my face. "Does that sound stupid?"

He shook his head. "Not at all. Your mom passed away?"

"Yeah. When I was twelve. Cancer."

"I'm sorry," he said quietly, and I could tell he meant it.

"Yeah, me too. My mom was great." Losing my mom left a gaping hole in my life that my dad tried to fill but sometimes he was at a loss. I still remember the panic on his face the first time I told him I needed tampons. It was almost comical. "She was a high school English teacher, but she was a good artist too. She taught me how to use watercolors and acrylics and how to sketch…I'm not sure how I would have treated her when I was a teenager. Probably horrible. But when I was young, we never had those mother/daughter fights like some of my friends did." I looked down at my coffee, wondering how much hurt one heart could hold. "I miss her every day."

"But it's nice you have good memories." He gave me a soft smile I'd never seen him use before. I'd caught the wistfulness in his tone, and I got the feeling he didn't have a lot of good memories from his childhood. I hoped I was wrong and he had hundreds of good memories, just like I did.

Turned out that an hour in Killian's company went fast, and we powered through so much coffee I was all jangly now. The summer shower had been a quick one and now the sun was shining again, and the air was hot and heavy. As promised, Ava was waiting outside the graffiti-covered art gallery, the bottom floor of a four-story brick apartment building. She looked cool and fresh in a 1950's-style black and white polka dot dress, flip-flops, and cherry red lipstick.

Ava gave Killian a little slug on the shoulder. "You should come with us. Get a little culture in your life."

Killian squinted at the art gallery and rubbed his jaw, like he was considering it, but his phone rang before he could give us an answer. He slid it out of his pocket and squinted at the screen. "I need to go."

He turned on his heel and headed down Bedford Avenue, his phone pressed to his ear. I watched him walking away. Correction. Killian didn't walk. He strode, stalked, or swaggered. Sometimes all at the same time. Ha-ha. Skills.

"So…how was your coffee date?" Ava asked as we entered the gallery, an all-white space with exposed pipes in the ceiling, and spotlights trained on the art pieces.

"It wasn't a date."

"No need to get all prickly. Did you have a good time?"

"It was fine. But Killian didn't appreciate being tricked."

Ava snorted. "Trust me, if Killian was unhappy about it you wouldn't have enjoyed your coffee. He wouldn't have stayed long enough to *drink* the coffee."

True. But he stayed. We talked about a million things, some of them deep, and some of them fun and silly. We laughed, we had a good time, and I got to see another side of him, a side I really liked. Maybe that was my problem. I thought about Killian all the time. He took up so much headspace it prompted me to stalk Luke on Facebook. Why? To remind myself that guys couldn't be trusted so I needed to guard my heart? Keep my walls up to protect myself?

It wasn't my nature to be cautious, but I needed to be smarter and guard my heart more carefully. Not that Killian had ever given me any indication he was interested in me. Except maybe the way he looked at me in the coffee shop, the way he listened to everything I said and gave me his undivided attention. It made me feel like I was someone special to him, if only for an hour.

Ava and I wandered through the gallery, checking out the

special exhibition called Destruction and Renewal. Abstract landscapes lined the walls and sculptures sat on Perspex cubes. I stopped in front of a sculpture made from scraps of fabric, recycled debris, wire, and string, all pieced together to create a three-dimensional art object.

Just as I was thinking that this *Destruction and Renewal* exhibit felt like my life, Ava beat me to it, "Looks like my life," she mused, almost to herself.

"I know the feeling."

"Did someone break your heart?"

"Yeah," I said with a heavy sigh.

"It sucks."

"Big time. But I'm working on rebuilding it." I hoped it was true and kind of felt like it was. Maybe I was gearing up to let go of the hurt and pain and move on to a new and better version of myself. Like the art exhibit, the destruction was behind me and now it was time for the renewal. "Did someone break your heart?"

"Yeah," Ava said. "But it keeps happening with the same person. I mean, he's still a big part of my life. I'll always love him. I just can't be with him."

"Did he cheat on you?" I couldn't think of any other reason not to be with a person you love. Which just went to show how narrow my focus was.

"No. He'd never do that. He's…damaged. I thought I could fix him. Like, maybe my love would be enough. But you can't fix another person. And now he's gone…and I have no idea if he's okay or not."

"Are you talking about Killian's brother?" I asked, taking a wild guess.

"He told you about Connor?" Her gray eyes widened in surprise.

"Just a few things. Not a lot. And nothing about you," I assured her.

"Wow," she said, shaking her head.

"What?"

"Killian doesn't open up to too many people. I mean, he talks to me and Louis because we've known him forever. But even with us, he holds a lot back. He's never been the guy to pour out all his thoughts and feelings. He keeps it locked up tight."

I'd already figured that out the day I met him. "He doesn't tell me that much. It's not like I *really* know him."

"But he drives you home after work," she pointed out.

"Only because he worries about my safety."

"Yeah, he's super protective. But he could just make sure you got in a taxi."

"He said my apartment is on his way home."

Ava shook her head like I still wasn't getting it. "Trust me. If Killian is driving you home, he wants to spend more time with you."

"I'm not looking for a relationship, and I don't think he is either."

"That's where you're wrong. Everyone is looking for a relationship. Fighting it and not wanting it are two different things. And trust me, Killian wants it. He's just too stubborn to give in to his real feelings. But hang in there. He's worth it," she said, as we exited the gallery.

"I'm sure he's worth it. But, like I said, I'm not—"

"You know what I think?" Ava said, as if I hadn't spoken.

"No. What?" If Killian was too stubborn and I was too gun-shy to start a relationship, where would that leave us? Nowhere.

"You're his unicorn."

"His unicorn?" I asked, glancing in the window of a vintage

clothing store.

"You know, the dream girl. You make him laugh and smile and it's so good to see. He's been in a bad way—" She clamped her mouth shut. I waited for an explanation. Instead, she forged on with her unicorn definition. "You challenge him and don't let him get away with everything. But you see the good in him. You genuinely care about him. And his friends love you. We're Team Eden." She gave me a big smile. "You make his life better."

"I don't think I do all that." I wasn't sure I did anything for Killian except drive him nuts with questions he usually doesn't want to answer. But he usually ends up answering, anyway, albeit grudgingly.

"You baked chocolate chip cookies for him. And he ate them."

"They were just cookies." I wasn't sure how this had anything to do with being someone's unicorn. Which I wasn't.

"He never eats cookies. Or any kind of dessert or junk food. Like, never ever."

"Why not?"

She shrugged noncommittally. "He just doesn't. But he ate your cookies. And I happen to think you're perfect for each other." Ava gave me a secret smile and now I knew what was behind it. Wishful thinking on her part, if you asked me.

Later that evening, while I was cooking spaghetti with jarred sauce in my postage-stamp-sized kitchen, I got a text from Killian.

How was the art exhibit?

Interesting

I sent him a photo of the sculpture.

He responded with a photo of a mountain of paperwork on his desk.

I piled a plate high with spaghetti and grated cheese and

sent him a photo of my dinner.

Where are the vegetables?

They're overrated.

Not even a salad?

I sent a photo of mini carrots and a cucumber, the only vegetables in my fridge. *Dessert.*

While I ate my dinner, sitting cross-legged on my living room floor, we texted back and forth about nothing important. I guess, for want of a better word, Killian and I were becoming friends.

Chapter Eleven

Eden

"You're all up in my space, dude," Zeke teased, as we both reached for the same bottle of tequila. He hip-bumped me out of the way, and I hip-bumped him back, grabbing the bottle before he got the chance. "I win."

He winked at me. "Only because I let you."

"Eden!" someone shouted over the indie rock band's music. I turned to look at Hailey who had worked her way up to the bar. "Congrats. You got the job." She leaned in for a high five, a big smile on her face. "How's it going?"

"Great. I owe you."

"Flowers are always welcome. Or chocolates." Hailey grinned to let me know she was joking. "I should get your number. We can hang out sometime."

I gave it to her, and she punched it into her phone and sent me a text, so I had hers too. "I'll buy you a coffee. Or chocolates. Or both."

"Totally not necessary."

"Did you need a drink?"

"Yeah. I'm with some friends." She looked over her shoulder then back at me. "They're watching the band." She pointed to one of the beers on tap. "Three please."

I poured the beers and set them in front of Hailey who was watching Zeke flirt with the girls he was serving. As if he sensed her watching him, Zeke looked over, and gave Hailey a big wink and his signature smile. She dragged her gaze away from him and handed me the money.

I rang it up and set the change in front of her. "Thanks," she said, leaving a tip on the bar. "In case you're wondering, I already know Zeke's a player. But I'm in it for the long game. Players have to stop playing sometime, right?"

I gave her a little smile, not convinced. Zeke had confided that he had no interest in settling for one girl anytime soon. "It's just a matter of how long you're willing to wait."

She groaned. "You're right. I could be old and gray by then." She tossed her hair and squared her shoulders as if preparing for battle. "In the meantime, I'm going to find someone else."

"Good luck," I said, laughing as she gave me a little wave and one last look at Zeke before she disappeared into the crowd.

A little while later, while we were side by side at the beer taps, Zeke asked, "Are you friends with Hailey?"

I told him how we'd met, and that Hailey had tipped me off about the job. "Why do you ask?"

"She seems cool. Sometimes she'll talk to me and it's all good. But other times, she'll totally ignore me." He scratched his head like this truly puzzled him. I smothered a laugh.

"Interesting."

"It's just weird." He shook his head like this had never happened to him before. It probably hadn't. "I don't get where she's coming from."

"Maybe she's not that into you," I tossed over my shoulder.

Louis chuckled and shook his head. "Reverse psychology. Works every time."

"Does it work on everyone?" I asked.

"That remains to be seen," he said cryptically. "Some

people need to be bashed over the head a few times before they see the light.

"Sounds violent. Are you doing the bashing?"

"I'm a lover, not a fighter."

"You've got some pretty big muscles," I pointed out.

He grinned. "For display purposes only."

It had been a long night, and we didn't lock up until four in the morning, but like all the nights I worked, I was running on adrenaline and I knew sleep would be impossible.

"Can I do a sketch of your face?" I asked Killian as we walked to his Jeep in the purple light of the moon.

He looked at me like I was crazy. I couldn't blame him. I surprised myself by asking. "Why?"

"You have an interesting face. And it's not unattractive." He snorted. "Will you let me do it?"

He narrowed his eyes, considering my request. "No."

"Are you scared?" I asked, trying out some of that reverse psychology. He didn't respond. If he was scared, that made two of us. It's an intimate thing to sketch someone's face. Maybe he didn't want me looking that closely. Maybe he had a lot to hide. I could almost see his brain ticking over, and I sensed he might be persuaded to change his mind. "All you need to do is sit on my sofa and chill out. It'll be like we're hanging out." I threw in a please for good measure.

He pulled up outside my building and gripped his upper lip between his teeth, weighing the pros and cons of letting this crazy girl get a glimpse of his soul. "You really want to do this?"

"Yes, I really do."

"Okay." He sounded uncertain, but I wasn't about to give him a chance to change his mind.

When we got inside my apartment, I flicked on the floor

lamp with a dimmer switch that cast a soft pool of light on the room. My apartment felt stuffy, and I always thought this city was noisy, but it was suddenly too quiet. I opened the two windows facing the street and scrolled through my playlists. Nothing felt right so I hit random shuffle and left it to chance. The Fray's "How to Save a Life" came on. Good choice? Bad choice? Kind of a downer, maybe, but I left it playing. Killian was standing at the window, looking outside, with his hands stuffed in the front pockets of his jeans.

"Just make yourself comfortable on my one piece of furniture. I'll be right back."

He nodded but didn't move from the window and all I had was a view of his back, and the rigid set of his shoulders. I escaped to my bedroom, closed the door, and dumped my bag on the floor. Why was I doing this, I wondered, as I changed into shorts and my favorite blue T-shirt, soft and faded from too many washings.

Taking a few deep breaths to calm myself, I gathered up my sketchbook, eraser, and pencils and walked into the living room.

Killian was standing behind my easel, studying the painting I'd been working on. He looked over at me and I felt so exposed I might as well be naked. "Not what I expected."

"What did you expect? Unicorns and smiley faces?"

He shrugged. "I don't know." He returned his gaze to my painting. "You like all the dark colors and the blues."

"I guess those are my favorite colors." I'd used a lot of different blues, bottle green and mossy green, black and shades of gray.

"Mine too. But I like that there's some hope there. With the burst of yellow."

I stared at him a few seconds, but he kept his gaze fixed on the painting, and he kept his face shuttered, so I had no idea what he was thinking. But it was interesting he'd seen hope in the citrusy yellow, and he'd commented on it. "That's the sun coming through."

He smiled, and it was just like the sun coming through, lighting up the drabs and dark colors, warming me up from the inside. I didn't mention that the painting was him, or rather, it reminded me of him. That would probably freak him out or send him running. I also didn't mention that I'd painted a few abstracts that reflected the way he made me feel, as if my paintings would somehow reveal everything he kept hidden.

"If you want to paint over it, feel free. Throw some glitter and fairy dust on it."

"I like it as it is," he said quietly. "I like it a lot."

And I like you a lot. Even with your dark colors and the drabs and the blues, there are moments when you shine, and let the light in, and it's so beautiful to watch.

"Thanks." It suddenly felt like the room was too small for both of us. He filled all the empty space and I just stood there, staring at him. Which it seemed I did a lot. Sometimes his looks still caught me off guard. In his fitted white T-shirt and faded jeans, the beat-up combat boots I loved. His dark hair unruly and tousled like he'd been running his hands through it. He looked like dirty sex and hidden pleasures. He radiated heat and tension and danger. Maybe he wasn't the kind of guy I should want or crave, probably the worst possible choice for me, but it didn't stop me from wanting him. He was right here, so close, yet so unreachable. Which always seemed to be the way with him.

I dragged my stool over and sat in front of the sofa, my sketchbook in my lap.

Killian sat on the middle cushion, his arms draped across the back of the sofa, his legs slightly spread. He dominated the room, but I had the feeling he'd dominate any room he entered. I studied his symmetrical face. The strong chiseled jaw. Broad cheekbones. His full, sensuous lips. Deep-set almond-shaped eyes. Straight nose. Thick, dark eyebrows. My gaze dipped down to the scar on his neck. I held my pencil horizontally and measured the distance between his eyes. A rough estimate but I could work with that.

I lowered my head and lightly drew the shape of his eye.

"I feel like an animal in the zoo," he said.

I laughed, feeling some of the tension lifting. "Which animal would you be?"

He thought about it for a minute. "A wolf."

I pictured him as a big cat. A panther or a tiger. A predator—sleek and powerful and graceful. But I guess he could be a wolf. "You'd be the alpha, leading the pack."

"Or a lone wolf."

A lone wolf. I could see that. Even surrounded by people at the bar, Killian appeared to hold himself apart.

"Or the big bad wolf," I teased.

"Sounds about right."

"Which animal would I be?"

"One of the big cats," he said without hesitation, as if he had already given this some thought. I wanted to tell him I felt the same about him, but I didn't. "A snow leopard. They're the rarest. And beautiful," he said, his voice low and husky.

My cheeks flushed with warmth. After a beat I said, "I think wolves are beautiful."

Were we talking about animals or each other? I kept sketching. Shading in his nose. Drawing the planes of his face. By the way he kept rubbing the back of his neck, I could tell it was making him uncomfortable and he didn't like me watching him so closely. But he was doing it. For me.

"This isn't meant to be a form of torture," I said.

He ran his hand through his hair and blew air out his cheeks. "Yeah, I know. It's just…"

"That you feel like an animal in the zoo?"

"Pretty much."

"Okay, I'll entertain you with a story. I can talk and sketch because I'm a multi-tasker."

"Prove it," he challenged, a teasing tone in his voice.

"Okay." I filled in his dark hair, and the off-center part that wasn't really a part but the natural way his hair fell. The ear-length layers in front, longer in the back. While I sketched, I told him about the time Sawyer and I were sword-fighting on the beam of our wooden climbing frame.

"We were into pirates that summer. The beam was our plank. The swords were two sticks tied together with string. When he stabbed me, I enacted a dramatic death scene. It was pretty sensational. I fell off the plank and got eaten by crocodiles. But Sawyer was disappointed. He was aiming for my eye and hoped I'd have to wear an eyepatch the rest of my life." Sawyer and I were using our own version of sailor jargon and we were pretending to be drunk on rum, so we were staggering and saying "aaargh matey" and "bloody hell" a lot. "He called himself Captain Mad Dog, and I was Captain Chicken Little."

Killian found the story hilarious. I'd never seen him laugh so hard. "Why Chicken Little?" he asked.

"He said I had scrawny chicken legs."

Killian's gaze swept over my legs, and I thought maybe he appreciated the view, but he didn't comment on it. "Are you and Sawyer still close?"

"Yeah. We're a lot alike and we're only fourteen months apart. Growing up, everything was a competition. He drives me crazy. But he was always my best friend and, secretly, I love him best. I worry about him all the time."

"Why?"

"He's a Marine. He's in Afghanistan right now. But he'll be home soon." My voice rang with conviction. I needed it to be true. He'd been there for six months already, and Marines rarely stayed longer than seven months. So, yeah, he'd be home soon, and he'd come home in one piece. The last email I'd gotten from him, he said it was quiet, routine stuff. But he always said that, even the last time when it hadn't been true.

We grew silent, and I continued sketching. The next time I lifted my head, Killian's eyes were closed. He'd sunk lower on the sofa, his hands folded over his stomach, his chest rising and falling in a slow, steady rhythm. I watched him sleeping as the sun rose in a burst of orange and purple then faded to a pale yellow. His face was at peace in a way it never was when he was awake, the frown lines smoothed out. With his guard down, he looked softer, more vulnerable, and achingly beautiful.

I longed to run my fingers through his hair, press my lips against his slightly parted ones. Sink into his lap and feel his arms around me. I wanted him so badly it hurt. If it had been any other guy, maybe I'd be bolder, and I'd close the distance between us. But this was Killian and he was unlike any guy I'd ever met so I stayed where I was and just watched him sleeping.

His eyelids fluttered open, and I averted my face, but not quickly enough. He knew I'd been watching him, that I'd stolen a little piece of his soul while he slept. Linkin Park's "Bleed It Out" was playing and he stared at my sound system for a few seconds before he stood and walked to the door, letting himself out without saying a word. I followed him to the door.

"Killian?"

He was out in the hallway already, his back turned to me, shoulders straight, head lowered.

"Yeah?" he said.

"Thanks for letting me sketch your face."

He turned towards me and opened his mouth as if to speak, but he shut it without saying anything. I stood inside my doorway and watched him jog down the stairs like he couldn't get away fast enough, before I closed the door and locked it.

I slid down against the door and sat on the floor, wondering why everything was so complicated with us. Why was I drawn to a guy who was emotionally unavailable? Why did I persist in trying to know him better? He ran hot and cold, and he had me up, down, and twisted around.

For the sake of my sanity, I needed to stop thinking about Killian Vincent.

Chapter Twelve

Killian

Mass had ended fifteen minutes ago. I slipped into the pew next to my father in the empty church. Growing up, Seamus had squired me and Connor to Our Lady of Angels every Sunday, intent on guiding us through our spiritual journeys. I'd stopped attending mass years ago, but today Seamus had summoned me. If I hadn't met him here, he would have turned up at my house or at the bar. I liked to keep my life separate from his. Sometimes I wondered why I still gave a shit about this man. Why did I still cling to the belief that he possessed a sliver of decency? That once, just once, he'd ask me how I was doing and care enough to listen to my answer without railroading me.

"You missed Mass," Seamus said, stating the obvious. He cast a critical eye over my faded jeans and black T-shirt. I kept my gaze focused on the green marble pillars supporting the archways—the cross above the painting of the Virgin Mary behind the altar. Finally, Seamus stood, knowing he wouldn't get an excuse or an apology. Facing the altar, he genuflected and made the sign of the cross before walking out of the church with me, the heels of his polished black shoes clicking on the tiles, the sound echoing in the empty church. As everyone knew, Seamus Vincent was a devout Catholic.

We exited the church and I slipped on my aviators to ward off the sunlight. I was operating on no sleep, except for the nap

I'd taken on Eden's sofa. When I'd woken up, I knew she'd been watching me, and I'd gotten the feeling she'd been doing it for a while. As if I hadn't felt exposed enough already, Linkin Park's "Bleed It Out" had been playing. My walkout song in the UFC. My cue to walk the hell out of her apartment.

"Why am I here?" I asked Seamus as we turned the corner and stopped by his black SUV. He always had an ulterior motive. A quick phone call would have conveyed the message, but he always insisted on seeing me face to face. An effort to exert control he no longer had.

"Still haven't heard from Connor?" he asked, loosening his tie. His muscles bulged under his dark suit jacket, threatening to split the seams. The man was built like an ox and had his Sunday suits tailored to fit his frame.

I shook my head. He squinted into the distance, searching for some choice words, no doubt. "He's probably too strung out to know where the hell he is. That boy is a sorry excuse for a son."

And you're a sorry excuse for a father. "You did this to him," I said, my voice low. I rarely called him out for his behavior. It was pointless. I'd never get an apology, and he'd never own up to anything he'd done.

His eyes narrowed into slits. "What did you say?"

"You heard me."

"I don't think I did. I thought I just heard you blaming me for your brother's lack of willpower and discipline. Must have heard you wrong." He poked his finger into my solar plexus. When my body had been his punching bag, he'd planted his fist in it plenty of times. "As soon as you hear from him, call me."

Seamus would be the last person I called. His mission would be to knock some sense into Connor. But I nodded as if I intended to comply with his wishes. He ran a hand over his dark, slicked-back hair. In the heat, the scent of his Bay Rum aftershave intensified. Funny how I used to think it smelled good. Now, I equated it with the scent of Pine-Sol.

"Truth is," he mused, getting into the real reason I was here. With Connor out of the way, it was time to focus on my shortcomings. "I never expected you to amount to anything. You weren't much of a student. Barely scraped by with passing grades. Always getting into trouble. But you had a good thing going with your MMA career…"

I exhaled sharply. He'd been badgering me about this for an entire year. It shouldn't have surprised me that he'd taken a keen interest in my career. After all, he'd raised me to be a fighter. He used to watch all my fights and call me afterward to critique my performance. I'd like to think he'd been proud of me, but the words had never come out of his mouth, and I'd given up trying to earn his praise a long, long time ago. "It's over," I said for the hundredth time. "I'm not going back."

"You're a damned fool for walking away. What if every cop quit the force after they got involved in an altercation? I didn't raise you to be a coward. Or a quitter."

There were a lot of things I could have said. Instead, I turned and walked away. He grabbed me by the collar, the fabric of my T-shirt fisted in his hand and yanked me back. My back slammed into his chest, his voice in my ear low and steely. "You don't walk away when I'm talking to you, boy."

I shrugged him off and rolled out my shoulders. "You're starting to sound like a broken record. Get some new material. We're done here."

"We're done when I say we're done."

I turned around and got right in his face, using the same voice he'd used on me. "If you want to get knocked on your ass in front of a fucking church in broad daylight, then keep talking, old man."

Heat flushed his face, turning it an alarming shade of red. The veins on his temples bulged. His pupils enlarged. Classic warning signs that Seamus was about to blow. I laughed in his face. His jaw clenched, and his chest heaved. If he were a cartoon character, steam would be coming out of his ears. There wasn't a damn thing he could do to me, and he knew it. How frustrating for him that he had no hold on me now. When I was sixteen, I started fighting back. By the time I was eighteen, I stood a decent chance of winning. There was nothing he could threaten me with or hold over my head anymore. Except one thing.

"If anyone's responsible for your brother's drug addiction, it's you," he said. "You moved him out of my house when he was still in high school. He never did drugs under my roof. That's all on you. You had *one job*…looking after him. But you fucked it up."

My hands curled into fists. His eyes challenged me. *Go on, do it,* they said.

I wouldn't stoop to his level. I strode away and climbed into my Jeep. Pulling away from the curb, I cranked up the volume on my music, trying to drown out my thoughts. There was a time I had loved that man. Held him up as a superhero, out saving lives and rounding up the 'bad guys.' Before my mom took off, I had hazy memories of watching him shave while I sat on the toilet with the seat down, listening to his stories of life on the beat. I'd been proud to call him my father back then. And my mother…I remembered thinking she was the most beautiful woman in the world. For a while, we'd been a family. Before the arguments started. Before Seamus started hitting the bottle. Before I caught my mother with another man.

"*This will be our little secret,*" she said, a pleading tone in her *voice that prompted me to keep my mouth shut, the first of many little secrets I'd kept.*

After she left us, everything fell apart. I learned how to gauge my father's moods, read his body language when he came through the front door. I knew when he'd had a bad day and would hit the bottle, and I knew when his mood would turn ugly. I'd been on constant alert, relaxing only when I saw he wasn't reaching for the whiskey. He didn't drink every night. Sometimes he went for months without touching a drop of liquor—the sign of a true alcoholic who couldn't quit drinking when he'd had enough—and I'd allow myself to get lulled into a false sense of security.

The first time he'd ever laid a hand on me, I was eight. Connor and I had been playing with action figures on the living room floor. Seamus, on the sofa, drinking Jack Daniels and watching the news. Without taking his eyes off the TV, he'd told us to get upstairs and brush our teeth. We'd kept playing. Then he'd said it again, in a voice I didn't recognize. Low and steely, more frightening than if he'd shouted. Connor had jumped up and ran right upstairs. He'd always been smarter than me. Even at four and half, he'd recognized the danger signs before I did.

Seamus had yanked me to my feet and backhanded me. The sheer force had sent me flying across the room. The coffee table broke my fall, my head hitting it with a *thunk*. It had happened so quickly, I was too stunned to react. Nauseous and dizzy, I'd stumbled upstairs and puked out my guts. The next day, it had been like nothing had ever happened. Months went by before it happened again, and by then, I'd put it out of my mind. The next time had been worse. I'd heard the bones crunching when his fist had connected with my ribs. After that, it had happened more regularly. I used to tell Connor to hide in the closet until it was over. When Seamus was done venting his rage, I'd been broken and bleeding on the kitchen floor. Coast clear, Connor would creep downstairs to help me clean up. He'd gotten good at tending to my wounds, taping my ribs, and patching up my bruises. And we'd both gotten good at hiding our dirty little secrets.

I parked down the street from the pre-war apartment building with a green awning across from Prospect Park. I wasn't sure what had brought me here today. Clearly, I was a masochist. I stared out the windshield, waiting and watching like a creepy stalker. Couples strolled past, and families with little kids on bikes and scooters headed to the park for a Sunday picnic or a game of Frisbee. Park Slope was so civilized, with its tree-lined streets and clean sidewalks in front of renovated brownstones, the perfect place for city-dwellers to raise a family.

I flipped down my visor to ward off the sunlight. Sweat trickled between my shoulder blades, the heat suffocating. If she didn't come out soon, I'd ask the doorman to call her from the desk. Yeah, as if she'd agree to see me. She might already be out. This was a crapshoot but still, I waited, my fingers drumming the steering wheel.

Twenty minutes later, my patience was rewarded. I sat up in my seat as she exited the building, pushing a stroller. Dark hair, high cheekbones, and curvy in all the right places, wearing shorts and a tank top. Relief washed over me. She looked like her old self. I still envisioned her at the funeral, six months pregnant and grief-stricken, her face ghostly pale.

I didn't even know the baby's name. He must be nine months old by now.

Fuck it. I needed to see her. I needed to see Johnny's baby. I got out of my Jeep and followed her to the set of traffic lights.

The lights turned red and she crossed at the crosswalk, with me following ten paces behind. When she reached the other side, I called her name. She froze in her tracks and turned slowly. I couldn't see her eyes behind her sunglasses, but her mouth was pressed in a flat line.

"What are you doing here?" she asked.

I snuck a glance at Johnny's little boy. He looked so much like Johnny, my breath hitched. Same black curly hair, mocha skin, and long, black lashes. Big, dark eyes studied my face, a rice cake clutched in his little hand. He was so beautiful. So pure and innocent. The vice on my heart squeezed and twisted. *I'm sorry, Johnny.* Fuck, he'd been so excited about becoming a father.

I swallowed hard, trying to find my voice. "What's his name?"

"Leo."

Leo Ramirez. "He looks like a Leo. Great name." I crouched in front of him. "Hey, Leo." He waved the gummy rice cake in the air in greeting. I reached for his hand and he grabbed my index finger, his grip tight, his brown eyes flitting over my face. "You're strong. Just like your—" *Daddy.*

"Killian," Anna said sharply, drawing my attention to her. I stood, and she tightened her grip on the stroller handles, her knuckles turning white.

"It was an accident. If I could go back and change—"

"You can't. Life doesn't work that way."

"I know that." I struggled to keep my voice even and lock down all the emotions swirling inside me. Anger. Pain. Overwhelming sadness at the fucking injustice of it all.

"You wanted to win so badly, you would have done anything it took."

I stared at her. She thought winning was more important

to me than Johnny's fucking life? "Johnny was my friend. What happened that night—"

"What happened that night was that you hit him so hard it jostled his brain." She glanced at my hands. Instinctively, I flexed them. "He was my husband. The father of my child… and because of you, he's dead."

Because of you, he's dead. "I'm sorry." What else could I say? "I'm so fucking sorry." Couldn't she see the guilt and sorrow and regret on my face, hear it in my voice?

"I begged him not to fight you. I had a bad feeling about it. You knew how to destroy him."

I glanced at Leo, trying to block out her words. He was squirming in his seat, struggling to break free of the safety belts. I was tempted to grant his wish, swoop him up and hold him in my arms. Just one minute of his sweetness and light to chase away the darkness in my soul. "I wasn't out to destroy him. I never wanted to fight him. I tried to talk him out of it."

She let out a harsh laugh like she didn't believe me, but it was the truth and Johnny knew it. Maybe he'd never told her. What did it matter, anyway? "I can't give you what you want. Maybe Johnny would have forgiven you. But I can't. I just…I'm sorry…I can't do it." She diverted her gaze, her voice so quiet I almost didn't hear the words. "Stay away from me. It hurts too much to see your face."

I closed my eyes. When I opened them, she was walking away, in a hurry to put as much distance between us as possible. I let her go. What more could I say? Her loss was so great she needed to hang on to her anger. When it came to Johnny, Anna had protected him fiercely but stood up to him when he was acting like an ass. He'd told me she made him a better man. They had the kind of love everyone envied, and few people found. But now all she had were her memories, an empty bed, and a son who would never know his father. Forgiveness was too much to ask. Being a part of this little boy's life, a piece of Johnny that still lived on, was out of the question now too.

If someone killed the person I loved, would I ever find a way to forgive them?

Chapter Thirteen

Killian

Eden spun around and rammed into me, two bottles in her hand. "I told you before…fucking watch where you're going," I said, through gritted teeth. "You're still making rookie mistakes."

She glared at me. "I was going to apologize, but if you're going to be an asshole—"

"I *am* an asshole. You should have figured that out by now." I'd been acting like a dick ever since she'd walked through the front door tonight, as if I held her personally responsible for my fucked-up life. If I stopped to analyze it, which I wouldn't, I'd understand the reason I was doing this. She made me want something I didn't deserve.

"I guess I'm a slow learner. Thanks for clearing that up for me, *Prince Charming*."

I gritted my teeth. I wish I'd had the foresight to work the outside bar, instead of being stuck inside with just her, the girl featured in all my late-night fantasies. When I was alone with my hand and visions of her.

"What did you need?" I asked, stopping in front of two blonde girls.

"Are you on the menu?" one of the girls asked in a Southern drawl.

Even her accent pissed me off. I glared at her. She flinched. "Drinks?" I asked brusquely. I had no patience for these sweet-as-pie girls. Or anyone else. Tonight, I hated the world.

"Oh yeah, sure. Um...." She scrunched up her nose as she read the specials on the blackboard. Then she consulted with her friend and they chatted about it. I'd reached my limit.

I turned to go. She grabbed my arm. I gave her a look that prompted her to release her hold. *Read the warning signs, baby. Danger Zone. Keep Out.*

"Wait. We know what we want." She looked at her friend, waiting for the answer.

"Two mojitos."

I looked at them more closely. Even in the dim lighting, I could see the thick layers of makeup on their faces. They were young, trying to look older. "I need to see some ID."

"We're twenty-two. Well, she's twenty-one but almost..."

I held out my hand and wiggled my fingers for them to hand over their IDs. They dug their licenses out of their wallets, and I checked their birthdates. Twenty-two and twenty-one. From Georgia.

I set two glasses on the bar mat and bashed the hell out of the mint leaves. By the time I was done, it looked like the mint had been chewed up and spit out.

I served the Southern belles their drinks and one of them handed me a card. "We're just visiting. It's our first time in New York."

Why was she still talking to me? Didn't my attitude make it clear that I was in no mood for chit-chat?

"We heard Williamsburg has a good party scene. Where do you hang out? Like...after work?" She twirled a lock of hair around her finger and licked her lips. I opened my mouth to say something that would effectively shut her up for the rest of the night.

"Yeah, Killian," Eden said, coming to stand next to me. Her

sunshine scent washed over me. It made me dizzy. Tendrils of hair escaped her ponytail, the column of her neck exposed. I wanted to kiss my way up it and sink my teeth into the soft flesh of her earlobe. Release the blonde waves of her hair from the elastic and fist it in my hand. Bury my face in it and breathe her in. *Fuck.* "Where do you hang out after work? I bet you know where all the good parties are, don't you?"

I gave her a tight smile. "Why don't you tell the ladies what to do for fun in Williamsburg?"

She flashed me a fake smile. "Certainly. I know all the hot spots."

I raised my brows. "You do?"

She nodded and brushed past me, stopping in front of the girls. Five minutes later, they were still talking and laughing. I tuned them out and made a concerted effort not to look at Eden's ass in her tiny black skirt. Or all that golden skin on display. Was all her skin that golden color or did she have hidden tan lines? Ava, in her infinite wisdom, had ordered tank tops instead of T-shirts for Eden. More skin exposure, bigger tips. Maybe I should fuck this mood out of my system. Bend her over the desk and take her from behind…. Jesus, I needed to stay away from her. She needed someone who wasn't so fucked-up. Eden wasn't the kind of girl you fucked and left in the middle of the night. And she certainly wasn't the doormat Prince Charming wiped his feet on. She'd proven, more than once, that she could hold her own.

For the rest of the night, I continued to be my charming self. She alternated between ignoring me and calling me out for my rude behavior. If she'd ever entertained any notions of getting closer to me, I was hell-bent on blowing those plans out of the water.

"I'm going home with Zeke," Eden announced after they

finished counting their tips at the bar, the two of them laughing and talking about God knew what. Even from the office, I'd heard their voices and laughter.

My gaze snapped to the doorway. "You're going home with Zeke," I repeated.

She nodded. "We're going to grab a bite to eat. Catch you guys later." She waved goodbye to me and Louis and sauntered away.

He arched his brows. "What did you do to piss her off, Romeo?"

I ignored Louis and followed Eden out into the hallway. "Where are you going?"

She stopped and turned to face me. I crossed my arms over my chest. She took a few steps closer and planted her hands on her hips. "If this is how you act after letting me sketch your face, I'm sorry I asked." She was beautiful when she was angry, her skin flushed and those green eyes flashing heat.

"You think everything is about you, princess?"

Her eyes flared. "I don't know what to think. How could I? You don't talk. All night you acted like…"

"An asshole. You said that already. A few times."

"I call it like I see it." She tilted her head, trying to make sense of my behavior. "Why are you acting like this?"

"Text me when you get home."

She let out an exasperated sigh. "Why?"

"So, I know you got home safely." How hard was that to understand?

Eden rolled her eyes. "I can take care of myself, and if you ever call me princess again, I'll—"

I leaned my shoulder against the wall and gave her a lazy grin designed to piss her off. "What will you do?" I glanced at her balled fists and laughed. "Punch me?"

Her chest heaving with indignation, she stormed off.

"Don't forget to text me," I called after her. She held her middle finger in the air as she rounded the corner. I chuckled under my breath. I loved it when she got feisty. How could I *not* find her irresistible?

I whipped out my phone and texted Zeke. *Make sure she gets home okay. And remember what I told you.*

Friends. No benefits. Got it, he texted back.

Five minutes later, he sent me a follow-up text. *She's not too impressed with you right now. If you're saving her for yourself, you're doing a shitty job of it.*

I didn't bother replying.

★ ★ ★

I swirled the amber liquid around in my glass before I downed it. The burn hit my throat and heat pooled in my stomach, the fire spreading throughout my body. I set my empty glass on the coffee table. Unlike Seamus, I knew how to control my whiskey consumption. The shootout scene in a basement tavern played out on my TV. I'd seen *Inglourious Basterds* before, so the element of surprise was missing. It was background noise—something to keep me company and pass the time.

I checked my phone again. It was three in the morning, and still nothing from Eden. Fuck it.

Are you home yet? I texted.

Seconds later, my phone buzzed with a message. *Yes.*

I told you to text me.

And I told you I can take care of myself.

How did you get home?

My two feet carried me.

You walked? At 3:00 in the morning?

I stared at my phone and waited for a response. I didn't get one.

Fucking Zeke. I swiped the screen and called him. When he answered, I heard music in the background. Something upbeat and loud. Party music. "What's up?"

"You let Eden walk home alone?"

"No. I walked her home."

I exhaled.

"Ugh. I burnt my tongue," I heard Eden say.

"You need to wait until the cheese cools," Zeke said.

Eden laughed. "I know. I do it every single time. When will I ever learn?"

What the hell? They were cooking? He was in her apartment? Zeke got party music, while I'd been treated to a dirge by The Fray that reminded me of Connor. My walkout song had been the cherry on top of the shit sundae. If I didn't know better, I'd think she'd chosen the music specifically designed to hit me where it hurt the most.

"Tell Killian the most dangerous part of my night is this grilled cheese sandwich," Eden said. Then her voice came over the line. "Killian?"

"Yeah."

"I got home okay. I'll see you at work tomorrow night. Oh...and I told Louis I wanted to work outside with Brody."

She cut the call without saying goodbye. Mission accomplished. It was better this way. Keeping my distance was the right thing to do. I leaned my head against the sofa cushion and closed my eyes. I saw her face. Her smile. Heard her laughter. I tried to imagine what it would be like to wake up with her every morning. To do simple, everyday things couples did. Go out for coffee. To dinner. A movie. I pictured her on the beach in Montauk, the breeze lifting her hair, her green eyes translucent in the sunshine. My hands massaging suntan lotion into her skin. I thought about all the stupid little things I'd never allowed myself to want before. Someone who knew me, all my faults and weaknesses, but loved me anyway.

Then I remembered who I was. A man who had killed his friend. Failed his brother. With no clue how to repair any of the damage. I had no idea what a healthy relationship would even look like. Why was I entertaining the possibility of a relationship with someone like her? She didn't belong in my world. She didn't need a guy who was carting around a shitload of baggage.

I needed to keep Eden out of my head, out of my bed, and out of my messy life.

For the next week, I succeeded in doing just that. At work, I treated her like an employee and nothing more. On our rides home, she didn't ask me what I was thinking about or ply me with questions I didn't want to answer. I was polite. Distant. Courteous. I gave her no reason to call me an asshole, and she had no cause to call me out on my behavior or accuse me of acting like a caveman. Until Friday night, when she decided she'd had enough.

"I hate this game we're playing," she said, as I was pouring gin from the bottle in my left hand and vodka from the bottle in my right hand. She pulled four bottles of beer from the cooler and flipped the caps. I grabbed the nozzle, poured tonic in three of the drinks, and opened a carton of cranberry juice for the fourth drink. Drinks served, I collected the money and waited for Eden to finish at the register. Normally, she was quick. Tonight, she was taking her sweet time. Considering it was three-deep at the bar, she needed to speed up.

I drummed my fingers on the counter. "Any day now."

The drawer swung open, and she counted out the change in slow motion before shutting it and stepping aside. "Why are you acting like we're strangers?"

I keyed in the order on the touchscreen and counted out the change. It took two seconds, tops. "Why aren't you serving customers?" I asked, brushing past her.

Minutes later, she was in my space again. The bar was long with plenty of room for me, her, Louis, and the bar back, Manny, who was so quiet and efficient, I sometimes forgot he was there.

Eden slammed the glasses down on the bar mat and scooped ice into them, her usual smile nowhere in sight. Meanwhile, I'd been downright pleasant all night. I side-eyed her as she served the customers. No smile. No engagement when they tried to draw her into conversation. No moving her hips to the beat of the music. In other words, she did not look happy. I shouldn't give a fuck. Unfortunately, I did give a fuck.

For the rest of the night, her bad mood didn't lift, and I felt solely responsible.

As we left the bar, she walked beside me in silence. Got in my Jeep and quietly closed the door, staring straight ahead, her hands folded in her lap. We drove in silence, my music playing at a higher volume than usual. Neither of us said a word until I pulled up in front of her building. "That painting on my easel… it was you."

Me? I ran my hand through my hair, not sure what to say. When I'd seen that painting, I'd studied it, trying to figure out why it affected me so much. It was just paint on a canvas. An abstract, no less. It had taken me by surprise that she'd painted something so dark and tumultuous. The only part that looked like her was the burst of yellow. Like the sunshine trying to break through a sky thick with storm clouds. It was the kind of painting people would hang on their wall and notice something different each time they looked at it. A storm at sea. Dark forces fighting the light. Beauty. Destruction. Nature at its most powerful. I'd wondered, at the time, which side would ultimately win the battle? The light? Or the dark?

And now she said the painting was me. Yeah, I had nothing. She wasn't waiting for a response anyway. She hopped out of the Jeep and closed the door behind her. I watched her fitting the key into the lock and only pulled away when she was safely inside.

She'd gotten it wrong. That painting wasn't me. It was us.

Chapter Fourteen

Eden

"A**NOTHER ROUND?**" THE WAITER ASKED. "Yes, please," Hailey said, fanning herself. "It's so hot and we're so thirsty."

After the waiter cleared our empty glasses, I grabbed a cheesy nacho, loaded with salsa and guacamole, and stuffed it in my mouth.

"Feels like we're in Mexico," I said, although when I looked out at the Midtown Manhattan skyline, it looked nothing like Mexico. Sunlight sparkled on the East River, a ferry churning up the water, passengers crowding the deck. The Rooftop was a trendy bar, on top of a hotel, and the place I'd been rejected on the day I met Hailey. It was a cool bar, the music was chilled-out, and we'd managed to score a table outside. What more could you ask for on a Saturday afternoon?

"Arriba," Hailey said, reaching for a nacho.

I slid my sunglasses up my nose and tipped my face to the sun. I felt all toasty and warmed by the sun and the alcohol coursing through my veins. This was the perfect thing to do on a sunny July day when you needed to relax and forget the world. And forget about Killian who worried about my safety but didn't give a damn about my feelings. He'd shut me out so completely. Did that day in the coffee shop or our late-night conversations on the drives home ever happen? Last night after he'd dropped me off, I told myself it was for the best and tried to convince myself it was true.

"If I did get with Zeke, I might find out he's not all that great and the illusion will be shattered," Hailey said.

Pretty sure she said something similar about five minutes ago. Or maybe it was an hour ago. Who was counting? I'd lost track of time somewhere after my first margarita. "Or maybe you two will fall in love and get married and live in a house with a white picket fence and a bunch of kids."

She wrinkled her nose. "I can't think of anything worse." Come to think of it, neither could I. Was that what I'd planned to do with Luke? Play house, have kids, get a teaching job with my English degree? While I enjoyed some of my English Lit classes, it wasn't my passion. Unlike my mom, teaching Shakespeare and the classics wouldn't have made me happy. "That is *not* my dream. One day I'll own my own restaurant and I'll hire all women. Restaurant kitchens are so male-dominated. I mean, I knew this from culinary school, but it still drives me nuts the way they strut around like they're so superior just because they have penises. What about you?"

I tugged down the hem of my white crocheted mini skirt. "I don't have a penis."

Hailey giggled. "I can see that."

I squinted at her and lowered my sunglasses for a more accurate color reading. "You told me to tell you if your shoulders are getting pink. They're getting pink." I winced. They'd passed pink and gone straight to red.

She slid the strap of her tank top aside to confirm it was a lot redder than the unexposed skin. "Ugh. I never tan. I just get more freckles." She whipped out her suntan lotion and slathered it all over her arms and shoulders.

When the waiter served our margaritas, I leaned forward and took a sip without picking up the glass. I licked the salt off my lips and settled back in my chair, sighing with contentment like a big cat.

"If you could do anything, and nothing was holding you back, what would it be?" Hailey asked.

I gathered my hair, slid it over one shoulder and loosely braided it to keep it off my neck. "I'd be an artist. There's this gallery I visit, and it's run by women. And all the exhibitions are by female artists." I secured the end of the braid with the elastic on my wrist.

"You need to get your own exhibition." She smacked my arm for emphasis. We'd bonded over margaritas and sunshine. "How cool would it be if everyone came to see your work?"

"I'm a long way from getting my own exhibition. There are tons of brilliant artists in this city."

"You could be one of those brilliant artists someday."

I mulled that over for a minute. The whole point of coming to Brooklyn was to start making my own dreams come true. I needed to start focusing on the things that really mattered.

Intent on doing just that, I whipped out my phone and sent a quick text without giving myself a chance to overthink it. Everyone needed to start somewhere. A wall was a good place to start. I had nothing to lose by asking. I tossed my cell in my handbag and guzzled my margarita, pleased with all the fabulous decisions I'd made today. I was taking my life into my own hands and making things happen. Why couldn't I be a brilliant artist someday? There was no reason to limit myself.

"You're absolutely right," I said. "We need to go for our dreams and not let guys get in the way."

"Absolutely." Hailey raised her glass. "Here's to our future. It's looking bright."

We clinked glasses and drank to that. Not that we needed

any incentive to down these drinks. It was hot, and we were thirsty.

"Hey." Hailey nudged my arm and lowered her voice. "Check out the guys who just came out. They're total hotties."

So much for leaving guys out of the equation. I looked over at the glass doors opened onto the roof terrace. My eyes locked on the guy in Ray Ban wayfarers, wearing a polo shirt, khaki shorts, and Sperry Topsiders. He looked like he'd just stepped off a yacht or a sailboat, one of his fancy toys, maybe. Adam's gaze landed on us, and I looked away.

"They're coming over here," Hailey said in a loud whisper.

"Mind if we sit with you?" his friend asked, giving us a big smile.

"We don't mind," Hailey said, returning his smile.

They pulled over chairs from other tables, and Hailey and I scooted over to make room for them.

"I'm Ben," the blond guy said. "And that's Adam."

"Hailey. And—"

"Eve," Adam said, flashing me a smile.

"So…you're Adam's Eve," Ben said, with a smirk.

"It's Eden," I said.

Adam chuckled. "I know."

"You guys know each other?" Hailey asked, surprised.

"Eden kept me company one night when I was drowning my sorrows," Adam said.

"I was working," I said, to erase any doubt it had been something more. "Adam came into the bar."

Ben called over the waiter. "Next round is on us. Since we invaded your space."

The guys ordered beers and asked if we wanted two more margaritas. "I'll have a beer," I said, thinking it might be safer. Hailey switched to beer too. We were so responsible.

"I was pretty drunk that night," Adam said, by way of apology, maybe.

"If it makes you feel better, I've had way too many margaritas already." I lost count. Was that our third drink?

"Good. So, tell Dr. Adam...what's fucked up about your life right now?" He propped his chin on his hand and gave me a mock serious look like he was planning to figure out my problem and fix it.

"Absolutely nothing. My life is perfect. I'm traveling light. Baggage free." Wow, I sounded so convincing, I almost believed it myself. But then, what was wrong with my life right now? I was buzzed on margaritas and drunk on life, looking down the road at my brilliant future. I wasn't letting guys get in the way—not a guy who looked like Luke, and especially not a guy who could start a brush fire just by looking at me.

"Damn. You're no fun," Adam said, leaning back in his chair and kicking out his legs. "Sounds like we need a few rounds of shots."

"Shots," Ben said. "That's exactly what we need."

Hailey punched the air. "Yeah, we do."

"Now look what you started," I told Adam.

"Oops." He grinned, not sorry at all then his grin faded. "Maybe I didn't make the best impression the first night we met. Give me another chance?"

"I—"

He held up his hand. "No pressure. I'd just to like to get to know you better." He leaned close and whispered in my ear, "You're even more beautiful in the light of day."

"Thank you."

"In case you haven't noticed, I have a crush on you. But it's a secret."

I laughed. Adam wasn't such a bad guy. Maybe I should give

him a chance. This could be fun and easy. "I won't tell anyone."

Just because the shots and beers were on our table didn't mean I was being forced to drink them. "You in?" Adam asked, lifting his tequila shot.

"I'll just have one." I licked the salt off the side of my hand, downed the shot and stuffed the lime wedge in my mouth. Whoa. That was tequila, all right.

★ ★ ★

"Eve. Eve. Evie, baby." Adam held his arms open like I was supposed to fall into them. He was waiting for me when I came out of the restroom, and while in there I'd decided that the fun had worn off for me. I was ready to leave. I needed to go outside and tell Hailey, but Adam was blocking my way.

"I need to go home. I'm not feeling so great." I made a conscious effort not to slur my words. My head was spinning, and the inside bar at The Rooftop was all shadows and eerie blue lighting I found disorienting. I should have gone home sooner and slept this off. Adam had been fun, and he'd been nice, until he'd stopped being fun and nice. It was like a switch had been flipped, and he'd gotten aggressive and cocky, and had been rude to our waiter.

"Let's go back to my place." Adam grabbed my hand and led me to a quiet corner. "I'll show you a good time."

I shook my head. "No, I just need—"

He pulled me against him and his lips crashed against mine forcefully. His tongue snaked into my mouth and his hands roamed my body. I was beyond drunk, but I knew with absolute clarity this wasn't something I wanted.

"Get off me." I shoved him away. He grabbed my upper arms and backed me against the wall. Nobody even glanced in our direction. The crowd was congregated around the bar, shouting over the thumping music. Gone was the chilled-out vibe from earlier.

"I'm ready to get off on you," he said, rubbing against me. "You know you want it."

"No. I don't."

His lips crashed against mine again, and his hand slid under my tank top. Putting my hands on his shoulders, I aimed my knee at his balls, but he blocked it with his hand. I stomped on his foot, but my flat, strappy sandals didn't do much damage.

"You wanna play games, Evie baby?" He pressed his body against the length of mine.

"Get. Off. Me," I gritted out. I gave him a shove and Adam flew backwards with a lot more force than I'd expected. When my vision cleared, I saw the reason for it. Even through my drunken haze, I could see that Killian was furious, his face hard and unyielding and scary as hell as he held Adam in a headlock.

"What the fuck, man?" Adam snarled. "Get your hands off me."

I leaned against the wall for support, my mouth gaping open. Killian turned Adam around and shoved him against the wall, holding him in place. I scooted out of the way and stood by Killian's side.

"She said no. Are you deaf or just stupid?" Killian said, getting right in Adam's face. "I told you to keep your hands off her." His voice was low, but I heard the undercurrent of steel running through it.

"Get your fucking hands off me," Adam said, shoving at Killian who didn't budge.

Adam narrowed his eyes at me. "I thought you said he wasn't your boyfriend."

"I just want to go home," I said, weary, defeated, and on

the verge of tears. I grabbed Killian's arm. "Killian. Just let it go. He's not worth it."

He looked at me then back at Adam. "Don't *ever* touch her again. If I see you anywhere near her or the bar, you won't get off so easy next time."

"Fuck. You," Adam said. Killian gave him a shove and then he took my hand in his.

"I'll take you home," he said.

I nodded. That was all I wanted right now.

Adam laughed harshly. "You'll let *him* take you home?"

His comment was lost on us because Killian was dragging me out of the bar. "Wait. Hailey. I need to get her—"

He didn't stop or slow down, just kept dragging me along with him. People got out of his way to let us through. It was like the Red Sea parted to let him pass. Either that, or they'd get mowed down. When we reached the elevator, Killian jabbed his finger at the down button. "I need to go back for Hailey. I can't just leave her."

"Stay here," Killian said, not releasing my hand. He pulled my phone out of my bag, entered my password, and scrolled through my contacts until he found Hailey. He held the phone to his ear and waited for her to answer. "This is Killian. I'm taking Eden home. Do you need a ride?" He waited for an answer. "Meet us downstairs." He cut the call and tossed my phone in my bag, jabbing at the down button again. Killian slammed the elevator door with the palm of his hand, frustrated when it didn't open upon his request.

"How did you know my password?"

"Your birthday."

"But I never told—"

"Are you okay to take the stairs?" Without giving me a chance to answer, he headed for the Exit sign above the stairwell, with me in tow.

"Eve."

Adam tried to grab my arm, but Killian moved me out of the way and tucked me behind his back, securing me with one arm. "What did I say? Keep your fucking hands off her."

It was hard to see because I was behind Killian, my back against the door leading to the stairwell, but I felt the impact of Adam's body or his fist or something slamming into Killian. The whole thing probably lasted two minutes, and Adam didn't stand a chance against Killian, although Adam kept coming at him, punching, and grappling with him. I looked over at Adam getting to his feet, wiping the blood off his mouth with the back of his hand, his eyes focused on Killian as he advanced towards him.

Without thinking, I jumped in front of Killian and then everything went black.

Chapter Fifteen

Eden

KILLIAN HELD ME IN HIS ARMS, STROKING MY HAIR, HIS TOUCH so gentle I thought I was imagining it. "Killian?"

He pressed his forehead against mine. "Why did you do that, baby?"

Did he just call me baby? Was he sitting on the ground? With his forehead pressed against mine? Mm, he smelled good.

"I didn't want you to get hurt," I murmured.

He pulled away and looked at my face. "I'm built to take a punch. You're not."

Did I get punched? I rubbed my head and felt a lump under my fingers. "My head hurts."

"I'm sorry." His voice cracked on the word, and his arms around me tightened. "I'm so fucking sorry."

"But what—" I looked over at two police officers who had just arrived on the scene. A small crowd had gathered, and everyone was talking at once. Why were the cops here?

"Killian," one of the cops said, like he knew Killian. "Do we need to call your father?"

His father? "Don't call *him*," I said, without thinking.

Killian gave me a little squeeze. "Shhh. It's okay." Somehow, still holding me in his arms, Killian got to his feet. I couldn't imagine what kind of muscles he needed to perform that maneuver so smoothly.

"No," Killian said, shaking his head at the cop. "That won't be necessary."

"Are you okay, miss?" the other cop asked.

"I'm okay." I had no idea what I was, except drunk and confused, and in Killian's arms where I felt safe.

"She's not okay," Killian said. "She needs a paramedic. She fell and hit her head."

"The paramedics are on their way," someone said.

"Can you tell me what happened?" the cop asked me. "How did you hit your head?"

"I don't know."

"We were told there was a fight."

Hailey rushed over and stood next to the cop. "I saw it. Killian tried to get Eden out of the way because that guy…" Hailey was pointing at something or someone I couldn't see. "Adam. He attacked Killian. And she jumped in to…I don't know what Eden was doing. But she would have gotten punched by that asshole if Killian hadn't pushed her out of the way. We've been drinking so she stumbled and fell," Hailey said, as if that explained everything.

Oh my God. I was an idiot. I closed my eyes. All I wanted to do was sleep. "You need to stay awake, baby." Killian's voice came from somewhere far away. "Open your eyes."

Baby. There it was again. Was I dreaming? "But I'm tired," I mumbled. "So tired."

"I know you are. But just stay awake for me. *Please*," he said, a desperation in his voice I'd never heard before.

"For you…" I forced my eyes open and snuggled against his chest. It wasn't a bad place to hang out. Not bad at all. "I'll stay awake."

The paramedics arrived and whisked me off to the hospital in an ambulance, despite my protests I was fine. Because Killian insisted I wasn't.

★ ★ ★

I woke up when I heard a door shutting and the locks clicking into place, still groggy, my mouth desert-dry, and a jackhammer pounding inside my head. A soft knock came on my bedroom door followed by the door opening. Killian was carrying a paper bag and two coffees, one of which was iced coffee, the exact shade of creaminess I liked it.

I pulled the sheet over my head and heard Killian chuckling. "I know you're in there, sunshine."

Sunshine. Right now, I felt more like a storm cloud. What was going on here? Baby repeated in my head, along with a million other things I'd rather not remember, some of which I didn't. My night still had gaps I couldn't fill in.

"I'm so embarrassed. I can't come out."

"Not even for coffee? With two sugars?"

I lowered the sheet. I was acting like an idiot, which seemed to be a trend for me lately. He pressed the cold cup in my hand. "Thank you," I said, unable to meet his eye.

He set the bag on my bedside table and fished my house keys out of his pocket, setting them next to the bag. I could only assume he'd borrowed the keys from my handbag. "What's in the bag?"

"Your barista buddy said you like the cinnamon rolls. But I also got you a superfood salad."

I opted for the cinnamon roll, and he looked disappointed in my choice. "You can eat the salad later," he said.

I didn't have the heart to tell him the salad looked about as appetizing as a superfood salad could look. Lots of sprouts and…I couldn't even identify half the ingredients, and I didn't want to.

Killian wandered over to my white minimalist dresser and checked out the silver-framed photos—Sawyer and I at Lejeune when he graduated boot camp, my entire family in Stone Harbor, a few more family vacation photos without my mom, and one that was just me and my mom. A framed oil painting my mom had painted, of the swimming hole we went to as kids, hung above my dresser. The bottle green water, darker in the middle where it was deepest, and flecked with sunlight. The wooded path leading up to the jumping-off rocks where we used to cannonball or do flips into the water. Standing up there, it used to look impossibly high. When my feet left the ledge, I used to imagine I'd soar above the trees.

"Yours?" Killian asked, referring to the painting.

"My mom's."

Sitting cross-legged on my bed, with my back against the headboard, I drank my coffee and ate my cinnamon roll. Killian sat on the floor, his back leaning against the closet door and drank his coffee. All the events of last night ran through my head while I ate and drank. As bad luck would have it, none of it had been a dream. Killian had been detained for questioning, so Hailey had ridden in the ambulance with me. When Killian arrived at the hospital, he sent Hailey home in a taxi. He'd gotten a little crazy and had persuaded the doctor to run every test and scan known to man. The tests revealed that I was fine, and the bump on my head was not a concussion, but even the doctor's assurances hadn't put Killian at ease.

He'd been a wreck, worried beyond what the situation had warranted. The part I'd played in ending up in the hospital was so mortifying I hadn't talked to him about it yet. All night in the ER, his forehead had been creased with worry. When they finally released me, he'd driven me home, and insisted on staying on the sofa in case I needed him. I didn't need him. I'd passed out as soon as my head hit the pillow, something he'd insisted I couldn't do while I'd been in the hospital, and now here he was sitting in my bedroom that suddenly felt too small and cramped.

"How's your head? Are you okay?" he asked, worry creeping into his voice again.

"I'm fine. Except for the hangover and the embarrassment. I'm sorry. Last night…everything that happened…it was all my fault."

"I pushed you out of the way. That's why you got hurt."

"So, I wouldn't get punched by Adam. That's why you did it. I heard Hailey tell the cops." And I vaguely remembered it.

He shook his head and exhaled, like he didn't believe me, and I could see the guilt written all over his face. Last night, Killian had dropped his guard around me and even my addled brain had seen his emotions on full display.

"It wasn't your fault. It was my fault for getting drunk. And it was Adam's fault for acting like a douchebag. You were trying to help me. He's the one who came after you. You just tried to defend yourself and me. You weren't looking for a fight." Which was true. Killian had tried to walk away, and he would have if Adam hadn't attacked him.

"I wanted to kill him."

"I'm glad you didn't. He's not worth a prison sentence."

Killian averted his head and clenched his jaw, the muscle in his cheek jumping. He was white-knuckling his cardboard coffee cup and I was surprised his grip didn't crush the cup and turn it into a handful of dust.

"Did you meet him there on a date?" he asked, making a concerted effort to keep his voice neutral. If he'd been on the phone, I would have bought it, but I could see all the tension rolling off him.

"No. Adam and his friend just happened to come in while

Hailey and I were there. And they sat at our table."

"Asshole."

"I know," I said, grateful he didn't tell me *I told you so*. Adam had two faces and I'd decided I didn't like either one of them.

"Did you know Adam was doing coke last night?" Killian asked, watching my face.

"No. I had no idea." Wow. Talk about stupid. I hadn't even noticed. That was probably why he'd gotten so aggressive. "Why were you at The Rooftop?"

"You called me."

I didn't remember calling him or talking to him. "Oh. Did we…talk?" I was so drunk. I dreaded to think what I said to him. He rubbed the back of his neck and I winced. Maybe I needed to hide under the covers again. Whatever I said had prompted him to leave work and come to The Rooftop. But whatever I'd said, he wasn't sharing it with me. I tried another tactic. "Why did you leave work?" According to Louis and everyone else, Killian *never* left work or took a night off.

Killian blew air out of his cheeks. "I was worried about you. I worry about you all the God damn time." He sounded angry that he'd been forced to admit it.

"I don't want you to worry about me."

"Next time someone is looking for a fight, stay out of the way, okay?" he said, his face softer than I'd ever seen it.

"I was trying to stop him."

"How? By taking a punch?" he asked incredulously.

Not one of my better ideas, I could admit that now. "It seemed like a good idea at the time."

"How much tequila did it take to make *that* seem like a good idea?"

I rubbed my aching head and groaned. "Too much. I'm never drinking again."

"Famous last words."

"Yeah." I snuck a glance at him. He was drinking his coffee, eyeing me over the rim of the cup. I should have stayed under the sheet. I could only imagine what I looked like right now, after my night of drunken debauchery and stupidity. Wearing a paint-stained T-shirt and cotton sleep shorts. In an attempt to look more presentable, I ran my fingers through the tangles of my hair but gave up. Even my hair hurt.

"I spoke to your dad," he said casually, like this was perfectly normal.

My eyes widened, and my jaw dropped, my hangover temporarily forgotten. "*What?* Nooo. You called my dad? Oh my God. What did you tell him?"

Killian chuckled which did not seem like the appropriate response. "That you fell and hit your head."

"Did you give him the details?"

"I'll leave that up to you."

Well, that was something, at least. "Why did you call him?"

"I needed your insurance information to fill out the paperwork."

I closed my eyes. "What did he say?"

"He wasn't surprised to hear you were in the ER. Sounds like he spent your whole childhood taking you and your brother in."

I let out a loud sigh, unable to dispute that.

"Did you think that jumping from the second-floor window onto a trampoline was going to end well?" he asked, sounding amused.

My dad was not a big talker. I was surprised he'd shared that story with Killian. Did they bond over tales of my childhood antics and injuries? "What he doesn't know is that I nailed the landing the next time. With my arm in a cast," I said triumphantly.

Killian shook his head and exhaled. "Trouble magnet. What am I going to do with you?"

I wanted to tell him exactly what he could do with me and once again, his hands, mouth and body were very much involved. But I didn't think this was the right time to get into that. Not after last night's disaster. Not to mention the way he'd been acting before last night.

My phone rang, and one glance at the screen told me it was my dad. "Ugh. I need a story." I picked up my phone from the bedside table, and Killian stood to leave. I held up my hand and sent him puppy dog eyes. "Wait. Don't go yet."

"Wait?"

I nodded. "Moral support." I answered my phone and squeezed my eyes shut, chewing on my lower lip.

"Hey, Dad. What's up?"

"What landed you in the ER?" he asked, cutting right to the chase.

"Oh, well, it was nothing." I cleared my throat and looked over at Killian who was leaning against my bedroom door frame, an amused expression on his face. He couldn't wait to hear how I got out of this one, I bet. "I tripped and fell and hit my head. The whole ambulance and ER thing was totally unnecessary." I waved my hand in the air even though he couldn't see me.

"Uh huh. What was your blood alcohol level?"

"My blood alcohol level?" I rolled my eyes, but that hurt too. "You're such a cop. I only had a couple margaritas." I crossed my fingers, ignoring Killian's raised brows. "It must have been the sun. We were sitting outside. And when I went inside to use the bathroom, it was kind of dark and I missed a step and tripped and fell. Health and safety issue, really." Killian's chest was rumbling with silent laughter and still, I kept going, digging myself a bigger hole. "In fact, I should register a complaint. I'll get on that today. Give them hell for it."

"I've been your father for twenty-two years. You think I don't know when you're lying?"

"Are you calling me a liar?" I asked, incensed. He grunted. Like a caveman. I should have been fluent in the language by now. "Whatever. The point is I'm fine, and I'm sorry you got that call. It was good talking to you. I'm sure you're busy."

He grunted again. "Sure you're okay?"

"I'm sure. I've got a hard skull. Tough to crack."

My dad chuckled. "Got that right." He paused, and I heard an announcement in the background. He was probably hanging out at Lowe's, stocking up on more tools or charcoal for the barbecue. "Who's Killian?"

"Oh...uh, Killian...he's...my boss. Or, you know, one of my bosses. I work for him. How's Kate? Did you ask her on a date yet?" I smothered a laugh. "You really should. She's got the hots for you. She's quite the catch, Dad. Better hurry before some doctor snatches her up. You'll need a nurse in your old age."

My dad muttered something unintelligible, then got back on topic, undeterred by my attempt at sidetracking him. "Killian was worried about you."

"Oh, well...he probably doesn't want me to miss any work. He's a slave driver. And you know I can take care of myself. Nothing to worry about here."

Killian and my dad snorted simultaneously. I rolled my eyes. Last night's antics didn't support my claim. At all.

"Getting drunk won't make you feel any better. Just forget about Luke," my dad said gruffly.

I chewed on my bottom lip. "I'm over it."

"Good. You deserve better." His voice was gruff again. My

dad wasn't great at discussing emotions or displaying them, but he'd always been in my corner, and I'd never doubted his love. "Call me if you need me, kiddo."

"Bye, Dad."

I cut the call and tossed my phone on the bedside table. Killian was still standing in my doorway. "He didn't buy my story."

"You're a shitty liar."

"I know. I've never mastered the art."

"That's a good thing. Your dad seems like a good guy."

"Yeah. He's the best." Killian gave me a little smile. Something the cop said last night came back to me. "Why did that cop want to call your dad?"

Killian rubbed the back of his neck. "He's NYPD. Chief of Police."

My jaw dropped. The man who came into the bar and insulted Killian was a cop? Not just a cop, but one of the head honchos. "Wow. That's—"

"Brody's covering your shift tonight," Killian said, cutting me off. He obviously didn't want to discuss his dad, and I couldn't blame him. "And your *boss* is leaving."

What was I supposed to call him? "I'm okay to work," I protested, following him out to the living room on somewhat shaky legs.

"Get some rest," he said, opening my apartment door. "You'll need your energy if you want to paint the wall in the courtyard."

The wall? I tried to make sense of what he said. Then, it dawned on me. I'd texted to ask if I could paint the wall and he was okay with it? I stopped in the open doorway. "Really?" I asked, barely able to contain my excitement. "You'd let me do that?"

"Sure. Why not?"

I gave him a big smile. "Thank you. For everything."

"No problem." He reached out his hand as if to touch me, but withdrew it, and I felt a pang of loss for something that never happened.

Chapter Sixteen

Killian

"Hey, Killian," Zeke called as I crossed the courtyard with the cash drawer. If I never had to hole up in an office with Louis again, balancing cash drawers, I wouldn't miss it. "You up for hanging out with us tonight?"

Us? "You're going out with Zeke?" I asked Eden, returning the drawer to the register.

"Yeah. Just to shoot some pool."

I shot Zeke a look. He started cracking up like I was a comedian who had just told him a good joke.

Eden looked from Zeke to me, no doubt confused as to why Zeke was so entertained by the scowl on my face. "We're all done here. I just need to change out of this T-shirt and brush my paint-splattered hair," she said. "I'll be right back."

"Hey, Eden," Zeke called after her. "Ask Hailey to come along."

She turned and walked backwards, a big smile on her face. "I'll text her." Eden re-directed her smile at me. "You should come with us. I mean…if you want."

After what happened with Adam the other night, I had no intention of letting Eden go to a bar at two in the morning without me. I didn't trust Zeke's ability to protect her from drunk assholes.

If that night at The Rooftop had happened a few years

ago, Adam wouldn't have gotten off as easy. I would have gone straight in, raining punches on him, and he would have been lucky to crawl out of that bar.

"Where are you going?" I asked Zeke, who was digging around in his backpack and came out with a clean T-shirt.

"Fat Earl's."

Fuck. No. The last time I was in Fat Earl's, I was twelve. It was the middle of the afternoon in January and Connor and I had a snow day. Fat Earl's was quiet, just Seamus and a few dregs sitting at the bar. He was putting back the Jack Daniels, I was shooting pool in the back room, and Connor was sitting in the back corner, drawing superheroes on a stack of cardboard coasters I'd swiped from the bar. I had the brilliant idea to finish an open beer I'd found under the pool table. It was flat and warm and tasted like shit, but I drank it anyway, liking the way all the edges blurred with each sip.

I knew damn well I was pushing the boundaries, and I'd pay for it. But I didn't realize how much I'd pay. Why hadn't I stayed hidden, and out of the way, like Connor? I was a God damn idiot, poking a stick at a bear, but there was no tree to climb, and no way to escape my punishment—swift, brutal, and bloody. Maybe, in his blind rage fueled by too much whiskey, he didn't realize what he'd done until it was too late. Who knows? We never spoke of it, not then and not in any of the years that followed.

"Hey, Killian," Zeke said, jarring me from my memories. "You coming with us?"

I looked at the doves exploding from the grenade on the wall Eden had started painting today. It amazed me that she could create something so beautiful with just a brush and some paint. This morning, when I took her to Connor's favorite art supply store in Bushwick, she was like a kid set loose in a candy store. Watching her face, so filled with joy and excitement, made me happy. Being with her makes me happy, and the thought of anything bad happening to her makes me feel sick inside.

"Yeah. I'm coming."

"Cool. So, what happened to Eden the other night?" he asked as we walked into the bar.

I pressed my lips together and remained mute. He should know by now I rarely talked about myself, let alone anyone else. Once again, Zeke laughed for no apparent reason.

"Hailey said she'll meet us there," Eden said, walking down the hallway toward us, her hair loose and falling around her shoulders. She was wearing a tank top with jeans and Converse. It didn't matter what she wore. Eden always looked beautiful. And fuck it. I wanted her, and I needed to do something about it. Tonight.

"How's Hailey getting there?" I asked.

"Um…" She chewed on her lip, a tell-tale sign. "She said it's only a ten-minute walk."

I let out an exasperated breath. Why did these women take stupid chances? Did they honestly believe nothing bad could happen to them in Williamsburg? "Call her. Tell her *not* to start walking. We'll pick her up."

On the way to Fat Earl's, the Jeep was noisy with chatter, but I had no idea what Zeke, Hailey, and Eden were talking about. I was too busy talking myself down from the ledge.

Growing up, most of the bad shit went down in my own house, and I had no choice but to live there every day, so this was no big deal. Better to face your fears than run from them. I wasn't twelve anymore. No need to trip down memory lane, a journey I rarely took.

As soon as we walked in the door, the familiar scent of fried food and stale beer assaulted my senses, making my stomach churn. Country music blared from the jukebox, and although the ownership and crowd had changed, the place still looked the same, right down to the year-round Christmas tree lights strung above the bar.

It was a long time ago. It's just a bar. Stop being a fucking pussy.

Deep breaths.

Chapter Seventeen

Eden

Fat Earl's ticked all the boxes for an after-hours dive bar. The floors were sticky, country music blared from the jukebox, and a film of grease coated every surface. But it was a good place for people-watching and the crowd was a lot more diverse than at any of the dive bars I'd been to in Pennsylvania. Bikers, hipsters, some guys who looked like rock stars, and from what Hailey told me, a lot of the people here worked in other bars and restaurants.

She and I were crammed in a corner near the jukebox and Zeke had gone to put our names on the list for a pool table. Killian hadn't made much progress. He was still by the front door, talking to Jared, and he kept rubbing the back of his neck. Even from across the room, I could see the tension rolling off him. He'd downed his first whiskey, a double, in two seconds flat and was working on the second one.

"This is known as a bar for bad decisions," Hailey said, taking a swig of her beer. We'd made a pact to stick to one bottle of beer, and I was nursing mine. I didn't need to make a fool of myself again.

I nudged Hailey's arm. "We're going to be sensible, remember?"

"Absolutely. I got my ass kicked in the kitchen tonight. I sweated out buckets. I'm not even sure how I'm still standing."

"I know the feeling." We both yawned at the same time, as

if to prove it.

"At this rate, we'll be asleep in the corner before this sad old country song ends," Hailey said. "No wonder they're always crying in their whiskey. If you sing like that, you deserve to have your woman done run off and leave you."

We both cracked up over that one. "Country music's big where I come from. In western Pennsylvania, all the rednecks drive around in pickup trucks, looking for things to shoot," I said. "Then they sit back on the couch on their front porch and get drunk on PBR and Wild Turkey."

"Where I come from, we make our own whiskey," Hailey said, referring to her Midwest upbringing. "After a big Saturday night of riding around on your boyfriend's tractor and making out in the cornfields, or rolling around the hay in the barn, everyone goes cow tipping for some real fun."

"You can't tip a cow."

She laughed. "I know. But it never stopped us from trying."

I looked over at a guy wearing a black leather vest and painted-on jeans with so many facial piercings I lost count. "We're not in Kansas anymore, Dorothy."

"I'll drink to that." She clinked her bottle against mine, and we drank to that.

"Zeke's the one who suggested I invite you."

"Really?" Hailey asked, surprised.

"Maybe you guys should try being friends first. He's a good guy."

"You think he'd be up for being friend-zoned?"

"He and I are just friends so he's capable of being friends with a girl."

"Maybe." She took a sip of her beer and scanned the room. "Killian keeps looking at you. Like, a lot."

I followed the direction of Hailey's gaze. Killian's eyes

caught mine, and he took a swig of his whiskey, still watching me. He was doing that thing he did, drawing me in with nothing but his eyes until I felt like I could barely breathe.

"What's the deal with you guys?" Hailey asked.

"If I knew the deal, I'd tell you." In the four days since that night at The Rooftop, Killian hadn't mentioned it. Two nights ago, we went to a twenty-four-hour diner after work. It was me and three guys crammed into a booth. Killian sat next to me, his arm draped across the seat behind me, his thigh pressed against mine. Like he was marking his territory but making no move to do anything about it. Today, when he'd driven me to the art supply store, he'd brought me an iced coffee and a cinnamon roll. We'd talked and laughed all the way and he'd gotten a big kick out of my excitement in the art supply store. But yeah, I had no idea what was going on with us.

"That night at the hospital was so swoony," Hailey said. "He took care of business, and he did it all for you."

"Yeah, well, he's a control freak. It was a little over the top."

"I'd love it if a guy went over the top for me. And if that guy looked like Killian, I'd be in seventh heaven."

"Hey," Zeke said, interrupting our conversation. "Our table's ready." He nudged my arm. "Ask Killian to be our fourth."

I weaved my way through the crowd and stopped in front of Jared and Killian. After greeting Jared, I asked Killian if he wanted to shoot pool with us. "Pool?" he asked, as if the concept was foreign to him.

"You need another drink?" Jared asked him.

Killian looked down at his empty glass as if he was surprised to see it was empty and shook his head. "Nah. I'm good." He squinted at the pool tables in the back and took deep breaths through his nostrils, like he was gearing up for something monumental. "Let's do this."

"Okay," I said slowly, watching his face. "Are you—"

He reached for my hand and held it in his. As we walked through the bar, I looked down at our joined hands. His warm, strong, calloused hand, the palm pressed against mine, my hand fitting so perfectly inside his made my stomach all fluttery.

I looked up at his face. It was shuttered, his jaw clenched, the muscle in his cheek jumping.

Zeke and Hailey paired up, and she looked all animated now, like she'd gotten a second wind. Killian had let go of my hand and I wasn't sure how I was feeling. All shaken up and confused, as usual.

We chalked our cue sticks, and a flip of the coin decided that Zeke and Hailey's team would break.

"How's your pool game?" Killian asked me.

"They don't call me Shark for nothing." I winked at him. What an idiot. Killian chuckled. "How's your game?"

"I've got skills," he said with a sexy grin.

I gripped my teeth between my lower lip. "I bet you do."

He nudged my arm and jerked his chin at the pool table, reminding me of the reason we were here. "You're up. Let's see what you've got, Shark."

What I've got is a racing pulse and a hammering heart. I stared at the pool table. Were we stripes or solids?

"Stripes," Killian said, his voice laced with humor as he answered a question I hadn't voiced.

"Yeah. I knew that." I walked around the table. My dad had taught me and my brothers to shoot pool on the table in our basement. Just concentrate, I coached myself. Line up the shot. Don't jiggle your cue stick. I leaned over the table and lined up an easy shot to the corner pocket and sunk an orange stripe.

Zeke and Hailey were good. Killian was better than good. I wasn't a bad pool player either. "You need some pointers?" I teased Killian as he leaned over the table, looking for his shot.

"What do you recommend, Shark?"

"The green in the corner pocket."

"Too easy. I'll leave it for you."

I smacked his arm and he laughed. "Step aside," he said. "I'll show you how it's done." And he did.

"Show-off," I teased.

He winked at me, and I decided that I liked this fun, cocky Killian, a big change from the stressed-out Killian from earlier. As the pool game continued, he was fun and sexy and flirty, and I gave it right back to him.

"This is for the win," he said, as we both studied the table, sizing it up. It wasn't an easy shot, but I was feeling confident. Or cocky.

"I've got this." I leaned over the table and positioned my cue stick. Killian was watching my ass, not the table. "Enjoying the view?"

"Oh yeah," he said, with another sexy grin, those dimples on full display.

Honestly, I didn't know how I was still carrying on with this pool game or how I'd be able to concentrate on my next shot. "Step aside, Hustler," I said. "I'll show you how it's done."

By some miracle, I nailed the shot. I stared at the table for a few seconds dumbfounded. "We won."

"Nice one, Shark." Killian and I went in for high-fives.

"Stop gloating," Zeke said, but I didn't think he cared.

I decided to be sensible and call it a night. Hailey and Zeke decided to stay a while, and Killian said he'd walk me home. As we were leaving, a willowy brunette in a black slip dress and silver stilettos walked in the door. Overdressed for a dive bar but she looked like a Victoria's Secret model. And Adam was right behind her. I grabbed Killian's arm. Adam's eye caught mine and he said something in the girl's ear.

"Fuck," Killian muttered.

Fuck was right. I didn't even know the half of it.

"Killian," the girl said, stopping in front of us. "Have you met my brother, Adam?" She smirked at Killian then her eyes narrowed on me. "You must be Eden."

I nodded like an idiot. What was going on here?

"I'm Joss. Killian's former fuck buddy. And Adam's sister. Small world, isn't it?" She laughed harshly, and her beautiful face turned ugly.

I glanced at Adam. He swallowed hard, not meeting my eye.

Killian took my hand and led me to the door. Shockingly, Adam stepped aside to let us pass. When we got outside, I took deep breaths.

I heard the door open, letting out the sound of country music and looked over my shoulder at Joss.

"I loved you, asshole," she screamed.

Killian stopped walking. He rubbed the back of his neck and turned to face her. "You didn't even know me," he said, sounding weary.

She erased the distance between us, her eyes narrowed on me again.

"Is this your new fuck buddy? Does he just call you for sex then leave afterwards? He never even stayed the night." She was crying now, her mascara leaving black trails down her cheeks. "What's so great about her that you and Adam were fighting over her?"

Joss lunged at Killian and slapped him across the face, the sound ringing in the air. She raised her hand to do it again, but Killian wrapped his hand around her wrist to stop her. "You got your one shot."

"Fuck you," she said, dissolving into tears again.

Adam stood back, watching this whole disaster play out. "Come on, Joss. Let's get out of here."

She glared at us before she turned and walked away. Killian took my hand again and we started walking. Something hard smacked against my shoulder blade. Ouch.

I turned just as Joss unleashed her other stiletto. Killian blocked it with his body. "Joss," he said through gritted teeth. He strode over to her and Adam and planted his hands on his hips. "Stay. Away. From. Eden." Killian leaned in and said something to Adam in a low voice I didn't catch.

I picked up Joss's shoes and tossed them in her general direction. Adam scooped them up, grabbed Joss's arm and led her away.

Killian stood his ground, hands on his hips and watched them until they were gone. I didn't know what to say or do about any of this, so I started walking. Killian fell into step with me but neither of us said a word.

When we reached my building, I stopped at the bottom of the steps. "I don't even know what to say about any of this."

He squinted at something over my shoulder. "I haven't seen her in months. She was never my girlfriend."

"Yeah, I picked up on that. You were just fuck buddies."

He sucked air in through his teeth. "I was honest with her. I never pretended it was something it wasn't."

"She seems to think she was in love with you."

"She's Adam's sister. What can you expect?" he asked, attempting to make a joke. It was kind of funny, but it was so messed-up I couldn't laugh.

He reached out and tucked a lock of hair behind my ear. His knuckles brushed against my skin and everywhere he touched was electric. "Killian," I whispered. "What are we doing?"

He cradled my face in his hands and lowered his head, his lips brushing against mine in an almost-kiss. I wrapped my arms around his neck and his hand glided through my hair, holding the back of my head. His other arm wrapped around my waist and he kissed me, his lips soft and warm, the stubble on his jaw rough against my skin. My lips parted to let him in, and our tongues swirled together, exploring each other's mouths, seeking, and searching. My fingers tangled in his thick hair, softer and silkier than I'd imagined it to be. He tasted like something exotic I'd never tasted before. Sweet forbidden fruit or a drug I'd craved without knowing it until now.

We were kissing with a fervent, urgent need, like it was the air we needed to breathe. My body trembled with adrenaline and we adjusted our bodies until there was no space between us, no way we could possibly get closer. My hip pressed against his rigid length and he groaned into my mouth, a low, guttural sound that sent heat pooling between my thighs.

I was coming undone. I'd never been kissed like this before, with so much hunger and intensity and so much of everything. The ground beneath me didn't feel solid. But I wasn't sure that Killian was someone I should want. I wasn't sure what kind of game we were playing or what was going on with us.

With those thoughts invading my brain, I pulled away from him and tried to catch my breath. I was shaking from head to toe and that kiss had left us both in a bad place. He adjusted himself in his jeans and ran a hand through his hair, letting out a ragged breath. I walked away from him on wobbly legs and lowered myself onto a step, in front of my building. Hugging myself, I closed my eyes. He sat next to me, and I felt him there, felt the heat of his body even though we weren't touching. I tasted him on my lips and with every breath I took, I inhaled his scent.

One kiss and he'd gotten under my skin. Made me yearn

for something I wasn't sure he could give me—more of himself.

"Killian…what are we? Because I'm not…I just feel like you're messing with my head."

"Let me come upstairs with you."

"Why? So, you can get me into bed?" I asked flippantly.

"If I only wanted sex, I'd tell you that."

Not that it worked with Joss. She'd obviously wanted more. "What *do* you want from me?"

He rubbed his jaw and squinted into the distance. I waited to hear what would come out of his mouth and hoped it would be a real answer. We'd been doing this dance for too long and this push and pull was giving me whiplash. "I can't get you out of my head. I think about you all the time."

It didn't answer my question, but I felt the same way about him. I was surprised he'd admitted it. We sat in silence, and I replayed the night in my head.

I'm Joss. Killian's former fuck buddy.

It was naïve to think Killian lived like a monk, but I'd prefer his former conquests to remain nameless and faceless. I'd rather not know that he'd just used her for sex and left afterwards.

Killian told me he didn't only want me for sex, and I still had no idea where that left us, but I was the fool who had always rushed headlong into danger. This time was no exception.

I bumped his shoulder with mine. "Do you want to come upstairs to *not* have sex?"

Chapter Eighteen

Eden

On the way upstairs, he asked to see the sketch I'd done of him. He'd never brought it up before, and I'd taken it to mean he didn't care.

I left him in the living room and retrieved the sketch from my bedside table drawer. Sinking onto my bed, I stared at the sketch in my hands. If I hadn't been the artist, and saw this sketch hanging on a wall, I would know it was him. I would think he was handsome. The kind of dark good looks that made you do a double-take, made you want to stop and stare if you saw him on the street. I did stop and stare the first time I saw him. I'd done it many times since then. Stolen glances, seeking him out across the room when I worked. But on closer inspection, I would see the way he was looking at the artist with hooded eyes. Did I notice the way he'd looked at me? I must have. And I would see the way the artist saw him. Now I understood why he'd never asked to see it. The sketch was too revealing.

I returned to the living room empty-handed. He looked at my hands, his brows raised. I shrugged. "I can't find it."

His mouth quirked in amusement and then he was laughing.

When he finished laughing, I rolled my eyes and took a seat on the sofa. "What's so funny?"

"You."

Yeah, he knew I was lying. My face gave everything away. I leaned my head against the sofa cushion and looked at the ceiling.

"My boyfriend cheated on me," I said, out of the blue. "He got my best friend pregnant and now they're living in my hometown." Killian sat next to me and slid down on the sofa, so he was at my level. I turned my head to look at him. Then I fixed my gaze on the ceiling again and told him the Luke and Lexie story and how they'd betrayed me.

"Should I beat him up?" he asked.

I laughed. "I took care of that. I mean, I didn't beat him up. Just his car. I went after it with a baseball bat." After the incident with Joss, my violent reaction was probably the wrong thing to confess.

Killian chuckled. "That's fantastic."

"It made me feel a little bit better at the time. But then I felt lousy again. Luke and I started dating in eleventh grade and we went to college together and everything. Instead of applying to art school in a city like I wanted to, I went to the same college my parents went to. The same college my boyfriend went to. The whole time I was at Penn State, I tried to convince myself it was something I wanted."

"But it wasn't?"

"No. It felt like a continuation of high school," I admitted. "I don't know…maybe he was right about me. He said I'm too much of everything. He used to tell me I should tone it down. I think he wanted a trophy girlfriend. Someone who looked good but didn't push back. Didn't argue. Didn't have so many opinions. Didn't let her temper make her say stupid things she regretted. I tried."

"Why?"

"Why?" I repeated.

"Why would you change anything about yourself for that asshole?"

"I didn't, really. I just tried, but usually failed. And he wasn't always an asshole, or I never would have been with him. Before the whole Lexie thing happened, he was everything you could want in a boyfriend. Everyone liked him…" I wracked my brain trying to remember the things I loved about Luke. It used to be easy to define, and if you'd asked me to name the guy least likely to cheat on his girlfriend, it would have been Luke. But now the only strong points I could come up with was a list of things that sounded good on a resume. Baseball team, high school quarterback, Class President, 4.0 average. Clean-cut. All-American. A politician in the making.

What made it so hard to accept was that Luke had acted like the perfect boyfriend. He never missed a birthday or holiday. He was polite with good manners. Opened car doors and respected authority figures. Teachers loved him because he followed all the rules. He'd never sat in detention or gotten a speeding ticket. I asked him once if he was ever tempted to shake up the rules or rebel against something. He'd patiently explained his views on the law and its place in society. Luke was not an anarchist or a rebel. He was a pillar of society. Yet he turned out to be a liar, a cheat, and a coward.

I'd never told anyone that I felt like Luke was trying to hold me back, trying to make me less of what I was but now all the words tumbled out. "He used to say little things in a passive aggressive way, and at the time I just brushed them off. Instead of standing up to me or pushing back when I argued with him, he'd just tell me I was being unreasonable, and he wasn't going to discuss anything with me until I calmed down and stopped acting like a toddler."

"He said that?" Killian asked, incensed on my behalf.

"Yeah. He used this voice like he was the adult and I was the toddler which infuriated me even more."

"You're better off without him."

"I didn't have much choice. It still hurts when I think about it," I admitted. "It made me feel like I was lacking somehow, and Lexie gave him something I couldn't. I felt so stupid that this was going on behind my back and I didn't even know about it. But I should have noticed. Towards the end, we never had sex. Unless I initiated it." After the words were out, I covered my face with my hands and groaned. "I can't believe I just told you that. I'm not even drunk. Now you think I'm pathetic."

"No, I don't. I like you just as you are."

I uncovered my face and snuck a look at him. He gave me a little smile.

"You do?"

"He's an idiot if he couldn't appreciate you. And to cheat on you? That's just wrong."

I sighed. We sat in silence for a while, and I was happy he stayed, happy he wasn't in a rush to get out the door. Something had shifted between us, not only because of that mind-blowing kiss, but because I'd told him things I'd never told anyone. And he'd listened, and he'd stayed, and he'd said exactly the right things. Maybe Killian was the last person I should trust, and maybe my moral compass was damaged, but he didn't pretend to be anything he wasn't. Killian wasn't a smooth talker who used his charm to win people over like Luke did. He wasn't a big talker, but he said what he meant, and he meant what he said. Maybe that's why I believed everything he did say.

"Will you tell me something about yourself?"

"What do you want to know?" he asked, sounding wary.

"Something you've never told anyone."

He was silent for so long that I didn't think he would. I kept my eyes trained on the ceiling because I thought it might make it easier to talk if I wasn't looking at him. He could have just said no, or walked out the door, or told me something unimportant but he didn't do any of those things.

"My mom left when I was seven and my brother was three. Connor doesn't even remember her. But I remember everything. The day she left…her bags were packed, waiting by the door. She kissed me goodbye and told me to take care of my brother. I chased after her, begging her not to go. I was barefoot, but I chased her taxi down the street. I kept chasing it until I lost sight of it. She never even looked back. Not once. When I got home, my feet were cut up and bleeding and I tracked blood across the kitchen floor. All I could think about was that my mom would be upset. She liked to keep the house clean. I put on socks and scrubbed the floor with Pine-Sol, thinking that if I got it nice and clean she'd come back. Whenever I smell Pine-Sol, I think about that day. I fucking hate the smell of Pine-Sol."

Oh, Killian.

I reached for his hand and took it in mine, entwining our fingers. He let out an exhale like telling that story had cost him a lot. While he'd been talking, his voice had been devoid of emotion, but I knew he had to feel it deeply. How could he not? What kind of mother would leave her two little boys to fend for themselves? "Thank you for telling me. And I'm so sorry."

"It was a long time ago." He brushed it off as if it didn't mean anything, as if it hadn't crushed him. My heart ached for him. I imagined seven-year-old Killian chasing the taxi and scrubbing the floor. His heart was breaking, and he was tasked with looking after his brother, but who was there for him? I didn't get the impression that his dad was the good guy mine was. Who tucked Killian in at night, kissed it better, baked cookies with him when he had a bad day?

After my mom died, my dad was there for us. He didn't always get it right, we pushed him to the limits of his patience more often than we should have, but my dad never gave up, never let us down, never faltered in his drive to succeed. And I realized that that's what real-life heroes are made of. They show up, day in and day out, and they do the heavy-lifting so the people around them feel safe and loved and secure in the knowledge that those strong shoulders can carry the burden. Even when their own hearts are breaking.

If Killian's mother asked him to look out for his brother, I was willing to bet Killian tried to protect him from every storm. It was his nature to protect people, to be their rock, to fight the bullies of this world, to make sure nothing hurt the people he cared about. Somehow, I'd become one of those people.

Outside a siren wailed but inside my bare white living room, it was still and quiet, a warm July breeze skating through my open windows. Killian and I sat like that for a long time, side by side, holding hands, our fingers entwined. I had that same feeling I'd had when I met him, like nothing bad could happen to me if I was with him. Killian knew how to take care of things. He was street smart and he was a fixer. He knew how to repair everything that broke down at the bar—toilets, leaky faucets, broken fans, a cracked paving slab in the courtyard. His to-do list was a mile long and had become a running joke amongst the staff.

Luke was book smart, but he wasn't a fixer. One time, Sawyer told me you couldn't trust a guy who didn't know his way around the engine of a car. When I laughed, he expanded on the topic, and reeled off a list of things every self-respecting guy should know how to do. *"Luke wouldn't know what to do with a wrench if it hit him on the head. If he got a flat tire, I bet he'd ask you to change it for him,"* Sawyer said. My dad had taught me how to change a tire, but when Luke had gotten a flat, he'd called AAA to take care of it for him. I wasn't there, or I would have offered to do it.

Luke said if he was meant to be a plumber or an auto mechanic, he wouldn't waste his parents' money on an education.

"But don't you want to learn how to do any of those things?" I asked.

Luke looked at me like I had two heads. "Not when I can pay someone to do it for me," he scoffed.

"If you got a flat tire, would you change it yourself?" I asked. It was an abrupt change of subject, considering that we'd been sitting in silence after Killian shared a piece of his soul with me.

"Who else is going do it?"

I laughed. "I could do it."

He snorted. "No."

"I've been thinking about DIY," I said. "What have you been thinking about?"

"I was thinking…" He squinted into the distance, and I thought he was going to wow me with something profound. "What would I do if I got a flat tire on my way home?"

I snorted laughter. "I hope you have a spare in your trunk."

"And a tire iron. It's Brooklyn."

"Danger lurks around every corner," I teased.

"Trouble finds us even when we're not looking for it."

I sighed. "That was all kinds of crazy."

Killian blew air out of his cheeks. "What were the fucking chances?"

Yeah, Killian didn't know Joss very well. He didn't even know Adam was her brother. Meanwhile, he knew all about my brothers and he'd even spoken to my dad on the phone. Weird.

I let go of his hand and stood. "Wait here. Don't go anywhere."

"Whatever you say, sunshine."

"Why do you call me sunshine?"

He tilted his head and closed one eye. "You want another confession? Two in one night?"

"I'm greedy like that."

"Hmm. Okay. You look like sunshine. And, to me, you smell like sunshine." He gripped his lower lip between his teeth. I hadn't expected that kind of honesty. Or any of the truths he'd revealed tonight.

"It's Orange Blossom by Jo Malone. That's the name of my perfume."

"I know. I saw it on your dresser."

Of course, he did. Ugh. We've had two crazy, drama-filled nights.

I walked into my bedroom, opened my bedside table drawer, and pulled out the sketch. Killian watched me as I walked toward him. I sat next to him and handed him the sketch. Pulling my legs to my chest, I wrapped my arms around them. He studied the sketch for a long time before he set it on the cushion next to him. "You have so much talent."

I shrugged. Accepting compliments about my art was difficult. Maybe it was because I'd always wanted to be good, but I never felt like I was good enough. Art is subjective. You could reach a level of technical proficiency but still fail to stir someone's emotions or entice them to linger over your work.

"Do you still want to go to art school?" Killian asked.

"I don't really want to go back for another degree. But I might take some classes. Or I might just keep experimenting on walls. It was my own fault that I didn't apply to art school. I can't blame anyone else. That was my decision." As I said it, I knew it was true. But now I was making my own decisions, boldly taking a leap into the unknown. It wasn't always perfect, not by a long shot, but moving to Brooklyn had been the right decision. I wasn't going to let one stupid drunken night overshadow the good things in my life—my job, my new friends, my art, and yes…Killian. Always Killian.

"Do you want to go on a date with me, Eden?" Killian asked.

A date. With Killian. It was so unexpected, yet it was the perfect ending to our imperfect, chaotic, messy, wonderful night. My lips curved into a smile. "I'd love to go on a date with you."

Chapter Nineteen

Killian

"I FEEL LIKE THE PROUD PAPA, SENDING MY BOY ON HIS FIRST date," Louis said as I changed out of my T-shirt and into a black button-down shirt in the office.

"Call me if you need me," I said, doing up the buttons. I was all thumbs.

"I won't be calling you. You're not allowed to come back to check on things. No calls either. What time's your reservation?"

"Nine."

"What you need to do is ask her questions about herself. Be that charming Killian I know you can be and—"

"Here's an idea. How about you get back to work and leave me in peace?"

"How about you stop acting like a jackass and listen to some good advice?"

"If I wanted your advice, I would have asked for it."

"But you took my advice," Louis said smugly. "Or you wouldn't be going out to dinner with her."

"You're taking credit for this?"

"If I hadn't said anything, you never would have pulled your head out of your ass."

That was a lie. I never did anything I didn't want to do. If this wasn't something I wanted, all his advice would have fallen on deaf ears. He knew that. But if he needed to take credit, let him. "Your job here is done," I said. "Now get back to your real job."

He held up his hands and backed out of the office. "Just wanted to give you a proper send-off. Be brave, warrior." He pounded his chest with his fist before he finally left me alone.

Be brave, warrior. Jesus.

Ava stopped in the doorway, holding a taco in a cardboard container. "So...big date, huh?"

"It's just dinner."

"Uh huh. Sure, it is." She looked me up and down as I cuffed my sleeves. "Is that what you're wearing?"

I looked down at my black shirt and black jeans. Clearly, it was what I was wearing so no answer was required. Did the whole world know I was taking Eden to dinner? The only person I told was Louis, and I regretted it.

"You wear that all the time," Ava said. "You wear too much black. You should jazz it up with a little bit of color every now and then." I eyed the loud colors of her psychedelic mini skirt. It was like a strip of fabric on acid. Just looking at it made my head spin. "You would look really good in a light blue shirt."

Everyone had an opinion. "I don't own a light blue shirt."

"Exactly. But you should. It would match your eyes. When Connor wears blue—" She stopped talking and we stared at each other for a few seconds before she lowered her head, but I saw the tears she was trying to hold back.

"I need to go," I said, brushing past her. I didn't need a reminder that Connor was still out there somewhere, but I had no fucking idea where. Every day I worried that I'd get that dreaded phone call from a hospital or a police officer, and every day I thanked God when it didn't come.

"I'm sorry," Ava said, her voice sounding small, but I still heard her. "You look great, Killian. Really. You always look great."

I raised my hand in the air and forced myself to keep

walking, right out of the bar and onto the street. I didn't stop or slow down or turn my head to see what the bartenders were doing. Progress. Louis accused me of being a control freak and a workaholic, but he knew the real reason I needed to keep busy—less time to think. And I liked taking care of problems I could fix. In my real life, I had a shit-ton of problems with no solutions.

When I got outside, I breathed in through my nose and out through my mouth. Deep breaths. On the drive to Eden's apartment, I tried to calm myself down. It was just dinner. I needed to chill the fuck out. I rolled out my shoulders. Even before a fight, I never used to get nervous. But this was uncharted territory, and I didn't want to screw it up.

Last night, I'd gotten a taste of Eden, and I knew it would never be enough. I'd never understood the power of a kiss before. She didn't taste like an ashtray or lipstick or dirty martinis. Eden tasted like warm honey. She smelled like…orange blossoms, I guess.

After she told me the story about her dickhead boyfriend, I didn't want to be another dick who screwed her over. I wanted to be someone worthy. I wanted to be someone special to her, not just some guy who fucks her and leaves. That was *all* I'd ever done in the past, something she got to hear about from Joss.

I should have known that nothing good ever happened at Fat Earl's. Being in that bar again twisted my stomach into knots. Eden noticed something was wrong. She always noticed. But I pulled myself together and by the time we finished our game of pool, it was all good. Until we ran into Joss and Adam.

I told Adam if he valued his life, he wouldn't get within a hundred yards of Eden. Wouldn't even glance in her direction. He'd make sure Joss did the same. Adam knew who I was, and what I was capable of, and that worked in my favor for a change.

He wouldn't mess with her again.

I climbed the stairs to Eden's front door and pressed the intercom. The lock on this door wasn't worth jack shit. She should talk to her landlord about this. I backed up on the landing and looked at her windows. Closed. I smiled when I heard her voice on the intercom, "Killian?"

"Good evening, ma'am. I'm one of Jehovah's Witnesses and I'd like to talk to you about the Lord's work."

She laughed that husky laugh of hers. "The Lord works in mysterious ways. I'd love to hear more about it. Be right down."

"I'll be waiting." I tried to get my dick to behave. Just hearing her laugh got me hard. I groaned and rubbed my hands over my face.

The door opened behind me, and I turned around to look at her. She gripped her plump lower lip between her white teeth and smoothed her hands over her dress. It was white, or something close to white. The sleeves wrapped around her biceps, leaving her shoulders bare. I'd never make it through dinner. I wanted to skip food and haul her back upstairs and ravage her body. The dress was deceptive. It appeared to be sweet and innocent, but on her, it was the sexiest dress I'd ever seen. My gaze traveled down her tanned legs to sandals that tied around her ankle. I wanted to rip open the laces with my teeth.

I lifted my eyes to her face. She was wearing her hair down, a blonde tumble of loose waves. She told me she keeps her hair long for her mom who said she never thought she was vain until she lost all her hair. I hope Eden never cuts her hair. I love that she doesn't wear tons of makeup so I can actually see her face. Her lips are naturally pink and lush and…fuck. I hadn't said a word since she stepped out of her door. "You look good." *Beautiful.*

She smiled. "Thank you. I changed my outfit about twenty

times. But I ended up wearing my first choice."

How cool that she admitted it. No pretense. No ulterior motive. Just pure honesty. "Good choice."

Eden reached for my hand and I clasped her smaller hand in mine, our palms pressed together. I'd never been a hand-holder before. When I used to take a woman to my hotel room after a fight, I always walked two paces ahead, like an arrogant asshole, and they'd have to jog a little to keep up. I didn't know what it was about Eden, or why everything was so different with her. It felt like I'd been living in the dark for too long and she'd turned on all the lights inside me. Like the world wasn't such a fucked-up place if she was in it.

The restaurant was French with vintage posters on the walls, hardwood floors, and low lighting. The kind of restaurant where you brought a date for a romantic dinner. Not overly fancy, but quaint I guess. After I turned down the first table they tried to give us—right in front, on top of everyone else, and not where I wanted to be—they led us to a candle-lit table in the back corner of the patio garden enclosed by ivy-covered walls.

I ordered steak and salad. She ordered chicken. I ordered a bottle of red wine, after asking her if she liked it. She said she did, but she'd need to wear her napkin as a bib. Which made me laugh.

Over dinner, she talked about art and the artist Jean-Michel Basquiat, and how he grew up in Brooklyn and dropped out of school. How Basquiat started as a graffiti artist before he moved on to painting. Then he died young, from a heroin overdose. As usual, every word out of her mouth fascinated me, even though I knew all about Basquiat already. He was one of Connor's favorite artists. Unfortunately, Connor had more in common with Basquiat than just art.

"You want to be a graffiti artist?" I asked her.

She had that same look on her face as she did when she considered getting a tattoo. I knew she'd say yes, even before the words came out of her mouth. "Yeah, I do. If I got arrested, would you bail me out of jail?" she asked, with a mischievous smile like the idea thrilled her rather than scared her.

"I won't let you get arrested. I'll be your lookout and your getaway driver." Hell, if I'd let her do that on her own. Bushwick was the best place to throw something on the wall. Connor used to do it back in high school. But graffiti needs to be done late at night, and no way was that safe for Eden.

"You'd do that for me?" she asked, her eyes lighting up. Her whole face lit up when she was happy.

She had no idea how much I'd be willing to do for her. Making her happy had become my new purpose in life. Maybe I didn't deserve her, but neither did Luke or Adam. I liked who she was—talented, beautiful, strong, argumentative. She'd suffered her share of loss and heartbreak, but she wasn't jaded or bitter. I liked it that she pushed back and questioned me about everything. I couldn't think of anything I didn't like about her. "Yeah, I'd do that for you."

"We'll be like Bonnie and Clyde," she said. "Without the guns and the bank robberies."

"So, nothing like Bonnie and Clyde."

She burst out laughing. "Guess not."

The waiter cleared our plates and handed us dessert menus. I didn't even look at mine, but Eden studied hers like it held the secrets of the universe. When the waiter came back to take our order, she was still pouring over the menu.

"Need some help there, sunshine?"

She lowered the menu and smiled at me. "That's exactly what I need. Thanks for the offer." Eden turned to the waiter and ordered two desserts.

"I got the molten lava chocolate cake and the apple tart," she told me, with a smug smile. "So, you'll need to help me."

Help consisted of her force-feeding me bites of each. "You like it, right?" she asked, after feeding me a bite of chocolate cake.

I closed my eyes and moaned like I was having an orgasm. "Mm. Best thing I ever tasted. I need more."

Her face flushed pink, and I smirked at her.

She held a forkful of apple tart in front of my mouth. "Tart?"

"And here I thought you were sweet and innocent."

She laughed. "Open up."

"Oh. It keeps getting better. What will you have me do next?"

"The night is still young," she said, with a wicked gleam in her eyes.

I opened my mouth, and she fed me. Eight years of a dessert-free, refined sugar-free diet, shot to hell by the temptress across the table. She watched my mouth as I chewed, and her gaze dropped down to my throat as I swallowed. Back to my mouth as I licked my lips, her eyes following the progress of my tongue. She lifted her gaze and her green eyes locked onto mine. "You made that innocent tart look downright sinful," she said.

"I'll feed you the chocolate cake, and you can return the favor."

Eyes still locked on mine, she handed me her fork and pushed the cake in front of me. Challenge accepted. Chocolate cake had never looked so sinful. I reached across the table and slowly dragged my thumb across her lower lip, feeling the tremor go through her. "You missed some."

She wrapped her hand around my wrist and guided my

thumb into her mouth. Holy fuck. Her lips wrapped around my thumb and she sucked on it, her cheeks hollowed, her tongue circling, her teeth grazing my skin. I reached down and adjusted myself under the table. I had every intention of dropping her off with a goodnight kiss and nothing more. For the first time in my life, I wanted to take this slow and do it right. But she was blowing all my good intentions out of the water. All I could think about were those lips wrapped around my cock.

Eden released my thumb, her eyelids at half-mast. "You taste good."

Chapter Twenty

Eden

H IS HANDS GRIPPED MY HIPS, AND HIS MOUTH TOOK COMMAND of mine. He kicked the door shut behind him, our mouths still melded, our kisses hot and wet and frantic, and drove me against the wall. His hand fisted my hair and the other one cupped my butt, his hard body pressed against the length of mine. He kissed me like he was starving, and I was his favorite food. And I kissed him back the same way, greedy and wanting more. It had all started in the restaurant—the bulge in his jeans had been hard to miss, but he didn't know how wet I'd gotten during that soft porn show…AKA dessert. He tried to say goodnight with a kiss and leave me at the door like a gentleman, but I asked him to come inside, practically spelling it out for him. Sex. Sex. Sex.

My hungry hands clawed at his back, my fingers digging into shirt and muscle.

"You sure about this?" he asked huskily.

I rocked my hips against him to let him know just how sure I was. I wanted him. Inside me. On top of me. Under me. Rough and wild. Slow and gentle. Every which way. I wanted it all.

His hand slid into my panties, rubbing between my slick folds. I moaned and bucked against his hand. Two fingers slipped inside me, reaching and curling, rubbing a spot that touched every nerve ending in my body. How did he know exactly where to touch me?

My fingers fumbled with the buttons of his jeans, and my hand found him inside his boxer briefs. Long, thick, rock hard. He groaned, the sound deep and guttural and so erotic it reverberated in my core. I slid my hand up his hard length, rubbing the pad of my thumb around the small slit at the tip.

"Fuck," he growled.

He lifted me off the ground, my legs cinched around his waist, and carried me into the bedroom. Setting me down on the end of the bed, he knelt in front of me and untied one sandal and removed it then moved on to the next, like he was in no hurry and we had all the time in the world now. When I reached for him, he told me to sit still and keep my hands to myself.

"Still issuing commands?" I asked.

"All for your pleasure."

And, oh yes, it was *all* for my pleasure.

His warm, calloused hands caressed my bare shoulders, my upper arms, my dress miraculously gliding down my body, his fingers brushing my skin. He reached around to my back and expertly unhooked my strapless bra, tossing it on the floor. Putting his hands on my shoulders, he pushed me back on the bed. My dress came off. My panties followed. And I was lying on my bed, my feet on the floor, stripped bare for him. I pushed myself up on my elbows.

"You're so beautiful," he said, his voice hushed as if we were in a church, still kneeling in front of me, his eyes worshiping my body. He pushed my thighs apart and put his head between them, gripping my hips in his hands. My back hit the bed. I couldn't hold myself up anymore. He tortured me with his tongue, coaxing and teasing, bringing me to the brink then slowing the pace. My hands fisted the sheets, and I pulled so hard that both corners came loose. His hand slid over my belly and rib cage and he squeezed my nipple between his fingers as his tongue continued to coax and tease.

"Killian," I whimpered. I was not above begging. "Please."

That was all it took. Fingers, tongue, mouth. What kind of sorcery was this? I didn't even know what he was doing to me, but I'd never felt anything like it. My whole body was trembling.

I was so…close. My eyes rolled back in my head. I had no control over the sounds coming out of my mouth.

"Killian," I said, in a strangled voice I barely recognized as my own. I came so hard I was practically crying.

I was still riding out the crest of the wave when I heard his boots thud against the floor. I opened my eyes as he was unbuttoning his shirt, exposing all that tanned skin and sculpted muscle.

"You want me?" he asked, tossing his shirt on the floor.

My gaze traveled down from his broad chest to the cut V-shape of his abs and lower, to the undone buttons of his jeans. I wanted more. I wanted him to fill me up inside, bring me over the edge again, like I knew he could.

I nodded. *Yes, yes, I want you.*

"I need to hear you say the words," he said.

"I want you."

He stripped off his jeans and boxer briefs and stood in front of me naked, in the dim shadows of my room and oh my God, I had never in my life seen anything as perfect as him. Every muscle was clearly defined, his cock long and thick and impossibly big. I wanted to touch every inch of skin and muscle, feel him in my hands, feel my body wrapped around his.

I cupped his balls in my hand, feeling their weight, and gave them a gentle squeeze. He sucked in his breath and gripped my shoulders, his fingers digging into my skin. I slid my other hand up the length of him, feeling the silky, thin skin and veins. He was so hard it must have been painful. Wrapping my hand around the base, I teased him with the tip of my tongue, running it up his length, and circling the tip. His hands on my shoulders tightened, his breathing ragged as I took him in my mouth.

He pulled away from me. "I need to be inside you." Fishing a condom out of his jeans pocket, he ripped open the packet, and rolled it onto his erection.

He hauled me up the bed and braced his arms on either side of me, lowering his head and kissing me hard. I tasted myself on his lips and his tongue. "You taste so sweet," he said, in his sexy, gravelly voice. "Better than any dessert."

I arched my back, my breasts pressing against his chest, my nipples getting hard on contact. Supporting himself on one arm, he rubbed his tip against my clit, the tight bundle of nerves getting taut, until I was all slick heat between my legs again. He kept kissing me. Kept teasing me until it was all I could do not to beg him to enter me already. How he exercised so much self-control, I had no idea. I was greedy for another orgasm, and he hadn't even had his first one yet.

He sat up and knelt between my legs, his hand caressing my inner thigh, wrapping around my calf, and lifting my leg onto his shoulder. My other leg wrapped around his thigh and when he finally, finally, entered me, I knew that nothing, absolutely nothing, had ever felt this good. I watched his unguarded face, the intense pleasure written all over it, his lips slightly parted. It gave me a thrill that I'd been the one to put that look on his face.

"I want you to come," he said, his thumb rubbing my clit. I was only my body. Skin, bones, muscle. I was moaning. And I was so…close. When I came, I was split wide open. Shattering into thousands of pieces. My muscles clenched around him as he thrust deep inside me. One. Two. Three times. He came apart, his body shuddering with his release, his arms wrapping around me, holding me close against him. We smelled like sweat and sex and dirty pleasures.

He buried his face in my hair. "You feel fucking amazing, sunshine." I smiled into the darkness. A beat later, he asked, "Does that air conditioner work?"

Chapter Twenty-One

Killian

I was so far gone I didn't have a hope in hell. One night and she was under my skin. Those were my first thoughts when I woke up the next morning, her warm body curled against mine. My next thought was that I was so hard my dick hurt. She pressed her ass against it, and I thought she did it in her sleep, until I heard her husky laugh.

"Evil temptress," I said.

"You called me a dirty angel last night."

"I called you a lot of things last night."

"Mm, you're creative." She turned around in my arms to face me. Even in the morning, make-up free and her hair wild and tangled, she was gorgeous. "Good morning."

Damn if it wasn't the best morning I could ever remember. I'd never slept in a girl's bed all night. I'd never woken up in one. I never wanted to leave this bed with its snowy white sheets and downy comforter. The shades were drawn and the air conditioner under her window clanked and hissed, but I'd closed her bedroom door, turned it on high, and it did the job keeping the room nice and cool. She leaned over and grabbed a condom from her bedside table. Last night, I was happy to see that the box hadn't been opened yet. "Round three?" she asked, with a wink.

"I don't know. You're a delicate flower. You sure you're up for it?"

"Looks like you're up for it." She pulled back the covers to reveal the evidence. "I'm sure I can make the effort."

She fisted my cock, and I watched her hand move up and down, exerting the perfect amount of pressure. My balls were drawn up so tight, I felt like I was going to explode in her hand. "Oh...God," I groaned.

"You can call me Eden."

"Eden. Eden. Eden." *What are you doing to me?*

She kept a grip on my dick and ripped opened the condom packet with her teeth. I snatched it out of her mouth, rolled it over my erection and pulled her on top of me. She took me in her hand and guided me inside her. She was already wet for me. I wrapped my hands around her hips, intent on controlling the pace. If she kept grinding against me like this I wouldn't last two seconds. But she had other ideas. "Hands behind your head."

I slid my hands up her sides and held her breasts in my hands, thumbing the pink nipples that hardened under my touch. "But think of all the things they can do for you."

She grabbed my wrists and pushed my arms down on either side of my head. "Let me show you what I can do."

"I love it when you talk dirty." I laced my fingers behind my head and let her take control. Her idea of taking control was taking control of me *and* herself.

I scowled at her. "That's my job."

"Just sit back and watch."

Oh fuck. She threw her head back, fingering her clit, riding me hard, and squeezing my nipple between her fingers, her palm flat on my chest for support. Her long blonde hair, silky and soft, flowed down her back and caressed my thighs. I rolled my hips and she let out a moan that would put porn stars to shame.

"Are you close?" I asked, my voice strained. I was barely

hanging on, and if she didn't come soon I'd lose it. "Baby…"

"Killian," she screamed. Her eyes closed, and her mouth dropped open, her muscles clenching around my cock. I sat up, wrapped my arms around her quivering body and exploded inside her.

Nothing had ever felt this good.

My back collapsed against the bed, my arms still holding her, bringing her down with me. I couldn't speak, couldn't move a muscle. She lay on top of me, her legs shaking like she had no control over them, her arms wrapped around my neck, her face pressed against my neck.

"I can't move," she mumbled.

"Don't. We'll stay here all day."

"Like Yoko Ono and John Lennon."

She lost me there. She climbed off me, and I reached for the condom, but she smacked my hand away and took care of it herself.

"Tell me I'm the best you've ever had," I said, in a teasing tone. I wasn't teasing though. I wanted it to be like that for her because it was for me.

"I just rode you like a cowgirl. What more could you want?"

An answer.

I watched her walk across the bedroom, naked, the condom dangling from her fingers. Jesus. I rubbed my hands over my face. One night will never be enough.

"You're the best I've ever had," she called from the hallway before the bathroom door closed behind her.

With a stupid grin on my face, I got dressed.

I was putting on my boots when she sauntered into the bedroom, wearing a short, silky green robe that matched her eyes. Jealousy seized me. Did her ex-boyfriend give it to her? Did she wear it after she had sex with him? How could anyone think there was something better out there than her? I'd been with too many women to count, but they'd all left me feeling cold. Or numb. Not Eden. She made me feel too much of everything. I wrapped my hand around her wrist and pulled her into my lap, wrapping my arms around her. "Listen…about last night…"

Her phone buzzed on the bedside table. A number with no name. She stared at it, chewing on her bottom lip then reached over and pressed the silent button.

"Was that him?" I asked. My arms tightened around her as if I were a human shield, protecting her from the evil forces.

"Yeah. But I never answer."

That surprised me. Eden wasn't scared of confrontation, and she wasn't the type to run and hide or stick her head in the sand. She called me out on everything and didn't hesitate to try and set me straight or push me for answers. "Why not?"

She shrugged.

"Why don't you answer?" I asked, really needing to know. Maybe the question was, why did he keep calling?

"What can he say to justify his actions? Nothing. And it's not like we'd ever get back together again. I don't know why he keeps calling. What's the point?"

"You never talked to him after you caught them together?"

"No," she said, chewing on her lower lip. That was her thing. She did it when she was nervous. "But I will talk to him. Eventually."

I couldn't blame her for not talking to him though. What could he say? The asshole never deserved her. But she might still be in love with him and that thought hit me in the gut. She'd spent five years in a committed relationship with the guy, so she must have loved him. I'd spent one night with her, and weeks before that trying to convince myself I should leave her alone.

Nothing I did worked. When I closed my eyes, I saw her face. After I downed a few glasses of Jameson, I wanted to call her and hear her voice. My hand didn't satisfy my needs. Nothing did. But now I couldn't imagine letting her go.

"What were you going to tell me?" she asked, and it sounded like she was steeling herself for bad news. "Because I don't want last night to be a one-night stand. I want to keep doing this. We don't need to be in a real relationship. We can just hook up."

"That's what you want?"

"Yeah. That's what I want." But I could hear it in her voice it wasn't what she wanted. "What do you think?"

I thought it sucked. It wasn't nearly enough. She deserved better, and I wasn't sure I could give it to her, but I wanted to be that guy. I wanted to be the guy who took her out to dinner, brought her flowers, and woke up with her in the morning. The thought of another guy doing that made me sick to my stomach. I'd never been jealous before, but now I was jealous of any guy who'd gone before me or any guy she might be with that wasn't me. "I think it's a bad idea."

Her shoulders drooped. "Oh. Okay."

"You're with me. Nobody else. This wasn't a one-night stand and we're not just hooking up."

"What? But you just said..." Her brows puckered. It was adorable. Everything she did was adorable. Yeah, I was fucked. "You want a relationship?"

Was that what I wanted? I couldn't deal with the alternative. Letting her go. Taking the risk that she'd find someone else. Or hook up with random guys. No. Not happening. "Yeah, that's what I want. You?"

She took a minute to think about it then she smiled and wrapped an arm around my neck and snuggled against my chest. "Yeah, I do. Hooking up just makes me feel kind of empty."

This morning, I felt a lot of things. Empty wasn't one of them. I gave her a little squeeze. "So why did you say it was what you wanted?"

"I don't know. I just...you're not a relationship guy."

"You'll have to show me how it's done," I said.

She turned her body towards me and looked me in the eye, her green eyes so clear and bright, searching for truth. Wanting to trust me, but not sure if she could. I knew what she was going to ask me before she said it. "I need you to promise me one thing."

"I won't cheat on you," I said, beating her to the punch, my specialty.

"Promise?"

"On my life." I was a lot of things, not all of them good, but I'd never go behind her back with someone else. I hadn't even looked at another woman or encouraged their advances since I met her. She watched me at the bar as much as I watched her, so she knew that. "If I did something like that, you'd have my permission to bash the hell out of my car and then swing the bat at my head."

"I'd never hurt you, Killian," she said softly.

The way she said it just about killed me. I knew she was saying she wouldn't physically hurt me, and she was looking at the scar on my neck while she said it. She looked at it a lot, her eyes filled with questions I had no intention of ever answering honestly. But I couldn't help feeling like she was talking about another kind of hurt, and that was a promise neither one of us could make. Life was messy and complicated. *I* was messy and complicated. Shit happened. Hearts got broken, intentionally or not. I'd always safeguarded mine, kept it out of danger by never getting too close to any woman. One-night stands and casual hookups had been a way of life for me and it had never been difficult to keep those boundaries in place. *Until her.*

I was as much at her mercy, as she was at mine. That, right there, was some scary shit.

Lifting her off my lap, I set her on the bed next to me, and leaned down to tie my laces. When I stood, she came to stand in front of me and took both my hands in hers.

"We can take it slow," Eden said, but I thought we'd already passed slow and moved into turbo-charge. Neither one of us was built for the slow lane, and once I committed to something, I never did it in half-measures. It was all or nothing for me, and I got the feeling she wasn't that much different. But I kept that to myself. All we could do was ride this out and see where it took us. I could only hope we ended up somewhere good.

"Ready to go?" I eyed her sexy little robe that told me she wasn't ready to go anywhere.

"Go where?" she asked, furrowing her brows.

I laughed. She'd forgotten all about painting the wall. When it finally dawned on her, she smacked herself on the forehead and groaned. "Just give me two minutes." She held up two fingers and flew to her dresser. After rummaging around in the drawers, she came out with shorts, a top, and a matching bra and underwear set—blue trimmed in silver. Now I'd know what was under her clothes. Pure, delicious torture.

Chapter Twenty-Two

Killian

She kept me waiting for fifteen minutes, but I didn't complain. I was impressed she showered, dressed, dried her hair and was in the Jeep so quickly. She was wearing enormous sunglasses, short shorts, and a Ripcurl T-shirt that skimmed her waistband and hugged her body in all the right places. She looked like a Hollywood starlet. A dirty angel. A California surfer girl. A modern-day fairytale. Eden Madley was sexy, sweet, gorgeous, and mine. How in the hell had any of this happened?

While I drove, she pulled all her hair on top of her head, twisted it around and around, and tied it in a knot that secured it in place. Wispy strands of hair escaped the knot and blew in the breeze from the open windows. Her bare feet propped on the dash, she tapped out the beat of Bedouin Soundclash's "When the Night Feels My Song" on the window frame. I had to agree with the lyrics—it was a beautiful day. An ordinary day, but a beautiful one. I didn't feel the weight of the world on my shoulders. I felt happy in a way I hadn't felt in so long. I wanted to hang onto it for as long as it lasted.

We picked up coffee from her favorite barista who put two and two together and came up with five. "So…you two, huh?" He put his hand over his heart and tapped it a few times. Then fluttered his eyelashes at both of us. "I knew there was something there from that first day. You two look so good together.

Just for the record," he said, putting his hand on my arm, "I knew you were straight. But it never hurts to look, right?"

Just give me the coffee and spare me the chat. Maybe I grunted in response. Who knows? Eden nudged my shoulder, prompting me to respond, so I mustered a smile and tried to be nice. "Right. Doesn't hurt to look."

"Have a good day," Eden said, with a big smile and a wave.

"You too," he said, giving us a wink like he'd been personally responsible for getting us together.

"Don't mess with my head any more, okay?" Eden said when we were back in the Jeep and she was drinking her caffeine laced with milk and sugar. She was saving her cinnamon roll for later, having shot down my suggestion to try one of the salads or the Greek yogurt.

I glanced at her. "How do I mess with your head?" I wasn't sure I wanted to hear it.

"You don't know how you mess with my head?"

I pulled up in front of the bar and left the motor idling. She unfastened her seatbelt and turned in her seat to look at me.

"If we're going to do this, we need to be open and honest with each other. I can't handle it if you're running hot and cold and I don't know the reason behind it. Like, after the time I sketched your face, why were you so closed-off? You acted really cold."

She was waiting for an answer, and I knew she wouldn't let me go until she got one. I rubbed the back of my neck. This wasn't going to be easy, but if I wanted to be with her, I couldn't fall at the first hurdle. I did want to be with her. But I didn't know how to answer her question.

"Is that why you were hanging out with Adam?" I asked. It was a dickhead move and I knew it. To her credit, she didn't rise to it.

"Killian. Look at me."

I looked at her. She pushed her sunglasses on top of her head and she looked at me, really looked at me the way only she could. Like she was an excavator digging out my secrets and lies and exposing them to the light.

"If you're not ready for this, tell me now before we get into it. I don't want you to jerk me around. I'm working on myself, and I don't need someone to make me feel bad about myself. I care about you, and I think you care about me too. But we need to start communicating better."

Like I said, she was strong and brave, and didn't shy away from confrontation. And I cared about her, more than she probably knew. The last thing I wanted to do was make her feel bad about herself. I leaned back in my seat and searched my brain for the right answer. Sex was easy. Intimacy was hard for me. "If you look too closely, dig too deep, you won't like what you find and that…scares the shit out of me." I swallowed hard, not sure how all this honesty made me feel. I wanted her to leave, so I could go work it out at the gym. Punch a leather bag with my bare hands until my knuckles were raw and bleeding. *That* was how it made me feel.

She leaned over the gearbox and wrapped her hand around the back of my neck, pulling me towards her for a goodbye kiss. My eyes closed, and she pressed her lips gently against my closed eyelid. It felt odd, but in a good way. Sweet and gentle and caring. She sat back in her seat and looked over at me, a small smile tugging on her lips.

"What was that?" I asked.

"An angel kiss. From a dirty angel. And I like what I see, even when I look closely. Let me see you, Killian. Don't shut me out." She hopped out of the Jeep and waved goodbye over her shoulder.

Yep. She hadn't Googled me. Fuck. What would she think about that? It didn't matter that they ruled it an accident. Or that they claimed there were pre-existing medical conditions. My hands were officially lethal weapons, and I was a man seeking salvation and redemption, without a clue how to find it.

On my way to the gym, I thought about what she'd asked me in the coffee shop that day we talked for an hour. What would be my first choice of career? For years, all I'd known was fighting. All my life, I'd been fighting—for survival, against the bullies, against authority. When I discovered Brazilian Jiu-Jitsu at fifteen, I was hooked. Not only did it give me the self-defense training I needed, it gave me a focus and a purpose in my life. MMA had been my passion, my art, my religion, my calling. For the first time in my life, I'd found a home, a place where I belonged. I loved the adrenaline rush. I loved the crowd. I loved the fans, especially the kids. When they asked for my autograph and told me they wanted to be just like me when they grew up, that I was their favorite fighter, their hero, I'd never felt more humbled or prouder of any achievement in my life.

But that life was over, and I couldn't go back to it. Now, if I could choose to do anything, I'd use my hands to do something good. To create something beautiful. To build something instead of knocking it down and destroying it. But it was pointless to think about what I *would* do when I'd already committed to the bar business. There were worse ways to earn a living, and I didn't hate it. I just didn't love it.

Later that afternoon, the enormity of what was happening hit me. Somehow, I'd talked my way into a relationship and I was happy about it. I leaned against the doorframe in the courtyard and watched her painting the wall while she talked to Zeke. I knew they were just friends, so I didn't need to be an asshole about it. Eden said I needed to make more of an effort to be nice to Zeke. Jesus. This girl will be ruling my life soon, as if she didn't already.

The mural unfolded before my eyes as she painted pink flowers. Poppies? Her talent awed me. When I saw the sketch she did of me, I felt like I was looking at myself the way she saw me, not the way I really was, but better. Like I was someone good.

Her art was different than Connor's. His was more graphic, I guess. He was into manga and anime. In his early teens, he'd been working on a comic book, but I didn't know what happened to it. I stared at my phone as if thinking about Connor hard enough would send him a telepathic message that he should call me.

My phone remained silent.

Unfortunately, Louis didn't. We were standing across the street from the bar, watching the construction guys working on the roof. Not that watching them would speed up their progress or lower the cost—we were Monday morning quarterbacks, critiquing their work and grumbling about everything we could do better. I took a swig from my bottle of water and squinted at the crew of men in hardhats doing jack shit, as far as I could tell.

"He hasn't gotten off his ass in twenty minutes," Louis grumbled. "What the hell is he doing?"

"Catching some rays on our tar beach." The guy in question was shirtless, with a beer gut and a red face he hadn't gotten from over-exertion, judging by the way he was sitting around like a fucking potato.

"Good thing we agreed on a price for the job," Louis said.

"We should have done it ourselves."

"Because we have so much roofing experience," Louis deadpanned. "With so much free time on our hands."

We could have done it, but we had enough work, running the bar, and standing around, doing nothing, like we were doing now.

"Speaking of hands, how was your date?" Louis asked.

"I kept my hands to myself." I smothered a laugh, thinking about Eden's no-hands command this morning.

"I call bullshit." He side-eyed me. My face gave him no clues to support his claim. Unlike Eden, I've perfected the art of keeping a poker face. A lifetime of secrets and lies taught me how to hide my emotions. "Did you tell her yet?" Louis asked, bursting my happy bubble.

I shook my head no.

"You should," he said, telling me something I already knew.

She'd find out eventually. Every bartender at Trinity Bar, except for her, had eventually found out what I had done for a living. I asked them to keep their mouths shut about it but one of those days it would slip out.

"Nobody judges you as harshly as you judge yourself," Louis said, trying to impart some words of wisdom.

Too bad it was bullshit. Anna Ramirez judges me, and one day when her son is old enough to understand, he'll judge me, and he'll hate me for what I stole from him. Sometimes, I tried to take consolation in the knowledge that Johnny loved MMA as much as I did. He ate, slept, and breathed the sport. He'd taken too many blows to the head, had suffered too many concussions, supposedly. If that had been the case, why did they let him fight me? Injuries were a risk we took every time we stepped into the cage. If you dwelled on what could happen, or let the fear get inside your head, you've already lost the fight before it started. To win, you needed to be mentally strong and you needed to be confident. There's no room for self-doubt.

Johnny was deemed physically fit and mentally sound. Even after that punch to his head during our fight, he'd passed the medical team's tests and was sent back in for two more rounds.

"If by some terrible twist of fate, I couldn't continue fighting, I wouldn't be Johnny Ramirez anymore," he'd told me once after a training session. "I'd be pissed off at the world, hating life, and impossible to be around."

"More than you are now?" I'd joked, but I had understood what he was saying because I felt like that too.

"You ain't no day at the beach, Vincent."

"Is that why you're always trying to cozy up to me?"

"We'll leave our bromance outside the Octagon. When I'm forced to fight you, all bets are off."

"I'm not fighting you." Johnny was five years older than me—my teammate, my mentor, my friend, and a contender in the same weight class. His career started peaking while mine was still getting off the ground. We didn't choose our opponents. The promoters did. But teammates fighting each other was contentious and not something I ever wanted to do. Ironically, Johnny had no problem with it.

"Your star is rising. Everyone's buying into the Killian Vincent brand," he'd said. "If you keep going like this, our day of reckoning will come."

"We'll refuse."

"Like hell we will. We're fighters. It's not only what we do, it's who we are. We're in the UFC because we want to fight the best of the best. If the day comes, I'll fight your sorry ass for the title. After I win, I'll shake your fucking hand and buy you a whiskey, so you can drown your sorrows in it."

By some terrible twist of fate, that wasn't how it happened.

We fought to win. Not to kill. Not to finish someone

off. We weren't gladiators in the Colosseum, fighting for our lives. We believed that we were men of pride and honor. Competitors in the Octagon, friends outside of it.

Once upon a time, I was a champion. Who, or what, was I now?

Chapter Twenty-Three

Eden

"Friend-zoned," Zeke said. He was lounging on a chair in the courtyard, soaking up the rays and drinking a Gatorade while I painted my poppy field.

"I friend-zoned you and that's working out fine."

"No offense but *I* friend-zoned *you*. Killian gave me strict instructions that you were off-limits. I want to keep my job. It's a cool gig."

"He actually said that? Why?" I turned to look at Zeke whose eyes were closed.

"Probably because he knows I'm the resident man whore." Zeke held up his hands. "I'm not even apologizing."

"I can't believe Killian. That should have been my decision, not his." Which was true. But did he feel like there was a connection from the first time we met? I'd never had sex like that. It was so intense, so mind-blowing, so much of everything. He knew how to play my body, how to get me begging for more. With him, I had a feeling I'd always want more. But last night was more than just the sex. He held me in his arms all night, my back against his chest, and it felt so right and so good. It was hard to believe we'd taken so many detours to get to this place. I belonged in his arms, in a way I'd never felt before, not even with Luke.

"You would have gone for me?" Zeke asked.

"No. You look too much like my brother Sawyer." He didn't really look like Sawyer, but Zeke didn't do it for me, and I didn't want to hurt his feelings.

"Your brother must be a stud," Zeke said.

"He'd like to think so."

Zeke snorted with disgust. "My ego is being bruised and battered. I've been relegated to brotherly love. And I've been friend-zoned. What the hell?"

"Just accept the challenge. Doesn't it get old going from one girl to another?"

"Nope. They're all different girls. That keeps it fresh. I like to keep my life simple. No complicated emotions to bog me down. If Hailey thinks I'm deep, she's sadly mistaken."

"Are you scared she'll find out you're just a pretty face?" I teased.

"Hey. That's not fair. I've got a hot body too. My body is my temple, and she should be worshiping at it instead of treating me as a…*friend*," he said, as if friend was a dirty word.

"Then just forget about Hailey. No one's forcing you to be her friend."

"I know you put her up to this."

I shrugged. "All I did was suggest it. This was Hailey's call."

Zeke sighed. "Like I said, my reputation precedes me."

I stepped back to study my field of abstract pink poppies.

"Your mural looks awesome."

I wasn't so sure, but it was nice to hear. "Thanks."

"I need to ramble," Zeke said, grabbing his skateboard. "Catch you later."

"See you."

A few minutes later, I looked inside the bar and saw Zeke talking to Killian. I smiled to myself when I heard them laughing.

I hooked myself up to my music and got back to my mural.

The brick was cracked in places, parts of the wall crumbling. I liked that it wasn't perfect and that my mural looked more like graffiti. When I finished this, I was going to work on my next piece—my street art.

"Time for a break," Ava called from the doorway.

"I need to finish."

She dragged me away and forced me to eat with her. I didn't realize I was so hungry until she unpacked the deli sandwiches and tossed me a bag of chips. She bought enough to feed a small country. I offered her money, but she waved it away. "Killian and Louis gave me money. They'll eat most of it anyway so get in there before they get here."

I knew all about fighting for food in a household of boys, so after checking out the selection, I grabbed a turkey and Swiss and ripped open my bag of chips.

"Wanna do half and half?" Ava asked, holding up half of her sandwich.

"What's yours?"

"Tuna melt."

I swapped half of my sandwich for half of hers and took a big bite of the turkey sandwich.

Killian and Louis came outside with bottles of water and Killian took the seat next to me, with Louis next to Ava. Killian's hand found my thigh under the table and he rested it there, on my bare skin, as if his hand belonged on my thigh. A little thrill shot through me. I loved that his hand belonged there.

"Yes!" Ava said, punching the air in victory. "My coffee arrangement worked."

Louis chuckled. "It takes a village."

Killian snorted. I concentrated on eating my food, but with Killian's hand branding my skin, it wasn't an easy task. My pulse was racing, and my stomach was all fluttery as I stuffed my face with food I wasn't hungry for anymore.

I side-eyed Killian. *Do you know that your hand is setting off a five-alarm fire inside me?*

He smirked. *Yes. I'm aware of what I'm doing to you.*

I tried not to think about his naked body or what it could do to mine. His hand drifted to my inner thigh and inched its way upwards. I squirmed in my seat and pushed his hand away.

"Chips?" Ava asked, dangling a bag in front of Killian's face.

He batted them away. She arched her brows at me, as if to say, I told you so.

"You don't eat chips?" I asked, plucking one from my bag and tossing it into my mouth.

"No chips," Louis said. "No cookies, candy, cake, brownies—"

"She gets the point," Killian said.

"He even has issues with sandwiches," Ava said. "Notice how he only went for the ones with the birdseed bread and raw vegetables."

I peeked at his sandwich choices. Sure enough, he'd chosen two that I'd passed up. One had birdseed bread and the other one was a wrap with raw vegetables and sprouts sticking out of it.

"I almost didn't order them," Ava said. "Out of protest."

"Save your energy for something that matters," Killian advised, as his hand returned to my thigh. His fingers traced the outline of my underwear and slipped inside, rubbing between my folds. I nearly choked on my sandwich and started coughing, my eyes watering. He removed his hand to give me a few helpful thumps on the back.

"Drink some water," Killian said, all innocence, offering me his water bottle. I coughed a few times then took a swig of my Coke, glaring at him. He pretended to cower. What a comedian.

"A turkey sandwich can be dangerous," Louis said, arching

his brows. He knew what was going down under the table.

"Especially when it gets stuck in your throat," Killian said, making it sound dirty.

"Even a *small* turkey sandwich can cause bodily harm," Louis said.

"Just think what a *big* one could do," Killian said.

"Choke you," Louis said. "Good thing *you* don't have that problem."

"Exactly," Killian said. "I don't eat turkey sandwiches. Something you need to share, Louis? Does Carmen know about this?"

I rolled my eyes.

"Are you guys done comparing the size of your dicks?" Ava said.

"What is she talking about?" Louis asked Killian.

Killian shrugged. "*Someone* has a dirty mind." He gave my thigh a squeeze. I smacked his hand away. He laughed.

Ava and I shook our heads at each other as we got up from the table. "We'll leave you guys to battle it out over the rest of my turkey sandwich."

"Too bad it isn't a fat sausage sandwich," Ava said.

I laughed. "Or a foot-long hot dog."

I returned to my mural, cracking up over that stupid conversation at the picnic table.

Hours later, I stepped back to survey the finished product. Doves exploded from a grenade and flew through the broken windows of a derelict warehouse and into a cerulean blue sky. I'd painted a cityscape, a little piece of Brooklyn, but mixed it up with an abstract field of poppies. Barbed wire zigzagged across the length of it. I wasn't sure what had compelled me to paint this peace wall or if it even made any sense.

"It's a conversation piece," Brody said, stocking the ice in the outside bar.

"Yeah, but I'm not sure how people will interpret it," I said.

"That's the beauty of art. They can interpret it any way they want," Brody said. "It's cool."

"Thanks, Brody." Brody was cool. Last week, we worked together, and he told me about his travels to far-flung places, seeking out good deep-sea diving spots. I asked him if the whole breathing thing ever freaked him out. He said you just had to keep your shit together and go with the flow.

"You need to sign it, Picasso," Zeke called out as I snapped photos.

Picasso? I wish.

I signed my name in lower case letters on the far right-hand corner. No need to shout it to the world. When I straightened up and backed up a few paces, I hit a brick wall. Killian's arms circled my middle and he pulled me back against him.

"It's amazing," he murmured in my ear, sending tingles up and down my spine. Zeke's eyebrows shot up to his hairline, but I pretended not to notice. He'd be grilling me for answers later, I was sure of it.

"Yo, Killian," Zeke called.

Killian looked over at him. "Yeah?" he said, as if holding me in his arms was a regular occurrence. I couldn't see the look on Killian's face, but it probably didn't look open to questions. Zeke chuckled and shook his head.

Killian walked me closer to the mural and studied every detail of it. "To paint like this…it's a gift."

Thank you. You're pretty gifted yourself."

"Oh yeah?"

"Mmhmm," I murmured. "You have skills."

He nuzzled my neck. "I'll be using them tonight."

Chapter Twenty-Four

Eden

"Ready?" I asked, tucking my rolled-up artwork under my arm. I reached into the back for my tote bag and Killian grabbed the bucket of wheat paste from my hand. I'd kept it between my feet on the drive to Bushwick.

"Born ready," Killian said, closing the hatch.

"How did I know you'd say that?"

He gave my butt a playful swat. "What do you need me to do?"

"Just stand guard. I've got this."

He leaned against the wall of the derelict warehouse I deemed perfect for my art after I had him drive around Bushwick a few times scoping it out, his arms crossed over his chest, booted feet crossed at the ankle. "Stop distracting me," I said, pulling on Latex gloves because this goop was messy. I was dressed all in black, like a ninja on a stealth operation. Killian was dressed all in black because that was his usual attire. "Why are you so sexy?"

Killian smirked then held his hand over his forehead like a visor and looked up and down the street. "Coast clear, Doctor Madley. Are you prepared for surgery?"

I snorted laughter and held up my glove-covered hands, palms facing me. "I'm going in."

He chuckled as I dipped my long-handled brush in the

bucket of wheat paste I mixed in my kitchen earlier and applied it to the wall in long, sweeping strokes. Who knew that graffiti with Killian at three in the morning could be this much fun? Who knew Killian could be this much fun?

In the three weeks since our date, everything had changed. For someone who had never been in a relationship before, Killian stepped into the role of boyfriend with ease. We spent most of our nights together now, and his talent in the bedroom was a bonus. My sex life had never been this active or this good. But his talents extended beyond the bedroom. Mr. Fix-It fixed things in my apartment I hadn't even realized were broken or in need of fixing. The hinges on my doors didn't squeak anymore, and he did something to the shower head that increased the water pressure. He fixed the fourth gas ring on my stove I'd never bothered using because it wouldn't turn on. Last week, I dragged him along on a shopping trip and came home with an overdyed vintage rug and some throw pillows that instantly cozied up my living room.

The same day I'd been bitten by the interior design bug, Killian drove me to the art store and I stocked up on butcher paper, acrylic markers, and X-ACTO knives.

Now I worked quickly—getting busted would be a bummer. My dad would not be impressed. I knew his view on graffiti. He considered it vandalism, not art. Unrolling my artwork, I stood on tip-toes to affix the top to the paste. Killian swatted me away. "Hey."

"I'll get the top. You want it here?" He didn't need to stand on tiptoes. He was a giant among men.

"Yeah. Just smooth your hands over the top to get the bubbles out and…" He didn't need further instructions. He was good with his hands. When he secured the top part, we worked our way down until the whole piece was glued to the wall.

Hopefully, it was on straight. This paste dried quickly, and I'd rip the paper if I tried to move it. After I'd finished sketching and painting the two separate pieces, I'd painstakingly cut them out, overlapped and glued them together, aiming for a 3-D effect.

I brushed on another coat of wheat paste over the top of my art to seal it, and it was done. I pulled my camera out of my tote bag. Killian took the bag from me and packed all my supplies in the back of his Jeep. "I hid the evidence," he said, joining me on the sidewalk.

"You're the best." I leaned in for a kiss. He lifted me off the ground, and I wrapped my legs around him, cinching them tight around his waist. This was quickly becoming my favorite mode of transportation. If Killian could carry me everywhere, he probably would. I chuckled at the thought.

"What's so funny, Chuckles?"

"You. We did it." I was so keyed-up I could barely contain the joy fizzing inside me.

What. A. Rush.

"*You* did it. And it's fucking amazing."

I jumped down to the ground. "I need to get some photos."

Not only was I thrilled we'd gotten away with it, but now my art was part of this wall, this street, the fabric of this neighborhood. My artwork won't last forever. Someone might paint over it. Deface it with vulgar words. The paper will eventually peel. The elements will attack it. Reminders that nothing lasts forever. But right now, my life-sized mom lives on a wall in Bushwick.

I had no idea what it felt like to see your artwork displayed in a gallery, but I wasn't sure how it could compare to this. A lot of street artists I read about said they do what they do, not only for the rush, but because art should be accessible to everyone. Art is subjective, so it would be conceited to think everyone will appreciate what I put on this wall. Putting my mom out there was such a personal thing. But choosing to make it accessible to the public was a risk I chose to take. No matter what happened, I wouldn't allow myself to regret it.

I snapped photos, zooming out so I could get the whole piece in one photo. My mom was wearing a blue headscarf, holding a thin paintbrush poised above the dark pink lotus flower of the mandala, as if she was putting the final touches on it. I spent the longest time working on her hands, to make sure I got them right—the long, slender fingers, the veins, the half-moons on her nails. Her green eyes were vivid, and a smile tugged at her lips, not fully formed. The gauntness of her face made her cheekbones stand out more prominently, and I remember thinking in the moments after she'd died that she had never looked more beautiful. Like she was at peace.

We were all there when she'd died, gathered around her hospice bed, and for a few moments, an eerie calmness had come over me. I felt like she was holding my hand and whispering in my ear that everything was going to be okay. Physically, she was already gone, but I felt her presence in the room like a strong vibration running through my whole body. One look at Sawyer's stricken face told me he wasn't feeling the same thing I was. A few minutes later, Sawyer stood and kicked his chair over. He kicked and punched every inanimate object in the room before announcing that he was running home and slammed out of the room. Garrett tried to go after Sawyer, but my dad stopped him. "Let him go. We all grieve in different ways."

When we got home from the hospice, I headed to the woods behind our house. I found him lying on the dead leaves, staring at the sky, his hands balled into fists. Still angry and most likely cursing a God he'd stopped believing in. I lay on the ground next to him and neither of us said a word. By then, those few moments of positive energy after my mom died had disappeared and been replaced with the reality—my mom was gone, and she wasn't coming back. All I felt was an overwhelming sense of loss and sadness.

"You okay?" Killian asked, jolting me out of my memories.

"Yeah. Just thinking about my mom."

He pulled me in front of him and wrapped his arms around my middle. "You look a lot like her. She was beautiful."

"Thank you."

"And so is your art."

"You think?"

"I don't think it. I know it. It's so vibrant with color. Like you. But it's kind of peaceful too. The way you make me feel sometimes."

I was so happy I made him feel that way that I nearly wept. Killian had changed a lot, and I didn't know if it was because we'd verbally declared our relationship, but now he spoke more freely. He didn't hold himself back like he used to, didn't lock down his feelings as much, and I loved it.

"Hungry?" he asked.

"Is that a trick question?"

"You and your dirty mind. You like empanadas?"

"I never had one."

"Oh man. That's just wrong."

"You'll have to show me the way."

* * *

I straddled him and pressed my lips against the scar on his neck. His breath hitched, and I could feel his pulse beating wildly against my lips. His arms around me tensed as I left a trail of feather light kisses, following the path of the scar, but he didn't push me away or try to stop me. "How did you get it?" I asked.

"A broken bottle."

"What happened?"

"I got in a fight with a junkie." His answer came out so smoothly, so well-rehearsed, that I knew it was the answer he gave anyone who asked. I also knew he was lying, but I didn't push him for the truth. Just like I'd never asked him what kind of fighter he was or what he did before he started running the bar, or what his relationship with his father was like. Some things, I decided, needed to come directly from him. Whenever he was ready, and without my prompting, I hoped he would trust me with the truth. I had a feeling that the things he kept locked inside had been there for a long time, and his pain ran deep.

He flipped me onto my back and braced his arms on either side of me. "Do you want me?"

"Always."

Killian held his weight on one arm and slipped two fingers inside me. "You're always so wet."

"Only for you."

He reached for a condom in the bedside table. I wrapped my arms around his neck and pulled his head down. "We don't need it. I'm on the pill," I murmured against his lips.

"I've never done it without a condom."

"Good. I can be your first."

"You sure?"

"Yeah. I never skip. Promise. I want to feel you inside me."

He pulled back and studied my face. I gave him a reassuring smile and wrapped my legs around his waist. He kept watching my face as he entered me. Just the tip. Then he glided in. Slowly. Slowly. Like he was in no rush. His eyes closed as he pushed all the way inside and stilled. "Jesus. You feel so good." I squeezed my muscles around him. "This is…fuuuck."

I thrust my hips against him, but he was controlling the pace, gliding all the way in and almost all the way out like he wanted to make it last forever. It built slowly, but it was so powerful, this gentleness. He opened his eyes and looked into mine. In the dim shadows of my room, I saw his raw emotions, his vulnerability and his need for me and something else I couldn't identify. I wondered if he saw the same thing in my face. If I was stripped bare, more naked than I'd ever been with him.

He lowered his head and kissed me, our tongues swirling together, our bodies moving in a graceful dance. Slow and rhythmic, almost like we were in a trance. My arms and legs held him close, my breasts pressed against his hard chest. Our rhythm sped up, and he thrust harder and faster, my hips rocking against him, desperate to get that sweet release.

"Killian," I screamed.

We came at the same time. In shockwave after shockwave, my body convulsed against his. He filled me up so completely, and I was everything and nothing all at once. Overwhelmed by the flood of emotions, unshed tears caught in my throat. It scared me how hard and how fast I'd fallen, and how I could no longer imagine my life without him.

I hung onto him, holding him close, loving the feel of his weight on top of me, and having him still inside me.

"You're killing me, baby," he said, his voice low and husky.

Baby. I loved the way it sounded rolling off his tongue. "Gently, I hope."

"Sometimes that's the worst way."

* * *

"Two margaritas," a brunette shouted over the DJ's music. I did a double-take. The girl looked a lot like Joss. Tall and willowy with high cheekbones and boobs spilling out of her plunging neckline. Thankfully, it wasn't her. "And a Cosmo."

"Maybe I'll have a Pina colada," her friend said.

"No salt on my margarita," her other friend said.

"Make mine a Long Island Iced Tea."

"Two margaritas, one without salt. A Cosmopolitan. A Pina colada. And a Long Island Iced Tea," I repeated.

"Wait," the brunette said. "That's like…" Her brow furrowed in concentration. "Six drinks."

"It's five," I said.

"Uh, duh." She tossed her hair and pulled a face like I was an idiot. "There's only four of us."

Uh, duh? Were we back in junior high? It wasn't my fault she couldn't count.

She turned to her friends to ask what they wanted but got sidetracked by a conversation about Brazilian waxes. She was all for them. "It's the only way to go. I know the best place on…"

I moved on to a guy who ordered three draft beers without turning it into a major debate. It made my job easier. No hassle, no fuss, no stupid questions. I couldn't count how many times people had stood right in front of the clearly labeled taps and asked me which beers we had on tap.

I poured the beers, set them on the bar, and collected the guy's money. When I returned with his change, Joss-lookalike snarled at me. "I was here first."

"What can I get you?" I asked calmly. Sometimes it took the patience of a saint to be a bartender.

"Like, maybe, a decent bartender."

I gritted my teeth and tried not to let it show that she was testing my limited patience. I was this close to lunging across the bar and slapping her. Not that I would. But it was tempting.

"Give me your order and I'll serve your drinks." I forced

a smile as fake as her boobs. Now I was just being catty. But I thought they were fake. They were hard to miss, and they defied gravity.

"A Cosmo. Two Long Island iced teas. And a margarita. Think you can handle that?"

What I couldn't handle was her snippy tone. Deep breaths. Stay calm. Physical violence wouldn't solve anything. Neither would a bad attitude. I repeated the order back to her in my most professional voice then asked, "Do you want the margarita with salt or without?"

"Whatever." She waved her manicured hand, fobbing me off. I set out the glasses on the bar mat. I'd do half the glass with salt and the other half without. If she was going to be rude about it, she could just suck it up. If I didn't have to worry about customer relations and professionalism, I'd put her in her place.

"Start a tab," she said when I set the drinks in front of her, then turned her back to me.

"I'll need your card."

She turned back around and pulled a face. "Like we ever pay for our own drinks."

"I can't run a tab without a card," I said firmly.

"Bitch," she hissed, digging around in her bag, and tossing two twenty-dollar bills on the bar.

Louis chuckled as I jabbed my finger at each item on the touchscreen with more force than necessary.

"Rise above," he said, something of a catchphrase for him.

"She called me a bitch," I muttered. "I seriously want to punch her."

He chuckled again and squeezed my shoulder. "Make art, not war."

I sighed. "I'll try my best."

For some reason, Joss-lookalike had chosen to be the bane

of my existence tonight. When I set her second Cosmo in front of her, she swung around and knocked it over with her elbow. "Oh my God," she yelled. "What is your problem?"

Once again, I gritted my teeth and bit my tongue as I threw down paper towels to sop up her spilled drink. It was taking super-human strength not to get all mean girl on her. I cleared her now-empty glass and tossed the towels in the trash.

"You owe me a drink," she said, as I wiped down the sticky bar.

"You knocked it over with your elbow," I reminded her. "So that will be ten dollars." I gave her a big smile and twirled my hair around my finger. So much for rising above. It was junior high all over again, and I was stooping to her level. "My math isn't that great. But I think that's twenty dollars if you want another drink."

She glared at me. "That's it. I'm sick of your attitude. I need to speak to—" Her eyes widened. "Oh. My. God. It's Killian Vincent."

I followed her gaze. Killian and Mitch, one of the bouncers, were escorting two guys out of the bar. "Hey, man, he started it," one of the guys said.

"I don't give a shit who started it," Killian said. "You're both out."

With that, the door shut behind them. A few minutes later, Killian returned alone and came behind the bar to speak with Louis. Meanwhile, Joss-lookalike had thrown a twenty on the bar as if paying for her drinks had never been an issue.

I set her new Cosmo in front of her, but she was too busy ogling Killian to notice.

She yelled his name and his head swung in her direction. "It's Darcy. I was in Vegas for a bachelorette party. We went to one of your fights and afterwards…remember? That was such a great night..." She beamed at him. *Beamed.*

My jaw dropped to the floor. Did he sleep with her? Killian ran his hand through his hair and muttered something under his breath. What the hell? I felt like I was going to throw up.

Killian wrapped his hand around my upper arm and tried to pull me closer. "Eden..."

Nope. Couldn't go there right now. I shrugged him off. "I'm busy."

Chapter Twenty-Five

Killian

I brought her to the waterfront under the guise of watching the sunrise. She knew it was bullshit and I wasn't trying to be romantic. I was just looking for a neutral location. We took a seat on a wooden bench on the boardwalk, the glass and steel towers behind us and an unobstructed view of the Manhattan skyline in front of us, the dusky blue sky streaked with red. She drew her legs to her chest and wrapped her arms around them.

"You really pick the winners," she said. "First Joss and now…Darcy." She pulled a face like just saying the name made her sick to her stomach.

Louis filled me in later while we counted the cash drawer in the office. Apparently, this Darcy chick had been bitchy to Eden. I only had a vague recollection of Darcy. I didn't even remember her name, but I doubted it would help my cause to mention that.

Darcy didn't mention Johnny, thankfully. Instead, she went on and on about the amazing night we shared. By then, she'd followed me to the outside bar where I was working, so Brody had gotten an earful, but Eden didn't have to hear about it.

"Did you tell Darcy I was your girlfriend?" Eden asked.

"Yeah, I told her."

Eden shrugged. "I guess that's something, at least."

"You have nothing to be jealous about."

"You seem to have a type and I'm not it."

She was focused on the one-night stand which was the least of my transgressions. "She means nothing to me. It was one night, nearly two years ago." I only knew that because Darcy filled me in. "Way before I ever met you."

Her shoulders slumped. "I know. It's just…ugh. I hate to think of you with someone else."

I knew the feeling. "Don't think about it. I told you I'd never cheat on you." At least that was a promise I could keep. I couldn't imagine walking in on Eden with another guy. Didn't even want to. I'd *never* do that to her. It nearly destroyed me when I saw my mother with another man. I was too young to understand what they were doing, but I knew it was wrong. I'd never breathed a word of it to anyone. Not even to Connor.

She rested her chin on her knees. I could almost see the wheels in her head spinning. "Your dad mentioned something about fighting…the night he came in. He asked if I was one of your groupies."

Fucking Seamus.

"I was waiting for you to tell me about it yourself. That's why I never asked."

I looked straight ahead at the skyline, at the lights that never seemed to go out, in offices and apartment buildings. All those people, living their lives, with their own dramas and hardships.

Fuck. This was so hard to say. I'd never told anyone. Never said the words aloud. Everyone who had been in my life before already knew, and nobody else needed to know. Until now. She needed to hear it from me, not from someone else.

"I used to be an MMA fighter. I was in the UFC."

"What happened?"

I needed to go right in, lay out the facts, and get it over with. Rip off the fucking Band-Aid.

"My last fight was against Johnny Ramirez. He was my teammate, my friend…. a great fighter. One of the best." I swallowed hard and forced myself to keep going. "I punched him in the temple. I usually tried to avoid head shots. I wasn't…" Out to kill him. He'd had me down on the mat, my legs locked. It had been a wild hook from a submissive position. I hadn't thought it would pack so much power. "The medical team gave him the okay to keep fighting. We went two more rounds and I won. Afterwards, he was pissed off that he lost, but he seemed okay otherwise. Walking and talking. Later that night, he complained he was dizzy and tired, and they took him to the emergency room."

"It was a subdural hematoma. Traumatic brain injury. They performed an emergency craniotomy and he was in a coma. Three days later, he died." My voice sounded automated, like I didn't give a shit. Like the words I was saying didn't affect me, didn't have anything to do with me.

"Killian," she said, her voice soft. "It wasn't your fault."

I shook my head and let out a harsh laugh. "It was entirely my fault." I held up my hands and flexed them. "I killed him."

"It was an accident. A horrible accident. You can't blame yourself."

I could, and I did. "He had a wife and a son who was born after he died."

Eden straddled me on the bench and wrapped her arms around my neck. My arms went around her waist. She couldn't do or say anything to make it better, but somehow, she did. Just by being here. The tension in my muscles relaxed and I breathed her in.

She pulled back and held my face in her hands. "What you told me doesn't change the way I feel about you."

I closed my eyes. "Eden." She pressed her lips against mine.

Neither one of us tried to turn it into a kiss. It was almost more intimate than a kiss.

When our lips separated, she climbed off me and sat next to me. I wrapped my arm around her and she leaned her head on my shoulder. We sat in silence as the blues and pinks of twilight became an orange glow that reflected off the buildings of the Manhattan skyline.

"It's a new day," she said quietly. "A world of possibility. Do you believe that?"

"I don't know." *But I'd like to.*

She didn't say anything for a few minutes. "Killian? What would Johnny have done?"

"What?"

"If the roles had been reversed…what would Johnny have done? Would he have mourned your loss and continued fighting? Would he have given up something he loved?"

I didn't have an answer because Johnny wasn't here to ask. "He told me once that if he had to give up fighting, he wouldn't be Johnny Ramirez anymore."

"Is that how it feels to you?"

"Sometimes." *All the time.* "But that life is over. I can't go back to it."

"Sawyer keeps going back to combat zones."

"He doesn't have a choice."

"He had a choice. He re-enlisted."

She couldn't wrap her head around that, but I got where Sawyer was coming from. I didn't know him, but I had a feeling that being in a combat zone was his new normal. People return to what they know. I'd never been to war, but sometimes I felt like I'd lived through one, so I understood why he didn't talk about it. It wasn't the kind of thing you shared with people who hadn't been there.

"Killian?"

"Yeah?" I asked, hoping she would drop it. I was done. I told her what I needed to tell her and now I wanted to put it behind me. I kept picturing baby Leo's face, his big brown eyes so trusting. He didn't understand pain and suffering yet. He didn't know that the world wasn't fair or that the people you love could be snatched away in an instant. I wanted to protect him from this fucked-up irrational universe. Ironic, really. I was the villain in Leo's fairy tale.

"Was MMA your passion? The thing you were meant to do?"

Yes. And no. It had cost me everything. "I used to think so."

"If you can't go back to fighting, you need to find a new passion. It's important."

"It's not one of life's necessities."

"Maybe not for everyone, but it is for you. Because you found it once and it was taken away from you."

"It wasn't taken from me," I said, through gritted teeth. She didn't heed the warning in my voice.

"Do you think Johnny would be punishing himself? Or would he recognize that it was an accident and keep doing what he loved? Do you think this is what he would want for you? To know that you gave up something—"

"Eden," I said, my voice hard. "Stop. You have no fucking clue what you're talking about." I rubbed the back of my neck, regretting that I'd ever told her. I stood and strode away, without waiting for her or looking back to see if she was following. I kept walking, straight up North Sixth Street, intent on getting in my fucking car and driving away.

She caught up but stayed two paces behind. I beeped my locks and yanked the driver's door open. She grabbed my arm to stop me. "What are you doing? Running away when things get hard? That's not who you are. It's not what you do."

"How the hell would you know who I am or what I do?" I removed her hand from my arm and climbed into the driver's seat.

She blocked the door with her body. "You're not leaving. Not like this."

I clenched my jaw. "Step aside."

"No." Eden crossed her arms, not budging. "I want you to come home with me. To Pennsylvania."

In three days, Sawyer was coming home on leave, and she didn't want to miss his homecoming. I'd offered her my Jeep, but now she wanted me too. I'd never been taken home to meet anyone's father before. And this seemed like a shitty time to bring it up.

She chewed on her lower lip. "Would you? My dad and brothers will really like you. And I want to celebrate your birthday with you."

My birthday. Hooray. Fuck birthdays. Fuck everything. I jammed my key in the ignition.

"Don't act like an ass. I need you."

I need you. I looked at her face. "Why?"

"I just…do. Killian, I asked you not to shut me out. What you told me was hard for you. I know that. But I was trying to tell you that you deserve to be happy."

"Yeah, I got the message. You're not that subtle."

"I never said I was. Maybe you should think about it. And maybe next time you tell me something important, you could consider my feelings."

"*Your* feelings?"

"I care about you. How clear do I need to make it? Should I graffiti the words on the walls of Bushwick? Across the

Brooklyn Bridge? Your words and actions affect me too. I'm sorry you had to give up something you loved. I'm sorry your friend is gone. I wish there was something, anything, I could do to make it better. But sometimes the only thing you can do is be there for the other person. And I'm here for you. Maybe you never had that before, so you don't know how it works. In a relationship, there are two of us. We're on the same team. I'll always be in your corner—"

I grabbed the back of her head and pulled her towards me for a kiss, effectively shutting her up. She kissed me back, her lips soft and warm. She gave, and I took. Tasting her sweetness, her body yielding to me as I stood and pulled her closer, my hand tangling in her silky soft hair. It was a new day. A world of possibility. And I was a dumbass because this girl…she was the best fucking thing that had ever happened to me.

"You kissed me to shut me up," she said when our lips parted.

I pulled her into another kiss. "Whatever it takes."

"Does that mean you'll come with me?"

I smiled against her lips. "Whatever you want, sunshine."

"I want you."

I walked her over to the sidewalk, my hands roaming the curves of her body.

"But first I need to show you the error of your ways," she said, as we climbed the steps to her front door, her body tucked against mine.

That should be fun. "What else are you going to show me?" I took the keys out of her hand to unlock the door.

"Ugh." She planted her hands on her hips. "I'm capable of opening my own lock."

"But you don't need to because you have me to do it for you."

"Do I? Have you?" she asked, on the way up to the third floor.

"You've got me. How can I prove it?"

"Groveling would be a good place to start."

"If you get on your hands and knees for me, I'll grovel."

"Deal." I masked my surprise. I hadn't expected her to give in so easily. But then, she expected me to grovel. "Better make it good."

"My thoughts exactly. Tell me what you're going to do to me," I said, as I unlocked her apartment door.

She waited until the door was closed and locked behind us to tell me. By the time we reached her bedroom, I was so hard my dick felt like concrete.

* * *

Hours later, I woke up to her fingers tracing the lines of the phoenix tattoo on my shoulder and back. I rolled onto my side, and she planted a soft kiss on my upper back then wrapped her arm around me and molded her body against mine. If I was going home with her, I needed to tell Louis. I grabbed my phone from her bedside table, but Eden took it out of my hand.

"It's all arranged," she said. "I talked to Louis."

I laughed under my breath. On top of her other talents, she was reading my mind and arranging my life to suit her needs. "When did you do this?"

"Two nights ago." I could imagine, without turning to look, that her smug smile matched her voice. "I asked him not to tell you."

"How did you know I'd agree to it?"

"I'm the optimist in this duo."

I couldn't argue with that. Even when shitty things

happened, her glass was half-full.

"You haven't groveled yet," she reminded me.

"I got sidetracked by the hot babe who asked for a spanking."

"Likely excuse," she said, and I looked over my shoulder because I knew, just knew, she'd be blushing. Yep. God, I loved that. She could talk dirty, have sex doggy style, ask for a spanking, and still blush. That's what made her so special. She was so many things all rolled into one perfect package—naughty and nice, sweet and sultry, dirty and innocent.

I turned around to face her and propped my head on my hand, tracing the curves of her face with my fingertips.

She raised her brows. "Still waiting for you to make good on your end of the deal. Quid pro quo."

"Look at you and your fancy Latin."

Eden rolled her eyes. "Stop procrastinating."

"How does this groveling thing work?"

"You apologize profusely. But it needs to be heartfelt and genuine."

Heartfelt and genuine. "I'm sorry I walked away."

She gestured with her hand for me to keep going.

"I'm sorry I shot you down when you were just trying to help. And I'm sorry I hurt your feelings."

Her face lit up with a smile. "Not bad for a rookie."

In my life, I rarely apologized for anything, even though there had been hundreds of times when I should have. I understood now, how a woman could bring a man to his knees. If I had to, I'd crawl to her, groveling, just to put that smile on her face. How had she infiltrated every facet of my life so quickly?

"Just for the record, before you met me…you had lousy taste in women."

"I could say the same about your taste in men," I countered.

She grabbed my index finger, guided it to her mouth and bit down hard. I laughed. "She-devil."

"Tell me I'm the best you've ever had."

"You're the best I've ever had." It wasn't a lie. She was the best, in every way.

"Will we ever be able to talk about this again?"

I knew what she was referring to—Johnny, my guilt, her quest to help me find a new passion in my life. "Someday. But not today."

Her eyes searched my face and then she smiled. "Okay. Someday sounds good."

The fact that I'd even used the word someday implied we had a future. And in three days I'd be meeting her dad. Jesus. Be brave, warrior.

That evening, I had a surprise for her. Judging by the look on her face when she walked into the office, it wasn't a good one. "You cut your hair," she cried. I thought she was going to burst into tears. "You look like...a GQ model now."

"She hates it," Ava said, stopping in the doorway. She offered Eden a Twizzler to ease her pain.

"I'm going to need more than one strip of licorice to get over this," Eden muttered, ripping the licorice with her teeth, and chewing furiously, her eyes still glued to my short hair.

Ava tossed her the whole pack, and Eden caught it one hand, without taking her eyes off me. Skills. "O-kay," Ava said, backing away. "I think I'm needed in the courtyard."

I scrubbed my hand over my hair. It hadn't been this short since my MMA days, which meant I looked more like I used to when I was a fighter. Not sure that would work in my favor. The idea was to make myself look more respectable. I had no idea how conservative her dad was, but he was a state trooper and they lived in a small town. Not much I could do about the scar or tattoos. I probably still looked like a thug who grew up on the wrong side of good. "Are you gonna leave my ass in Brooklyn, baby?" She was still staring at me, speechless.

"No. Your ass comes with me. But I want you to grow your hair back."

I chuckled and leaned back in the swivel chair. "You're so shallow. Had I known you were just with me for my hair…"

"Shut up." She came to stand between my legs. "I'm not just with you for your looks or your body although…well, they're a nice bonus. You're still beautiful. It's just…you look so different."

I captured her hands in mine and tugged her closer. "Did you call me beautiful? I'm not a girl. I'm a man. Have a seat on my lap. I'll show you I'm still the man I was before I got a haircut."

She rolled her eyes, but she couldn't hide the smile. "I need to get to work." She put her hands on my shoulders and kissed me. "My boss will get angry if I slack off on the job."

"Your boss might give you a spanking," I murmured against her lips.

Her tentative fingers sifted through my hair. "Not much to hang onto."

"I've got plenty of things to hang onto. You're welcome to all of them." I guided her hand to my crotch where, as usual, I was hard for her. "This is for you. All. The. Time."

"Sounds like a problem. You should get that checked out."

I swatted her butt. "Get to work before I lock the door and take you right here. Right now."

"I'll meet you back here at the end of the night," she said, with a wink. Then she sashayed out of the office and left me wondering how I'd make it through the next nine hours with a raging hard-on. She was starting to feel like an addiction. Eden was my crack. Which got me thinking about Connor. Which got me out of the office and behind the bar where I could stay busy and not have to think about anything.

Chapter Twenty-Six

Eden

I CAUGHT A GLIMPSE OF DESERT CAMOUFLAGE MAKING ITS SLOW and torturous way down the escalator in the Pittsburgh airport. He was behind two massive guys wearing baseball jerseys and ball caps, slurping oversized drinks. Sawyer stepped off the escalator and gave me a big grin that reminded me of the boy he used to be. I rushed over and wrapped my arms around him, practically knocking him over. His arms came around my waist to steady us both.

"Whoa. Easy, girl. You'd think I'd been to war or something."

"Shut up. That's not even funny."

I held him—all six feet, two inches of solid muscle—too tightly and for too long. He hugged me back without complaining or pulling away. When I was sure he was real and solid, I released him and gave him a little slug on the shoulder.

"I should have brought balloons and a marching band," I teased.

"I'm sure as hell glad you didn't. But you could have brought the cheerleaders. Give me a proper welcome." He waggled his eyebrows at me.

I snorted. "You're such a horndog."

He laughed but didn't bother denying it.

"It's good to have you home." I looked into his green eyes, so much like my own, but I didn't like what I saw in them.

"Good to be here," he said, but I knew he was lying. Home didn't feel like home to him anymore.

We made our way to the baggage claim and stopped in front of the carousel to wait for his bag.

"So…I met someone," I said, because I hadn't filled him in on my love life. Or anyone in my family. "He's part owner of the bar where I work and he's waiting for us outside. He's staying with us for a few days."

Sawyer chuckled. "Does he know he's getting Garrett's old room?"

I rolled my eyes. "I'm twenty-two and I live on my own. Dad won't make us sleep in separate rooms." He totally would. Whenever Luke was over, I had to keep my bedroom door open if we were in there. As usual, my dad turned a blind eye whenever Sawyer and Garrett had girls in the house. Yet another example of the inequality between the sexes, I'd always argued. It had gotten me exactly nowhere.

"Not another preppy, entitled asshole, I hope."

"Not even close." I cleared my throat like I was making a major announcement. "His name is…Killian Vincent."

I glanced at him to see if the name rang a bell. It did. Sawyer was an MMA fan. So was Garrett. So was my dad. I hadn't told them Killian's last name yet, so it would be a surprise. Yay!

"Killian 'The Kill' Vincent? As in, UFC superstar Killian Vincent?" It was funny. Sawyer looked a little star struck. Very few people impressed Sawyer but by the look on his face, I guess Killian's fighting prowess was impressive.

The Kill? Ugh. "Uh, yeah, that's the one."

"Well, damn," Sawyer said, and then he started laughing. A huge belly laugh. It was a good sound, but I felt like I was the brunt of a joke I hadn't heard.

"What's so funny?" I asked, planting my hands on my hips.

He shook his head, still laughing too hard to answer.

"You're an idiot." I rolled my eyes and crossed my arms, waiting for him to pull himself together.

"Does 'The Kill' know he's dating Chicken Little?"

"Don't call him 'The Kill,'" I muttered. "He's not a fighter anymore."

His humor faded. "I know. I watched that fight. He was good though. One of the best."

"Was he...he feels guilty, like it was his fault."

"It wasn't his fault. But that doesn't make shit like that any easier."

"I didn't see the fight," I said. "Or any of his fights. I've never Googled him."

"You shittin' me?"

I shrugged. "No. I never felt the need."

"You're the one who used to snoop around looking for the Christmas presents."

True. The anticipation used to kill me. My dad kept finding new and creative places to hide the presents. One year, he set a booby trap. When I pulled down the ladder to the loft in the garage, I got doused with a bucket of cold water.

Sawyer was laughing, probably remembering the same thing I was.

"That was funny as hell," Sawyer said.

Sawyer's sea bag dropped down the chute and he grabbed it from the conveyor belt, slinging it over his shoulder. He walked tall and proud, shoulders square, head held high, and a whole lot of swagger.

We exited through the sliding glass doors into glaring sunshine. I slid my sunglasses from the top of my head to my face and Sawyer slipped on a pair of aviators.

"It's the Jeep Wrangler." I pointed to Killian's Jeep parked by the pick-up area where nobody was supposed to park and wait but we did it anyway.

Killian met us on the sidewalk and Sawyer shocked me by pulling Killian into a guy hug, handshake combo. He was rarely demonstrative. That hug in the airport had been a stretch for him. He'd never so much as shaken hands with Luke but here he was getting all chummy with a perfect stranger. "Good to meet you, man," Sawyer said.

"You too," Killian said, opening the hatch and Sawyer stowed his bag inside. I looked at them standing side by side, with similar powerful builds, all lean muscle, and Killian was maybe an inch taller, but it was barely noticeable.

"Hey, Killian," I said. "Give me the keys. I'll drive."

Sawyer snorted. "How brave are you feeling today?"

"Hey, I resent that," I said. "I'm an excellent driver."

Sawyer shook his head no. "She's a shit driver," he said, climbing into the passenger seat. No matter who was driving, Sawyer had already claimed shotgun. Typical. Actually, that wasn't true. Anytime we went anywhere together, Sawyer claimed the driver's seat.

I ignored Sawyer's comment and wiggled my fingers for Killian to turn over the keys. "You've been driving for six hours, and I slept most of the way. You barely got any sleep last night."

"Whose fault was that?"

I wrapped my arms around him, sweetening the offer. "You can sleep in the back. You'll have it all to yourself and you won't miss a thing. It's a boring drive. And you might need your energy for later." I gave him a big wink like it was a promise of good things to come.

He turned over his keys which surprised me—he must have been more tired than I thought.

"That was easy," I couldn't resist telling him.

"I'm like Samson. All my strength was in my hair."

I snorted laughter. "That makes me your Delilah," I tossed over my shoulder. I liked the sound of that. And I was getting used to his hair. He still looked gorgeous, just more grown-up, his face more chiseled.

I climbed into the driver's seat and adjusted it to accommodate my shorter legs. Sawyer was already eating the sandwich from Panera Bread we'd brought him. And I'd left a sweet tea in the cup holder for him. "Don't say I never gave you anything."

"You got a cold beer to go with this?" he asked.

"Don't push your luck."

"How's your life insurance?" Sawyer asked Killian as I pulled away from the curb.

I gave Sawyer the finger and Killian chuckled. They talked amongst themselves for a while, and it made me happy they got along, just as I suspected they would. Fifteen minutes later, it got quiet, and I checked the rearview mirror.

"He's out," Sawyer said. "You must have worn him out with all that talking you do."

"I slept most of the way." Leaving Brooklyn at seven in the morning was not my idea of fun, especially not after two hours of sleep.

I blasted the music and weaved in and out of afternoon traffic while Sawyer ate his sandwich and drank his tea. As soon as we exited the tunnel, Sawyer turned off the air con and we both rolled down our windows.

He scrubbed a hand over his dirty-blond hair, short on top and shaved around the sides. I hated his military haircut. I hated the way his face looked harder and his eyes looked haunted, like he'd seen too much, and he couldn't shake the images.

"Did you volunteer for this last mission?" I asked.

"I'm a Marine, Eden. I go *where* they tell me to go. I go *when* they tell me to go."

I didn't know how the Marines operated, but I'd be willing to bet a week's tips that he put himself forward for this last deployment. "No one deploys back to back like that. You only had a few months in between…" I let my voice trail off. It had been five months, to be exact, between him losing his best friend and shipping out again. But I didn't know a damn thing about what the Marines did and didn't do. They did whatever the hell they wanted. Unbelievably, after five years in the Corps and three deployments, Sawyer was still drinking the Kool-Aid. This was the guy who used to believe that rules were made to be broken. He'd spent so much time in the principal's office, the secretary made a label and stuck it on a chair: Reserved for Sawyer Madley.

Sawyer looked out at the river and the bridges of Pittsburgh, and I wondered how different the world looked to him now. After balling up his empty sandwich wrapper and tossing it in the bag, he whipped my phone out of my purse and entered my password, giving him total access to all the information on my cell phone. I needed better security. Everyone, as in Killian and Sawyer, knew my password and they weren't afraid to use it.

I watched in my peripheral as Sawyer scrolled through the photos of Mom on the wall.

"Next time give her hair," he said.

"Next time she's getting wings."

"Dad see this?" he asked

"No. He'd be pissed."

"Secretly, he'd think you did good."

I knew that was Sawyer's way of telling me *he* thought I did good. *Secretly, I love your guts too, Sawyer.*

He moved on, to a few candid shots of Killian I took last week and a few selfies of us together. Killian hated having his picture taken but he humored me. Uh oh. Sawyer had found my peace wall. I kept sneaking glances at him, trying to gauge his reaction.

"Where is it?"

"At Killian's bar. In the courtyard."

"The world is a fucked-up place," he said, sounding weary and far older than his twenty-three years. If I could replace his sorrow with joy, I'd do it. I'd do anything to see his eyes sparkle with mischief or light up with happiness like they used to. But I didn't have that kind of power. I didn't know how to do it for Sawyer or for Killian. Maybe that was why I felt like I understood Killian so well. I'd seen something in him that reminded me of Sawyer, and it made me want to soothe his troubled soul.

He tossed my phone in my purse and leaned back against the seat, arms crossed over his chest. We fell into silence, lost in our own thoughts as I drove on autopilot. Why was the world such a fucked-up place?

I took the Wayne Avenue exit, a road I knew so well but Indiana, Pennsylvania looked so different to me now. It didn't have the grittiness or the cool factor or the architecture of Brooklyn. Everything looked sterile. Manufactured. Boring.

Over the music blasting from the speakers, I heard a siren. I checked my rearview mirror and groaned. The state trooper was riding my tail, lights flashing.

"Must be your welcome wagon," I shouted over the music.

"Yeah, it's good to be home," Sawyer said. We shot each other a grin, and this time I believed he meant it.

I pulled over onto the shoulder, cut the music, and looked in my side mirror at the approaching officer. He snagged us two miles from home. Wasn't that always the way? "Doesn't he have anything better to do?"

"He lives for this shit. Were you speeding?" Sawyer asked,

not particularly concerned.

"I have no idea how fast I was going."

Sawyer shrugged. Neither one of us was paying attention to the speedometer. We both had lead feet.

The officer stopped outside my open window, and I flashed him a big smile. He scowled at me. "Hello, Officer. Is there a problem?"

He put his hands on his hips. "Do you know how fast you were going?"

"Not fast enough," I said. "You caught me."

Sawyer snorted, and Garrett gave us a stern look that cracked us up.

"I'll need to see your license and registration."

"Seriously?" I looked at his face. Either he was serious, or he was good at role-playing because he hadn't broken character. He looked like Dad—brown hair, square jaw with a cleft, hazel eyes. My brother Garrett looked like Superman, and nothing like Sawyer and me. "You're taking this too far."

He held out his hand and wiggled his fingers for me to hand over the documents. I rolled my eyes as I retrieved the license from my purse and Sawyer handed over the registration from the glove compartment. Killian's registration, might I add. "Put a guy in a uniform, and it goes right to his head," I muttered.

"Eden Madley. Give me one good reason I shouldn't give you a ticket today." He didn't even bother to inspect the license or registration.

"Hmm…let me think." I snapped my fingers. "I'll give you two good reasons. This isn't my car so I'm not responsible for speeding in it." Sawyer snickered. "And our wayward son is back. So, we need to get home and get this party started." I slid my sunglasses down my nose and gave him a big wink.

"A party's not a party until we show up," Sawyer crowed,

and I turned in my seat to high-five him.

Garrett shook his head at our display. Nothing's changed. He was always the sensible one. Mom used to tell us he felt left out, that three's a crowd. But Garrett was four years older, and infinitely wiser, and never showed any interest in joining our *shenanigans*, as he called them. "You're damn lucky it was me."

"Oh please," I scoffed. "I saw you a mile away. Dad is way better than you are." It was no joke. Our dad snagged Sawyer and me more times than we cared to remember. Not that I saw Garrett, but I didn't mention that. "If you were attempting to hide and catch unsuspecting victims, you did a shitty job of it."

"Watch your mouth, girl. You're speaking to an officer of the law."

"You look like you've got a stick up your ass in that uniform," Sawyer said.

"Nice haircut," Garrett said. "Someone get after you with a buzz saw?"

They went back and forth, sharing their own brand of brotherly love. When they exhausted their arsenal of insults, Garrett wagged his finger at me like the stern big brother giving me hell. "You shouldn't be speeding. Whose car is this?"

"You got us arrested, sunshine?" Killian asked. All three of us turned to look at him as he sat up, running a hand over his much shorter hair.

"Pfft. Happens all the time in this neck of the woods," I said, waving it off. "This officer is overzealous. Needs to meet his quota for the week."

Killian rolled down his window and I looked over at Garrett whose jaw had nearly dropped to the ground.

"Killian 'The Kill' Vincent?"

"Guilty," Killian answered, shaking the hand Garrett offered through the back window.

"Don't call him 'The Kill'," I muttered, but nobody was paying attention. Garrett was too busy introducing himself, shaking Killian's hand, and fangirling all over him.

"Did he call you sunshine?" Sawyer asked me, while Garrett ran through some of the highlights of Killian's career, as if Killian wasn't fully aware of his stats. I had no idea Garrett was *that* big of a fan or that knowledgeable on the subject but, sadly, he was.

I nodded. "I'm Killian's sunshine."

Sawyer snorted laughter. "You're more like a hurricane or a tornado."

My fist connected with his bicep. It bounced right off, though, and Sawyer snickered at me. "Nice try, Chicken Little." Yep, just like old times. But it made me happy when Sawyer acted like a teenaged idiot.

"Can we go now, officer?" I asked, drumming my fingers on the steering wheel.

"Drive safely," Garrett said. "No more speeding."

"Catch me if you can," I yelled out the window before I pulled off the shoulder and rocketed down the road. But I eased off the accelerator and stuck to the speed limit. If Garrett caught me again, he wouldn't let me off easy. My dad never did, so Garrett had big shoes to fill.

I pulled into the driveway of our brick and white-sided split-level house with the perfectly manicured lawn. Dad prided himself on his lawnmowing skills—the lines were as straight as always. Sawyer looked up at the stars and stripes, blowing in the breeze from the flagpole in our front yard. I wondered if he was tempted to salute it.

I hopped out of the Jeep and wrapped my arms around Killian. "Are you up for this?"

He kissed me on the lips. "Bring it on."

Chapter Twenty-Seven

Eden

"Y<small>OU DECENT?</small>" S<small>AWYER YELLED ON THE OTHER SIDE OF</small> my bedroom door as I gave myself a onceover in the full-length mirror on the back of my closet door. My dad always threw a welcome home party for Sawyer and tonight was no exception. Sawyer barreled into my room without waiting for a reply, an open beer in his hand and two more cans stuffed in the pockets of his cargo shorts. His eyes were glossy, and I wondered how much he'd already had to drink.

He tossed me a beer and I caught it in one hand and tapped the top before I popped it open, catching the foam in my mouth. Sawyer collapsed on my bed, in no hurry to join this party. I looked out my bedroom window at the backyard—our two-acre property extended back to the woods where we used to spend a lot of time as kids.

My dad and his friends were huddled around the grill on the deck below my window, and the smoke curled up into the air, the aroma of grilled burgers and hot dogs coming in through my second-floor window. Dad's music—classic rock—was blasting from the speakers and Springsteen was singing about busting out of school and not surrendering. Kate, pretty and petite in a yellow sundress, her dark hair smooth and glossy, tapped him on the shoulder. When he saw her, the smile on his face matched hers. He wrapped his arm around her waist and kissed her on the mouth. I turned away from the window, with a little smile.

I sank into my oversized beanbag and tugged down the hem of my blue cotton mini dress. "Have you seen Killian?" As predicted, Killian had been instructed to stay in Garrett's old room. After we'd arrived, we took naps separately and I hadn't seen him since.

"He's in the shower," Sawyer said, guzzling his beer like he was on a mission to see how fast he could get drunk. He downed his beer and tossed the empty can in the wastepaper basket next to my dresser then cracked open another beer. "You love him?"

Love. That was a big word. But I felt like I could love him. Killian would be easy to love. Easy for me to love. "I don't know. I'm crazy about him, though. I feel like..." Sawyer and I had never discussed our love lives before. As close as we'd always been, that was an area we never ventured into. "On paper, Luke was perfect, you know? But with Killian, I feel like he accepts me for who I am, my faults and weaknesses, and he's not trying to change me."

"Well, you are his sunshine."

I grinned. "Exactly."

"Glad you're happy," he said gruffly.

"Thanks. Are you—"

"Yoo hoo," I heard on the other side of my door and then Cassidy was in my room, with Brianna and what looked like the rest of my old cheering squad.

"Oh. My. God," Brianna whispered, her eyes wide. "Who is that?"

I looked over at Killian standing in the doorway. Shirtless. "Where's your shirt?"

"In the room."

"Go put it on." I shooed him out the door with my hands,

although I was clear across the room, still ensconced in my beanbag.

He chuckled and pranced down the hallway. Half the cheerleading squad swiveled their heads to watch him. The other half ogled Sawyer lounging on my bed, and Brianna dove on top of him. "Hey, baby," Bri said, planting a big kiss on his lips. "Missed you."

"Oh yeah? Wanna show me how much?"

I groaned, and seconds later a bunch of guys from Sawyer's high school football team crowded into my bedroom. It was too small to accommodate all the sweat and hormones, not to mention the aftershave someone had used too liberally. Cameron, the former linebacker, and Sawyer's best friend from high school, pulled me out of the beanbag and threw me over his shoulder. "Put me down." I pounded his back. He was built like a refrigerator, almost too wide to fit through my door.

This was one of his party tricks. He wouldn't put me down until I was outside in the backyard, after he'd run a victory lap. This used to be my life. Sigh. "Killian," I called out as Cameron trotted past Garrett's old room. "Rescue me from this brute." Since I was laughing, I didn't think Killian took it seriously.

Cameron spun around in a circle. I lifted my head and looked over my shoulder at Killian standing in the doorway. I was happy to note he'd donned a T-shirt. "Holy shit," Cameron said. "I'm a big fan, dude."

I groaned. Killian managed to avoid this in Brooklyn but a few hours in western Pennsylvania and he was being subjected to his worst nightmare. Killian Vincent fever had reached a high pitch. But I saw my exit strategy, and I was an opportunist, so I took it. "Cam, let me down. I'll introduce you."

Cameron let me down without a struggle and Killian tucked me close to his side. I felt like he needed the support more than I did.

I made the introductions and Killian got to meet the football team and the cheerleaders. He was ogled at and fangirled over in equal measure.

"I was her first kiss," Cameron informed Killian when we'd all gotten outside, with beers in our hands.

"Most awkward kiss on the planet," I said.

"She's exaggerating." Cameron winked at me. "But not by much."

We all drank and made merry, talked, and laughed, and everyone got over the fact that Killian was a former UFC fighter. Nobody mentioned Luke or Lexie or the baby that must have been born by now either.

Killian slung an arm around my shoulder and I looked up at him, a big smile on my face. "It's so weird to see you here. But in a good way."

From the deck, the opening chords of Linkin Park's "Bleed It Out" blasted from the sound system. Cameron was manning the music and pumped the air. "Tune," he yelled, pointing his arm at Killian.

A look passed between Sawyer and Killian who was rubbing the back of his neck.

"Change it, Cam," Sawyer instructed.

"It's okay," Killian said.

"Change it," Sawyer said again.

Cam looked perplexed, but he changed the music.

"What's wrong with that song?" I asked Killian.

"It was my walkout song. It's not a big deal."

I wrapped an arm around his waist and took a sip of my beer. "Is this hard for you?"

He kissed me on the lips. "No."

But I didn't believe him. Everyone was reminding him

about the life he'd had before, a life he'd loved but couldn't go back to because he felt too guilty. If, for some reason, I couldn't do my art anymore, I'd be a little lost. Maybe it wasn't the same, and you couldn't compare it, but art was my passion in the same way MMA had been for Killian. Since I'd moved to Brooklyn, it had become even more important in my life. Jared asked me to paint a mural on the side of his tattoo shop when I got back to Brooklyn. I knew it was Killian's idea, and that he'd asked Jared if I could do it. I only knew that because Jared told me. I wanted to find a way to help Killian find a new passion, but I had no idea how to do that.

He pulled me in front of him and wrapped his arms around me, my back against his chest. "Stop worrying," he murmured in my ear.

I leaned back against him and we talked and joked with my old friends and my brothers.

"Eden was the queen bee of our high school," Cassidy said, and I caught a tone in her voice that crossed over the line of friendly. She was obviously in Lexie's camp now.

"Well, duh," Brianna said, coming to my defense. "Eden rocks."

"We rocked it together," I said.

"Yeah, we did, babe." She grinned at me, then jerked her head towards Cassidy, raising her eyebrows.

I shrugged. Sawyer and Garrett recounted a few stupid childhood tales, all at my expense might I add, that got us all laughing and dispelled whatever tension Cassidy had created.

"She was hell on wheels," Sawyer told Killian. "Hope you know what you've gotten yourself into."

"I've calmed down a lot. I'm a mature, responsible adult now."

Sawyer and Killian cracked up over that one, although

I hadn't been trying to be funny. I elbowed Killian in the ribs. "Just for that, you're eating cake tomorrow."

"No cake."

I smirked. "You're getting the Eden Madley birthday special."

He leaned down and whispered in my ear. "Your naked body wrapped in a bow?"

"That can be arranged."

"You're the gift that keeps on giving."

"And don't you forget it."

Later that night, alone in my bedroom, I watched through my open window as Sawyer and Killian disappeared into the woods behind our house, a bottle of Jack Daniels in Sawyer's hand. They'd bonded just like I'd hoped they would.

I changed into a tank top and sleep shorts and lay on my bed like a starfish, my body sticky from the August heat and humidity. It was so quiet here. I missed the noise of the city, the lullaby that rocked me to sleep now—the early morning garbage trucks, sirens, and the constant hum of voices and traffic. I missed the smell of Brooklyn—the pungent aroma of cheese from the shop across from Brickwood Coffee, roasted pork from Jimmy's taco truck, garbage and asphalt, the scent of freshly baked bread in Greenpoint on early Sunday mornings when I stayed at Killian's.

As much as I love my family, being back here made me realize that Brooklyn is my home now. I was grateful that I wasn't stuck in small-town Pennsylvania, living with Luke's parents, looking after a baby at the age of twenty-two.

Luke had done a shitty thing and he'd hurt me, but my heart wasn't broken like I thought it was. I'd wanted to be a different girl, expand my horizons, and explore the great beyond, but with Luke I'd stayed in a holding pattern, not growing, or changing. I'd held so much of myself back from him, confined to that box he'd kept me in.

With Killian, I'd been myself right from the start, not holding anything back. And he liked me just as I was.

* * *

Of course, I snuck into Garrett's room and stayed with Killian. What my dad didn't know wouldn't hurt him. Unfortunately, a six-thirty a.m. wakeup call came in the form of Sawyer pounding on the bedroom door. I burrowed under the covers as the door burst open. Privacy, in our house, was a joke.

Something hit my arm, forcing me to blow my cover which hadn't been much of a cover at all. I pulled back the covers, grabbed Sawyer's Nike and pelted it at his head. He ducked, and it hit the bedroom door with a thwack. "This is war," I declared. "You asked for it."

Sawyer laughed at my ridiculous statement, and so did Killian. I glared at one and then the other before I threw back the covers, jumped out of bed and flew at Sawyer, trying to knock him over. Fat chance of that. He threw me over his shoulder and deposited me on the bed.

I flopped back on the bed. This was all too much for this early hour. It was barely light outside. I sniffed the air. "Is that bacon?"

"Dad's on KP duty," Sawyer said then looked at Killian. "Ready for that run?"

"Give me two minutes," Killian said.

"Meet you out back."

"Did you guys make this plan without me? I'm going with you," I said, even though running at this hour was the last thing I wanted to do.

"What did I tell you?" Sawyer asked, and Killian chuckled, sharing an inside joke I wasn't privy to. "She hates to be left out of *anything*."

"Tell me about it," Killian said.

After Sawyer left, I elbowed Killian in the ribs. "You're on my team. No defecting to Team Sawyer."

"Whatever you say, sunshine."

"Happy birthday, baby."

Chapter Twenty-Eight

Killian

"**H**ow do you like your steak, son?" Jack Madley asked, as he fired up the barbecue. A tray stacked high with five of the biggest, thickest steaks I'd ever seen sat on the shelf next to the grill.

I looked at Sawyer who was carting a cooler of beer onto the deck and then at Garrett who was fiddling on his phone. Neither of them answered.

Eden's dad chuckled. "I know how they like their steaks. I was—"

"Killian likes his steak rare," Eden said, setting a salad on the table, and pulling a face. "Yuck."

She wasn't a big fan of steak but had chosen the menu, designed specifically for me. I was getting the Eden Madley special birthday treatment, and the Madley men were more than happy to go along with it. They loved steak, the bigger the T-bone the better.

"Sorry, sir, I thought—"

"It's Jack," he growled. He'd corrected me a few times last night, but I kept reverting to sir, for reasons I couldn't understand. I'd never called anyone sir in my entire life, but the man deserved my respect. Jack Madley had embraced me as his daughter's boyfriend, without judgement. I didn't know how to handle that, any more than I knew how to handle this whole situation. Eden might have wanted to get away from home, and I could understand why she didn't want to live in a small town or anywhere near that jackass, but this house was a home. It was clear within minutes of meeting her family that they all had her back, and she'd been raised with love.

I was drinking a cold beer on the deck in the early evening sunlight because I'd been told birthdays are special in the Madley house which meant I wasn't allowed to lift a finger to help. I looked out at the green expanse of her backyard and into the woods where I'd hung out with Sawyer last night after Eden had gone to bed, a cunning plan to make it look like she was honoring her dad's wishes.

"Do you ever get that feeling when you're surrounded by people having a good time, and you feel like you're not really there? Like, you're numb?" Sawyer had asked me.

"Yeah, I know that feeling."

"I'll be twenty-four in October, but I feel like I'm decades older than the guys I grew up with."

"I know that feeling."

"I thought you might." He took a swig of whiskey and stared at the bottle in his hand. "My second deployment…we were out on patrol, crossing a field. Me and my buddy Casey had metal detectors, scanning the area. We were just about to cross a dirt road. It looked like fresh earth had been dug up, so I told Casey and Jonesy to stay back and I'd inspect it. Next thing I knew, I was blown off my feet. I woke up in the field, and I stared up at the blazing sun. For a minute, I thought I was dead. It was so fucking quiet. But then I heard voices and I knew I wasn't dead. The IED had blown a crater in the road waist deep. I jumped in and the first thing I saw was a leg. Then I saw Jonesy. Both his legs were blown off, but he was telling me about the car he planned to get when he got home. His fucking legs were gone, and he was talking about a car and I was telling him it's gonna be all right. You'll get that car. A few guys jumped in to help. In my head, I was telling myself that Casey O'Malley is somewhere in that field. And he's okay. But I saw his boot sticking out of the dirt and I started digging him out…"

While he'd been telling me the story, he'd used that same automated voice I used when I told Eden my Johnny Ramirez story.

"We carried Casey back to base camp in a black body bag. My best friend was dead, Jonesy got his legs blown off, and I got away with a twisted ankle and some scrapes. I've replayed this thing in my head so many times, and I always ask myself what I could have done differently. Did I trigger that IED? Why did that happen to them and not me?"

Jesus Christ. How did he live with those images? I closed my eyes and leaned back against the trunk of the tree. "It wasn't your fault," I said finally, and I meant it.

I tipped back my head and looked up at the stars reeling in the night sky. Unbelievable that the world kept spinning. The stars still came out at night. The sun rose and set every day in this fucked-up irrational universe.

"I never told my family or friends that story," Sawyer said quietly.

"Why did you tell me?" Although I had some idea.

"You look like you've been to hell and back."

"I look that good, huh?" I joked.

"Ridden hard and put away wet," he joked right back at me.

"You shouldn't talk about your sister that way."

He held up his hand. "Spare me the details."

"You weren't gonna get any."

"She traded up, that's for damn sure," Sawyer said.

"Is he as big of an asshole as I think he is?"

Sawyer passed me the bottle of whiskey, and I took a swig.

Jack Daniel's, not my favorite. I passed it back to him and crossed my arms over my chest, waiting for an answer. "I never liked him. Everyone in this town treated him like he was God's gift. They called Luke and Eden the golden couple, but it was high school bullshit. Luke is shallow. He never knew the real Eden. She's a pain in the ass but my sister is cool as shit."

I already knew that.

Eden placed an armload of wrapped presents in front of me. Oh hell, no.

"What's this?" I asked.

"What does it look like? Your birthday presents."

"I told you not to buy me anything."

"Yeah, well, you're not the boss of me so I ignored you."

Sawyer and Garrett snorted and took a seat at the table. "Get used to it," Jack Madley said, throwing the steaks on the grill. "She's been ignoring my good advice for twenty-two years."

Eden rolled her eyes. "I get such a bum rap around here." She smacked me on the shoulder. "Open your presents. They're not just from me."

"The T-shirt is from me," Sawyer said.

"The whiskey is from me," Garrett said.

"You guys are the worst," Eden huffed. "It's supposed to be a surprise."

They shrugged and settled back with their beers. Eden sat across from me and snapped a photo. I held up my hand. "No."

More snorts in unison from the Madley men.

"Fine." She scooted her chair closer to me. "Open your stupid presents."

I opened the Jameson and thanked Garrett who informed me that Eden told him what to buy. Opened the box with a black Harley Davidson T-shirt and thanked Sawyer. "Picked it out on my own," he claimed. Since we'd spent the entire day out, doing 'guy stuff' and shopping for Sawyer's new motorcycle, I found that hard to believe. As a birthday present, he let me take his Kawasaki Ninja on a joy ride. I used to have a Ducati, one of the few things I'd ever bought myself, but I sold it after Johnny died.

"That looks a lot like the T-shirt I bought you for your birthday two years ago," Eden said.

Sawyer snickered.

"You re-gifted something I gave you?" Eden asked.

I tossed the T-shirt to Sawyer. He caught it and tossed it back to me. "It's a cool T-shirt," he said, to soften the blow. "But I've got a million T-shirts and no time to wear them."

"It'll look better on Killian, anyway." Eden crossed her arms and slumped in her seat.

The next present I opened was a stainless-steel Leatherman. "Dad, I gave you that for Christmas," Eden said.

"I didn't need two of them, kiddo."

By now, the guys and I were dying laughing. Eden threw her arms up. "You guys are hopeless."

Two unopened presents remained—a long cylinder and a small box.

"I bet she rolled up my old naked girl posters and re-gifted them," Sawyer said as I unwrapped the cardboard cylinder.

"Like I want Killian to plaster his walls with naked girl posters," she scoffed.

I popped open the plastic lid. I knew what was in there, and I almost didn't want to take it out. But she gave it to me and she wanted me to have it, so I slid it out, and I unrolled it, and looked at the painting I'd seen on her easel the night she sketched my face. "You can stash it in your closet," she said, chewing on her lower lip.

I put my arm around her and kissed her on the cheek. "It's

not going in the closet. I love it. Thank you."

"You're welcome." She gave me a big happy smile. "When we get home, I can stretch it and put it on a frame. If you want."

"You can do that?"

"Yeah. It's easy."

The last gift was a key chain—a silver globe. She turned it over in my palm to the smooth side, so I could read the engraving. *Every new day is a world of possibility.*

"I know it's totally corny." She shrugged. "But I went with it. They had to make the writing small to fit it all in. I always have too much to say."

"No shit," Sawyer said.

I had nothing to say. Not a God damn thing. The torture of an Eden Madley birthday special continued. After dinner, she carried out the cake, lit all twenty-seven candles, and sang Happy Birthday to me, insisting her dad and brothers join in.

When the song finally ended, she nudged my arm, laughing. "You look like you're in pain."

I rubbed my hands over my face. I was in pain. Nobody had ever done this for me before. I stared at the cake, the wax from the candles dripping into the icing, then at her face, all lit up in the glow, her green eyes shining. So fucking beautiful.

"You need to make a wish and blow out your candles, birthday boy."

A wish. I looked at her again and made my wish. I wanted every new day to include her. *She* was a world of possibility and it was a world I wanted to live in.

The next day, before we left, Jack Madley asked if he could have a word with me. I was stupidly nervous he'd give me hell for sleeping with Eden under his roof after he'd given me instructions to sleep down the hall from her. I followed him out to the deck and waited for him to lay into me. We stood side by side, facing the woods. It was so fucking quiet here. I could hear the birds chirping from the oak tree in their backyard and the hum of a lawnmower in the distance.

Jack clapped a hand on my shoulder and I startled. He chuckled. "I didn't peg you for the jumpy type."

I laughed. "I'm not usually." He dropped his arm to his side. I wiped the sweat off my forehead with the back of my arm. It was only nine in the morning, but the heat and humidity were already stifling.

"I wasn't sold on her idea to move to Brooklyn alone."

"I can understand that."

"She might think she's all grown up, but she'll always be my little girl."

I side-eyed him. Was he going to tell me to stay away from her?

"Look out for her," he said. "Make sure she stays out of trouble."

My shoulders relaxed. "I will."

He nodded and asked me to take his number. I entered it into my phone and pocketed it. "With any luck, you won't be escorting her to the ER anytime soon. But in case of an emergency, make sure you call me. Raising a daughter is a hell of a lot different than raising sons. I worry more about her safety. Always have." He shook his head. "She'd call me a sexist for saying that."

I laughed, remembering the time she'd accused me of the same thing. "I won't let anything happen to her."

"Good. I'll hold you to it. And don't mention we've had this little chat or I'll be getting an earful from her."

"I'll keep it to myself."

"And next time you visit, your doors will be booby-trapped. Nothing like a bucket of ice cold water falling on your head in the middle of the night."

I bit my bottom lip to keep from laughing. God, I loved this family. They were everything I'd never had but had always wanted. Supportive. Funny. Loving. Protective. Loyal. Even though Eden's mom had died much too young, this family didn't fall apart. Her dad hadn't hit the bottle to drown his sorrows. He stood strong, like that oak tree in the backyard. And he had passed that strength on to his kids.

I aspired to be a man like Jack Madley. Someday. Maybe.

Chapter Twenty-Nine

Eden

Jared wanted a skull, roses, and wings so that's what I was painting on the side of his two-story brick building that housed the tattoo parlor on the first floor and his apartment on the second floor. It was the Tuesday after Labor Day, but it still felt like summer in Brooklyn. Sweat trickled between my shoulder blades and I was fantasizing about a cold shower when Zeke yelled up to me.

"Yo, what's up, Picasso?"

I looked down at Zeke from my perch on the mini-scaffold tower. He was wearing a flowered Hawaiian shirt, plaid Bermuda shorts and Vans, his skateboard under his foot. Somehow, he made the crazy outfit work for him. He'd just returned from a week-long vacation in Martha's Vineyard with his family, and was sporting a golden tan, his hair bleached lighter from the sun and saltwater. I set down my paintbrush and climbed down the scaffolding to give him a big hug. "I missed you," I said, treating him to my sweaty, grungy self.

Zeke grinned. "Missed you too. Get my postcard?"

"Wish you were here," I quoted which was all the postcard said, and I found out he sent the same message to every bartender and Ava too, because he sent all the postcards to the bar and we compared notes. "Good trip?"

"Excellent. Spent time with the fam. Hooked up with a hot chick. Did some sailing. Life is good in Zeke's world."

"Is it ever bad in Zeke's world?" I teased. It was impossible not to love Zeke. I kept waiting to catch him in a bad mood, but I never did.

"Nope. My life is awesome."

I laughed and shook my head but right now, my life was awesome too.

"Speaking of awesome," Zeke said. "This wall is the bomb."

I backed up on the sidewalk to look at what I'd done so far. Last week, Killian had power-washed the wall and helped me paint the undercoat because he was the master of all trades. My skull was twelve feet tall, with roses in the eye sockets, around the base, and a banner underneath for the name of Jared's tattoo shop: Forever Ink. The wings, which I was working on now, extended from each side of the skull and spanned the width of the wall.

"Thanks, Zeke."

"You want me to grab some lunch for you and bring it back?" Zeke asked just as Killian pulled up to the curb. He cut the engine and stepped out of the Jeep, giving Zeke a onceover. His gaze swung to me and he gave me a big smile like he was happy to see me, and it had been a long time. When we'd woken up together only a few hours ago and he'd dropped me off here with an iced coffee, a bagel, and bottles of water to keep me hydrated. He'd hung out for a while, talking with me and Jared while I painted.

"Hey, baby," he said, pulling me into his arms.

"Hey." I leaned into him and gave him a kiss. "I'm all hot and sweaty," I murmured against his lips.

He nuzzled my neck. "I love your sweat." He tucked me close to his side and walked us over to Zeke who had a big smirk on his face.

"How was Hawaii?" Killian asked. I elbowed him in the ribs.

"Martha's Vineyard," Zeke said with a grin. "It was all good." He waggled his brows. "But I feel like I've missed a lot… living in the permanent friend-zone."

Killian spun his globe keychain around his finger. "Hope you're enjoying your stay."

"Like I had a choice."

"There's always a choice," Killian said. "You made the right one."

"Plenty of fish in the sea of Zeke." Zeke grinned at us, then flipped his skateboard over. "I'm going fishing. Catch you later."

"Bye Zeke," I called after him, as he took off down the street, his arm raised in the air.

Killian shook his head. "What the hell is he wearing?"

I burst out laughing. "His fishing outfit. Obviously. You should be nicer to him."

"That was me being nice. If I wanted to be mean, I would have asked him what the hell he was wearing."

I eyed Killian's cargo shorts and gray T-shirt. "His wardrobe has more colors than black, white, gray, and khaki."

"You want me to wear different colors?"

"No. I like you just as you are."

Pulling me against him, he cupped my butt in his hand. "I like these little orange shorts and this little blue top. And *all* the colors of your skin."

I laughed. My shorts were coral, my tank top was navy, and my arms and legs were splattered with paint dots. Killian tugged my lower lip between his teeth and sucked on it. I whimpered and pressed my body against his and wrapped my arms around his neck.

"Mm." I bit his lip and ground my body against his. He backed us up, so he was leaning against the door of his Jeep.

"You taste so good. I want to eat you for breakfast, lunch, and dinner."

"I love it when you talk dirty," he said, working his kisses down my neck.

"I learned from the best."

"Wanna hear what I'm going to do to you later?"

"Yes."

Someone cleared their throat and I turned to look at Ava. "Am I interrupting?"

"Yes," Killian said, turning me around in his arms so I was standing in front of him, with my back against his chest. Most likely to cover the raging hard-on he was sporting. I pushed my butt into it and laughed when he groaned.

"I don't know how Eden gets any work done with all her visitors," Killian complained.

Ava smirked at him. "We don't distract her as much as you do."

"I welcome *all* distractions." I wiggled my butt against him again.

"You're going to pay for this later," he whispered in my ear.

"I look forward to it."

Ava clapped her hands together. "Who's up for some lunch?"

"Killian is up for anything," I said.

"I bet he is," she said, arching her brows. "Shake Shack? Burgers, fries, shakes."

"It's a salad day," Killian said, extracting himself from me. He opened the hatch and came out with a bag that no doubt contained Tupperware containers filled with salads. He'd been bringing me lunch every day, which was how I'd learned just how big of a health nut he was. Lean protein, lots of greens, and grains I'd never heard of, all prepared by him in his kitchen.

On today's menu, we had a quinoa salad with chicken, pistachios, dried cranberries, and mint. And a green salad with tons of raw veggies and a mustard vinaigrette dressing. Yesterday we had couscous with roasted vegetables. The day before was a wild rice salad with salmon. The day before that was a Greek salad.

Ava rolled her eyes as he unpacked the salads. "I knew the cookies were a one-off," she grumbled.

"Next time I'll bake brownies and we can eat them all," I told her.

She high-fived me. "Now we're talking a language I understand."

We sat on the ground with our backs leaning against the wall and ate our salads al fresco which had become our little routine. Ava turned her nose up at the salads, but she hung out and talked while Killian fielded bar-related phone calls and I stuffed my face because I loved his salads.

"Pick you up at four," Killian said, giving me a chaste kiss goodbye. Anything more started a fire inside me, and I needed to focus on painting my wall. Not to mention I needed to conserve my energy for work tonight. The sun and heat and Killian turned me into a limp noodle.

After they left, I climbed back up the scaffold and got back to work. While I painted, I tried to remember a time when I was this happy, and I couldn't. Unless I went all the way back to childhood, but that was an entirely different kind of happiness. My life was so good now it was scary.

Any feelings I'd harbored for Luke had vanished. I'd finally spoken to him on the phone and he'd tried to explain his side of the story. While he'd talked, I'd waited for the hurt to dig its claws in. When it didn't, I'd smiled into the phone, grateful that I'd put it behind me and had moved on.

Now I was painting a wall in Williamsburg, had a bartending job I loved, cool friends and best of all, I had Killian. Hard to believe that we'd ever done that push-and-pull because now we were all in.

* * *

I was lying naked on the chopping block island in Killian's kitchen, my hair fanning out around me like a mermaid washed up on the beach, my legs draped over his bare shoulders. My body was his banquet to feast at and I was Lady Bountiful.

A David Guetta remix was playing on his sound system, the ceiling fan spinning above me. A cool breeze blew across my skin, and a delicious shiver ran through my body. I wasn't cold, though. I was a raging inferno.

His tongue circled the rim of my belly button and dipped inside. Around and around. Heat pooled between my legs. My muscles clenched, and a low moan escaped my lips. His tongue glided up my belly, slow and torturous. The stubble on his jaw grated against my skin, making all the neurons in my body fire on all cylinders. His tongue circled my nipple, flicked over it. Glided over the swell of my breast and moved on to the next one where he continued to torture me.

My back arched, and I was moaning, writhing. He's working me into a frenzy. It wasn't enough. It was too much.

"You need to stop," I whimpered.

"You want me to stop?" he asked, lifting his head to look at me.

"Yes. I mean, no. I want…more than you're giving me."

He chuckled. "So greedy and impatient."

He was trying to kill me, I was sure of it. His tongue glided up my inner thigh. Inching its way up to where I wanted it. My body was quaking, my palms sweaty. He stopped short of the mark and started on the other leg. The tip of his tongue found my clit and flicked over it once. My body spasmed. He did it again. And again. Two fingers slid inside me, curling, reaching, rubbing against the spot he didn't need a map to find. I was all nerve endings and slick heat. Throbbing, pulsing, aching need.

"I. Want. You," I gritted out.

Taking himself in his hand, he rubbed the tip between my slick folds.

I lifted my head to watch him. His eyes were on my face, his lips slightly parted as he guided himself inside me. Slowly. Slowly. I closed my eyes and all thoughts evaporated as he moved in and out filling me up. Again. And again. He pushed deep inside me.

"Oh…God." I yelled hoarsely.

My body exploded, my muscles clenching around him, convulsions rocking my body. As if from somewhere far away, I heard his ragged breathing. His hands tightened on my hips, fingers digging into my flesh, as he came. He pressed a kiss on my belly, the stubble on his jaw brushing my skin, before he pulled out of me.

My legs felt like rubber as he lowered me to the ground, and I got dressed in my tank top and underwear.

He took my hand and led me upstairs to his bedroom. Unlike me, he hadn't bothered to put on clothes. I got a good look at his perfect ass, firm, and round, and deserving of a photo plastered on the Brooklyn Bridge. On billboards across the country. It was that good. My gaze traveled upwards to the dimples on his lower back and to the phoenix tattoo.

"How are you going to make your salads on that island now?" I asked.

"Tomorrow's salads will be extra salty."

"Oh God," I said, laughing.

We took turns in the bathroom and met up in his bed. I hadn't seen Connor's bedroom, but Killian's was small, with two windows facing the backyard. His room was clean but basic, with a queen-sized bed, a dresser, and bedside tables. I lay back on his forest green sheets and looked at my painting on the wall. I'd stretched the canvas onto a wooden frame and he'd hung it across from his bed, so it would be the last thing he saw before he went to sleep and the first thing he saw when he woke up.

Killian slipped under the sheets, flicked off the lamp, and pulled my back against his chest. He bent his knees, bringing mine with them, and I snuggled into the curve of his body. His hand found mine and he laced our fingers together. This was how we fell asleep every night. We didn't wake up this way. Killian slept on his stomach, his arms wrapped around the pillow. I usually woke up on my side, arm under my pillow, facing him. But this was how we fell asleep and I loved it.

"Goodnight, baby."

"Goodnight, Killian." I had barely gotten the words out before I drifted off to sleep with a smile on my lips.

I was woken the next morning by a tongue swirling around my nipple. Twenty minutes later, we emerged from the shower together, a cloud of steam billowing behind us.

Fifteen minutes later, we were on our way to Jared's tattoo shop, an iced coffee in my hand. I'd braided my wet hair and bravely donned white shorts and a light blue T-shirt because I had a laundry issue, as in I needed to cart all my dirty clothes to the laundromat. Which, sadly, I planned to do tonight, on my night off.

"We'll pick it up now," Killian said, when I mentioned it.

"Why?"

"I'll take it to my house."

"Why?" I asked, still not cluing in.

"I have a washer and dryer. I'll throw your stuff in while I make lunch."

"You can't do my laundry, make my lunch, run the bar, drive me all over town and—" I was still protesting when he stopped in front of my apartment building.

"Go. You're burning daylight."

"Burning daylight?"

He drummed the steering wheel with his fingers. "I've got shit to do."

"Exactly my point," I said, not making a move to leave. "You don't have time to do all this other stuff. I'll buy lunch at the deli today. And if you let me hang out at your apartment tonight, I'll do my own laundry and I'll be waiting for you when you get home."

He perked up at that suggestion. "Naked?"

"Maybe."

"Naked," he repeated.

"Okay. Fine." Although I had no intention of sitting around his house naked. "I'll cook dinner too. We can eat at two in the morning."

"Yeah?"

"Yeah. But you'll have to eat whatever I cook."

He grinned. "Deal." He leaned across me and pushed open my door. "Get your laundry."

Chapter Thirty

Killian

CONNOR WAS HOME. HE CAME TO THE BAR THIS AFTERNOON, showing up at the door as if he'd never been away.

"Where in the hell have you been?" I roared when I opened the door and saw him standing on the other side, a duffle bag slung over his shoulder, with a fucking suntan. A suntan? Had he been lying around on a beach all this time?

"Miami."

"Miami," I repeated, looking into his eyes. They were clear. Focused. He looked good, like he'd put on some weight and muscle. "How did you get there and back?"

"Greyhound."

What the fuck? His Harley was still parked in the backyard, covered with a tarp. But his mode of transportation was the least of my concerns. "They don't have phones in Miami?" I inspected his arms for fresh track marks. There weren't any.

"I'm clean. Have been for six months. I didn't do any drugs after I got out of rehab."

That didn't make sense. If he'd been clean this whole time, why had he stayed away for so long? "So, you just took off on a little vacation. Fuck everyone else. Is that it?"

He looked over my shoulder. "Ava here?"

"No."

Connor lowered his head and rubbed the back of his neck, letting out a breath. "Are you going to let me in?"

"Are you going to tell me what the hell you've been doing for five months?"

He pushed past me. I slammed the door shut and followed him out to the courtyard. "Place looks good. Did Ava do that?" he asked, jerking his chin at the honeysuckle climbing the wood trellis on the side wall.

Ava planted it, along with the mint and lavender that kept getting trampled by drunks and watered with beer and cocktails. But she tended to it every day. Like Eden, Ava was an optimist. "Yeah."

Connor's gaze swung to the wall Eden painted. I watched his face as he took in every detail. He crossed the courtyard and crouched in front of the wall, studying her mural up close and at eye-level. Connor looked at the world through an artist's eye. He noticed things I didn't, but he missed a lot too. When we were kids, he lived inside his head, a dream world he'd created to escape reality.

Sometimes I used to think it took balls to do drugs right under Seamus Vincent's nose, but other times I recognized it for what it was—yet another way for Connor to escape the real world. When he was high, he didn't care who he hurt or who he let down. All he cared about was chasing his next high. He'd stolen from me, lied to me, and asked for my help. I'd always gotten to Connor before Seamus did, which was nothing short of a miracle. But then, I got all of Seamus's attention, and Connor got none. I was Connor's human shield, his invisibility cloak.

"Now that I'm back, I'll start going to NA meetings," Connor told the wall. "And I'll get a sponsor."

"I'm giving you one last chance, Connor. If you screw up again, I can't help you." Who was I kidding? I'd keep giving him chances until he got it right. But if he disappeared again or went back to drugs, I didn't want to go through that again. I'd helped him detox at home a few years ago. I'd stayed up with him through the night. Held his body in my arms to try to stop the shaking. Cleaned up his vomit. Helped him into the shower, holding on to his arm so he didn't fall and crack his head open. I'd talked him down from wanting to kill himself when all he'd wanted was to die. Horrible didn't even begin to describe those awful days and nights when I'd guarded over him. Finally, I'd taken him to a detox clinic and they'd dosed him with methadone, something we should have done from the start. A month later, after going to hell and back, he started doing drugs again.

He nodded. "I know. It's something I need to do for myself."

Maybe I should have questioned his answer, but it was the first time he'd acknowledged this was his responsibility. I wanted to believe in him. I needed to believe in him. Taking care of Connor was my job, and I hated it that I'd failed him.

"I'll do everything in my power to support you," I said.

"You always do," he said, still looking at Eden's wall. "I don't know how you do it, Killian."

"Do what?"

"Be you." He turned around to face me. "I don't know how you fucking do it. Do you just turn off a switch? Block it out? Lock it down? Is it all inside, eating away at you? Or did you punch and kick your way out?"

I clenched my jaw. "I've got shit to do. I don't have time—"

"I'm not the only one with an addiction problem."

"I don't have an addiction problem."

"You're addicted to pain."

"Fuck you." I left him in the courtyard, stalked down the hallway and into the office, slamming the door shut behind me.

You're addicted to pain.

Who did this to you, Killian?

I'd never hurt you, Killian.

The door swung open and Connor filled the doorway. "I'm not leaving again. I'm done running." I didn't answer. "Did you hear me?"

"I heard you. Do you want a medal? Should I throw a party?"

"Who painted the wall?" he asked. "Who's Eden?"

Who is Eden? She's everything. But she still had no idea how fucked up I was. Every day she made me happier than the day before, and every day I worried that I'd ruin us. That a guy like me wasn't cut out for a healthy, functional relationship. I had no guidelines, no blueprint to follow, no role models to emulate. All I had was my gut feeling that told me this was real, and it was good, and I'd never known anything like it. I wanted to hang onto it for as long as I could before the house of cards came tumbling down.

"I hired her in June," I said. "She's a bartender."

"A bartender?"

As if on cue, my cell phone rang. "Hey, baby," I answered, without thinking.

"Hey baby right back at you."

"Everything okay?"

"Just taking a water break. Someone told me I need to stay hydrated."

"Someone's giving you good advice."

"I always take it too."

I chuckled. "No you don't."

She laughed. "Usually."

"How many visitors since I last saw you?" Friends were always stopping by to hang out with her—Hailey, Ava, Chris, Brody, Zeke...even her favorite barista delivered coffee. Not to mention Jared and the other tattoo artists popping out for a chat.

"Not so many. I'm almost done."

"Call me when you finish. I'll pick you up."

"Okay," she said. "Gotta go. Jared's here to inspect the damage."

"Not the damage. The masterpiece."

"I stand corrected."

"See you soon," I said.

"Can't wait."

When I cut the call, Connor smirked at me. "Holy shit. I can't believe what I just heard. Killian Vincent, the walking one-night stand, has a *girlfriend?*"

I narrowed my eyes at him. "Don't say that shit in front of her."

"Whoa. You're serious about this girl. Is she an MMA fan?"

"No."

"She's a bartender. And an artist," he guessed. "Eden?"

"Don't fuck this up for me, Connor."

"You act like I don't want you to be happy."

"Why would I think that? Your disappearing acts? The money you stole from me? The lies and the drugs? You have a gift, Connor. You had a scholarship to art school. And you had Ava. You had *everything*. But you threw it all away."

"I told you. I'm getting my shit together. And I'm going to pay back every cent I owe you."

I didn't give a shit about the money. I needed answers. "What were you doing in Miami?"

"Working at a tattoo parlor."

This wasn't adding up. Why did he go to Miami when he had a job here? A job he loved. "Why didn't you call me?"

"I was working through some stuff and I needed space," he said, not meeting my eye. He was lying about something, but I didn't know what or why. "I needed time. But I swear on my life, everything will be different now. I'm going to do the work. I know my word's not good anymore. But I'm going to prove it to you. One day at a time. I'm just asking you to have a little faith in me."

Have a little faith. Yeah, I guess that was what I needed to do. No matter what he did, he was still my brother, and there was nothing in this world I wouldn't do for him. He knew that.

"I need to talk to Jared," he said. "See if he'll take me back."

"He will. Eden's there now."

"She's a tattoo artist too?"

I met his gaze. "No."

"Jared's wall," Connor said, working his jaw.

That's what happens when you skip town.

It was supposed to be Connor's wall to paint. Jared wanted to wait for Connor to come back. Despite all the drugs Connor had done over the years, he'd somehow managed to hold down his job. The way Jared talked about Connor, you'd think he was a prodigy. An artistic genius. Brilliant with a streak of madness. A free spirit, Jared called him. Junkie was the word he left out.

I talked Jared into letting Eden paint the wall. He wouldn't have said yes if he didn't think she was good, but Eden didn't need to know that Jared promised the wall to Connor. Jared asked her to paint a skull, roses, and wings—Connor's idea. But Connor never sketched anything in advance, so Eden could do her own version of it.

"She's good," Connor said.

"I know."

"Killian," Ava sing-songed. "I've been shop—"

"Ava Blue," Connor said. He called her Blue for Bluebird. Connor loved birds. No mystery there.

"Connor," she said, her voice hushed.

He wrapped her up in his arms, and she looked so tiny, and

so fragile.

"I hate you," she whispered.

"I know."

They disappeared, and I placed an order with the beer distributor. Fixed a broken soap dispenser in the men's room. Conducted an inventory in the liquor room. Jotted down a to-do list for Ava. I knew the drill. She'd be a wreck for the next few days, and her organized brain would be thrown into chaos. After today's talk, she'd refuse to speak to Connor. Sometimes that went on for weeks or even months. They'd broken up over three years ago, right around the time Connor had gotten clean the first time, but I'd given up trying to figure out their screwed-up relationship.

Eden called to tell me she was done so I headed out. I didn't know why I spent so much time working at the bar, taking on all the problems. Louis said I was a workaholic. Connor said I was addicted to pain. Eden said everyone had their own coping mechanisms. Keeping busy, taking care of problems I could fix, was what I did.

"Wait up," Connor said, as I was on my way out the door. "I'll come with you."

We drove in silence. I watched him in my peripheral, trying to gauge his mood. I couldn't think of a damn thing to say that wouldn't come out sounding angry, so I kept my mouth shut. Up ahead, I saw Eden across the street from her wall, snapping photos. The way the sun hit her, she shimmered like gold, I swear to God. I eased off the accelerator as we approached. If I were an artist or a photographer, I'd want to capture her at this very moment.

"Jesus Christ," Connor said. "That's her?"

"That's her."

I pulled into a spot farther up the street, so I wouldn't ruin her photos, and cut the engine. She lowered her camera and looked over at the Jeep, her lips widening into a smile. Her gaze swung to the passenger seat and her mouth formed an O.

"Does she know about me?" Connor asked.

I nodded. Eden didn't know everything. But she knew about the drugs and rehab, and she knew how worried I'd been that he hadn't contacted me.

"She's beautiful," Connor said.

"Yeah, she is."

"Is that a smile?" he asked. "Holy shit. It's a smile. Can I get a photo?"

I punched his arm, he punched me back, and we grinned at each other like two idiots. Then we got out of the Jeep and joined Eden on the sidewalk. Being Eden, she welcomed him with open arms and told him how happy she was he came home. She said all the things I'd wanted to say to Connor, but didn't—couldn't.

★ ★ ★

I unlocked the front door and stepped inside. Laughter and music drifted from the kitchen and I stopped in the hallway, listening. I didn't know what Eden cooked but whatever it was, it made this crappy house smell like a home. It felt like a home. All because she was in it. I didn't know what to do with this feeling, so I walked back out the door I'd just entered and stood on the front steps. Warehouses lined the street across from me, their corrugated metal doors closed for the night. The old water tower rose up behind them, next to a derelict eight-story warehouse with burnt-out windows. Out here, it smelled like burnt rubber and motor oil. Inside, it smelled like home.

I took a few deep breaths and went back inside.

"Killian?" Eden called. She walked into the hallway, barefoot in a little blue cotton dress, loose waves of blonde hair falling around her shoulders. Her face lit up with a smile just for me, and it felt like someone sucker punched me in the stomach. She jumped into my arms and I caught her, holding on tight as she wrapped her legs around my waist. Eden held my face in her hands and peered into it, seeing too much, as usual. "Hey. Are you okay?"

"Yeah." I forced a smile. I wasn't okay, but I didn't know how to articulate what I was feeling. She wouldn't understand why happiness scared me. In my life, whenever anything had gone well, I was always waiting for the other shoe to drop. It always did. But maybe this time it would be different. Connor was home, he wasn't using, and Eden and I were on our way to something so good I didn't have a word for it.

"I hope you like lasagna," she said. "I also made salad and brownies, but Connor ate half the tray of brownies."

"She wouldn't let me touch the lasagna until you got home," Connor yelled from the kitchen. "So, get your ass in here. I'm starving."

Eden laughed and kissed me on the lips. She slid out of my arms, took my hand in hers and led me into the kitchen. The island was set for dinner with two wine glasses, and water for Connor.

"Eden did all the laundry." Connor grabbed a cucumber slice from the salad and tossed it into his mouth.

"What do you mean by *all* the laundry?" I asked.

"Hers, mine, yours. All of it."

"I don't want you to do our laundry."

"Sit down and be quiet," Eden said, dishing up the lasagna.

I pulled up a stool across from Connor. "What were you doing while she cooked and did all the laundry?"

"Connor helped me," Eden said, setting a plate of lasagna in front of me.

Connor shook his head no.

"You carried the grocery bags. And helped me shop. And you kept me company."

"And he ate half the fucking brownies," I grumbled.

"You don't even eat brownies," Eden said, sitting next to me.

"Not the point."

"Nobody's ever taken care of Killian. He doesn't know how to handle it," Connor said, shoveling a huge bite of lasagna into his mouth.

He wasn't lying about the drugs. When Connor was doing drugs, he didn't eat like he was starving. And he was right. I didn't know how to handle it.

Eden poured wine into my glass and gave Connor an apologetic smile.

"I told you it was okay," he said. "Really. I don't even like wine."

It was probably true. Alcohol had never been his problem.

Eden nudged my arm. "Eat your dinner and drink some wine. And get used to it. I like doing things for you."

Connor grinned at me. "Eden is the best thing that ever happened to you."

She laughed like it was a joke, but Connor wasn't joking. It was the truth.

After the night she cooked for me and Connor, Eden was pretty much living with us. Her shampoo, conditioner, and shower gel lived in our shower, her toothbrush in the holder, her makeup and perfume on my dresser top, her clothes in a duffel bag on my bedroom floor. After four days of watching her dig through her bag to find clothes, I cleared space in my closet and gave her one of my dresser drawers. She unpacked her things and put them away. We'd never discussed this new living arrangement, but she knew I worried about leaving Connor on his own every night and I wanted to spend my nights with her.

"Are you guys getting tired of me yet?" she asked one rainy, lazy Sunday afternoon, about a week into this new living arrangement while we were watching one of the *Fast & Furious* movies. Connor asked us to pause it while he tended to his microwave popcorn. Eden and I were on the sofa, her head resting in my lap, and I tipped my chin down to look at her face.

"I don't think I'll ever get tired of you," I said, and I meant it. I couldn't imagine a day when I wouldn't want to see her face, listen to her conversation, just *be* with her.

She smiled. "It's nice to see you relax."

"You told me it was mandatory."

"Do you ever get scared?"

I wrapped a lock of her hair around my fingers. "Of what?"

"Us. It's just…everything is so good with us. It feels so right."

I looked over in the corner, at the artwork she rolled up when she wasn't working on it. She wanted to paste it on the concrete tower on top of the eight-story burnt-out warehouse. So far, she'd sketched the curl of wave with a surfer girl inside the barrel. It looked like the wave was about to crash over her head. Or, if you were an optimist, the girl would ride it out. Eden called it: Finding Peace in the Chaos.

"That scares you?" It surprised me she had the same fears I did.

"Sometimes. Now that I have you, I don't want to lose you. I think…" She chewed on her lip. "My heart would break for real."

Jesus. "You're not going to lose me. You're stuck with me." I hoped it was a promise I could keep.

"Popcorn?" Connor asked, holding out the bowl. Eden sat up and dug her hand in the bowl, coming out with a big handful.

"Thanks Connor."

I waved the bowl away. Connor always melted tons of butter on it and sometimes he sprinkled sugar and cinnamon over it. "Mm, sweet and buttery," Eden said. "This is sooo good."

Connor smirked at me and collapsed in his chair, setting the bowl on the coffee table for him and Eden to share. She scooted closer for better access to the popcorn and I hit play on the remote and pretended to watch the movie.

Before Eden, I didn't know what love felt like. Now I did.

Chapter Thirty-One

Eden

THE CREDITS WERE ROLLING, AND I WAS SNUGGLED UP AGAINST Killian's side. Connor was asleep on the chair, his long legs kicked out in front of him, arms folded over his chest. He looked like the younger version of Killian. Dark hair cut short on the sides and spiky on top, and the same electric-blue eyes. Straight nose. Chiseled jaw. Equally beautiful. With one dimple, instead of two.

The tattoo sleeve on his left arm was birds in flight and fish that fit together like a jigsaw puzzle inked in blue and black.

"M.C. Escher," Connor had said, when he'd caught me staring at his tattoo sleeve the day we met. "It's based on *Sky and Water*."

Killian pointed the remote at the TV and turned it off, plunging the room into silence. "I've been thinking about getting another tattoo," he said.

I perked up at that. I'd become a big fan of ink, especially on Killian's body. He had the perfect canvas to work with. "Where?"

He took my hand in his, curled it into a fist, and held it over his heart. "Will you design it?"

My breath caught in my throat. A tattoo over his heart, and he was asking me to design it. That was kind of huge. I turned my head to look at his face. "What do you want?"

"Whatever you design. Connor can work from your sketch."

A tattoo designed by me and inked by his brother. I knew Connor had designed all of Killian's tattoos. I also knew Connor was supposed to paint the wall of Jared's shop. Jared had let it slip. The other day, when I was alone with Connor, browsing through his sketchbooks, I'd asked him if he was okay with it. I felt like I'd stolen something that had been promised to him. Connor had assured me he was cool with it, and it was his own fault for skipping town.

"Connor was supposed to paint the wall," I said.

"He told you that?"

"No. Jared did."

"You weren't supposed to know about that."

I ran my hand down his chest. "I was right. Underneath that tough exterior, you're a marshmallow."

"How do you figure that?"

"You were trying to protect my feelings." I put my fingers over his lips. "Don't even try to deny it."

He growled and bit my finger. "Let's go upstairs." Before I could respond, he was off the sofa, hauling me to my feet and dragging me up the stairs.

"I'm surprised you don't pull me around by the hair."

"Would you like that?"

I laughed. "No."

He kicked his door shut, swept me off my feet, and tossed me on the bed. Then he was on top of me, his body covering mine. Arms wrapped around me, he rolled onto his back, bringing me with him. Cool, damp air came in through his open bedroom windows. Outside, the skies were gray, and the rain had tapered off to a drizzle, but the backyard looked like a mud pit.

I rolled off him and tugged up the hem of his T-shirt. "Take it off."

His lips quirked in amusement, but he pulled the T-shirt

over his head and tossed it on the floor. My fingers danced across his bare chest like I was playing a piano, a finely tuned instrument. I studied the tattoos on his upper arm and imagined the design extending to his left pec. I smoothed my hand down his chest, over the ridges of his muscles, his skin smooth and warm.

Propping my head on my hand, I traced the curves of his face with my fingertips. I knew his face and his body by heart now. If I were blindfolded and could only identify it by touch, I'd know it was him. I thought he brought me up here for sex, but now I realized it was more than that.

He rolled onto his side to face me. "Eden, what you said before…I don't want to break your heart. I don't want to do anything that will ruin what we have."

"I won't let you," I said.

"Promise?"

"Promise. I love you, Killian."

His eyes searched my face, and I held my breath. I hadn't planned to say that, even though I'd known it for a while. He rolled onto his back and stared at the ceiling. The room was so still and quiet, the air heavy with my words still hanging between us. "I love you too," he said so softly, I almost didn't hear him. "You own me, Eden. Body, heart, soul. I'm yours."

I nearly wept at his words. He turned his head to look at me. "That's some pretty deep shit for a lazy Sunday."

I laughed, and he pulled me on top of him, wrapping his arms around me, my cheek pressed against his chest, right above his heart. "So, what's this tattoo gonna be?" he asked a few minutes later. I'd just been lying on top of him, breathing him in, lost in my own happy love bubble while his hands massaged my back, making me purr like a kitten.

"My name," I teased.

"Yeah?"

I laughed. "No. I'll give you something better than that."

"You can work it into the design."

"You'd tattoo my name over your heart?"

"I love your name, so…yeah."

Wow. Just, wow. Ink was for life. This was almost more monumental than hearing him say "I love you." Hearing him tell me I owned him. I didn't think anyone had ever owned Killian. I lifted my head, and he tipped his chin down to look at me.

"Killian," I whispered.

"I know." He put his head back down on the pillow. "This is all kinds of crazy." He started laughing, his chest rumbling under my body, the sound filling up the quiet room. I was laughing with him, and I had no idea why, but it felt good to be this happy. My heart expanded like a balloon, filling up so much, I thought it might burst from joy.

Our laughter was interrupted by a pounding on the door. Connor yelled up the stairs that he'd get it. I heard the door opening, followed by a voice I knew all too well, even though it had been months and we'd only spoken for a few minutes in a noisy bar.

"What do you want?" Connor asked, sounding so much like Killian.

"Stay here," Killian said, heading for the door.

"Where have you been, you piece of shit?" Seamus asked Connor.

Downstairs, I heard a scuffle, followed by a grunt.

"Get your hands off him," Killian roared.

I hopped off the bed and stood in the open doorway, listening, my heart racing.

"Just like old times," Connor said. "Why did you do it, Killian? Why did you always need to be the hero?"

"Shut up, Connor," Killian warned.

"Shut up, Connor. Hide in the closet until I come for you, Connor," Connor mimicked.

"Why are you here?" Killian asked.

"I told you to call me when your brother got back. I had to hear it from someone else. Answer me. Where have you been?"

"You really have no idea?" Connor asked.

"Don't play games with me, boy. Where've you been?"

"Just took a road trip to nowhere special. Traveled around. Kept moving."

Connor was lying, but Killian didn't deny it. I didn't catch Seamus's response, but I heard the next part loud and clear.

"Saw you and your little girlfriend the other day over at the tattoo parlor," Seamus said, and I tensed. "What's wrong with you, boy? Artists are fucked up. Look at your brother here. Screwed up in the head. Got their wires all crossed."

"Whatever sick and twisted game you're playing, leave her out of it," Killian said.

"You're the one who's screwed up in the head," Connor said. "What did Killian do to piss you off so much you attacked him with a broken bottle? There was so much fucking blood. He was unconscious."

My hand flew to my mouth. Oh my God. No. *His father did that to him?*

"Shut up," Killian warned.

"That's not what happened, boy," Seamus growled. "It was that junkie. You know that."

"He was twelve years old," Connor said. "You made everyone believe it was that junkie. We kept your secrets. Told lies to protect you. Killian hid all his bruises, and everyone thought it was another street fight. He was scared nobody would believe him if he told the truth. Scared we'd go into foster care and get separated. That's why he took it. Over and over and over. How many punches did you take, Killian? How many times did he knock you out? Break your ribs? Leave you unconscious on the kitchen floor?"

"You don't know what you're talking about," Seamus said. "You've done so many drugs, your brain is scrambled."

My feet carried me to the stairs without my permission. I sat on the top step and leaned my shoulder against the wall, getting a clear view of the hallway and the three men standing in it.

"You tried to break him, but you couldn't," Connor said. "I'll never forgive you for what you did to him, and I'll never forget. You can go fuck yourself."

Seamus lunged for Connor, but Killian blocked him and pinned Seamus to the wall, getting right in his face. "You touch my brother or come anywhere near this house or my girlfriend, and you'll regret it."

"Is that a threat?" Seamus asked.

"It's a promise."

Seamus shoved Killian away and glanced up the stairs. Our eyes met for a split second. I hoped he could see how much I hated him.

"Think long and hard before you mess with me, boy," Seamus threatened before letting himself out and shutting the door behind him.

"Killian—" Connor said.

Killian held up his hand. "Don't talk to me."

"It needed to be said," he called after Killian, who was charging up the stairs, his face murderous. "You can't keep pretending it never happened."

"Not. Another. Fucking. Word."

I made myself small to let Killian pass and looked down the stairs at Connor. He hung his head and leaned against the wall. I was torn between wanting to make it better for Connor and going after Killian. I chose Killian and stood in the doorway, watching him.

"You ready for work?" he asked, pulling on a black T-shirt.

"Work?" I repeated.

"You have five minutes." He pulled jeans out of his drawer. Socks. His combat boots from the closet.

I stood there, staring at him, my feet rooted to the spot while he got dressed as if nothing had happened. His face was shuttered, and now I understood why he'd perfected the art of locking it down. My heart was breaking for the boy he'd been, for the man he'd become, burying all the hurt and lies and secrets deep inside.

"Killian—"

"I'm leaving in three minutes," he said brusquely.

I glanced at the clock on his bedside table. "It's only three forty-five."

He pulled out his wallet, laid a twenty-dollar bill on the dresser, and sat on the edge of his bed to put on his boots.

"What's that for?"

"Taxi money."

"I don't need your money. We need to talk about this."

"Either you come with me or you take a taxi. Your choice." He stood, and I slammed the door shut, blocking his exit with my body.

"I'm not talking about the taxi and you know it."

He crossed his arms over his chest. "I told you to stay in the room. You didn't. I told you to get ready for work, so I could give you a fucking ride. You're not doing that either."

"Why didn't you tell me?" Silent tears streamed down my face. "You claim you love me, but you kept this huge secret from me and—"

"I don't have time for this shit." He lifted me off the floor, set me down, then opened the bedroom door and walked right out. I heard his footsteps on the stairs, his boots hitting every step in staccato like he was sprinting down them.

"If you leave now, I'm packing my stuff and leaving," I said loud enough for him to hear. I didn't want him to leave, and I didn't want to leave him either. His footsteps stopped, then started again. "Please come back," I whispered, wrapping my arms around myself.

The front door opened, and I strained my ears, listening. There it was…the sound of the door closing behind him and the locks clicking into place. I lowered myself to the floor, drew my legs to my chest and wrapped my arms around them, Connor's words echoing in my head.

How many punches did you take, Killian? How many times did he knock you out? Break your ribs? Leave you unconscious on the kitchen floor?

You tried to break him, but you couldn't.

My silent tears turned into sobs that wracked my body.

Chapter Thirty-Two

Eden

I HEARD FOOTSTEPS ON THE STAIRS, SLOWER AND MORE LABORED than the way he'd descended them and then he was standing in front of me. He pulled me to my feet and wrapped his arms around me, holding me close. Killian had always made me feel safe. But he'd never been safe, not even in his own house. I wanted to be strong for him, but I was the one breaking down, crying for Killian's lost childhood, and he was the one holding me together.

How could anyone hurt beautiful Killian? His father was a monster.

I took a shaky breath. "I hate him for what he did to you."

"It was a long time ago."

It didn't matter how much time had passed. It had happened, and his father had gotten away with it. Killian hadn't wanted me to hear any of that, just like he'd never wanted me to hear the conversation with his father at the bar. If Connor hadn't said something today, would Killian have ever told me?

"Don't be mad at Connor," I said. "He loves you so much."

Killian exhaled sharply. "He should have kept his mouth shut."

"He's right. It needed to be said."

"How can it help to dredge up ancient history?"

"I don't know. Just…he should be made responsible for his actions."

"It was a long time ago," Killian said, sounding weary.

I pulled away from him a little and put my hands on his chest. He took my face in his hands and ran his thumbs under my eyes, wiping away the tears. "Don't cry for me," he said, softly kissing my lips.

"I can't help it." My fingers traced the scar on his neck. He wrapped his hand around my wrist and pulled my hand away. For fifteen years, he'd lived with this reminder. For fifteen years, he'd been telling a lie about how he got it.

"I'm okay," he said.

I didn't know how that could possibly be true. But I loved him even more now than I did earlier. I loved him for his scars and wounds and his battered heart, for his strength, and his loyalty to Connor, and now I understood the meaning of the phoenix tattooed on his back. Killian had risen from the ashes and he'd made something of his life, despite the shitty hand he'd been dealt.

"I wish I could make things better for you."

His hands moved to the side of my neck. "You already do." And then he was kissing me, his fingers sliding through my hair, his hand holding the back of my head. He tugged down my drawstring shorts and underwear. I stepped out of them and kicked them aside, unbuttoning his jeans. We pulled apart long enough to shed the rest of our clothes in haste. Killian walked me backwards, his lips on mine, our tongues swirling together, until the back of my legs hit the side of his bed.

I scooted back on the bed and lay down on his pillow, and he covered me with the weight of his body. I gave him my body, my heart, and my soul. I gave him all of me. For a little while, the world disappeared, and it was just the two of us living in a beautiful moment. With no past, no tears, no sadness, or pain. We were our bodies—skin, muscle, bones. We were our hearts—strong, resilient, steadily beating. We were our souls—pure, yearning, connected. We were everything.

Afterwards, we held each other close and the world came rushing back.

"You good now?" he asked.

"Yeah." I wasn't one hundred percent good, because of everything I'd heard downstairs. But I was okay because he came back, and he didn't run away from me, even though he wanted to. I meant something to him. My feelings mattered to him. After all his secrets had been revealed, he stayed. For me. But, still, I couldn't just let it go. "Are you hiding anything else from me?"

"You looking to rattle more skeletons in the closet?"

"Are there any?"

"No." He lifted his head and looked over my shoulder at the clock on his bedside table. "We need to go."

He was dressed and ready in two seconds flat. While I finished getting ready for work, he lounged on the bed, doing something on his phone. Most likely he was checking in with Louis to make sure everything was okay without him. I changed into jeans, a Trinity Bar T-shirt, and my motorcycle boots. Ran a brush through my hair, applied a few coats of mascara, brushed blush onto my cheekbones, and slicked on some pinky-brown gloss. I was ready in five minutes. Not bad.

Killian was still lounging on the bed, his fingers laced behind his head, watching me. "What?" I asked.

He shook his head. "Nothing. Ready?"

"Born ready." I gave him a flirty wink, but his face was serious. I wondered if he was thinking about what happened earlier with Seamus, or if he was taking a bad trip down memory lane.

"What are you thinking about?" I asked, knowing full well guys hated that question. My brothers clued me in years ago.

Garrett told me sometimes guys aren't thinking about anything, but girls always assume they're thinking something heavy, deep, and real. Sawyer never bothered to explain anything. He usually told me to get off his case, or he'd just walk away without answering.

"You," Killian said. "I was thinking about you."

"Good things or bad things?" I asked as we walked down the stairs. The TV blared in the living room, and it sounded like an action film with things getting blown up.

"Good."

"Bye, Connor," I yelled into the living room.

"Bye, Eden. Catch you later, Killian."

Killian didn't respond. I nudged his arm, but he guided me out the door without saying goodbye.

"Let's stay at your place tonight," he said.

"But Connor—"

"He's a big boy. He doesn't need a babysitter."

I climbed into the Jeep and fastened my seatbelt. "You need to talk to him," I said, boldly venturing into dangerous territory. "He's your brother. He was trying to defend you and—"

"I don't *need* anyone to defend me." Killian pulled away from the curb, his jaw clenched. I sighed loudly. Killian turned up the volume on the music to cut further conversation. I promptly turned it down. He glared at me. I ignored it.

"This is what you do," I said. "You shut down and shut people out."

"Did I shut you out?"

"You tried." I sat in silence for a few seconds, trying to come up with the right words, but maybe there weren't any. I just needed to share my opinion. "What happened to you growing up was horrible—"

"I thought we were done talking about that."

"Just let me finish. It was horrible for you, but it must have been horrible for Connor too. He feels guilty about it. You never let him—"

"Fucking hell, Eden. I was trying to protect him. Am I supposed to feel bad about that?"

"No. That's not what I'm saying. He loves you for protecting him, for always being there for him, but he wants to find a way to make it up to you."

"You've known him…for what…a week?"

Eleven days, but whatever. "We talk on the nights you work." Connor felt guilty about the drugs and all the times Killian had to clean up his mess, but now I knew it went deeper.

"You talk," Killian said sarcastically. "Of course you do. He probably pours out all his thoughts and feelings. I bet you love that. Sorry to tell you, I'm not Connor. I don't sit around analyzing every detail of my life and throwing myself a fucking pity party like he does."

I took a deep breath to calm myself. "Connor doesn't—"

"Fuck Connor. You said we were good. Why are we talking about him?"

"Because I don't want you to shut him out. You need each other. He's the only real family you have. I know you know that, so I don't need to tell you…"

"But you're telling me anyway."

I shrugged. "Yeah."

He parked down the street from the bar and cut the engine. "Anything else?"

"I think I covered it."

Killian gripped his upper lip between his teeth. "I've been this way most of my life so don't expect miracles overnight."

"I won't. But you're getting better."

He chuckled and shook his head. "You think?"

"I don't think it. I know it."

Killian turned in his seat to look at me. "How do you always know the right things to say to me? And all the things you do…just for me…. Eden, what do I do for you?"

"You don't know what you do for me?"

"Other than being a pain in the ass and making you cry… I'm drawing a blank."

He was serious. I turned my body, resting my shoulder and my cheek against the seat. "You gave me back my art. The day I came in, asking for a job, I hadn't painted or drawn anything in months. After the whole Luke thing happened, I just…I don't know, I kind of gave up on it. Maybe I shut down because I didn't want to feel anything. You asked if art was therapy, yet I hadn't turned to my art. I only started painting again after the first night I worked with you. Because even then, you made me feel so much of everything. It's hard to explain…"

"Try," he urged, and I knew this was important to him, so I tried to put it into words.

"When I'm with you, even on bad days, even on perfectly ordinary days, there's nowhere else I'd rather be. That's never happened to me before. I spent most of my life dreaming about places I'd rather be. But with you, I realized it has nothing to do with location…if I'm with you, it doesn't matter where we are. When I'm with you, I see all the colors. And I'm not scared of the darkness, because there's so much light inside you too. When you let me see you, really see you, there's nothing in this world more beautiful than you, Killian."

"It's not beautiful inside me. It's a fucked-up place to live."

"I'd rather live there, with you, than anywhere else on the planet. I wish you could see yourself the way I do."

"I wish every person on the planet could look at the world the way you do. I don't know what I did to deserve you, but I'm going to try my best to make you happy."

"You already do," I said.

He leaned across the gearbox, wrapped his hand around the back of my neck and kissed me softly on the lips. "You're beautiful, sunshine."

Chapter Thirty-Three

Eden

FRIDAY AFTERNOON, I WAS SITTING ON A STOOL IN FOREVER INK, watching Connor tattoo his brother's chest. I came to offer my moral support which Killian probably didn't need anyway. Two hours into his tattooing session, and Killian was unfazed by the needles piercing his skin. He didn't flinch and barely moved a muscle. He hadn't been joking about the tough skin but, then, he'd been through worse pain than this, I guess.

It had taken a few days before Killian talked to Connor again. But as I'd come to learn, Killian had a big heart and once he let someone in, he was generous with it. Despite the grief and worry Connor had caused Killian over the years, Killian kept giving him chances to get it right because he wanted Connor in his life.

I watched the concentration on Connor's face as he tattooed Killian's skin. Connor didn't want to mess it up, but I knew he wouldn't.

"You've got your serious artist face on," Killian joked.

"Eden will beat me up if I make a mistake," Connor said.

"She's pretty fierce," Killian said.

While they joked around, I thought about their mother and wondered what she'd think of the men they'd turned into. Good men, in my book. How could she leave her two boys behind?

My thoughts drifted to Anna Ramirez. A few days ago, I'd taken her number from Killian's phone and called her when he was at work. I figured nine-thirty would be a good time—not too late, but the baby would be asleep by then.

"Hi, Anna. My name is Eden. You don't know me, but I'm Killian's girlfriend and—"

"Killian has a girlfriend?" she asked, unable to conceal her surprise.

"Um, yes. He doesn't know anything about this phone call."

She remained silent, so I rushed in, "I can't pretend to know what you've been through, and maybe if I were in your shoes, I'd never be able to forgive the person responsible…but Killian loved Johnny. He feels so incredibly guilty. It was a horrible accident, and I am so, so sorry for your loss. And for your son's loss. But Killian needs your forgiveness. You have no idea how much it would mean to him if you could just… forgive him."

Once again, she was silent. I checked my phone to make sure our call was still connected. "Anna?"

"Do you love Killian?"

"Yes. I do. He's a good man. I mean, sometimes he acts like an asshole, but, you know, for the most part…he's great."

She laughed a little. It made me smile and gave me hope, so I forged on.

"I called you because I care about him. So much. And if there's anything I can do to make his life better, I'll do it."

"That's how I felt about Johnny."

"Then you know how it feels…" I let my sentence drift off, not sure if I was saying all the right things or all the wrong ones. "Will you at least consider it? It would mean the world to him if you—"

"I need to go," she said, cutting me off. "I'm glad Killian found someone who cares about him."

Anna cut the call and I looked at Connor who was standing in the open doorway of Killian's bedroom. "I didn't even hear you come home."

"I move like a ninja," he joked. He ran his hand over his hair and let out a ragged breath. "What did she say?"

There was no point in pretending. He'd obviously heard my end of the conversation. "I'm not sure she'll ever forgive him."

He crossed the room in a few long strides and sat next to me on the bed. "I think he needs to find a way to forgive himself. People don't always act the way we want. They don't always say the words we want to hear. Sometimes…you just need to find a way to make your own peace with that."

Connor's face was sad, contemplative. He was speaking from experience. These guys had never had it easy. Abandoned by their mother. Abused by their father. Instinctively, I reached for his hand. He pulled me to my feet and into a hug. "You make him happy and you've given him something he's never had," he said, releasing me. "Don't underestimate the power of love. He'll be okay."

My ringing phone interrupted my thoughts. "Hangover rating on a scale of one to ten," Hailey said when I answered.

"Mine is on the low spectrum. I'll go with a three." Last night, Hailey, Ava, and I had a girls' night out. It started with barbecue in a converted garage and ended with drinks at a bar that played nineties hip-hop. At two in the morning, Killian met us at the bar and chauffeured us home. No major incidents to report, thankfully. "How's yours?"

"Not bad," she said, sounding surprised.

"That's because we were smart this time. The key is to pig out on ribs and all those sides we ate. It soaked up all the alcohol. We were so sensible. We should be commended, really."

Killian snorted. I glared at him. "Baby, you were wasted."

"I was not," I said indignantly.

"You always come home, singing "Nasty Girl"?" Connor asked.

"Of course. Everyone loves The Notorious B.I.G.

Hailey laughed at our banter. "Where are you?"

"Forever Ink. Killian needed someone to hold his hand. You know what a big baby he is."

That earned me more snorts all around.

"Have you heard from Ava yet?" she asked.

"Uh, no." I eyed Connor who was too busy breaking into a sweat and focusing on his masterpiece to notice. "She's probably not on the low end of the scale."

"Yeah, she was pretty wasted," Hailey said. "Is Connor doing the tattooing?"

"Yep."

"Okay. Talk to you later. I need to get ready for work."

After we hung up, I sent a quick text to Ava, asking how she was feeling. Last night, she went from happy drunk to crying drunk in a nanosecond, so maybe I should rethink the part about no major incidents. The reason for her tears was sitting directly across from me, his steady hand holding a tattoo machine.

Two minutes later, my phone rang, and this time it was Ava.

"Hey, Ava. Are you okay?"

She groaned. "Stop talking so loud."

"Sorry," I whispered but she probably couldn't hear it over the buzzing of the tattoo machine and the rock music.

"Where are you?"

"Um, Forever Ink."

"Oh." Ava went silent for a few seconds. "In that case, I'll talk to you later."

"I can go outside, if you want."

"Ava," Connor said. "Stop ignoring me."

"Did you hear that?" I asked Ava.

She sighed. "Tell him he's an asshole. He has no idea what he put me and Killian through. I'm never speaking to him again."

"If she's saying she'll never speak to me again, tell her—"

"Enough," Killian said, cutting him off. "You and Ava sort it out on your own time. Stop putting me and Eden in the middle of your shit."

"I guess you heard that too," I said into the phone.

She sighed again. "Loud and clear. *Asshole.*"

"No, he's not," I said, jumping to Killian's defense.

"Sorry," she mumbled, and I thought she'd say goodbye but in the next beat she asked, "What's the tattoo of?"

I was pretty sure she was there last night when Hailey asked, but maybe she hadn't heard. I looked at Killian's chest, as if I needed to remind myself. "Well, it's…wings. With two rows of feathers and there's a star outline on each side of the wing tips…" It was hard to describe the design. It was dark ink, like dark angel wings spanning his upper chest, which wasn't my original plan. Initially, I'd drawn one wing for his left side to go above his heart, but Killian said if he was going to do it, he was all in, so I re-did my sketch and now here we were, watching it come to life. "It's very manly, though. No wimpy angel wings for Killian."

Killian chuckled.

"It's awesome," Connor said, loudly enough for Ava to hear.

"Connor is an awesome tattoo artist," she said, but not loudly enough for him to hear.

"Yeah, he's pretty awesome," I agreed. Killian raised his eyebrows and I smiled. "So, are you," I told him.

Ava and I said goodbye and I cut the call.

"She said I was awesome?" Connor asked, his voice hopeful.

I repeated what Ava told me and he smiled, feeling like he'd scored a small victory, no doubt. If I repeated everything she said last night, he wouldn't be too happy, so I vowed to keep that conversation to myself.

"What else did she say?" Connor asked.

Killian clenched his jaw. "Don't answer that."

I didn't answer that. Killian was right—Ava and Connor needed to talk to each other.

Connor lifted the machine and sat back. "Dude, you need to sit still."

"I am sitting still."

"You're flexing your pecs."

I rubbed my index fingers together. "Naughty boy. Flexing your pecs. You should be ashamed of yourself."

"Tell Connor to stop stressing me out."

"Connor, stop stressing him out."

"How am I stressing you out?" Connor asked.

Killian held up his hand. "You need to speak through Eden. She'll relay the message."

I laughed. Connor shook his head.

"Point taken," he said, getting back to work.

Killian reached for my hand and held it in his, and over the buzzing of the tattoo machine and Led Zeppelin's "Rock and Roll", I could hear my heart slamming against my chest. I'd fallen fast, and I'd fallen hard, and I was literally inked on his skin for life. The tattoo on his chest was my design, my name was on it, and it had been inspired by his calling me a dirty angel. But it was also because I wanted to give his heart wings, instead of stabbing it with a dagger. I didn't explain the symbolism to him, but maybe he understood it without my having to tell him.

★ ★ ★

Sundays had officially become our lazy day, although Killian and I went running this morning and he went to the gym but only for an hour. I was on his living room floor with my surfer girl piece spread out in front of me. Killian had pushed back the furniture and stacked the coffee table on the sofa to accommodate my twelve-foot-long street art piece. When I sketched this piece, it was like my brain was telling me to do one thing, but my hand was doing something entirely different. But I thought my surfer girl riding inside the barrel of the wave was turning out to be a good thing.

From the kitchen, I heard the whirring of the blender. Uh oh. Not again. *Please don't test my gag reflexes with another healthy smoothie.* They were godawful. No joke. Yesterday's delightful concoction was kale and God knew what else. I took one sip and it was one sip too many.

"How is it?" he asked.

I forced myself to swallow, even though I wanted to spit it in the sink. "Terrible. It tastes like…mud…and grass. Ugh."

I kept my head down, and painted my psychedelic waves, hoping he would drink the whole batch himself.

No such luck.

"You're gonna love this one," he claimed, coming into the living room.

"I'll pass."

"I made it especially for you."

Ugh. Why did he have to sound so sweet?

My gaze traveled up his sculpted calves, to his cargo shorts, and up his bare chest, my tattoo inked on his skin, and up to his clean-shaven face. I loved his face with stubble, I loved it smooth, I loved it framed by short hair or longer hair. I especially loved it with that adorable smile. Who could say no to those dimples? Not me, apparently.

He pressed a gigantic glass of something green and frothy into my hand and watched as I took a tiny sip. He frowned at my pathetic attempt to placate him, so I took a bigger sip. At least it didn't activate my gag reflex. It wasn't bad. Another sip confirmed it was pretty good.

"Well?" he asked, prompting me to deliver my verdict.

"It's not as good as…say, cinnamon rolls or brownies…but it's drinkable. Which is a huge improvement over the last few you tried to force on me." I softened the blow with a smile.

"Drinkable? Admit it. You love it."

I took another big gulp. Love was a stretch, but I *liked* it, and it was drinkable. "Yum. I feel healthier already."

"It's good protein," he said, lowering himself onto a chair at the kitchen table nobody ever ate at. Probably because it was in the living room and covered with Connor's sketchbooks, a stack of Connor's paperbacks, a laptop, and a pile of bills Killian was sorting through.

"What's in it?" I asked.

"Kale, spinach, cucumber, green apple, hemp seeds, mango, coconut oil…" I stared at him as he continued reeling off a list of approximately six-thousand ingredients, and he remembered to name every single one.

"O-kay. You sold me on it." Because, really, anyone who had gone to so much trouble to get something healthy into my body deserved some respect for their efforts. The least I could do was drink the smoothie, so I leaned my back against the sofa and drank it while I looked out the window at the burnt-out warehouse.

Yesterday, Killian and I had walked the perimeter, casing it out. The lot adjacent to the warehouse is fenced in with chain-link but we found a gap between the two metal bars of the padlocked gate like someone pried it apart.

"It's meant to be," I'd said, thrilled we'd found an entry point which didn't require further law-breaking. But since we'd gone during the day and the sign clearly said No Trespassing, we hadn't attempted to enter. Yet. Once I finished this piece, we were going in under the cover of darkness. If we pulled it off, it would be an even bigger rush than the first piece had been.

I finished my smoothie, reveling in the heat and sunshine streaming through the windows. The temperatures had hovered in the mid-eighties for the past three days and even though it was fall, it felt like a summer's day. My phone buzzed with a reminder to attend Zeke's chill-fest, as he called it. Following swiftly on the heels of that, my dad texted to make sure I was alive and well. Ava texted to ask if Killian and I were going to Zeke's party and, if so, could she get a ride. Then Hailey texted to ask if we were going to Zeke's party and, if it wasn't too much trouble, could she bum a ride.

When I sought out Killian to inform him of our plans, he had his head stuck in the cabinet under the kitchen sink and was doing something that required a toolbox and a lot of muscle flexing. Not a bad view—his bare torso was on display. I hopped onto the counter to watch while I brought him up to speed. "We'll leave here at two, pick up Ava first, and then Hailey which is a little out of our way but not by much, and we'll hang out at Zeke and Brody's party for a couple hours. Zeke's not working tonight but we can give Brody and Chris a lift to work when we leave."

"What?" he asked, from inside the cabinet. There was a clanking noise going on down there, so he probably missed every word I said.

I sighed. "At one fifty-five, you need to put on a shirt and shoes. I'll give you further instructions then."

"Babe, I heard what you said. I'm a multi-tasker, remember?"

"Yeah, I remember. But you weren't listening because you

asked, 'What?'"

His head popped out, and he stood and turned on the faucet. Apparently, he'd fixed whatever problem I hadn't noticed existed because he turned off the water and packed up his tools, satisfied with his work. He came to stand between my legs and ran his hands up my thighs. I watched his blue eyes darken as his hands continued their journey, all talk of the party forgotten. I wrapped my arms around his neck and asked him to repeat what I said. He did, and he got it right, but he used fewer words to convey the message.

"So, why did you play dumb?" I asked.

"I didn't. You never told me about this party. Neither did Zeke or Brody."

"It's an impromptu thing. They decided last night. They told me to tell you."

He raised his brows. "And did you?"

Ooops. "Uh huh. Five minutes ago."

"Sounds like a communication breakdown."

"Hmm. How can I make it up to you?"

He nuzzled my neck and murmured, "I'm sure you'll think of something." He brushed a kiss on my jawbone, and then his lips met mine. My legs cinched around his waist as he deepened the kiss, and my body responded the same way it always did with him. I craved him like a drug I could never get enough of. I was starting to understand addiction because Killian was quickly becoming mine.

"Pretend I'm not here," Connor said. I pulled away from Killian and looked over his shoulder at Connor who scrubbed his hand over his hair and yawned. Connor slept a lot, I'd noticed, and I wondered if it had something to do with giving up drugs. Like Killian, he was shirtless and wearing nothing but cargo shorts. After being in Florida for five months, his skin was bronzed darker than Killian's. I had to say the view of Connor's torso wasn't bad either.

Connor stuck his head in the fridge, slammed it shut, opened, and closed every cupboard, and returned to the fridge, as if he was expecting something new and different to jump out at him. I could save him the trouble of looking for something quick and easy. Everything in this house was healthy and required cooking or preparation. There was no junk food, no empty carbs, and nothing with refined sugar.

Having reached the same conclusion, Connor grabbed a bottle of water from the fridge and guzzled it. "What are you guys up to?" he asked, wiping his mouth with the back of his hand.

"We're going to an impromptu chill-fest." Without thinking it through, I invited Connor to join us.

"Ava gonna be there?" he asked.

I nodded.

"I'm coming."

Uh oh.

Killian turned around to face Connor and crossed his arms over his chest. "Just so we're clear, do not drag Eden or me into your drama." Connor opened his mouth to speak, but Killian held up his hand to stop him. "I work with these guys. So, keep your mouth shut about my personal life."

Connor adopted the same crossed-arm pose. "I never told anyone outside this room jack shit, and you know it. What happened with Seamus was a long time coming and I apologized to Eden and I apologized to you. But I'm not sorry I said it. He needs to be reminded of what he did. If you want to move on from something, you can't bury it inside. You need to shine the light on it. You need to work through it before you can let it go."

That was very true, and I thought Connor was brave and

smart for voicing it. I sat still, barely breathing, as they faced off. This could go either way but neither of them backed off or stalked away which was a good sign. Neither of them said a word for a few long moments either. Killian's shoulders were rigid, and I could feel the tension rolling off him.

"You learn this in your NA meetings?" Killian asked finally.

"Yeah, I did."

Killian lowered his head and rubbed the back of his neck. "Okay."

Connor nodded. "Okay."

And that was the end of it. They'd made their peace, and Connor pulled a frying pan out of the cupboard and eggs out of the refrigerator. He stuck birdseed bread in the toaster and asked us if we wanted any food, which we declined. I went upstairs to get ready, and Killian found a few odd jobs to do around the house. At one fifty-five, Killian joined me in the bedroom, donned a shirt and shoes, packed a duffel with our work clothes, and it was time to go.

No major drama occurred on the drive to the chill-fest or at the chill-fest itself. We hung out on Zeke and Brody's patio, drinking Zeke's special watermelon slammers on a sunny September day, with a reggae soundtrack that gave the whole atmosphere a chilled, happy vibe. Zeke's washed-out orange T-shirt said "Life is Good," and as I looked around at my friends, laughing and talking, and at Killian whose arm was slung over my shoulder while we talked to Brody about his world travels, I couldn't agree more.

Life was good.

"What's your favorite place for a vacation?" Killian asked later, when were behind the bar, chopping fruit.

"The beach."

"Me too. Ever been to Montauk?"

I shook my head. I'd heard people at the bar talking about it, so I knew it was in the Hamptons, but that was all I knew.

"You'll love it. I'm taking you there," he promised, and I knew it would happen because Killian's promises were never empty.

Chapter Thirty-Four

Killian

F OUR DAYS AFTER HIS PARTY, ZEKE ASKED ME TO MEET HIM FOR coffee.

"The things I do for you," I told Eden, my phone pressed to my ear as I left the bar to meet Zeke. "If he's wearing that flowered shirt, I'm leaving."

Eden laughed. "I think it's sweet. You and Zeke are bonding."

"I'll see him at work in less than an hour," I said, striding up South Fourth Street. "Why does he need to drag me away—"

"Be nice."

"Yeah, yeah. What are you wearing?"

"I'm naked," she said, in her sexy, sultry voice.

"Jesus. Don't tell me that. You're doing your art naked?"

"Mm. I'm covered in paint. *All* the colors."

"I'm coming home. Fuck coffee."

She laughed. "Connor's here. You really think I'd roll around on your living room floor naked in front of your brother?"

Good point. She'd better not. I stopped outside a real estate agent's office and glanced at the photos and listings. I already knew what I wanted, and it wasn't in this window. "You almost done with that piece?"

"I'm hoping to finish it tomorrow. Will you be ready to trespass and help me paste illegal artwork tomorrow night?"

"I think you know the answer to that." Although, if the

fire escape on the side of the warehouse wasn't sturdy enough, we'd need to find a new spot. I didn't mention that, though. She had her heart set on pasting that piece on the tower above the warehouse.

I heard Connor in the background asking Eden if she wanted pizza tonight. "Sounds good. Pepperoni?"

"Hell yeah," he said. "I'll even let you pick the movie."

"You're too good to me. It's a date."

"Hey," I said, getting her attention. "Remember which brother you get naked for. The one who loves you."

"Ooh. You're pulling out the big guns."

"Oh baby, you know it. Size matters."

"I never realized how much until I met you."

"Luke had a small dick?" I asked, unable to help myself.

"Well…it was normal. Not…you know, like you."

Damn, I wished I could see her face. I bet she was blushing right now. On my end, I was stupidly happy I'd won the biggest dick contest.

"Just for that, I'm going to treat you to the Killian special tonight."

"What's on that menu?" she asked.

"Dessert. A lot of it. I'm starving."

"You don't like sweet things."

"I like *your* sweet thing." I let out a low moan. "You taste so good."

"Okay, you can stop now. It's getting hot in here."

I chuckled. If I hadn't already reached the coffee shop, I would keep teasing her. "I'm at the coffee shop." I saw Zeke through the window, busy doing something on his phone.

"Say hi to Zeke for me, and if Daniel's there, tell him I missed him today."

I snorted. Like I'd pass on that message. I stepped inside the shop, the bell over the door alerting him to my presence, and Daniel's gaze swung to me. Was he the only one who worked here? "I'm not your social secretary," I said. "I don't have that kind of time."

"Love you," she said.

"Ditto."

"Ditto? What kind of answer is that?"

"I'm in the coffee shop, standing in front of Daniel."

Daniel who just winked at me and was doing a full-body scan. Daniel whose name I'd never known after one year of ordering coffee from him. But now I knew it because Eden was all chummy with him. She probably gave him updates on the progress of our relationship.

"Okay, it's not like we need to say it every day," she said, but I heard the disappointment in her voice.

"I love you, Eden," I said, loud and clear.

"Sa-woon," Daniel said, gripping the counter for support after Eden and I said our goodbyes. A little over the top there, Daniel.

I exhaled loudly. He didn't get the message. He kept staring at me while he chatted about my relationship with Eden. "Coffee," I reminded him, jerking my chin at the brewed coffee behind him.

He shot me a finger gun and winked. "Gotcha."

What felt like a million years later, I had the coffee in my hand, and took a seat across from Zeke.

"Thanks for meeting me," he said, with more formality than I'd ever heard him use before. It immediately put me on the alert. "I wanted to catch you alone. There's something I needed to talk to you about."

Oh shit. Zeke and I had two things in common—work and Eden. I'd only discuss one of those things with Zeke, and it wasn't Eden.

"You unhappy at work?"

He shook his head. "No. Not at all. Listen, I could be off-base here, but I don't think I am. I've known you for over a year now and…"

"Zeke." I motioned with my hand for him to get on with it.

"Right." He took a deep breath and let it out. This did not look good. I'd never seen this serious expression on his face before. His leg kept bouncing up and down. I wanted to reach under the table and smack it down. Instead, I took a drink of my coffee. "Okay, here's the deal. I want to be a partner in the bar."

"Come again?"

"I want to invest in the bar. What are your thoughts on that?"

I had a lot of thoughts on that, but I voiced the most obvious one first. "Why isn't Louis here? He's my partner."

"Yeah, I know. But if you want out, I'd like to buy your share."

I crossed my arms and narrowed my eyes at him. "What makes you think I want out?"

"Just a hunch," Zeke said.

Just a hunch. Right. In the form of a conversation with Eden, no doubt. What had she said to Zeke? I'd talk to her about this later. She could have warned me in advance.

"Eden didn't say anything, in case that's what you're thinking."

"You just came up with this on your own?"

"Yeah, I did." He looked me right in the eye, with an open, honest face. Nothing to hide. Zeke wasn't bullshitting me.

"Assuming I did want out…" I did want out, but I had no idea what I'd do if I weren't running a bar. I'd been thinking about buying a loft in a converted warehouse on the waterfront in Greenpoint. If I bought a two-bedroom, Eden could move in with me and Connor, and stop paying rent on her place. I still had a lot of money from my fighting career, but I'd always been a saver. If I spent the money in my account, I worried I wouldn't be able to replace it. "Where are you going to get that kind of money?" I asked, although I didn't know why I bothered. Daddy was loaded.

"My dad is looking to make an investment," he said, confirming my suspicions.

"Right."

"I know how that must sound to you, but he made it clear this would be a loan. I'd pay him back. Eventually."

I let that one go. None of my business. "I thought you didn't want the aggravation," I said. "Or responsibility."

"I didn't. But things have changed. I'm ready to man up."

I didn't bother pointing out that getting your daddy to invest in your latest passing fancy wasn't exactly manning up.

"How much was your initial investment?" he asked me.

I didn't answer. Zeke was undeterred by my silence. "Half a million?" he guessed. He was pretty damn close. It was north of that, but not by much.

"Close enough." I leaned back in my chair and gave him an appraising look. Zeke still looked like a rich kid who'd lived a good life and had never wanted for anything. He was only two years younger than me, but life had gone easy on him, so the age difference felt more like a decade. Zeke was carefree and easygoing and even if I'd consider letting him buy me out, I didn't know how well he'd handle the responsibility.

It was one thing to show up for work on time, follow the rules, and do a good job, but when the night was over, so was his job. He didn't need to worry about renewing the liquor license, paying the taxes, doing the shitload of work required to keep a bar running day in and day out. Louis was over there right now, dealing with a beer distributor who had jacked up the prices. I told the guy we were taking our business elsewhere. Louis claimed I'd been too hasty. We'd see how far he got by 'calmly discussing the situation'. Chances were, we'd take our business elsewhere.

As I was thinking this, Louis texted. *Fuck him. I'm calling other distributors.*

I chuckled and sent him a reply. *Good plan. Why didn't I think of that?*

"There's something I never told you," Zeke said.

Oh Jesus. I didn't need to hear Zeke's confessions. "Unless it's job-related, I don't need to hear it."

"It's kind of related. I've been to a lot of your fights. I even met you once about five years ago. And I followed you on social media."

I stared at him. What the fuck?

"I wanted to tell you during our interview, but you were… it wasn't a good time to mention it."

No shit. I met Zeke one month after I walked away. Not a good time for anything. "You're an MMA fan?"

"My dad's company was one of your sponsors. Sterling Technologies."

It was the first sponsorship I'd gotten, and it was a big one. Fuck, I had no idea Zeke's dad owned that company. I rubbed my hands over my face. This coffee meeting was full of surprises, and not all of them were good. "What do you want from me?"

"Maybe you should look at this differently. It's what I could do for you." He held up his hands. "Just hear me out. My dad chose you personally. Out of all the fighters he could have sponsored, he wanted you. Not just because you won more than lost.

But because you had a presence in and out of the Octagon, and you made a positive impression in both places. When we met, you were a different person than the guy on social media, the guy I met the first time, and the one who used to be a fighter."

Why was everyone trying to analyze me? This shit was getting old.

"I'm sorry I disappointed you," I said sarcastically.

"The point I'm trying to make is you don't belong in the bar business. But I do. And I'm not just a pretty face. I have a business degree from Columbia. I'm a better people person than you because I actually like people whereas you're more…selective. I notice shit that's going on around me. I know your beer distributor is ripping you off. Just like I knew Chad was. And Ava deserves a raise. She built the business through her social media savvy, just like she built your brand in the UFC."

I raised my brows. "How do you know that?"

"Good guess. You're not that tech savvy."

"And I guess you are."

"You'd guess right."

I'd underestimated Zeke. In fact, I barely recognized the guy sitting across from me. If he'd told me any of this a few months ago, I would have shot him down within the first two seconds. But now I was listening to his opinions. What had the world come to? I was declaring my love in coffee shops, considering a move to a waterfront loft so Eden had good light in a building with good security. I'd gone rug shopping with her and hadn't complained about it. I didn't slam out of my house when she overheard all the shit that went down in my life. I made peace with Connor even though I was tempted to kick him out, punch him in the face, or stuff his head in the toilet bowl to shut him the fuck up.

The house of cards had fallen, but I was still standing, and

Eden was still standing by my side. Despite everything, she loved my fucked-up self and accepted me exactly as I was. I had nothing to hide from her anymore, and I'd never known this kind of freedom. Now, I was listening to Zeke. Unbelievable how much my life had changed.

"Just think about it. That's all I'm asking. This could be a win for both of us. Louis likes me. I'm sure he'd come around when he figured out I'm serious and I could be an asset to the business. Not saying you're not good. You're very good at what you do. But it's not your jam."

"Not my jam."

He gave me one of his shit-eating grins. "Nope. I'm offering to lighten your load. Free you up for something you're better at."

"And what's that?" Jesus. Was I asking his advice now?

"You still have all the skills of a fighter and your name holds currency. Use it."

Yeah, that's what I thought. Not happening. I was a one-trick pony.

When are you gonna smarten up and get back to fighting? It's the only thing you're good at.

But I promised Zeke I'd think about his offer. While we prepped the bar for opening, I did think about it. I also thought about what he'd said about my fighting skills. I'd never step foot inside the Octagon again, but that didn't mean I couldn't teach other people those skills. As I worked next to Zeke, I felt something taking hold—something I hadn't felt in so long, I almost didn't recognize it. Hope. Possibility. *It's a new day and a world of possibility.* I was starting to believe in this world of possibility.

Throughout the night, my belief grew. Until I got the phone call from Eden that changed everything.

Chapter Thirty-Five

Killian

"THESE GUYS ARE IN THE HOUSE...THEY SAID...IF THE cops come, they'll kill Con—" Eden broke off on a sob.

Ice froze my spine. I pressed the phone closer to my ear. "Where are you?"

"Locked in the bathroom."

"I'm on my way." I ignored the customers and held out my hand to Zeke. "Your phone."

"My phone?"

I wiggled my fingers. He handed it over, a perplexed look on his face. I didn't have time to play nice or make explanations. "Baby, it's going to be okay."

"Okay," she whispered.

I pushed past Louis and strode out of the bar. On her end, I heard a pounding on the door and she whimpered. A man's voice said, "Call the cops, and you're as good as dead."

Fuck, fuck, fuck.

"I'm just using the toilet," she said, her voice strong. "Who are you and why are you here?"

I climbed into my Jeep and jammed my keys in the ignition, trying to think fast. The bathroom was the worst room to be trapped in. The only window was above the shower. Too high to reach and too small to climb out of.

"Baby, listen to me...don't say anything. Everything is

going to be okay. I'm coming for you. If they get to you first, use everything at your disposal…spray them with deodorant… anything. Put your phone in the cabinet. Turn on the shower and flush the toilet." What the fuck was I saying? Nothing helpful, that was for damn sure. She did as I asked, and I waited until I heard the water running and the toilet flushing before I called Seamus on Zeke's phone.

He was a shitty excuse for a father, but he was a good cop. He answered on the second ring, and I wasted no time with greetings. "I need you. At my house. They've got Connor and… Eden," I said, keeping my voice low.

He didn't hesitate, and for that, I was grateful. "Who? How many?"

"I don't know."

"Armed?"

"Yes." It was a guess but probably a good one. "They said no cops."

"I'm on my way. Wait for me. Don't go in without me."

I cut the call and turned onto Kent Avenue, listening for anything I could hear on Eden's phone. The sound was muffled, but I heard her screaming. They'd gotten to her. Fuck, fuck, fuck. Please God, no, not her.

What have you done, Connor?

This was no time to think about the worst-case scenario or I'd lose my shit. I needed to stay focused. As much as I wanted to bust through the door on my own, Seamus was right. I needed to wait for him.

Thankfully, he wasn't far behind me. When I climbed into the passenger seat of his black SUV and shut the door, I smelled the whiskey on his breath. Shit.

"Under your T-shirt," he barked, handing me under armor. The vest was lightweight, Kevlar I guessed. Vest on under my T-shirt, he handed me a Glock 17. "Remember how to use it?" he asked.

"Yeah." I checked the safety before I tucked it into my back waistband while he barked out more instructions. It boiled down to following his lead and not losing my shit.

"Leave your emotions outside the door," he said, and I briefly wondered if that was what he used to do when he came home at night all those years ago.

"If you help them, I'll do anything you ask. Anything you want…I'll do it."

He didn't answer until we were two doors down from my house. "Forgive me," he said, his voice gruff.

I gave him a look. He was serious. I'd say anything right now, make a deal with the devil himself if it meant he'd help me. "Done."

Seamus nodded once to indicate he'd heard me. I didn't have time to think about what he'd asked of me or what I'd granted him. In the SUV, he said we were lucky—if the men had been smart, they would have taken Connor and Eden to a remote location. We still didn't know what they wanted, but we both suspected it was drug-related, and whatever Connor had been doing in Florida, the trouble had followed him here.

These men might be idiots, but that didn't make them any less dangerous.

Chapter Thirty-Six

Eden

When I came to, I was lying on the living room floor, curled on my side, bound at the ankles, my arms behind my back and my wrists bound. My head was too heavy to lift off the floor. I tried to bring my eyes into focus. Everything was blurry. *Connor.* Oh my God. I wished I had stayed unconscious. He was bare-chested and tied to a kitchen chair, his face almost unrecognizable—pulpy flesh and so much blood. My stomach heaved, and I vomited on the floor. Nobody noticed. They were too busy meting out punishment to worry about me.

"Not so pretty anymore, pretty boy," a man with dark hair and a goatee said. Another man with ginger hair stood behind Connor. "You know what we do to snitches? We carve them up and feed them to the fish."

The man with the goatee flicked open a switchblade and made a cut in Connor's chest. Oh my God, no.

Connor's head lolled to the side. He didn't make a sound as the man carved his chest with the blade of a knife. I prayed, for his sake, he'd lost consciousness and couldn't feel the pain. I heard footsteps headed in my direction. I closed my eyes and feigned unconsciousness. I was lying in a pool of my own vomit.

"What are we gonna do with her?" a man's voice asked. "She's a pretty thing."

"She's got puke all over her. I hate puke," the other man

said. I recognized his voice. He was the one who kicked down the bathroom door.

"What did you do to her head?"

"I clocked her with the butt of my gun."

"What'd you do that for? Nobody said nothing about a girl."

"She fucking blinded me with deodorant and kicked me in the nuts."

"Pussy."

Someone picked my head up by the hair and dragged me across the floor. "Shame for her she was in the wrong place, wrong time."

He released his grip, and my head hit the floor with a clunk.

"Maybe we should have our fun with her before—"

I opened my eyes and snarled at him. "Get away from me."

"Or what?" he taunted, crouching in front of me. He wasn't the guy who broke down the bathroom door. This one looked like a big teddy bear with light brown hair, a beard, and warm brown eyes. Maybe I could appeal to his softer side.

"You seem like a nice guy. You don't want to hurt anyone. How did you get messed up in all this?"

"Shut up, bitch," the other guy said.

"Who are you guys? And why are you here?"

The guy in front of me reached out a hand and tucked my hair behind my ear. "Let me go," I whispered. "I won't say a word to any—"

"I told you to shut the fuck up," the other guy said. He lifted me into a sitting position. I didn't even see it coming. His fist slammed into my cheekbone. My head flew back and hit the wall behind me. Tears sprang to my eyes and I squeezed them shut.

I slumped onto the floor, unable to summon the energy to

hold myself upright. "You won't get away with this," I said, my teeth gritted. He kicked me in the stomach, knocking all the air out of my lungs. I groaned and drew my knees to my chest. My stomach heaved, and I vomited again. Coughing and gagging on the bitter bile, the only thing left in my stomach.

The guy crouched in front of me, getting right in my face. "You gonna shut up now?"

Using every ounce of strength left in my body, I lifted my head off the ground and spit in his face. His meaty hands wrapped around my throat and squeezed. This was how it would end. This was how I was going to die, I thought, as stars danced behind my closed eyes.

"Get your fucking hands off her," Killian roared.

Killian came for us.

The man's body was ripped away from me. I coughed and took big gulps of air. Connor and I would be safe now. Killian would make sure of it.

Shots rang out and I forced my eyes open.

A bullet hit Killian in the chest. He staggered backward, and another bullet ripped through his chest. I was screaming but gunfire drowned out my voice.

I squeezed my eyes shut and curled into a ball as the world blew up all around me.

From somewhere far away, I heard police sirens wailing, shouts and heavy footsteps.

I let the darkness suck me under.

Killian was dead.

Chapter Thirty-Seven

Killian

THE BULLET EXPLODED FROM MY GUN AND HIT HIM IN THE chest. His eyes widened in surprise as he fell to the ground, landing on top of Eden's curled-up body. For a second, I froze and stared at the gun in my hand.

"I said no cops!" a man shouted. I swung my gaze to him. He held his gun to Connor's head. "Nooo!" I roared. I lunged for him and knocked him off balance, my gun clattering to the floor. I was about to finish the job, but someone got me into a rear headlock. I locked in his leg with my foot, turned, and threw him to the ground. Shots rang out behind me. The man who'd been holding a gun to Connor's head staggered and fell. Seamus moved closer and stood over him, putting another bullet in the man's chest.

"Police. Drop your weapons."

The words were barely out when another shot was fired. And another. One hit Seamus in the neck, and the other one in the head. I looked at the man with dark hair and a goatee, the last one standing, the one I'd thrown to the ground. He met my gaze and drew his gun. He was three feet away, and I was unarmed. Slowly, I raised my arms in the air. The fucker shot me in the chest. All the air got knocked out of my lungs. Staggering from the blow, I hit the floor as bullets riddled the man's body.

Everything around me played out in slow-motion as I got to my feet, wheezing and clutching my chest. Officers and paramedics spurred into action while I stood still amid destruction and chaos. My eyes met Deacon Ramsey's across the room. He gave me a little nod, acknowledging he'd just saved my life, before he crouched behind Connor's chair and cut off the ties binding him.

I hauled the dead man's body off Eden and checked her pulse. It was faint. I pressed my ear to her heart, needing to hear it was still beating. Pulling her into my arms, I sat on the floor, holding her. I looked down at her face. Bruised and battered. Her hair matted to her head, vomit clinging to her golden-blonde locks.

Her eyelids fluttered open. "Killian?" Her voice was hoarse and so quiet, I strained to hear her. "Are we dead?"

All around us was a sea of blood and dead bodies.

"Baby…" Oh God. "Everything will be okay. Everything will be…." My voice cracked. She closed her eyes. I leaned my head against the wall and cried like a fucking baby. I'd cried twice in my life before this. The day my mother left, and the day Johnny was pronounced dead. All those times Seamus had knocked me around, I never shed a fucking tear. But now it felt like I would never stop crying.

An officer crouched in front of me and put her hand on my shoulder. I knew her. Officer Healey. "Killian, we're taking Connor to the hospital." I watched the paramedics get Connor onto a stretcher, his face so bloody and battered, it looked as if he'd been Mike Tyson's punching bag, and the word SNITCH carved in his chest. "We'll need your statement…" she continued, but I only heard half of what she said as she cut the ties off Eden. I rubbed Eden's wrists and hands, trying to get the circulation back. "The paramedics will take her out—"

"I'll carry her to the ambulance."

She studied my face, then nodded.

I winced as I got to my feet, struggling to get enough air into my lungs. Getting shot at close range hurt like a motherfucker. At first, the adrenaline had blocked out the pain, but it was hitting me now.

Officer Healey eyed my T-shirt, riddled with bullet holes. I'd been shot three times, but I'd gotten so damn lucky they'd gone for the chest every time. "They'll check you out in the ambulance," she said. "You probably cracked a few ribs."

* * *

Four, as it turned out. With bruises all over my chest. Other than taping up my ribs, there was nothing they could do. On the ride to the hospital, the paramedics hooked Eden up to an IV, explaining she was dehydrated after vomiting so much, and tested her vitals. I washed Eden's face with a damp cloth and tried to get the vomit out of her hair the best I could.

"Can you tell me what your name is?" the paramedic asked Eden. He shone a light in each eye, checking her pupils.

"Eden," she mumbled, her eyes closing.

"Good. Can you tell me what day of the week it is?"

She didn't answer for a few seconds. "Sunday?"

I closed my eyes. Fuck. "We went to Zeke's party on Sunday. Remember?"

"Yes," she said, but it came out sounding more like a question.

"Four days ago," I prompted.

"It's…Wednesday. No…Thursday. Right?"

"Right." I glanced at the paramedic, worried it was a bad sign she didn't know the fucking day of the week. He continued asking questions, his facial expression giving nothing away as to the severity of her head injury. She didn't get all the answers right. She wasn't even sure why she was in an ambulance.

"It's post-traumatic amnesia," he told me, as if this should set my mind at ease.

"I can still smell him," she whispered. "He's suffocating me."

Why hadn't I gotten that man's body off her immediately? She'd been buried under the weight of a dead man who weighed at least two hundred pounds.

The bruise on her forehead scared the shit out of me. It was raised and swollen. She whimpered as I pressed the ice pack on it. It looked as if someone had planted their fist in her face too, bruising her cheekbone. And the paramedics had cut open her T-shirt, exposing another bruise on her stomach.

"Tell me she's going to be okay," I said to the paramedic as the hospital came into view. My voice sounded strange. Like a desperate man, begging for a sliver of hope. A ray of sunshine on a bleak day. *She* was my sunshine. Didn't they know I'd be lost without her?

He flung open the back doors of the ambulance. "We'll get her in for an MRI."

That didn't put my mind at ease. Memories of Johnny flashed through my head as I walked into the emergency room, holding Eden's hand. I'd never seen her face this pale. All the color had been drained out of her.

"Killian?"

I squeezed her hand. "I'm here, baby."

Her eyes filled with tears. "I love you. So much."

"I love you too."

She clung to my hand like it was her lifeline. "Don't leave me."

"I won't leave you."

Unfortunately, I couldn't keep my promise. They whisked

Eden away to run tests, and I was told Connor had been taken into surgery to repair his fractured jaw with titanium plates and screws. I was left behind to fill out paperwork for Connor and Eden. After I filled it out, including Eden's insurance information I'd stored in my phone, I was relegated to the waiting area. It smelled like BO and chemical air freshener. Two guys sitting across from me were stuffing their faces with McDonald's. The smell made me nauseous on a good day. Tonight, I wanted to wrestle the bag out of their hands and throw it out the door. I moved to the farthest corner of the room and leaned against the wall. I called Louis and then Ava. I told them the same story. There'd been a break-in. Connor and Eden were being treated now but they would be okay. I said it because it was what I needed to believe.

"I'm calling an Uber," Ava said, her voice shaky, on the verge of tears. I hadn't even given her the details yet. I'd wait until I saw her in person to try to prepare her for the shock of seeing Connor. "See you soon."

I stared at the phone in my hand, knowing I needed to make another call, but I dreaded it. I closed my eyes as the phone rang. Once. Twice. And then his voice in my ear. "Killian."

"Hello, sir. It's…Eden." I swallowed hard. "She's going to be fine," I said quickly, to set his mind at ease.

Please, God, don't turn me into a liar.

"What happened?" Jack Madley asked.

"There was a break-in at my house. Eden was there with my brother, Connor. I was at work."

"A break-in?"

"I don't know the whole story yet. We just got to the hospital."

"Tell me what you do know."

I told him what I knew, keeping my voice low so nobody

else in the ER waiting room could overhear. As I said the words, I felt like I was talking about someone else, not me. I'd killed a man. Five men were dead, one of which was the man who had raised me. Jack listened without interrupting. "I'm on my way," he said when I finished my story. "Text me the address of the hospital. I'll be there as soon as I can."

I pinched the bridge of my nose. "Okay."

"And Killian?"

"Yeah."

"I'm sorry about your father."

"Thank you."

"But as a father, it's my duty to protect my daughter."

"I understand." I'd promised to keep her safe, but I'd failed. All I'd ever wanted was to keep her safe, but it turned out I was the biggest danger. If she'd never gotten involved with me, she wouldn't be in the hospital.

"Good. We'll talk about this later."

He cut the call. I closed my eyes and took a few deep breaths. "I need to get your statement." I opened my eyes and looked at Deacon Ramsey. You'd never know he'd just been involved in a shoot-out. Ramsey looked cool, confident, and unruffled. Even his dirty-blond hair looked like he'd just styled it for a night out. We'd gone to high school together. Back then, he had been more into partying and breaking the law than enforcing it. Seeing him in NYPD blues still took me by surprise. "You look like you could use a coffee."

"I could use something a hell of a lot stronger than coffee," I said

He grinned. "Left my hip flask at home."

We walked to the vending machines in the hallway, and he fed money into the slot. I watched the cup drop and fill up with 'gourmet coffee' according to the machine. He handed me the cup and got one for himself.

"Getting shot hurts like hell," he said, eying my ripped-up T-shirt as he took a sip of coffee.

Like getting hit in the chest with a hammer. "I've had worse."

"I bet you have. Shame about your old man," he said, not sounding sorry.

I side-eyed him. To hear most of the cops talk, you'd think my father walked on water.

Two kids and a woman stood in front of the vending machines, studying their options. Ramsey jerked his chin, gesturing me to follow him for some privacy.

"Any idea what Connor was involved in?" he asked when we got outside, standing a good distance away from the parked ambulances.

"No."

"Where's he been for the past few months?"

"You've been keeping tabs on Connor?"

"Just looking out for him."

Before tonight, the last time I'd seen Deacon Ramsey, he'd been first on the scene of Connor's motorcycle accident. It had been a hit and run and it hadn't been Connor's fault. Thankfully, he hadn't been driving under the influence, but he'd been in possession. Ramsey had called me, instead of busting Connor. I'd hauled Connor's ass to rehab. Three days after he got out of rehab, Connor disappeared. And now here we were, six months later, outside a hospital because of whatever the fuck Connor did in Miami.

"He was in Miami," I said.

"You think he was working as an informant?"

"I don't know." It was what I suspected. Which meant he'd gotten busted for drugs and cut a deal with the cops. Which also meant he'd lied to me.

"Tell me what happened tonight."

I told him everything, including the details I'd left out when I'd given Jack Madley a summary.

"He had his hands wrapped around her throat," Ramsey said, trying to get his facts straight. "And when you ripped him off her, he drew a gun."

"Right," I said, looking him in the eye. "He shot me twice. I shot back."

He nodded. "It was self-defense. But it might come back to haunt you."

I killed a man, but this time I didn't feel any guilt. I'd do it again if I had to just to save Eden. "Thanks," I said, rubbing the back of my neck. "For what you did."

"Just doing my job."

By doing his job, he'd saved my life. And Seamus had saved Connor's. It had been his final act and I wondered now, if he'd had a premonition he would die tonight. Why else would he have asked for my forgiveness when he'd never shown any signs of remorse before? Did I forgive him? I wasn't ready to think about Seamus or our complicated history yet. I wasn't ready to unravel all my tangled-up emotions either.

Right now, all I needed was to know Eden and Connor would be okay. All the rest of it…I'd deal with later.

Chapter Thirty-Eight

Eden

I FELT LIKE I WAS UNDERWATER TRYING TO SWIM TO THE SURFACE. I opened my eyes and blinked. The fluorescent lights hurt my head. I looked down at the IV attached to my arm and at the hand holding mine.

I turned my head to look at him. His eyes were red-rimmed like he'd been crying, and his face was ravaged. But it was him. His beautiful face, his beautiful everything. My gaze drifted down to his chest. The faded blue T-shirt said Martha's Vineyard.

"Why are you wearing Zeke's T-shirt?" I asked, my voice sounding hoarse like I hadn't used it in a long time.

"Because…" His eyes searched my face.

I closed my eyes, remembering. My ears were still ringing from the shots fired. My stomach hurt. My head hurt. Everything hurt. "They shot you. I thought…you were dead."

"I was wearing a bullet-proof vest."

Thank God. "Why am I in the hospital?"

His fingers brushed over my cheekbone and he swept my hair off my forehead. His touch was gentle, but I winced. "You have a concussion."

I started laughing, but it bordered on hysterical. My laughter turned into sobbing that wracked my body and made everything hurt even more. Killian climbed onto the bed and held me the way he did before we went to sleep. He kept holding me until, eventually, I calmed down and my breathing regulated.

"You're in shock," he said quietly, stroking my hair. "The brain can only handle so much information..." He was trying to help me make sense of something that didn't make any sense. I lay there, letting him stroke my hair and hold me. I listened to the sound of his voice but not the words.

I pressed my body closer to his. He flinched, sucking in his breath. "You're hurt." I remembered my dad and Garrett talking about it once. Bullet-resistant vests might stop a bullet, but it would still hurt like hell.

"I'm fine," Killian said. I knew he'd say that no matter how much it hurt. He reached for my hand and laced his fingers in mine.

"Is Connor...is he...?" I whimpered.

"He'll be okay."

"But he...what..."

"Miss Madley, we need to ask you a few questions," a woman's voice said. Two police officers were standing by my bed.

"She's not ready to talk," Killian said.

"I'm sorry," the female officer said. "But we need to talk to her."

"It's okay," I said.

The female officer asked the questions, and I told her what I remembered...which wasn't much. But I wanted to help Connor, so I tried my best to remember everything I could.

"I was upstairs changing into a clean shirt when they came. I'd been painting..." Which was totally irrelevant. "Connor was downstairs. We were about to watch a movie..." More useless information. "We thought it was our pizza delivery. Before he opened the door, Connor asked who it was. I heard the guy say the name of the pizzeria we ordered from... so Connor unlocked the door..."

"Fuck," Killian muttered under his breath.

"What did the men say when they came inside?" the police officer asked.

"They called him a snitch. And they said…" I took a deep breath. Connor was alive. He was going to be okay. "…they came to kill him. I heard a scuffle and they were…they must have been beating him up. I was on the phone with Killian. I called him right away."

"And, where were you at this point?" she asked.

"In the bathroom. With the door locked. I didn't know where else to go. It's the only door upstairs with a lock."

"Then what?"

"I heard someone coming up the stairs, checking the rooms. He…" I stopped and swallowed. "Knocked down the bathroom door. I sprayed deodorant in his eyes which kind of stunned him. Then I kneed him in the junk," I said, feeling kind of proud of my handiwork. Killian chuckled under his breath, but his humor was short-lived. The police officer prompted me to continue.

I took a deep breath and let it out as the memories washed over me. "I ran out of the bathroom, but he caught me and…" My whole body was trembling.

Killian's arms tightened around me. "What did he do to you?" he asked, his voice low.

"He just…" *The cool metal of the gun pressed against my forehead. "Boom", he said, and laughed.* "He hit me in the forehead with his gun."

I told her the rest of what happened, what I remembered, and the officer took it all down and said she'd contact me if they needed more information.

"How are you holding up, Killian?" she asked.

"Except for my girlfriend getting dragged into the shit

storm of my life...fucking great."

"I'm sorry about your father. We all looked up to him."

I felt Killian nod and when the cops left my room, I asked, "What happened to your dad?" I didn't even realize he'd been there which just went to show how much I'd missed.

"He was shot," Killian said.

"But...so were you."

"He was shot in the head."

Oh my God.

I hated that man, but he came to our rescue, right along with Killian. Now he was dead. It seemed strange we survived, but the police chief died. "And...what about those men?"

Killian either didn't know or he didn't want to tell me. "You don't need to worry about them anymore."

"And Connor...shouldn't you be with him now?"

"Ava is with him."

I felt better knowing he wasn't alone. I tried not to picture his face, the pulpy flesh and blood, or the knife cutting into his chest. What did he do to deserve that? They were going to kill him after they finished torturing him. They were going to kill me too, probably. Wrong place, wrong time.

"I love you, Killian. I love you so much."

He let out a ragged breath. "I love you too."

"Don't leave me."

"I'm not going anywhere."

Chapter Thirty-Nine

Killian

I unlocked the front door of Trinity Bar and held it open for Jack Madley. "Eden told me you take it black," he said, handing me a large cardboard cup from Brickwood Coffee.

"Thanks." I'd already had three large coffees today, but I took a sip of the one he offered me and locked the door behind him. "How's Eden?"

"Ava's with her now." That didn't surprise me. In the past three days, Jack hadn't left Eden's side. She'd texted me, complaining about his helicopter parenting. He was sleeping on an air mattress on her living room floor, scared to let her out of his sight. I couldn't blame him. If I had a daughter, I'd be the same way. As it was, I'd hoped to be the one by her side, helping her through this, but I hadn't had five minutes alone with her since we'd left the hospital. "She's waking up with nightmares every night."

I lowered my head and rubbed the back of my neck. Eden hadn't mentioned that. She kept telling me she felt fine and didn't understand why everyone was making such a fuss. "I'm sorry."

He didn't respond. He looked around the inside of the bar, taking it all in. He'd asked to see where Eden worked, and her mural on the back wall, so I ushered him outside to the courtyard and sat across from him at a picnic table, drinking my coffee while he studied the wall. I couldn't tell what he was thinking.

I couldn't even tell if he liked it or thought it was any good. It pissed me off that he didn't comment on her mural, but I kept my mouth shut and waited for him to introduce the real reason he'd stopped by.

"How have you been doing?" he asked, focusing his attention on me.

"Fine." *Shitty.* This morning, I met with my father's lawyer to go over the will. Seamus had left everything to me and Connor, to be divided equally, which had surprised me. When I saw how much money he'd left us, I'd nearly fallen off my fucking chair. How had a cop accrued so much money? Granted, he'd been on the force for thirty years with a chief's salary for the last five years and all his life he'd been frugal, but that still didn't explain the three million dollars in his account. The house was mortgage-free and even though it was a crappy house, the realtor said we'd probably get a million for it. Allegedly, it was a good family home in a coveted neighborhood.

After I'd left the lawyer's office, it hit me. I didn't know anything about Seamus Vincent.

Had he been a dirty cop? Had he been getting kickbacks? His work on the force had been the one thing that had redeemed him in my eyes. His sense of right and wrong when he'd put that uniform on. But now, I wasn't certain he'd even been a good cop.

"Eden and I talked this morning," Jack said. "She told me about your background. Only because I pushed her for answers. She didn't want to betray your confidence."

My chest tightened. I'd been keeping those secrets for so long, from everyone, and it wasn't something I was comfortable talking about or even acknowledging. I wasn't thrilled Eden's father knew about my background. It felt like the odds were stacked against me. After everything that had happened, and everything he knew about me, how could I be deemed a suitable boyfriend for this man's daughter?

"I grew up in a tough neighborhood in Philly," he said. "My old man was a con artist and a gambler."

My brows raised. I hadn't expected that. Jack chuckled at my reaction. "He used to swindle old ladies out of their savings. A real stand-up guy. He'd take the winnings to Atlantic City and blow it at the craps table. Sometimes he'd win, and we'd get shiny new toys, and my mom would get a piece of jewelry. Other times he lost. And when he lost, he lost big. My mom's jewelry went to the pawn shop. She'd take on extra hours at work, clean houses, do whatever she could to put food on the table and a roof over our heads. She was always threatening to leave him. But she never did." He looked off into the distance, caught up in his memories.

"All my life, I wanted to be everything my father wasn't. When I went to Penn State, I told myself this is it. A fresh start. But I wanted to have a good time and party and all the things I wanted cost money. So, I came up with all kinds of schemes. I used to drive into Jersey or New York. The drinking age was only eighteen in those states at the time. I'd load up the trunk with cheap liquor, drive back to campus, and sell it at a huge profit. Turned out I had a knack for poker and shooting pool too. And I was a damn good hustler. By the time I was a senior, I thought I was a legend. Then I met Eden's mom. We didn't exactly travel in the same circles, but she knew who I was by reputation and she didn't want to get anywhere near me. But, for me, it was love at first sight and I wasn't about to let her go. So, I told her I'd go straight. No more shady dealings. No more hustling. That worked out great for a while. I got the girl. She kind of liked me. Up until her birthday in April. We were graduating in a month, and I decided to give her a big diamond engagement ring. But I needed money. So, I went back to my old ways. Made a shitload of cash, bought her a big shiny ring, and took her out to dinner. I proposed. She said no."

He shook his head and chuckled. "She was stubborn, that woman. And she was pissed off like you wouldn't believe."

I smiled, thinking about Eden who was also stubborn. "I can believe it."

"Yeah, I guess you can. Eden's a lot like her mother."

"So, how did you win the girl?" I asked, curious despite myself. I wondered if Eden had ever heard this story. It surprised me that Jack Madley hadn't always been straight-edge, but I respected him even more now. He'd turned his life around and had gotten out from under his father's shadow. Built a good life for himself and his family.

"The hard way. I lost the girl. She told me I had no direction in my life and I needed to get my act together. She went off and got a teaching job. I went back to Philly and fell in with my old friends again. My old man died. Heart attack. And I thought I wouldn't feel a damn thing. But months later, it hit me like a freight train. At the end of the day, he had still been my father. But what hit me the hardest was I was becoming just like him. So, I got my ass in gear and by some miracle, they accepted me into the Police Academy. Now, you'd think she would have welcomed me back with open arms. But no. I had to fight to win her back. That woman made me wait until I'd graduated from the academy before she finally decided I was worthy. It was the best thing she could have done for me. If she'd taken me back right away, I might never have finished what I'd started."

He met my gaze across the table, and I knew by the look on his face I wouldn't like what he was about to tell me. "This isn't personal, son. I like you. And I know you love my daughter and she loves you. But you have a lot of things in your life to work through."

"You're telling me I need to get my shit together."

"That's what I'm telling you."

"Before I'm worthy of Eden," I said, filling in the words he'd implied.

"I'm not saying you're not worthy. I'm saying you have a lot to deal with. And I don't want my daughter living alone in Brooklyn. I haven't told her yet but after the funeral, she's coming home with me."

My stomach twisted into knots. It didn't sound like he was talking about a short visit. I'd known this was coming. It was what I'd been dreading since I'd called him from the ER. But still, I'd held out hope he'd prove me wrong. That, for once, the other shoe wouldn't drop. "She won't be happy about that."

"You'll need to convince her it's for the best."

"You're asking me to give her up." He wasn't asking me, he was telling me.

"If it's meant to be, time apart will make your love stronger."

Time apart. I didn't want to be without her. Not for a single fucking minute. The past three days had been hard enough on me. But that was me being selfish and not putting her needs first.

"I'm going to offer to pay for art school," Jack said, sweetening the deal. He'd obviously given this a lot of thought, probably worked it all out on his three-hundred-mile drive to the hospital on Thursday night. "They have a good art school in Pittsburgh. She can live at home and do something she loves."

I was tempted to beat him to the punch. Call Eden and tell her I'd buy us an apartment and pay for her tuition at Pratt Institute. She wouldn't need to work at the bar anymore. We didn't even need to stay in Brooklyn. We'd move to the mountains or the beach. Somewhere with a good art scene. We could live anywhere she wanted to live. But this man was her father. He was a good man who only wanted the best for his daughter. He was doing this out of love. How could I argue with that? I couldn't. Any more than I could keep her safe when I'd promised him I would.

I nodded, my heart heavy. I wanted him to leave now, but he stayed, and he kept talking, telling me more things I didn't want to hear.

"I'm going to get her counseling," Jack said. "And I recommend you do the same. You've been through a lot. It helps to talk through it with a professional."

I nodded again, although I had no intention of seeing a shrink.

"I'm serious," he said. I'd been slipping lately. He'd seen the skepticism on my face. That was what happened when you bared your heart to the person you loved. I needed to start locking down my emotions again, shuttering my face so nobody could read it. "I told Sawyer the same thing. He's gotta deal with his PTSD and so do you."

"Okay," I said, to make him happy. I'd rather go nine rounds with Mike Tyson with my hands tied behind my back than sit in a shrink's office and let him analyze me.

"Good," he said, as if it was all settled and he was satisfied with the outcome. "I'm counting on you to make this plan work. Eventually, you'll realize this is the best thing you could do for her."

Jack Madley was a clever man. He knew how to use the emotional artillery in his armory against me. He was appealing to Killian, the caretaker, not to the boyfriend who felt like he'd be ripping out his own beating heart to let her go. We stood, our conversation over. Jack, at least, seemed happy with the outcome. I had that feeling of numbness inside—that nothingness I used to feel before Eden came into my life.

Before he left, Jack clapped me on the shoulder. "You ever need me, call me." I heard the sincerity in his voice. The offer was genuine, like he truly cared. "I don't usually talk this much but I'm a pretty good listener. And you're always welcome to visit Eden in Pennsylvania."

Fucking perfect. I'd get to *visit* Eden and sleep down the hall from her. And I'd been tasked with convincing her it was for the best. How could he ask so much of me yet still act like he gave a damn about me?

"Thanks." I tried to sound like I meant it even though I didn't feel an ounce of gratitude.

But I needed to remember why we'd had this chat in the first place. If Eden hadn't gotten involved with me, she wouldn't have been in my house that night. She wouldn't have had a gun held to her head. She wouldn't have been knocked out, tied up, and beaten. And she wouldn't be waking up with nightmares every night. Jack Madley wasn't the bad guy in this scenario. That honor fell to me…and to Connor, who I still couldn't bring myself to visit. If I went to see him right now, I might be tempted to strangle him with my own two hands.

Don't fuck this up for me, Connor.
You act like I don't want you to be happy.
Yeah. Why would I have ever thought that?

Chapter Forty

Killian

"Nice of you to stop by," Jared said when he opened his apartment door, his voice dripping with sarcasm.

"I've been busy," I said, even though I didn't feel I owed him an explanation. "Someone had to clean out my father's house. I summoned the housecleaning fairies, but they didn't come."

He scowled at me. "Me and Ava have been taking care of him. He's on a liquid diet. But maybe you already know that."

I knew because Ava had told me. She'd laid into me for not 'giving a shit about my own brother.' So much for hating him. Ava had been by his side since she'd arrived at the hospital. Every time I saw her now, she burst into tears. Jared glanced at the suit bag I was carrying before he brushed past me. "He can text if he needs me. His sponsor, Tate, will be stopping by in an hour to check on him." I was about to close the door when Jared turned and faced me. "What's the deal, man? He needs you."

I closed the door and locked the deadbolt, shutting out his face and his words. The deal was I hadn't trusted myself to be alone with Connor. My moods had run the gamut this week. Angry. Hurt. Sad. Part of me wanted to rip him from limb to limb and vent my rage at his carelessness. His total disregard for anyone except himself. The other part of me wanted to make this better for him, protect him, help him heal. I'd been at war with myself and I still wasn't sure which side was winning.

Taking a few deep breaths, my ribs screaming in protest, I climbed the stairs. I'd never been in Jared's apartment. It was bigger than I'd expected, open and airy with dark hardwood floors and white walls. I laid the suit bag on the dark blue velvet sofa next to Connor and took a seat on a leather chair across from him. His face was swollen, mottled with greenish yellow bruises, his eyes bloodshot with dark circles underneath like he hadn't slept all week. I averted my gaze. I couldn't bear to see him like this. He pointed the remote at the TV and turned it off, plunging the room into silence.

"I brought you a suit, shirt, tie…for the funeral tomorrow." I gestured to the bag next to him as if he couldn't figure that out for himself. I glanced at the whiteboard and marker on the coffee table. "Can you talk?"

"Hurts," he said, his voice raspier than usual. He wrote something on the whiteboard and held it up for me to see. *I'm sorry.*

Sorry wasn't good enough. Not this time. "You *lied* to me. You put Eden in danger…" I stopped talking and tried to contain my anger. Tried to shove the memories of that night to the back of my head. But they kept replaying, like a movie on an endless loop. I could still smell the metallic tang of blood. Hear the bullets exploding. See the life drain out of that man's eyes when I shot him. *I killed a man.* I watched my father die.

I wrapped an arm around my ribs to protect them. Breathing hurt. Thinking too much hurt even more.

"I need you to tell me what happened in Miami. No bullshitting me."

He wrote something on the board and held it up. *Got busted for weed and ecstasy. Cut a deal with the cops.*

It didn't surprise me, but I was disappointed my assumption had been correct. "You told me you were clean. You told me you hadn't touched drugs since you left rehab. Talk to me. With words."

"I didn't do drugs," he said, forcing the words out. He winced, and I knew it was painful for him, but right now, I didn't give a shit. Because of his actions, too many people had suffered.

"How can you look me in the eye and continue lying to me?" I asked. "After everything that happened, you're still fucking lying."

He shook his head. "Not lying."

Yeah, right, okay. He bought drugs, got busted, and they confiscated the drugs. But weed and ecstasy? Those weren't even his drugs of choice. Maybe that was his idea of getting clean. Fuck if I knew. "Who were those guys who came to the house?"

"Don't know. Never saw them." He erased the board and wrote another note. I took it from him and read. *The cops killed the drug dealer in Miami. Confiscated enough coke and weapons to grant me freedom. Told me I'd be safe. Nobody would come after me.*

"Informants *always* pay the price. You should have known better. If you had told me the truth, I would have tried to help you. And I never would have let Eden stay in that house had I'd known. All of this, everything that happened, was because of your addiction. You didn't give a fuck about anyone else. All you cared about was yourself. And scoring drugs."

"No. You've got it wrong."

"Tell me how I've got it wrong. Give me something. Anything," I pleaded. I wanted him to make this better. Somehow. Some way. I needed him to redeem himself.

He swallowed, not meeting my eyes. He couldn't give me

what I so desperately wanted—a reason to believe in him. "You just need to trust me. I never meant to…hurt anyone. Or get you involved…"

"*Trust you?* I can't trust you. And you did hurt people."

I forced myself to look at him. Behind the bruises, I saw the little boy who'd tended to my wounds, tagged behind me everywhere I went. The sweet, innocent boy who I would have done anything to protect. Chased away the monsters when he'd had bad dreams. Relegated him to the closet to keep him out of harm's way. I saw Connor at sixteen, so grateful I'd moved him out of our father's house. He used to clean the apartment and cook our dinner because I was training six hours a day and bartending at nights to pay the bills. He'd gotten a part-time job at the grocery store, stocking shelves so he could help with expenses. In the winter, Connor would buy scarves and blankets for the homeless people because he couldn't bear to see anyone suffer. He'd filled the pages of his sketchbooks with their faces. Where was that boy? The artist who portrayed human suffering and turned the ugly into something beautiful and dignified? The dreamer who wanted to make the world a better place?

Across from me sat a man I barely recognized. A liar. An addict. A person whose actions had caused so much damage I couldn't even wrap my head around it. I had never been a saint, but I would never look my brother in the eye and feed him lies. He was asking for my blind faith, but I couldn't give it to him. For the first time in my life, I needed to turn my back on him. Maybe all these years I'd been enabling him. Cleaning up his messes. Making his bad choices go away.

"You're on your own, Connor. You'll have plenty of money in your account. Seamus left us everything." I wrote the dollar amount on the whiteboard and tossed it on the coffee table. He didn't even glance at it. He'd never cared about money, only the drugs he could buy with it. "You can take off and go wherever the hell you want. I'm done cleaning up your messes. Straighten out your own fucking life."

I walked away, that vice on my heart squeezing and twisting. It hurt so fucking much I could barely breathe. *Why, Connor? Why did you ruin us?* Growing up, all we'd had was each other and I'd always thought if we stuck together through thick and thin, we'd come out on the other side okay. I'd been wrong.

I'd lost everything and everyone I had ever loved. My mother. My career. Johnny. My brother. And I was losing Eden. Jack Madley had been right. I needed to get my shit together. I needed to let her go. It was the best thing I could do for her. I had nothing to offer her except a shitload of baggage. I felt like I was sinking under the weight of it all.

* * *

I pointed to my empty glass. *Keep 'em coming, mate.* The bartender poured me another whiskey. He should save himself the trouble and just leave the bottle. We'd bonded. His name was Ian. Or Liam. Or Craig. Whatever. The bar was dark. The customers were scarce. And the whiskey was flowing. I had everything I needed. The door opened, and Louis walked in.

He pulled up a stool next to me. "Drowning your sorrows at an Irish pub?"

"They've got whiskey. And Flogging Molly," I pointed out. "Gotta love Flogging Molly."

"You about to break into an Irish jig? Going back to your roots?"

I snorted and took a swig of my drink. "I'm a tree without roots. What does that make me?"

"A dead log," Louis said. I laughed so hard my eyes

watered. That was the beauty of alcohol. I was too numb to feel the pain in my ribs. Louis shook his head. "I came to haul your ass home."

I didn't have a home. "It's early. Drink with me."

"It's two-thirty in the morning and you've got a funeral tomorrow."

"Don't piss on my parade." I flagged down my buddy. Ian-Liam-Craig. Louis ordered a beer. "Make it two beers and two more whiskeys," I told the bartender.

Louis muttered something under his breath. I might have caught the word asshole, but it didn't stop him from drinking the beer *and* the whiskey when it was served. I hoisted my glass in the air and sang the final chorus of 'The Cradle of Humankind.' Two guys at the end of the bar lifted their beers and toasted me. I clinked my glass against Louis's glass. "Bottoms up." I knocked back my whiskey and slammed the empty glass on the bar. I made a twirling motion with my hand. Ian-Liam-Craig got what I was saying. Refills at the ready. This man would be getting a big-ass tip.

"Eden's worried about you," Louis said. Why was he always bursting my little happy bubble? Couldn't he see I was a man on a mission? The goal: get so shit-faced I wouldn't remember Eden's name. Her voice. Her smile. Her...everything. "She said you didn't answer her calls today."

I guzzled some beer. "Better this way. I'm no good for her."

"Wallowing in self-pity too. You're going all out tonight."

"Go big or go home. Have some peanuts." I pushed the bowl in front of him. Normally I wouldn't touch them with a ten-foot pole. All those germy hands digging in there. But tonight, the peanuts had been my dinner and they'd tasted just fine.

Louis and I ate peanuts and chased our beer with whiskey.

Thankfully, he did more drinking than talking, which I appreciated. At four in the morning, they turned on the lights in the bar and kicked us out. We stumbled back to Louis's place and I crashed on his sofa. I slept with one foot on the floor to stop the room from spinning.

This was going to be my life now. A life without sunshine.

Chapter Forty-One

Eden

THE STREETS WERE A SEA OF BLUE AS OUR LIMO MADE ITS SLOW progress behind the hearse. Even though it was a funeral and the past week felt like a bad dream, I could still appreciate how handsome Killian looked in a dark suit, pressed white shirt, and royal blue tie. His hair was growing out and it curled a little at the ends where it met his collar. He was sitting right next to me, my thigh pressed against his, but it felt like he was miles away.

Connor and Ava were sitting across from us, Ava's arm tucked in his. It was hard to look at Connor's face, a visual reminder of what those men had done to him. I knew under his dark suit jacket and blue dress shirt, his chest was carved with letters. His nose was swollen, and greenish yellow bruises mottled his entire face. A metal plate and screws held his broken jaw together. He shouldn't be here, but he felt it was his duty to attend. More guilt heaped on the Vincent brothers' shoulders.

Killian refused to even look at Connor, and Connor didn't glance in Killian's direction. Because of their rift and the occasion, we'd ridden to the church in stony silence.

Killian blamed himself for my being there. He blamed Connor for withholding the truth.

Connor blamed himself for everything.

I blamed those men for coming after Connor.

My dad wasn't impressed with any of it. He threatened to

take me home to Pennsylvania after the funeral. I wasn't leaving Brooklyn, and there wasn't a chance in hell I'd leave Killian, so my dad would just need to deal with that.

Our limo stopped in front of Our Lady of Angels in Bay Ridge. Thousands of police officers saluted as the flag-draped coffin was removed from the hearse by the honor guard who had walked alongside it.

The limo door swung open, and Killian stepped out, offering me his hand. As we followed the casket, officers stepped forward, offering their condolences, and shaking Killian's hand. I glanced over my shoulder at Connor. His head was bowed as if to hide his face, but he was getting the same handshakes and condolences as Killian.

The media didn't get hold of the real story. It must have been a police cover-up. Seamus Vincent, of course, came out looking like a hero. Allegedly, it was a robbery gone wrong. Junkies looking for quick cash. Seamus would have appreciated that story.

The church was packed, scented with incense and lilies, and sunlight streamed in through the arched stained-glass windows. We slid into the first pew, and I turned around to look behind me. My dad, who had driven out here as soon as Killian called him, and Garrett who had arrived yesterday, were in dark suits… and Sawyer in his dress blues?

"Sawyer," I whispered.

He gave me a little smile. "Hey, Chicken Little," he whispered. Tears stung my eyes at the tenderness in his voice and the expression on his face.

I blinked back the tears. "You look so handsome." It was true, and Ava seconded that.

"Chicks dig it. But it's itchy as hell," he complained.

Ava and I laughed. Typical Sawyer. Killian leaned across the pew and pulled Sawyer into a guy hug as the bagpipes played "Amazing Grace." Was there ever a sadder sound than bagpipes? Ava and I exchanged a look. Her eyes filled with tears, but I knew they weren't for Seamus. She shook her head a little and exhaled, trying to pull herself together. I didn't know what was going on with her and Connor, but this week hadn't been the right time to ask. My gaze drifted to Connor. Back straight, shoulders squared, head bowed.

Killian squeezed my hand, and I turned my attention to him as the priest began the funeral Mass. Killian stared straight ahead. I wondered what was going through his head, how he felt about his father's death. Conflicted, I guess. Despite Killian's abusive childhood, at the hands of his father, Killian had called Seamus for help and he came because his sons needed him. As I studied the painting of the Virgin Mary surrounded by cherubs behind the altar, I entertained the notion that their mom would come to the funeral. It would be like something out of a movie. She'd cry and ask their forgiveness. She'd beg to be a part of their lives and she'd find a way to make up for all the hurt and pain she'd caused.

But that didn't happen.

The funeral seemed to go on forever, and now, Seamus was in the ground and we'd all gathered at his house. Connor and Ava left directly after the burial which left Killian playing host to our friends and what appeared to be the entire NYPD. I was standing in the wood-paneled kitchen on the same green linoleum floor Killian had scrubbed with Pine-Sol the day his mom left. The kitchen table and counters buckled under the weight of hams and casseroles. It reminded me of my mom's funeral. Why did people always bring ham?

Friends surrounded me—Zeke, Hailey, Louis, his girlfriend Carmen who I'd met a couple times, Brody, Chris. Garrett had left a little while ago to take Sawyer to the airport. Thankfully, my dad was bonding with some of New York's finest which made my life easier. My dad had attached himself to me like Velcro. Every time I made a sound during the night, even in my sleep, he was on the other side of my bedroom door, asking if I needed anything.

"Stop being a helicopter parent," I'd complained. This wasn't like my dad but, then, I guess this situation wasn't entirely normal.

Louis hugged me. "We're out of here, beautiful."

"I'll be back at work soon."

He gave me a skeptical look.

"I will."

Louis held up his hands. "Take it up with Killian and your dad."

Killian and my dad? I'd certainly be taking it up with them. Chris, Brody, and Zeke took turns hugging me goodbye because they had jobs to get to. As did Hailey who pulled me into an extra-long hug.

"I'm glad you're okay." Hailey released me, her gaze lingering on my forehead.

"Do I need to touch up my makeup?" I'd covered the bruises on my cheekbone and forehead with foundation and thought I did a pretty good job of it. On the day I left the hospital, my forehead was swollen to the size of a baseball, but the swelling had gone down and now it was an ugly greenish yellow. Like Connor's entire face.

"You look fine," Hailey said, giving me a little smile. Then she was laughing.

"Well, that's not very convincing."

She shook her head. "I'm sorry. I was just thinking there's never a dull moment with you."

I sighed. "I'm a trouble magnet."

After my friends left, I looked around for Killian, searching the living room and the backyard, but I didn't see him anywhere. I climbed the stairs to the second floor, feeling like I was trespassing, and passed two closed doors before I came to one slightly ajar. I peeked my head inside and saw Killian sitting on the mossy green carpet, his back leaning against a double bed, cradling his head in his hands. In that moment, I saw Killian, the boy. My heart hurt for him. And it hurt for me too. I was losing him. I could feel it in the pit of my stomach. I knew it yesterday when he hadn't returned my calls. I knew it last week when he'd said goodbye to me at the hospital and I'd climbed into my dad's SUV.

A bottle of Jameson and a tumbler of whiskey sat next to him, like they were the only companions he needed.

A whimper escaped my lips. Killian lifted his head, his eyes meeting mine. They were empty. Vacant. He wasn't even in this room. I stood in the doorway, my gaze sweeping over the bedroom that must have been his when he was growing up. Neat and tidy. No photos on the dresser, no posters on the walls, nothing that gave me a clue as to who he'd been or what he'd liked when he was a kid. A cross hung above his bed and I wondered if he'd put it there or if Seamus had. I erased the distance between us and lowered myself onto the floor next to him, crossing my ankles and smoothing my hands over the skirt of my black dress. It was sleeveless and probably too short for a funeral, especially with my four-inch heels, but Ava had gone out and bought it for me because my dad had kept me locked in an ivory tower.

"Don't leave me," I whispered. I'd said it so many times at the hospital, and he'd always replied the same way. *"I'm not going anywhere."*

This time, he said nothing. He wrapped his arm around my shoulder, lifted the glass of whiskey to his lips, and drank.

★ ★ ★

Later that night, my dad, Killian, and I gathered in my living room. A few days ago, Killian, brought over a leather chair from the bar so my dad had somewhere to sit and read his newspaper while he guarded me all week. I loved my dad, but I was ready for him to get back to his regularly-scheduled life and let me do the same.

My dad was sitting on the chair, and Killian and I were on the sofa across from him. I had a bad feeling I did not want to hear what my dad was about to say. He had that look on his face he used to get whenever I was in trouble and we needed to have "a talk." And to make matters worse, Killian was on the opposite end of the couch, with a cushion separating us. There might as well have been an ocean between us.

"I'm not going back to Pennsylvania," I said, before he could speak. "It's not happening. I'm staying here with Killian and we're going to…I don't know…get back to our lives and…"

"Eden. I'm your father and that gives me the right—"

"I'm old enough to make my own decisions. I'm absolutely fine."

Killian leaned forward and rested his elbows on his thighs, his hands steepled, index fingers pressed against his lips. I glanced at Killian's face, but it was shuttered.

No. No, no, no. Don't do this, Killian. Not after everything we've been through together.

"Killian. Tell him—"

"Let your dad speak."

I crossed my arms and slumped against the back cushion, probably looking more like a petulant child than a mature adult.

"I spoke with Killian and he agrees with me," my dad said.

"You need some time to process everything that happened. What you've been through was traumatic."

"It was traumatic for Killian and Connor. I barely got hurt. I feel fine."

"Having nightmares every night is not fine," my dad said. "Waking up in a cold sweat is not fine."

Even though I wanted to deny it, I couldn't because my dad slept with one eye open. My bad dreams were always the same though. Not the exact same dream. But I always woke up right before Killian died. In a car flying off a cliff. In a fiery explosion. In a war zone, his body riddled with bullets.

"Killian agreed you'd both benefit from counseling," my dad said.

I stared at Killian, my mouth gaping. "You agreed to counseling."

"I insisted on it," my dad said. "Like I said, we talked." My dad's gaze swung to Killian and softened. I couldn't believe this. They'd been going behind my back, chatting like old chums, making plans for me without my consent, and even speaking to Louis on my behalf.

"Fine. We'll go to counseling." I had no objection to it and if Killian agreed to speak to a shrink, it might really help him. "So, we're good, right?"

"No," my dad said. "We are not good. You're leaving Brook—"

"No. Absolutely not. My life is here. My friends are here. My job…my art…Killian…everything is here. I'm sorry, Dad, but you can't make that decision for me. It's my life, and it's my decision. The only way for me to get better is to take control of my own life. I'm not helpless or broken, and I'm tired of you guys making me feel like I am." My dad kept opening his mouth to interrupt, but I kept talking, not letting him. "Did you tell Sawyer he wasn't allowed to enlist in the Marines? That he wasn't allowed to re-enlist? No, you didn't." I was just getting started, really warming up to my argument. I wasn't going down without a fight.

"You're a state trooper, so you know bad stuff happens everywhere. Even in Pennsylvania. I've heard your stories about shootings and domestic violence and horrific car crashes. Mom got cancer. You couldn't prevent that from happening, no matter what you did. And, Killian, if you feel guilty, talk to a shrink about it. Talk to me about it. But don't you dare throw us away because of what happened. It was not your fault. Dad, don't make him feel guiltier than he already does. Killian does not need more guilt in his life." I turned my attention to Killian. "Don't do this. I love you. You made me promise I wouldn't let you ruin us. Don't ruin us. Please—"

"Eden," Killian said, cutting me off. I opened my mouth to protest. "I was thinking we'd take that trip to Montauk."

A trip to Montauk? *What?* "As in...you and me?"

"A vacation," my dad fumed. "That's not what we talked about."

"I love your daughter, and I want what's best for her. I would never knowingly put her in danger. I would gladly risk my life to save hers. Eden showed me what love is. She's strong and she's brave and she stands up for the people she believes in. And, for some crazy reason, she believes in me. She chose me. And I choose her. Always. I'm not leaving her, and I'm not letting her go. I'm a wild card. I know that. I come with a shitload of baggage. I've done a lot of things in my life I regret. But loving her isn't one of them. I can't promise life will be smooth sailing, but I can promise I'll do whatever it takes to help her put this behind her. I'll do the work, and I'll do it with her at my side. Because life without her is unthinkable. I'm sorry if you think I'm being selfish, but that's what I need to do. For her. For me.

For us. When you love someone, you don't run away, and you don't leave them when things get hard or messy or fucked-up. When you love someone, you fight for them. And I will always fight for Eden."

I stared at Killian the whole time he spoke, making vows and promises. I'd never heard him say so many words at once, and all his words were perfect. They were everything I wanted to hear and more.

"You love me," I breathed.

"Fiercely. You're mine and I'm yours, so it looks like you're stuck with me."

"I love being stuck with you." I moved closer and leaned in, about to kiss him.

My dad cleared his throat. Oops, I forgot about him. I dragged my gaze away from Killian and to my dad. "Don't worry about me, Dad. I'm going to be okay." And I knew it was true. The only way I wouldn't be okay was if Killian had let my dad call the shots. Not that I ever had any intention of taking orders from my dad, but if Killian hadn't been in my corner, he wouldn't be the right man for me. He wouldn't be the man I'd come to depend on and believe in. And that would have broken my heart, for real.

My dad shook his head and exhaled. "You don't know what you put me through, kiddo."

Considering all the hovering he'd done in the past week, I had some idea, but I kept that to myself. I could see he was struggling, waging his own internal battle, but I also knew he'd concede defeat. And he did. My dad didn't raise us to be quitters. He didn't raise us to run away from our problems either. He taught us to stand up for the people and the things we believed in, and that's what I was doing. I was taking back control of my own life, and I was doing it with Killian at my side.

Chapter Forty-Two

Killian

THE LOT ADJACENT TO THE BURNT-OUT WAREHOUSE WAS fenced in with chain-link but luckily, nobody had bothered to fix the gap in the metal bars of the padlocked gate. I pushed the bucket of wheat paste through the gap, shoved Eden's tote bag inside, and fed the rolled-up artwork covered in bubble wrap and brown paper through it.

"Ready?" I asked.

"Born ready." She slid through the gap easily and once inside, tucked stray blonde locks into her black beanie and pulled up the hood of her black sweatshirt.

I sucked in my breath and squeezed through the tight space. Fuck. Discomfort, not pain, I told myself, leaning over to pick up the bucket. "I forgot about your ribs," she whispered. "Are you okay?"

"It's been a month. Good as new."

"In your world, maybe," she muttered.

I propped the artwork onto my shoulder and secured it with my arm. Glass crunched under our feet as we negotiated the scrap heap of twisted metal, cinderblocks, and broken window frames. I should have known Eden wouldn't give up on her goal to paste artwork on this tower, but I was so damn proud of her.

When we reached the metal fire escape that led to a flat roof, giving us access to the tower, I tipped back my head and looked up at the eight-story building. Eden adjusted the straps of her tote bag on her shoulder and nodded, her chin set with determination, a look I knew all too well by now. "Let's do this," she said.

"Let me test it." Ideally, I'd walk up all eight stories on my own to test it, but she was right behind me, and I knew nothing I could say would dissuade her from following me. The metal fire escape creaked under our weight, but it felt strong enough to hold us.

We climbed in the dark, slow but steady, our way lit by a big orange moon. I paused halfway up and looked at her over my shoulder. She was right behind me, her cheeks pink from exertion and the chill in the air. "You okay?"

"Yep." She gave me a big smile to prove it and looked up at the tower. "Almost there. Keep your eye on the prize."

I winked at her. "That's what I'm doing."

Her smile grew wider, and she let out a laugh. "You've been hanging out with Zeke too much." She prodded my back to indicate we should keep going. "Picking up all his corny lines."

I groaned as we continued our climb. "You think I'm corny now? I've reached an all-time low."

"I think you're sweet and gooey. Like marshmallow fluff."

"I think you're crazy. Like peanut butter."

"How is peanut butter crazy?"

"It's made of nuts."

She burst out laughing. "You're nuts."

"About you," I said, embracing these corny lines.

It was her turn to groan. "You need to stop now. You'll lose your street cred."

"I'm still a badass."

"Yeah, you are," she said, her tone more serious. Over the past two weeks, she'd binge-watched my fights on YouTube.

According to Dr. Eden Madley, it was part of my therapy to watch them with her. I felt like I was watching someone else, someone I barely recognized, and I thought she felt the same way. Eden watched my final fight alone though, and I knew she watched some of Johnny's fights too. But I couldn't watch them either.

When we reached the top, I inhaled deep breaths of crisp fall air while she rooted around in her bag. Coming out with the flashlight she flicked it on and swept the light across the flat concrete roof that appeared to be intact. "Need help getting up?" I asked, referring to the three-foot wall in front of us.

She rolled her eyes at that suggestion, placed the palms of her hands on the wall and levered herself onto it. I handed her the art piece and joined her on the roof.

While I trained the flashlight on the wall, my appointed job, she removed the packaging from her art and unrolled the top part, leaving the rest rolled up. She pulled on a pair of latex gloves and applied the paste to the wall with a long-handled brush until the entire surface was covered.

"Babe, let me do that," I said, when she tried to affix the top of the art piece by standing on tiptoes and extending her arms as high as they could reach. The struggle was real. I handed her the flashlight and affixed the top to the wall.

With the top part secured, we worked our way down and over the whole piece, smoothing out the bubbles. When it was firmly in place, I stepped back, and she applied a coat of paste over the top to seal it.

"We did it," she said when she finished, her voice filled with awe and joy. "We actually did it."

I wrapped my arms around her, and pulled her back against my chest, letting her have this moment. The art was amazing, and I didn't tell her this, but I liked it better than the first one.

This surfer girl didn't look like she was about to get sledgehammered by the wave. She was riding the crest of the wave, and she appeared to be in total control. Although I knew that was never possible, that we couldn't control every aspect of our lives, Eden's new art piece gave me hope we could find our way through any situation life threw at us. Maybe, somehow, someday we'd find peace in the chaos.

Over the past month, I'd been trying to get the vision of that night out of my head. Trying not to think about everything that *could* have gone wrong. If she'd taken a bullet instead of me. If that guy with his hands wrapped around her neck had squeezed the life out of her. A million what ifs invaded my brain, and I kept trying to shut them out. Just like I tried to shut out the memories of watching Seamus get shot in the head, of the bodies and the rivers of blood on the living room floor.

In Montauk, Eden and I watched the sun rise over the ocean every morning and we walked the beach to Ditch Plains to watch the surfers. It was cold, but we had sunshine every day for the week we spent there, and it was quiet, not overrun with summer tourists. I rented a beachfront house with ocean views from our bedroom windows. While we were there, living in our own little world, I understood the allure of running away from it all. We tried to forget everything that had happened, and for the first few days we didn't talk about it. But reality caught up to us, and we couldn't hide from it forever. We needed to sort out our lives and figure out a way to move on.

In the two weeks we'd been back in Brooklyn, living in her apartment, she painted her new art piece. We worked at the bar. We tried to get back to a normal life. And after discussing it with Eden, I spoke to Louis about Zeke buying me out. Louis wasn't overly surprised, and said he was cool with it. Louis and I met with Zeke and his dad, and the deal went through two days ago.

On that same day, I took Eden to look at the loft apartment on the Greenpoint waterfront. She loved the soaring ceilings, the exposed brick walls, the amazing light. The view of Manhattan, the chef's kitchen, and the walk-in shower. So, I bought it.

"I need to pay you rent," she said.

Like I'd take her money. "You're not paying rent. So, get over yourself, sunshine."

"But this place is super expensive. I can't just live here for free."

"I don't need your money."

"I don't want to be a kept woman."

I laughed. She pursed her lips and crossed her arms.

"I'll pay for the food and the utilities," she said.

Oh God. Stubborn woman. "We'll see." That was a no.

"We should call Connor. Ask him to come and see it," she said, her voice hopeful.

Connor wouldn't be living with us. Eden knew that, but she kept trying to change my mind. Three grueling, painful shrink sessions under my belt, and a lot of conversations with Eden, but I was nowhere near ready to forgive Connor. The only thing I'd ever asked of him was honesty. When he first came back from Florida, I suspected he was hiding something, but because he'd been drug-free, I pushed it to the back of my mind. Stupid me.

I still hadn't come to terms with my father's death either. Did I truly forgive him? I wasn't sure. And Johnny, well, I was working on trying to forgive myself.

I had my work cut out for me, but in a lot of ways, I was in a better place than I'd been before I met Eden. All I wanted now was to make sure she never regretted choosing me. After my conversations with her dad, I came so close to walking away, thinking it was the best thing I could do for her. Call me selfish, call it whatever you want, but I couldn't do it. I meant everything I said that night in her living room. She was mine, I was hers, and I wasn't letting her go.

"Ready?" I asked, taking a final look at her surfer girl.

"I'm ready for anything," she said as we climbed down the fire escape, with me leading the way.

"Living with me, you'll need to be."

"I just thought of another way to help out with rent."

"Daily blow jobs?"

"Are you a mind reader?"

"Only when you're thinking dirty thoughts. Keep 'em coming, and I'll keep reading."

She laughed loudly then clapped a hand over her mouth. Her eyes widened at the sound of glass crunching. We stopped at the bottom of the fire escape and she pressed her body against my back. I felt her trembling as her arms wrapped around my middle for support. I hated that something unknown had the power to scare her. I wanted to make her fearless again, but the shrink said it wouldn't happen overnight. Shit like this takes time.

"Dude, we need to climb to the top," a voice said.

"Totally."

The voices were male, but they sounded young. "It's okay," I assured her.

"I know," she whispered, but she didn't loosen her hold on me.

The two guys were tall and skinny and scared shitless when they came face to face with me. "Oh…hey…um…" one of them mumbled.

I glared at them. "It's not safe to climb." I pointed to the gate. "Leave the way you came."

They exchanged a look before they nodded and scurried away, with us following a short distance behind them. When we were on the other side of the fence, and the kids had taken off down the street, I pulled Eden into my arms. "Tomorrow morning we're starting those self-defense lessons."

She nodded against my chest. "Okay."

"I never want you to be scared again."

Eden took a deep breath and let it out. "Fair warning. Tomorrow morning I'm going to kick your ass."

I chuckled. "I'm looking forward to it."

"Afterwards, I'll kiss it better."

"I'm looking forward to that part even more."

She tipped her face up to look at me. "I'm looking forward to everything with you."

Epilogue

Eden

SOMETIMES SNOOPING WAS ILL-ADVISED BUT, IN MY DEFENSE, I wasn't looking for it. I heard the shower turn off and slipped the little velvet box back in the zippered compartment of Killian's gym bag. I stowed it on the shelf on his side of our closet and slid the door along the track, hiding the evidence. Oh my god. Oh my god. Oh my god.

I forgot all about getting ready for our dinner date and collapsed on our king-sized bed, staring at the exposed-wood ceiling beams. Today was the one-year anniversary of the day we met. I let my thoughts wander back in time. To the early days when he tried to keep me at a distance. And to all the hours and the days when he became mine. Heart, body, and soul. Our life together wasn't a fairytale. It was real, and sometimes hard and painful, but there was magic in the everyday too.

I couldn't pretend the night that man held a gun to my head didn't affect me, but I'd sought counseling and worked through it. I was stronger now. Killian gave me the tools to physically fight my own battles if I needed to. He was an amazing teacher with far more patience than I'd ever expected. Mentally and emotionally, I felt stronger too. For Killian, the counseling hasn't been as easy. He had always believed he needed to lock down his pain, but he sees his shrink once a week, and it's getting better. He doesn't come out of it looking like he's ready to punch a wall or shut himself in a room anymore.

Killian strutted into our bedroom and crossed the hardwood floor, a plush white towel slung around his hips. I rolled onto my side and propped my head on my hand. My gaze traveled up the length of him. Now that he owned a gym, Defiance MMA & Fitness, he'd found his passion again and loved his job and, unbelievably, he was even leaner and fitter than he was when we met. Beads of water trailed down his bare chest, and I raised my gaze to his freshly-shaven face. I stared at him, mesmerized, as if I'd never seen his face before. I wanted to spend the rest of my life with this man, and there was no doubt in my mind we belonged together.

"You going like that?" he asked, eyeing my silky green robe. I couldn't form the words to answer him. All I could do was smile so big it practically split my face in two. I watched the towel drop to the floor and caught the wicked gleam in his eye. "Let's have our dessert first."

I laughed. Killian still didn't eat dessert. Or junk food. But I kept my own stash in a cupboard next to his whole grains and birdseed.

I wrapped my arms around his neck. "Do we have time—" The rest of my sentence was swallowed up in his kiss. As it turned out, we didn't need a lot of time. It was quick and dirty, and I was screaming his name a few minutes later.

He collapsed on top of me and kissed my neck. "Love you."

"Love you more."

"It's not a contest."

"If it were, I'd win."

He chuckled and braced his arm to support his weight. I looked into his blue eyes and I could swear they twinkled. He lets me see him now—his joy, his pain, his sadness, his love. It was written on his face, reflected in his eyes, and I loved that he trusted me with all his emotions.

"The answer is yes," I blurted out. What an idiot. Filters, Eden.

Killian raised his brows. "What are you saying yes to?"

"Anything you ask me, I'll say yes." I smiled, all innocence. I didn't fool him for a minute.

He started laughing, the sound coming from deep inside, his chest rumbling against mine. He was laughing so hard tears sprang to his eyes.

"What's so funny?"

Killian rolled off me and scrubbed his hands over his face. "What am I going to do with you?"

Yeah, I ruined the surprise. My own stupid fault. "You should have booby-trapped it."

"You shouldn't have been looking through my bag."

"I was going to leave you a little love letter."

I leaned over the side of the bed, fished the proof out of my robe pocket, and placed the letter on his chest. He tipped down his chin and unfolded the notepaper, holding it up so he could read it. It was corny, but it put a smile on his face.

Dear Killian,
You once asked me what you do for me, so I made a list:
- *You always put the toilet seat down.*
- *You do all the nasty jobs around the house, like cleaning my hair out of the shower drain.*
- *You give excellent massages, guaranteed to have a happy ending.*
- *Your smoothies are hit-or-miss, but you don't force me to drink them…so thanks for that.*
- *You support all my crazy ideas, even when I insisted on cutting down our own Christmas tree (in Indiana, Pennsylvania AKA "The Christmas tree capital of the world"). I might have*

underestimated the difficulty of transporting a twelve-foot Blue Spruce on the roof for three-hundred miles. But hey, the tree looked amazing in our loft. Next year, I say we go bigger.
- You didn't get angry after that unfortunate fender bender with your new Range Rover.

For all these little reasons and the big ones too, you're my real-life hero. My white knight, my wish on a star, the wings of my heart.

I love you more today than I did yesterday.

Yours,

Eden

"So yeah," I said, when he folded it up. "I was going to put the letter in your gym bag, so you could find it tomorrow and... well..."

He was off the bed, reaching into the dresser for his boxer briefs. "Get dressed. We need to go."

My mouth gaped as he casually got dressed like nothing major was happening. "What? But..."

"We have a reservation."

"I know. But don't you have something to ask me?"

"You already said yes to anything."

Huh. Me and my big mouth. I grabbed my clothes and retreated into the bathroom to get dressed and do my makeup. Dressed and ready in a silky jade green dress with an open back, I gave myself a onceover in the mirror before I joined Killian in the bedroom. He was lounging on the bed, doing something on his phone. He was wearing the white linen button-down shirt I loved on him, with dark jeans and a newer version of his old combat boots.

He stood and erased the distance between us. "You look gorgeous."

"So, do you."

He dropped down on one knee in front of me, and it didn't matter that I'd spoiled the surprise. This was a huge surprise. I hadn't expected anything so traditional, but here he was, taking my hand in his as he knelt in front of me. I could barely see him through my tears.

"I love you, Eden. All your crazy ideas. Your optimism. Your stubborn determination. Your stellar driving skills…we'll work on them. Doesn't matter. I love you just as you are. You're my home," he said softly. "Will you marry me?"

You're my home. I put my hand over my heart and tried to swallow past my tears. God, that was beautiful. I nodded, incapable of speech. "Yes," I said, my voice barely a whisper. "Yes, I'll marry you."

He slid the ring on my finger and then he was on his feet, his hands cradling my face, his thumbs brushing away my tears.

Fifteen minutes later, I was still living on cloud nine, and couldn't stop looking at my engagement ring—an emerald, surrounded by sparkly diamonds. It was perfect.

"How did you pick this ring?" I asked.

"If you want a diamond, we can take it back—"

"No! I love it. It's perfect."

I looked out the window as he pulled into a parking space a block from the bar. "I thought we were going to dinner at our little French place."

"We have time for one drink." He guided me down the street, texting while we walked. I still worked at Trinity Bar, but I worked day shifts now. When Zeke bought out Killian's share, he and Louis made a few changes. One of them had been to open the bar during the day. Zeke and I were still good friends, and he had helped Killian put together a five-year business plan, as well as putting him in touch with foundations that helped him get grants for his at-risk-youth program.

Killian ushered me inside the bar, and it took me a minute to process what was going on. When I did, I was on the verge of happy tears again.

"Killian." I covered my mouth with my hands.

He smirked at me. "Surprise."

Ha! He got one over on me, not an easy feat. All our friends were gathered at the bar—Louis, Zeke, Chris, Brody, Hailey, Ava, Jared, Connor…even Daniel was here.

I stared at everyone, speechless.

"So why are we all here?" Connor asked.

"Uh, duh," Ava said. "You didn't see the rock on her finger?"

It was the most Ava had said to Connor in eight months, and the only time they'd been in a room together. Connor shot her a look, but she studiously ignored it, and carried on talking to Hailey. He shook his head and pulled me into a hug, congratulating me.

When he released me, I gave him a soft smile which he returned. We'd been through so much together and we'd gotten so close over these past months. Connor was like a brother to me now. I just wanted him to be happy, but it wasn't that easy. He was still working on rebuilding the trust he'd destroyed. My history with him didn't reach back as far as it did for Killian and Ava, so I guess it was easier for me to believe in him than it was for them.

"Love you, girl," Connor said.

"Love you too."

Connor gave me another hug and Louis pressed a glass of champagne into my hand.

The rest of the night was a blur of music, champagne, tacos, and everyone telling stories about how they were the ones responsible for getting us together.

Hours later, I was toasting Hailey who had just landed her

dream job in San Francisco where the head chef was a woman. "Here's to making our dreams come true," I said.

"I'll drink to that."

We clinked glasses and drank to that. I downed the rest of my champagne and set my empty glass on the bar.

Arms wrapped around me from behind and I leaned back against Killian's chest.

"I love you in that dress…" he murmured in my ear. "But all I can think about is getting you out of it. Wanna hear what I plan to do to you later?"

"How are you going to top this?" I asked, flashing the ring at him.

"I've got skills."

"Mm, I know you do."

"Let's go home," he said.

Home. That had to be one of the most beautiful words in the English language. Maybe life wasn't a fairy tale, but Killian and I were getting our happily ever after.

Acknowledgements

I owe thanks to so many people who helped bring Beneath Your Beautiful to life. To my family, for your unending patience and support. Thank you for believing in me, and for putting up with all the hours I spend with the fictional characters in my head. To my beta readers—Petra Gleason, Maddie Andrews, and Annie Dyer—thank you for your time, your thoughts, your encouragement, and for loving Eden and Killian as much as I do.

To my editors, Chelsea and Madison, for sharing your talent and advice. And to Monica Black, for performing miracles on a tight schedule, and polishing the words until they shone.

Sarah at Okay Creations, thank you for creating a gorgeous cover. To Stacey Blake of Champagne Formatting for the interior design. To Ena of Enticing Journey for arranging the promotions, and all the book bloggers who took the time to read and review.

And finally, a huge thank you to all the readers who took a chance on an unknown author. I hope you enjoyed reading it as much as I enjoyed writing it.

If you want to be contacted when Emery Rose's next book goes live, please go to the link below.
goo.gl/forms/W8jKfHsjyEUA1CfW2

Connect with Emery

Website: www.emeryroseauthor.com

Facebook: www.facebook.com/EmeryRoseAuthor

Twitter: twitter.com/emeryrosewrites

Printed in Great Britain
by Amazon